Janette Paul is an internationally published author of contemporary women's fiction and romantic comedy, and is the alter ego of award-winning suspense author Jaye Ford. Her first novel won two Davitt Awards for Australian women crime writers and her books have been translated into nine languages. She is a former news and sport journalist, was the first woman to host a live national sport show on Australian TV and ran her own public relations consultancy before turning to fiction. She now writes from her home in Newcastle, New South Wales.

Also by Janette Paul

The Summer Place

The View from the Balcony

Janette Paul

MACMILLAN
Pan Macmillan Australia

Pan Macmillan acknowledges the Traditional Custodians of Country throughout Australia and their connections to lands, waters and communities. We pay our respect to Elders past and present and extend that respect to all Aboriginal and Torres Strait Islander peoples today. We honour more than sixty thousand years of storytelling, art and culture.

First published 2025 in Macmillan by Pan Macmillan Australia Pty Ltd
1 Market Street, Sydney, New South Wales, Australia, 2000

A catalogue record for this book is available from the National Library of Australia

Typeset in 11 / 15.5 Palatino Regular by Post Pre-press Group

Printed by IVE

The author and the publisher have made every effort to contact copyright holders for material used in this book. Any person or organisation that may have been overlooked should contact the publisher.

The paper in this book is FSC® certified. FSC® promotes environmentally responsible, socially beneficial and economically viable management of the world's forests.

To Paul

Part 1

The Accident

Coral

'Hi, Mum,' Coral called as she let herself in, flicking off lights as she walked through her mother's house. 'Mum?'

'I'm looking for something.'

Coral followed the sound of her mother's voice, depositing a casserole in the fridge on her way to the walk-in pantry. She stood for a moment, surveying the near-empty shelves. Her mother was kneeling on the floor, foodstuffs and storage containers stacked in neat towers around her. 'What are you looking for?'

Val pulled a tin of tomato soup from a shelf, inspected the label, set it on the floor and said, 'A sock.'

'Among the tinned asparagus and desiccated coconut?'

Val glanced briefly at the items around her as though only just making the connection. 'Well, of course not,' she snapped. 'I *was* looking for a sock.'

'And now you're . . .?'

'Tidying up.' Gripping a shelf to pull herself up, Val adjusted her glasses and glared at Coral as though her daughter was being ridiculous. 'I was looking for a sock in here and noticed how disorganised it was. You must have been just pushing things aside when you put the shopping away. You know I like to keep the vegetables separated from the fruit, and the baking ingredients on the shelf above.'

Of course it was Coral's fault. All that shopping and putting away she did was so annoying. Casting an eye over the cans and containers again, Coral thought about the stack of bedsheets on the floor outside the linen closet last week, that Val had claimed could 'benefit from some refolding'. Which Coral had done, under supervision, in that extra half an hour she didn't have.

'Why were you looking for a sock in the pantry?' she asked now.

'Oh, don't be so pedantic, Coral.' Val shooed her out of the doorway. 'Are you staying for coffee?'

Coral glanced at the wall clock and did a quick calculation, weighing up the time she had before her meeting and her guilt about leaving the country. 'A quick one. I'll get it,' she said, knowing it would be faster if she made it.

While Val was occupied finding placemats, Coral did a hasty reorganisation of the pantry, lining up the cans with the labels facing out, fruit to the right, vegetables to the left. Rolling her eyes, she gave it the once-over and repeated the question she'd been asking herself for months now: was old age intensifying her mother's lifelong habits of tidying cupboards and correcting Coral, or had the falls and hospital stays over the last year done more than make her a bit stiffer and slower?

Dipping a biscuit into her coffee, Coral said, 'Summer's looking forward to helping you sort through your old china while I'm away.' It was a bit of an exaggeration, but Summer had suggested it, so close enough.

'What does she want to do that for?'

'Remember the two of you decided it would be your project?' Okay, perhaps Coral was more excited about the concept than her daughter or her mother. 'She's organised for Oliver to spend a day with his other grandmother so he won't be the bull in Nana's china shop, so to speak.'

'You're not going to America today, are you?'

'Not for ten days, Mum. It's on your calendar. I'm just going to Sydney today.' Coral couldn't help adding, 'Pre-conference meeting.'

'I don't know why they have to send you there. It's such a long way to go for a meeting.'

'Sydney or New York?'

'Sydney.' Val flapped a hand, making it clear what she thought of that. 'But New York. For a meeting?' She shook her head. The conference was the other thing Coral was more excited about than Summer or Val.

Coral wasn't sure whether her mother's exasperation was about the distance and money involved, or the fact that Coral had been invited. 'It's a conference, Mum. A week of big-deal meetings.' Coral was over the moon about going, and not just because it meant almost two weeks to herself. 'I'll be doing my presentation on day four.' Sick with nerves before, basking in glory afterwards, and quaffing expensive, well-earned champagne before she came home.

Val gave her usual raised-eyebrow response, managing to convey both pride and a hint of cynicism. As usual, Coral tried to focus on the pride, although that hadn't stopped her trying to decipher the cynicism. Either it was doubt that Coral had done anything worthy of being invited to present a paper at an inter-national conference, or a suspicion that 'international conference' was just a fancy term for being flown to New York for a couple of meetings at head office. *Whatever,* Coral told herself again.

Adjusting the sparkly rings on her left hand, Val asked, 'Did you decide what to wear?'

At least her mother understood how much consideration that had needed. Grateful to move on to a topic that didn't hold quite so many landmines, Coral described the outfit she'd spent a small fortune on: peach-coloured skirt suit, off-white blouse with flattering draped neckline, latte-coloured heels and matching handbag. She'd found the outfit on one of her Sydney trips, sent copious photos to Summer and made sure it was all returnable if her daughter didn't give her the thumbs up.

Val took it all in and said, 'That colour won't make you look big?'

Coral instructed her face to stay neutral. 'Summer thought it looked great,' she said, turning to carry the dishes to the kitchen. Actually, her millennial daughter had said, *No, Mum, the colour doesn't make your bum look big*, in a tone that suggested it was ridiculous to ask. Couldn't win either way. It didn't help that Val had started telling Coral she should dress more like a sixty-year-old. That she had three years left of her fifties made no difference, or that Hollywood icons Julianne Moore and Jamie Lee Curtis were just fine as fashion inspiration, and they had five years on Coral.

Glancing at her watch, she checked the fridge. 'I've left a chicken casserole for you,' she said, taking out last week's sandwich meat and a dead-looking carrot. 'There's enough for two meals. A minute in the microwave each time will be enough.'

'Alright.'

Dropping the food-poisoning hazards in the bin, she pulled out the liner and replaced it. 'Don't forget, there are still a couple of those small containers of pumpkin soup in the freezer.'

'I know.'

Coral cast an eye around again, emptying the dish drainer and straightening the tea towel hanging on the oven door. 'And a few of those ready-to-heat meals.'

'I'm perfectly capable of feeding myself.'

'Yes, I know.' Only she wasn't. Or didn't. Coral wasn't sure which. Either way, she was worried about how Val would get on while she was in New York.

Coral was still wrestling with her daughter guilt as she pulled up outside her Newcastle office. She texted Jessica and waited, reminding herself for the hundredth time that it wasn't her fault Val would have to cope on her own. Or that her daughter Summer, who was seven-and-a-half months pregnant, had to keep an eye on her grandmother while Coral was in New York.

Val had qualified for home assistance after her first nasty fall a year ago, but was refusing any help. According to Val, she didn't need a cleaner, or someone to shop for her, or a companion. She was eighty-five and perfectly capable of looking after herself.

She was also blind to how much Coral was doing for her. Or in denial that it was her daughter who made sure the bills were paid, the sheets changed, the vacuuming done, the shopping and a thousand other things seen to while Val 'took care of herself'. Whatever it was, Coral was fifty-seven and exhausted. Guilt or no guilt, she couldn't wait to get on the plane and just sleep.

'Can we stop for coffees?' Jessica called as she wedged her laptop and briefcase into the front seat footwell.

'Caffeine hit has to wait until we're on the motorway,' Coral said as Jess slid in beside her, bringing a waft of perfume and toothpaste. Always so well put together, thought Coral, feeling the need to fix her hair in the rear-view mirror.

She pulled into the street, thinking about how many frozen meals her mother would need while Coral was away.

'I'm having lunch with Brandon's mum next time she's down. Just the two of us.' Jessica shot Coral a grimace.

'You'll be fine.'

When they weren't talking work, Jess tended to steer the conversation to her favourite topics: her fiancé, their wedding, his parents and her career. It wasn't as though Coral was a success story on any of those fronts, but Jessica seemed to think Coral's life experience was to be mined at every opportunity.

Coral didn't mind, it gave her something to think about beyond her mother–daughter stress. Besides, it was nice to be appreciated for her wisdom, instead of just being the backstop for everyone else in her life.

Today, though, Coral was only half listening while she added bullet points to her pre-conference to-do list. Ask Summer to check for bills when she visited Val. As well as expiry dates in the fridge and phone messages.

'I'm thinking that new cafe down by the harbour,' Jess continued.

'Sounds good.' Buy a portable charger. Let the neighbours know she'll be away.

'Have you been there yet?'

'Not yet.' When did Coral have time to relax in a cafe? New York, that's when. Write *Relax/cafe* on the to-do list.

'Brandon and I went to check it out the other day but there were a heap of police still there after that guy drove into those pedestrians.'

'Oh yeah, that accident sounded awful.' Send email to clients with away dates. Oh, Stockholm. 'Hey, how's the Stockholm delivery looking?' The job had been booked for months by one of Coral's long-term clients: a small engineering firm that had been contracted to deliver two specialised diamond-tipped drill heads to an unnamed, hush-hush project in Sweden with a very specific deadline. One of the fun cloak-and-dagger jobs that cropped up sometimes. But the client had delayed the pick-up of the package several times and delivery status was heading towards urgent.

'It's on track for Monday, apparently.'

Coral frowned at yet another delay. 'When did you hear that?'

'There was an email this morning.'

Coral aimed her frown across the car.

'I forwarded it to you.' There was both defensiveness and censure in Jess's reply, a combination of *I covered my arse* and *Haven't you seen it?*

Coral's neck prickled with irritation that the news wasn't the first thing Jessica mentioned when she got in the car. But her thoughts were already skipping to the client and the drill heads. 'They must be having a collective heart attack over there.'

'What's their deadline?'

'The following Monday.' The day Coral flew to New York; the two events had been side by side in her calendar for six months. She did a quick calculation: on-time delivery was still possible without the need for someone to run through an airport yelling, 'Urgent package!' Theoretically, it would arrive with the weekend to spare, but even with the best contingency planning, things went wrong. 'Okay, we shift it up to urgent now. I don't want to be dealing with that drama while I'm getting on a plane.'

'I can manage it.' Annoyance in the pitch of Jess's voice.

Coral held back a sigh. Jess was in a hurry to climb the ladder and had a confidence that awed Coral at times, mostly because it was a skill set she'd never acquired. To Jess's credit, she had a degree and was good at what she set her mind to, but she'd only been in the job for a year, and had a tendency to overstate her capabilities and side-step her mistakes. Coral wasn't comfortable leaving a high priority, possible disaster-waiting-to-happen in Jess's inexperienced hands.

'These guys have been with me from the beginning,' Coral told her. 'I would feel obliged to be there for them if the shit hit the fan.'

Coral kept their focus on the Stockholm job until she pulled into the big service station on the motorway. Checking her phone while they waited for their coffee, she found the email, and chided herself for dwelling on her issues with Val instead of going through her inbox.

There was also a text from Summer: photos of Oliver that gave Coral the strange heart-soaring sensation she experienced whenever she saw her beautiful grandson. Had her own mother felt that way when Summer and Wade were little? When she saw them now? Val had never said, but then, Val didn't talk about things that made her heart sing.

They spent the rest of the trip going over the checklist of things to be done before and during Coral's trip to New York. Jessica had done a great job on Coral's slide presentation for the conference, working up much better-looking graphs and pie charts than Coral was capable of.

'I've uploaded the slides to the cloud, downloaded them onto USBs for both of us and emailed the updated versions to you just now,' Jessica said, laptop balanced on her knees.

'Brilliant, thank you. Glad to have that done before next week.' It was a rare thing in her business for everything to go off without a hitch, so as far as she was concerned, done wouldn't really be done until she walked off the stage in New York.

'Wish I was coming with you.'

'Your turn will come.' A lot faster than it had for Coral, and on a much less cluttered path.

Twenty-three years ago, Coral had never imagined that volunteering to hand-deliver an urgent package of thoroughbred racehorse sperm from the Hunter Valley to Perth would mark the start of a career in logistics. Back then, she didn't even know what logistics was. A friend's husband had needed a courier at the last minute, and she'd been grateful for the money, and for something to fill a few days while the kids were with their father. The journey had been a disaster: a huge storm cell, flights cancelled and redirected, connections missed, a bus to another airport, overly hopeful assurances she'd get there, terrified she wouldn't. Her own luggage had been lost, but she'd held on to that esky like she was handcuffed to it, and got the horse semen into the right hands, only half a day behind schedule.

The story was the opening to her presentation in New York, the crazy adventure that revealed her hidden talent for organising the hell out of a complicated journey.

⚓

Coral had been knee-shakingly nervous the first time she'd gone to Sydney for the group meeting. For a long time, she'd been the most knowledgeable fish in a very small pond, then the company she worked for was bought out and she found herself sitting at the table with the six directors of other global divisions. She'd been dumbstruck for about half an hour, until she realised she knew more than they did about moving small, sensitive packages around the country when they couldn't just be flown from large airport to large airport.

'We didn't buy you out because we liked the logo,' one of the directors had told her afterwards.

Today, Granger Holliton had been talking up her conference presentation as he sipped wine at the drinks and nibbles that followed the meeting. 'How long are you staying in New York after the conference? I'm putting together some post-conference sight-seeing options.'

Like a menopausal flush, disappointment made tiny beads of sweat break out on Coral's upper lip. 'Unfortunately, I have to get back. My mum's not doing well and my daughter will be only a few weeks from giving birth to my second grandchild.' She forced a smile, but the truth was she would have loved to stay and explore the Big Apple and mix with the movers and shakers of the company.

Granger's eyebrows rose, as though she'd made a curious choice. 'Next year's conference is in San Fran, maybe you can schedule some extra time after that one. You're still on for dinner in Manhattan, right?'

'So long as it's after my presentation. I don't want to be—' she stopped herself from saying *tired*, like an almost-sixty-year-old, 'to have a hangover any time before I'm on.'

He flashed a grin. 'You'll love it, and you're going to do great.'

Her smartwatch vibrated with an incoming call and Coral frowned at the name on the screen. Had Val already forgotten she was in Sydney? 'Excuse me, I've got to take this.'

Making her way to the main office outside, she felt a strange sort of detachment about being considered an automatic invite to the next conference. After five years of being the country cousin to the Sydney directors, of course she was gratified, and not least because she'd been overlooked twice before. The idea of another year in the trenches with an all-expenses-paid five-star conference at the end of it was tempting, but it was also tempered by a decision she'd made that she was yet to tell anyone.

New York was going to be her swan song. She'd loved her job for twenty-three years, but in the last twelve months, she'd been feeling too old and tired to be chasing deliveries around the world in other people's time zones. This job had saved her financially, put her kids through school, paid off her mortgage, bolstered her super and reminded her during the hardest years after the divorce that she wasn't a failure. Her speciality was the complicated and urgent jobs, the ones that meant sitting on the phone in the middle of the night and watching the computer on weekends, stressing about deadlines and the clients whose contracts, sometimes make-or-break contracts, relied on her. Being recognised at an international level – for her knowledge and experience, if not for the stress and hours – felt like the perfect high note to end on before exiting stage left at the end of the year. Just three months away now.

She hadn't said *Retirement* out loud yet and couldn't contemplate what it might look like, but she was tired of her life being held hostage by other people's deliveries. She'd need to dedicate some brain space to thinking about it once the conference was over. Maybe she'd do a course, or read the thousand books she hadn't had time to open, learn a language or just contemplate her navel whenever she felt like it. All she knew was that time for herself had been a very rare commodity for a long, long time.

She tapped her phone as she moved to a quiet corner. Eyes on the Sydney skyline, she listened through half a dozen rings before she heard muffled voices.

'Mum, it's Coral. Can you turn the TV down?'

'Hello?' A man's voice. 'Is that Coral?'

'Yes, who's this?'

'My name's James, I'm an ambulance officer. I'm with your mum, Valerie. She's had a fall.'

☕

Later, Coral felt bad that her first reaction hadn't been to gasp, 'Is she alright?' Instead, she'd screwed her eyes tight and clenched her teeth for three long seconds before digging deep and forcing herself to focus on her mum and not the twenty things that needed to happen before she could get to a hospital.

Five minutes later, Coral was pacing back and forth, waiting for Summer to answer her phone.

'Hey, Coral.' It was Summer's husband Dan. He sounded calm, but he didn't usually answer Summer's phone, and his voice shot another bolt of alarm through Coral's nerves.

'Is Summer okay?'

'She thinks she's coming down with something so I'm doing dinner and bath time for the kiddo while she has a rest.'

'Right.' Coral closed her eyes, trying to find sympathy, but her mind was already running through alternative options.

'What's up?'

'Mum had a fall. She's on her way to the hospital in an ambulance and I'm in Sydney.'

'Hang on, I'll put Summer on.'

There were muffled voices, then Summer's voice, husky from sleep. 'Is Nana okay?'

'You first. Are you alright?'

'My throat's scratchy and I'm a bit achy. Hopefully just tired.' She cleared her throat. 'What happened with Nana?'

'Apparently she was taking the garbage bin out to the kerb and . . .' What was Val doing taking it out on her own? It wasn't even bin night.

'And what?'

'I don't know. Someone found her on the driveway. The ambo said she was conscious but confused, bleeding from a graze on her head, and there's something wrong with her ankle. I thought you might be able to meet her at the hospital, but it sounds like you should be in bed.'

'What about her neighbour?'

'She's away.'

'Her best friend?'

'She needs a walker and won't drive at night.' Possibly shouldn't be driving at all. 'It's fine, don't stress. I'm heading back now.'

'I'll catch the train home later,' Jess said, her eyes straying to the others gathering for a post-meeting dinner that Coral would now miss. 'You don't mind, do you?'

Mind? Coral huffed silently, pushing paperwork into her brief-case as she gave in to a moment of silent griping. She'd listened to hours of Jess's relationship issues and twice picked her up when her car broke down. Then she shook her head. 'No, it's fine.'

In the end, she was glad Jess hadn't come with her: it gave Coral a chance to panic on her own as she drove along the dark motorway. There'd been similar rushes to the hospital. Once Coral had aban-doned a trolley full of groceries at the checkout, and another time she'd needed to use someone's breathalyser before getting in her car. Each time, she'd spent hours at Val's bedside, comforting, reassuring, worrying and waiting. Endlessly waiting – for nurses, doctors, information, pain relief, bedpans, a bed in a ward, coffee. Then follow-up appointments and rehab; updates repeated over and over to her kids, her brother Andrew in Tasmania, Val's neigh-bours and friends, and to Val herself, who was either increasingly in denial or unable to comprehend.

Coral had juggled it all with a full-time workload, overnight emails, increasing stress levels and decreasing tolerance. But now, she was going to New York in a week and there was no-one but Coral to manage the time-burning, patience-destroying, smile-or-you'll-cry process.

Andie

'Do you need more pain relief?'

Andie swivelled her eyes to the voice at the side of the bed. Her friend Vivian looked like shit. No make-up, hair scraped back in a ponytail, eyes huge behind thick glasses. Viv hated wearing her glasses.

Andie licked her lips. 'What time is it?'

'Three-ten.'

'In the afternoon?'

'In the morning.'

Without moving her head, Andie walked her gaze around the chaos of medical equipment and curtains, beds and patients, doctors, nurses, beeping machines. The stand beside her own bed with its tubes running into her arm. Her other one wrapped in a bandage. She lifted it and winced. 'What's wrong with my arm?'

'You haven't had X-rays yet but the elbow doesn't look good, apparently.'

It hurt. So did her head. She wished it would stop spinning, and pounding like it wanted to explode out of her ears. 'What happened?'

Vivian's magnified eyes held hers. 'There was a car accident.'

'Did I . . .?' *Oh god.* 'Was it my fault?'

'No, honey. You were hit by a car.'

Hit? By a car? Andie couldn't remember but somehow, in the spinning and thumping in her head, it seemed to make sense. 'Am I okay?' She felt numb and achy and she was in a hospital with a tube in her arm so, obviously, not okay. But it was all relative.

'You don't remember what the doctor said?'

'There was a doctor?'

Vivian gave Andie's hand a gentle squeeze. 'It's okay, you've got a concussion. You bumped your head pretty bad and your memory is . . . a bit off.'

Andie looked her friend over again. 'Are you okay?'

'I wasn't there.'

'Are you sure?'

'I was at home.'

'There was someone.'

'Yes, there were—'

'Was it Zack?'

Viv's eyes welled. 'Andie, he's been gone two years.'

Yes, of course, she knew that. She wasn't that concussed, but for just a moment it had felt like . . . Now Andie felt a different kind of pain. Blinking hard, she focused on sudden activity at the nurses' station. Several people in scrubs made a dash to a bed in the next bay, a nurse concealing the scene with the swish of a pale curtain.

Alarm tightened in Andie's chest. 'Who was I with?'

'You don't remember me telling you?'

'When?'

'Before. A couple of times before.' Vivian gave Andie's hand another squeeze. 'Four people were injured.'

Andie's eyes slid around again, dread thumping through her veins. Was it people she knew? People she cared about? 'Four?'

'There might be more. Or less. It's just what I last heard. One of them isn't doing so well.'

Andie wanted to ask who and where and how, but the questions were swept aside by the efforts going on behind the curtain around the bed opposite. Had she been with someone else in the moments before they died?

There wasn't a chance to ask. An orderly arrived to wheel Andie to X-ray, telling Vivian it could take a while. Viv looked tired and anxious, and undecided about whether to stay or leave. It was almost four o'clock in the morning, and apparently Andie had been drifting in and out of sleep the whole time. No point Viv waiting around for more of that. So Andie told her friend she loved her, and loved her even more for coming to the hospital in the middle of the night, and now she'd love her to go home and get some rest. Maybe in the morning she'd only have to explain once, or once more, what the hell had happened.

␥

'But why was I there?' Andie asked again, rolling her head on the pillow and wincing at the pain from the lump on the back of her skull. 'At eleven o'clock on a Tuesday night?'

'I don't know,' Vivian said again.

Andie had spent the day sleeping through slabs of time, dragged back to consciousness by nurses taking obs, Emergency Room noise, a couple of times to throw up. Sometime in the afternoon, she'd been wheeled to a ward room; sometime after that wakefulness had arrived, along with a pressing need to know. 'But I walk at five-thirty on Wednesday mornings. Why would I be out that late?'

Vivian shrugged.

'And on my own? It doesn't make sense.' Andie sighed, resting her chin on the cushion of a neck brace. 'I don't do alone.'

Vivian made a face that said she knew, she knew why and she didn't like it. 'All I know is what you texted me last night. And that you should probably be resting, not worrying about what you don't know.'

Andie had rested all day and felt exhausted and sore. She'd fractured her olecranon, the bony tip of the elbow; it had split the skin, but aside from a few stitches, it was a clean break with no floating fragments and no need for surgery. According to the doctor, it had probably been caused by landing on her elbow, rather than the impact with the car, which somehow felt better. A CT scan of her head had shown no damage, but memory loss, vomiting and a stiff neck was enough to make the head doctor keep her in overnight, which she wasn't going to argue about.

Vivian had arrived with flowers, fresh clothes and get-well wishes from a thousand people – poor Viv had been fielding calls all day. It was weird how fast word spread, and lovely that people had tracked down her best friend to send kind thoughts. Even better that no-one she knew had been injured, but all Andie wanted to know was why she'd been where she was when a car ran out of control.

She'd heard bits and pieces about the accident in Emergency, but she'd been woozy from concussion and pain meds, and she wasn't sure how much of it she'd dreamed. Googling would have been an option if she had a phone, but she'd arrived at the hospital with her handbag, one shoe and no mobile, which was assumed smashed under the tyres of the car that had veered off the road and over the kerb she'd been standing on. Better the phone than her, but it made it hard to get information. She'd garnered some details from nurses and the tiny TV at the end of her bed, but it wasn't until Vivian arrived that Andie started to get a clearer picture.

She'd gone to the bar to meet a fellow recruiter from Sydney, who'd been in town for a conference. The drink had been arranged the day before. Andie remembered the details after Vivian reminded her, but the actual night was a hole in Andie's memory.

According to Viv, Andie had kept forgetting whether her colleague's name was Michael Mitchells or Mitchell Michaels. She'd met him once at another conference and had to look up his profile to remember what he looked like. He'd emailed out of the blue to say he was in town and she'd only agreed to meet him because her ceramics class was on a term break. Vivian had kept calling it a date, Andie had pretended that was funny, and they'd both agreed if the fake-date wasn't worth a second drink, she'd go back to Viv and Theo's for takeaway.

According to Vivian, Andie had texted to say Mitchell Michaels hadn't turned up. She'd declined Viv's offer of the takeaway and several hours later, a car had veered off the road outside the bar and ploughed into several pedestrians, including Andie.

Googling on Vivian's phone, they worked out that four other people had been taken to hospital. Two were discharged with scrapes and a sprained ankle, a man was admitted after suffering a heart attack, and another man was in intensive care, listed as serious but stable.

The police weren't saying whether the driver hit them on purpose or by accident, but he was currently in a bed somewhere in the hospital.

Andie had no memory of any of it. She knew the bar, at the end of a strip of eateries by the harbour, and the road that ran past it, so she attempted to prompt her memory by conjuring up an image of the footpath at night. But the horror of a car barrelling into a group of people made her push the image away, unwilling to invent a set of screaming, crying memories to add to the ones she already had.

'Read the texts to me again.'

Vivian cast Andie a doubtful look before holding up her phone. 'At eight-oh-eight, you said he didn't show. I suggested Thai at my place. Twenty minutes later, you said: "Chatting. Just ordered risotto. Talk tomorrow."'

Note to self: send more detailed texts in future. 'So I stayed and ate risotto until eleven pm when my alarm was set for five the next morning.' Andie didn't like the early start, but she had a record to uphold – she was the only person who hadn't missed a morning since she'd started the walking group eighteen months earlier.

Mitchell Michaels had been among the people who'd tracked Vivian down after the accident. He'd lost track of time at the conference and felt awful that Andie had ended up in hospital.

'You'd think whoever I was chatting to would have tried to get in touch. Nothing on social media?' she asked again.

Vivian shook her head. 'Maybe they didn't know your name.'

'Maybe they were leaving town and flying to, I don't know, Helsinki.'

'Gah, Helsinki.'

Andie and Viv had flown home from there once, and thanks to missed connections and delays, it had taken days. 'Maybe they haven't seen any news from here. Maybe they'll reach out when they get wi-fi.'

'Sure.' Viv's tone suggested that either she thought Andie should leave it alone or she'd lost interest in questions she couldn't answer. Viv wasn't into detail, not like Andie. Andie had always thought that was one of the reasons they'd stayed friends through six and a half years of travelling the world: Vivian could see the grand plan of where to next, and Andie could work out how to make it happen.

Of course, Vivian wanted to move on. But Viv didn't have a big, black hole in her memory. She hadn't done something that didn't make sense, something that had made her wake up thinking of Zack.

☕

Night-time in the hospital was the kind of dark and quiet that made Andie's heart thump with dread. Her head and elbow hurt, she had assorted grazes and wrenched muscles and she was tired to the core, but her mind kept trailing off to the other dark places that kept her awake at night.

Around three, she asked a nurse, 'Is there anyone from my accident on the ward?'

'Sorry, we're not allowed to give out patient details.' She checked Andie's chart and bag of fluid. 'Can I get you anything?'

'Something for the headache?'

As the thumping eased, sleep finally came and Andie slid in

and out of dreams about Zack, smiling and jokey, as though he'd dropped by to cheer her up. So different from the way he usually came back to her. Then it wasn't Zack, but a sort of dreamworld sense of him that made a chuckle rise in her chest, and when she leaned into his warmth, she got tangled in the bars on the bed.

As dawn filtered around the edges of the window, Andie wondered if the presence she sensed from the accident *was* Zack. Not a ghost, she didn't believe in those, but an essence of him that she'd held on to all this time. Perhaps she'd imagined him into so many moments of her life in the last two years that when her brain had thought she was about to die, it had imagined him there with her.

She wanted to be comforted by the idea that he was with her when she needed him, but she couldn't help thinking there was something innately stupid about wasting time conjuring a dead man instead of getting the hell away from a speeding car.

☕

There was a uniformed police officer at the door when Andie returned from the bathroom, dressed for the first time since she'd woken up in Emergency and ready to fling the hospital gown to whatever hell it had come from.

'Sorry I'm so early but I was here on another matter,' the young woman said. 'I thought I'd see if you were up to answering some questions.'

'Sure, anything for company.'

After asking how Andie was feeling, the officer said, 'When you spoke with officers after the accident, you were unable to remember what happened.'

'I spoke with officers?'

'A constable at the scene and another officer while you were in Emergency.'

'Did I tell them what I was doing at the bar?'

'You didn't make an official statement and I don't have details about that, but my flatmate is the constable who sat with you at the scene. She said you were worried about some money. You kept looking for it in your handbag.'

Andie frowned. 'How much money?'

'Five dollars.'

'Five . . . oh, wait. That's the fine for not turning up to my Wednesday morning walking group. Maybe I'd decided not to go and was planning to pay.' Her glee at remembering sobered at the thought she'd been worried about her social activities while people around her had been hurt. 'What about the other people who were injured? How are they?'

The two who'd been discharged on the night had been injured running out of the vehicle's path. The driver was the man who'd had a heart attack, assumed at this stage to be the cause of the accident. The other patient, a forty-one-year-old man, had been standing near Andie on the kerb and had been thrown ten metres by the force of the impact. He'd suffered multiple fractures and was in an induced coma, still serious but stable.

Andie had a hand pressed to her chest by the time the officer finished. 'I was near him?'

'On the kerb, yes.'

'Do you have his name?'

She checked her notes: 'Benjamin Davison Cameron. Do you know him?'

Andie worked in recruitment, she knew a lot of people. She wanted to know Benjamin Davison Cameron. She wanted to know what she was doing outside a bar at eleven o'clock at night near Benjamin Cameron. She scrolled back through the client database in her mind, then shook her head. 'No.'

'He's from Perth.'

It didn't help. 'Is he going to be okay?'

'I can't answer that, I'm sorry.'

'What was he doing there?'

'I don't have those details. He hasn't been able to give a statement.'

Heat welled in Andie's eyes. He was two years older than her, he'd been standing on a kerb with her and he'd been thrown ten metres. It could have been *her*.

'You'll need to provide a statement for the investigation, but I know it can be upsetting to hear the details, and you don't have to do it today. We can contact you again in a few days.'

'What if I can't remember?'

'Your statement can be recorded as "no memory of the events".'

Andie rubbed the bump on the back of her head, eyeing the sling on her arm. She'd been hurt, and so had others. She wanted more than a black hole in her memory to be her final say.

'Can I take the few days option?'

The doctor removed Andie's neck brace and cleared her for discharge on his morning rounds. Vivian picked her up an hour later, saying as she turned into her own street, 'It makes sense to come to ours. You're meant to have someone to keep an eye on you for a few days and you can't drive for a week. Besides, you're already part of the family.' So while Viv shouted to Theo that lunch was on, Andie moved back into her old room down the hall.

'You look like hell,' Theo said, avoiding the sling as he gave her a hug.

Andie touched her cheek, where even her freckles didn't camouflage the bruise, and patted down her bird's nest of ginger hair: impossible to tame that curly mass with one hand. 'Thank you for the confidence builder.'

'Always glad to help.'

Andie had met Theo twelve years ago as they queued for coffee in an internet cafe in Amsterdam. It took thirty seconds for her intuition to kick in and she'd steered him across the room to meet her best friend. The rest was Theo and Vivian's history. He'd joined them on their travels through Europe for six months, worked in factory jobs with them outside Prague when the money ran low, and then when Viv fell pregnant and wanted to go home, Theo decided being a Frenchman in Australia would be an adventure.

Andie travelled for another three years on her own and came home at thirty-one with barely a dollar to her name and no useful job experience, ten years after finishing her degree. Theo talked her into a job in recruitment, a profession that she now loved and that had saved her twice – back then, when she needed a new beginning, and again two years ago when she needed something to hold her together.

Both times, Viv and Theo had been her backstop. When she returned from her travels, Andie spent six months living in what was now Theo's office; the second time, Andie and her grief had holed up in their spare room. Now, at thirty-nine years of age, she was back in the room down the hall, and as comforting as it was to be staying with her best friends, it felt like a giant step backwards to a place she'd worked hard to move on from.

Not that her feelings on the situation were going to kickstart her into recovery. She was exhausted by concussion, medication and whatever else her body was working through. She'd imagined healing would involve the people and activities that normally kept her in company outside of work hours. Only when her head had hit the pavement, her brain had been tossed hard enough into her skull to cause a frontal lobe concussion. It was probably the reason for her memory loss, but it was also causing thumping headaches and fatigue that made Andie's body feel like it weighed a tonne. She got dizzy if she moved too fast, bright light hurt her eyes and loud noises made her ears ring. She was weepy, had trouble doing anything more complicated than watching the telly, and phone calls left her with an urgent need for silence.

Andie had been told there was no knowing how long her symptoms would last, so while she did little more than slump on the sofa, Vivian, Theo and twelve-year-old Camille carried on with life around her, apparently fine with stepping back to when Andie was the broken person in their house.

The upside was that she wasn't alone. She wasn't sure she could handle being alone in that state. Not just because of her usual anxiety; the puzzle over what she couldn't remember had added another layer of angst.

To help, Theo set up a new phone for Andie, and when her bruised brain couldn't remember what to do, Camille tapped through it, mining it for information. All they discovered was that she'd ordered an Uber a couple of minutes before the accident: for one passenger, going to Andie's home address.

Meanwhile, Vivian worked her marketing job from home, kept Andie fed and clothed and tried to convince her to focus on the fact that she'd survived.

A week after waking up in Emergency, Andie went back to her own home. Light and sound weren't bothering her as much, the head-aches had dulled, her concentration was improving and she only needed the sling to give her arm a rest. The townhouse, though, felt dark and solemn.

'I could put some washing on,' Vivian said as she stacked ready-to-eat meals into the fridge.

'You've washed everything but the clothes on my back.'

'Then get that lot off and give me something to fuss about.' Vivian grinned, but there was an anxiousness to it. She was worried about handing the reins over to Andie. So was Andie.

When Viv had gone, Andie filled the yawning silence with television voices, clattering about in the kitchen as though there was urgent reorganising to be done. When a Constable Bess Paterson phoned to ask about making a statement, Andie told her to come on over.

'It's good to see you looking a lot better,' Constable Paterson said, shaking Andie's hand.

She was thirty-ish and lean, waist bulky with the paraphernalia on her uniform belt. There was nothing familiar about her, but

Andie liked the kindness in her gaze. 'I'm sorry, I don't remember you.'

'I was with you at the accident scene. You were pretty confused.'

'Another officer told me about that. Thank you for being there. I don't remember, but you seem like a good person to be with in a bad moment.'

They sat with coffee at either end of the sofa, Andie holding her mug between both hands as she said, 'Do you mind if I ask some questions first?'

'Sure.'

'Did I tell you why I was there?'

'You were a bit all over place.' Bess flipped through some pages in a notebook. 'You talked about the money you couldn't find, we discussed charades, and there was something about a hen.' She touched the bottom of the page with her index finger. 'Not a chook, a hen. You said that several times.' She looked back at Andie to see if any of that made sense.

'Charades and a hen.' She rolled her eyes. It was bad enough that she'd forgotten the important stuff, but it seemed like a different kind of failure to resort to stupid, pointless conversation as soon as she went into shock. What was the evolutionary point of that? 'Clearly I was talking gibberish.'

'You weren't making much sense, but I wrote it down. Nothing about why you were there, though. You don't remember?'

'None of it.' Andie nodded at the notebook. 'Will the gibberish go into my statement?'

'It wasn't a formal interview. I thought you had a concussion and I didn't want you to go to sleep, so I tried to keep you talking until the ambos could get to you.'

Maybe Bess was the *someone* Andie had thought she was with, that she'd thought was Zack? 'Was I conscious the whole time?'

'You were when I found you. You were away from the impact site, sitting with your back against the wall of the bar, holding on to your handbag.' She crossed her arms over her chest, demonstrating a desperate clutch. 'I don't know if you got yourself there or someone moved you, but I was on site for five or ten minutes before I saw you.'

Maybe the *someone* had helped her away from the car. Or maybe she'd stumbled about until she fell over, blathering about hens and charades. She'd travelled the world for ten years, staying calm and practical through more than a few tense moments, but she'd changed since Zack. She was breakable now. She shook her head, then asked, 'How is Benjamin Cameron?'

'You remember him?'

'No, but the last I heard, he was serious but stable while I'm—' she swept an arm around the room, 'here.'

The young woman nodded. 'He's still in ICU. The detectives are hoping he'll be well enough to be interviewed in a few days.'

'And the driver?'

'He had heart surgery a couple of days ago. It's possible there'll be charges, but at this stage, it appears his heart attack was the cause of the accident.'

Andie closed her eyes, thinking about the randomness of having a heart attack behind the wheel, of standing on a kerb just as that happened, of the fact that a few steps in one direction or another was the difference between minor injuries and being put in a coma.

'There's something else.' Bess flipped a few pages in her notebook. 'The accident wasn't caught by the bar's CCTV cameras, so until yesterday, we only had eyewitness accounts of the incident. But some vision has come in that shows what happened.' She paused to roll her lips together. 'I thought you might want to know that Benjamin Cameron pushed you out of the way.'

Andie's hand flew to her throat.

'You were in the path of the car and he,' Bess held out both hands and mimed a shove, 'pushed you sideways.'

'The car was going to hit me?'

'Yes.'

'Not him?'

'That's hard to determine from the footage. But he clearly sees it, turns towards you and shoves. It was pretty hard, you were lifted off your feet and pushed far enough to avoid being hit full-on by the vehicle.' Bess nodded towards Andie's elbow. 'Obviously it still didn't miss you.'

Andie shook her head. 'The injury is from landing.' She swallowed hard. 'He was hit instead of me?'

'Yes. The driver managed to get his foot off the accelerator before the vehicle reached the kerb, so it had slowed, but yes, Mr Cameron was right in front of it.'

Andie pressed both hands to her chest and breathed hard. She tried to speak, but her throat had closed.

'Can I get you some water?'

'No. I'm . . . It's . . . a lot to take in.' She blew out a breath, smoothed down her hair. 'Is he still in a coma?'

'An induced coma. I think it's possibly for broken ribs.'

Andie squeezed her eyes shut but couldn't stop the image of the street outside that bar, her body flying sideways while the car slams into the man beside her. 'I need to . . .' How do you make up for that? 'Thank him. Can I? Meet him? When he's awake.'

'That's not up to me. His family hasn't released his details yet. But I could let them know you're interested in talking to him. Is that something you'd want?'

'Yes. Please.'

☕

After Constable Paterson left, Andie lasted an hour in the solitude of the townhouse then took some painkillers, ditched her sling and walked to the pub on the corner, needing company to stop the dark thoughts from rising. She greeted the owner with a hug as she headed into the restaurant, her head ringing with the noise, but the rest of her body more relaxed.

The next morning, home felt like punishment. Andie had been

told to take a month off work to recover from the concussion, which meant three more weeks of rest and recovery. Only Andie needed to keep her mind occupied, and was uneasy about being alone. Bess Paterson had said she'd call when there was news from Benjamin Cameron's family, and the waiting added another layer to Andie's anxiety, on top of the guilt that he was in intensive care instead of her.

She filled the rest of the week with friends, meeting up for coffee and lunch and returning home bone-tired. Her head ached, but she went to book club on Thursday night regardless. She was greeted with hugs and baked goods, offers of lifts and advice for bringing out and covering up the bruising on her cheek. Andie's eyes welled with every new utterance of empathy and care. But she'd done enough crying with these women over the last two years.

'I'm fine, really,' she said on repeat, grateful to have these girl-friends, to fill her mind with their smart, funny, supportive voices. Because she wasn't fine. Not really. She felt as though the hit to her head had shaken something loose that was now floating around like a free radical; bumping about inside her, threatening to disturb emotions and memories that, if she wasn't careful, would push her back to the dark place she'd worked so hard to pull herself from.

On Friday, she got in her car for the first time since the accident and drove to her doctor's office to have her stitches removed. She'd been told not to drive for a week after the head injury, and not until she had good movement in her elbow. Afraid of causing an even longer recovery, she'd taken a few extra days to make sure the dizziness was gone. The glare hurt her eyes and the steering made her elbow ache, and by the time she got back to the townhouse, she was exhausted and cursing: cursing the driver who'd had the heart attack, and the concussion for making her brain hurt, and herself for being stupid enough to stand on a kerb and risk rekindling cruel memories.

Andie had started the Saturday morning coffee crowd eighteen months ago as a way to fill her weekends with people, but today her head ached and her concentration was off, and the idea of sitting with fifteen or so people and their post-cycling/walking/swimming energy was too much. Instead, she suggested to Vivian a quiet cafe somewhere else.

'I feel pretty good today,' Andie told her as they sat at a table.

'Yesterday you were going to shave your head.'

'You try doing my hair with one arm.' Andie gave her curly mop a flick.

'How'd you go writing those emails?'

Phone conversations still made Andie's head ache and Vivian was still fielding inquiries about her best friend, so writing group emails with updates on her progress had seemed like an easy solution for both of them. Until Andie tried. 'My head and fingers aren't talking to each other yet.'

'Brain fuzziness.'

Vivian said it like she was ticking a box on the list of indicators for frontal lobe concussion. Andie wasn't sure if it was meant to make her feel better about the symptoms, but this morning it only seemed to rub in how useless Andie would be at work and how long it might be before she got back there. Without warning, Andie burst into tears.

Viv reached a hand across the table. 'You're doing great.'

Andie turned her fingers to clasp the familiar presence.

'I thought you were feeling more positive today?'

'I was.' She wiped her eyes with a serviette. 'I am. That just came out of nowhere.'

'Probably another symptom of the concussion.'

'Blubbering in public places?'

'Mood swings, being over-emotional.'

Andie sighed, staring out the window at the drizzle that had been uplifting a few minutes ago. A moment later, her eyes welled again.

'Andie?'

She wiped her nose. 'I feel like I'm back where I was two years ago.'

'You've got a concussion. It's not the same.'

'Yeah, but...' She stirred her cappuccino. 'You know how it was after Zack.'

A fleeting frown. 'This is about Zack?'

'No. Kind of.' Andie sat back, folded her arms. 'Two years ago, a terrible thing happened and I sat around like a zombie. *This* feels like *that*.'

Vivian pulled in a breath, as though wanting to say something but wary of upsetting Andie more.

'It's not about Zack,' Andie said before Viv could speak. 'Not in the grief kind of way. It's the stuck-ness. I don't want to get stuck again.'

'It hasn't been two weeks yet.'

'But I keep thinking about what happened, about what might have happened. Seeing it in my mind, like I used to see Zack that night. Over and over. I don't want this to go round and round in my head for months too.'

Vivian watched her a moment. 'Have you heard anything more about Benjamin Cameron?' She wasn't changing the subject: Benjamin Cameron had become their symbol of Andie getting closure.

'I texted Bess Paterson again yesterday, but still no word from his family about speaking to him.'

'You'll feel better when you can talk to the man who pushed you out of the way.'

'I hope so.'

'Have you thought any more about what you want to say to him?'

'Sorry you're messed up, no idea how that happened.' Andie made a face. 'Anything I come up with just sounds like not enough.'

'Why not tell him you can't remember what happened but you'll never forget what he did.'

Andie smiled up at her. 'That sounds so much better. Thank you.'

Viv clasped her hand again. 'Then you can close the door on this random bloody event and move on. Back to where you'd got to.'

Andie nodded. She really wanted it to happen that way.

Mara

'WHY ME?' MARA made no effort to hide the alarm in her voice.

'Did you talk to her?' Laura spoke without looking up from the pages she was compiling. 'I told you not to talk to her.'

'Well, I . . .' Mara winced. 'Gave her a lift home on Friday night.'

Laura shook her head as though Mara was a lost cause.

'She was trying to get an Uber,' Mara explained. 'But she couldn't work the app on her phone. I think she'd had a couple of drinks.'

Mara had only gone back to the office to pick up her car keys. It had been dark and creepy-quiet, and she'd let out a yelp of fright when Estelle Collings, the senior law partner, had stepped into the dim corridor. Possibly more than a couple of drinks, Mara had thought at the time; she'd smelled the Scotch when Estelle got close enough to shove her phone in Mara's face. The app had needed a password, the older woman hadn't a clue and Mara figured it would end badly if she just left her in the office on a Friday night. The woman was seventy-two, after all. Hence the lift. 'And I was going her way.'

'She lives down by the harbour.'

'I was picking my brother up at the station. He's back home after a year out west.' Mara smiled, remembering his hug on the platform as he'd lifted her off her feet. He'd grown up and out after nine months working on a farm, no longer her little brother just out of school.

Laura quirked an eyebrow at Mara. 'Well, you've done it now, haven't you?'

'Done what?'

'Put a big, fat target on your back. Estelle believes it's her duty to crush all kindness in the office. She feels more comfortable when everyone in the room is on the same page. The one she wrote on mean-spirited hostility.'

'Great.'

Closing the thick bundle of papers into a file and securing it with a pink ribbon, Laura dumped it in Mara's hands. 'Did you get the instructions for her apartment?'

'Yes.'

'Make sure you follow them.'

'And you're sure she meant me?' Mara was a lowly clerical assistant, unlike Laura, who was an actual lawyer.

'The email said Mara with an M.' Laura gave her a pointed look. 'She sent it last night, obviously advance planning for the kindness crushing.'

Mara with an M was how she'd ended up being Laura's friend. After only three weeks in the job, Estelle had walked into the kitchen and called out, 'Laura!' Mara had ignored her because, well, she wasn't Laura. They both had straight, ash-blonde hair but Mara was a head shorter than Laura, and not pregnant. After some irritated confusion on Estelle's behalf, Mara, like a normal person, had explained that her name was Mara, to which Estelle had barked, *I beg your pardon!* 'I'm Mara, with an M,' she'd said with a smile perfected over the gazillion times she'd corrected the pronunciation and spelling of her name. And so, the scary litigation lawyer had spent the next two months making a point of calling her Mara-with-an-M.

Calling Laura a *friend* was probably overstating it, Mara thought as she walked to her car. Laura was more of an overworked, cynical colleague who enjoyed a chuckle with Mara at Estelle's expense. But banter was the closest thing to friendship that Mara had these days.

Driving through the CBD to Estelle's apartment, Mara thought about the unsettling sight of Estelle Collings on Friday night without a jacket or shoes. Sure, it had been the end of the week, the staff had left – some, like Mara, for the pub across the road – and if it had been anyone else, Mara wouldn't have thought twice. But it was Collings Law Firm folklore that Estelle had never been seen without her uniform of Chanel-style suit, coordinating shoes and slash of red lipstick. In three months, Mara had never seen her look anything other than flawlessly attired, except for the lipstick, which had a tendency to bleed into the cats-bum lines around her lips. So when she'd spotted the stockinged feet and a creased shirt that had slipped to reveal the strap of her bra, Mara had let out another yelp of fright.

Mara had assumed that after being witness to her unkemptness and phone helplessness, Estelle would ignore her forevermore or, worst case, find a reason to get rid of her. Instead, she'd specifically requested Mara to deliver documents to her home on the very next working day – documents that she could have accessed via the Collings' internal network.

Parking out the front, Mara looked up at the exclusive apartment block and wished she'd left the scary woman to find her own way home. It was one of the old, establishment buildings that had been converted to apartments around the city. This one was down by the harbour, not far from where some pedestrians had been hit by a runaway car last week.

Following the instructions on her phone, Mara buzzed open the street doors with a security fob, her heels clacking through the marble foyer to the lift. According to Isna, Executive Assistant to Vaughn Collings, Estelle owned the entire top floor, and when the lift doors opened, Mara would step into a small entrance area where 'approved staff' could leave files without having to enter

Estelle's private domain. Although Mara had been told to knock and wait for further instructions, which she did, her eyes sliding around the white marble floor and walls.

After a full minute, she knocked again. A muffled sound made her lean a little closer. All she got was more silence, but as she straightened, she thought she heard it again. Was it a . . . thump? Turning her head until her ear was almost pressed to the door and hoping Estelle didn't choose that moment to open it, she held her breath and listened.

Nothing. She stepped back, glanced around. Maybe the senior partner had gone to grab a coffee and left a dog inside. Or a cat. Maybe she should leave the files at the door. With a note. That included her phone number. Or just a note that said she'd been and would come back. She sighed and knocked again.

The next sound she heard made the hairs on her arms rise. The noise was dulled by the connecting door, but it was most definitely a voice. A single, indistinct word. Not *Hello* or *What?*, not really even spoken; something closer to a low howl. Mara wanted to be wrong, wanted it to be a dog growling or a cat with a throat problem, but what it really sounded like was: *Help!*

Crap. Crapola.

Her hand hesitated over the doorhandle. If she burst in, Estelle might be furious. If she didn't burst in . . .

Well, there was no bursting – the handle didn't move. Mara scanned her instructions again: letting herself in wasn't even mentioned. She took a closer look at the keypad with no clue where to start, then pulled the security fob from her pocket. She'd never lived anywhere with more security than a key, but she'd been around enough of her dad's fancy home renovations to know a code wasn't the only way in. She tapped the fob against the device, heard a buzz and felt the handle release.

Stepping into a short corridor, she followed sunlight into a huge, open-plan room that made her breath catch. Wow: the view, the leather furniture and glossy white surfaces, the tasteful splashes of colour in interesting frames. Then the voice came again, sounding more strident and distressed, now that she could hear it properly. Mara took a few more steps, peering around another corner, her eyes sliding over a chrome and glass staircase in front of floor-to-ceiling windows. She only had time to think, *Two-storey-high windows!* before she heard Estelle's voice.

Not that it was anything like her usual snap of authority. It was the crumpled body on the floor that told Mara who owned it . . . and the blood smeared around her that made Mara gasp and rush to her side.

'My. Leg.' Estelle pushed the words through gritted teeth, although they were unnecessary. It was exceedingly obvious the leg was the problem.

The major problem.

'Yes. Yep. Okay.' Mara did a panicky, feet-shuffling dance as she took in the situation. Estelle was arranged at the bottom of the stairs like a murder victim in a horror movie. Pale like a mannequin, her tall, gangling frame bent at the wrong angles. Her shoulders were on the floor, torso twisted onto one hip, her top leg raised and anchored where her shin was caught between two treads several steps from the bottom.

Mara didn't want to look, but she stepped gingerly around the mess of body fluids and tangled limbs and lifted the edge of Estelle's blood-soaked dressing gown from where it covered her thigh. 'Oh . . . It's . . . The bone . . .'

'Has it?' Estelle asked.

Mara nodded, covering it again, swallowing hard. 'I'll, um . . .' She'd pulled her mobile from her pocket without realising. 'Call an ambulance.'

She'd imagined a rush of sirens and efficient officers, but got put on hold. With rising alarm, she set the phone on speaker and squatted beside Estelle, careful not to get the knees of her trousers anywhere near the mess on the floor. As well as blood, there was a yellow puddle on the white marble that Mara didn't want to think about. Her hands hovered over the older woman, wanting to release her leg, only not sure where or whether to touch her. 'Are you hurt anywhere else?'

'Left shoulder.' Her voice was hoarse. Maybe she'd been calling out for a while. 'My head.' The words were clipped as though they were an effort. She lifted a trembling hand, and Mara's stomach jolted at the bloody gash through the middle of it. She grabbed the phone as the ambulance service connected.

'How long has the patient been there?' the operator asked when Mara had explained the situation.

She looked at Estelle, who licked dry lips. 'One am.'

Oh, geez. 'Since one o'clock. No, I just found her.' She answered more questions, raised her eyebrows at Estelle to confirm she'd given the address correctly. Finally putting the phone down, she mustered what she hoped was an encouraging smile. 'Just twenty minutes more, okay?'

Estelle rolled her eyes closed.

Mara couldn't tell if it was relief, despair or pain. 'How do I let them in?'

'Security panel at the front door.' The hinge at the side of her jaw bulged as she took a breath. 'Tap the screen.'

'Okay. Just a minute.' Slipping off her shoes, not wanting to walk blood and . . . whatever else through the white apartment, Mara went to make sure she could work the panel before returning. 'Can I get you something?'

'Pillow.'

Mara looked over at the leather lounges she'd seen on the way in and the pale, expensive-looking cushions. Best not. 'They said not to move you. Are you cold? Can I get you a blanket?'

'Upstairs.'

Mara skirted the blood on the lower stairs and bolted upwards, reaching a narrow landing suspended like a parapet over the floor below, the sparkling view of the harbour stretching in every direction. She hurried past a guest room and a bathroom and another room. No time to search for a linen cupboard, she grabbed a neatly folded rug from the end of a bed, towels from a bathroom and ran back down the stairs.

Wadding a small towel around Estelle's bleeding hand, she set a larger one on the floor to soak up the . . . fluid. Estelle sucked in a breath when Mara tucked the blanket around her shoulders. 'Sorry, sorry. Can I call someone for you?'

A small shake of Estelle's head.

'A friend?' Mara pressed. The woman was seriously injured, someone who cared about her should be here. 'Vaughn? Other family?' *No.* 'Someone at the office?' *No.* 'Someone who could meet you at the hospital?'

'I said *no.*' Estelle closed her eyes.

Mara wondered if Estelle had no-one who'd care or if she didn't want anyone to know what had happened. Pulling in a breath, her gaze followed the upward curve of the staircase. 'Were you going up or down?'

Estelle opened her eyes again, but kept her focus on the ceiling way above them. 'Down,' she said. 'My slipper caught.'

This time Mara followed the downward curve of the stairs, all the way to where Estelle's leg was caught, and imagination tightened her face into a horrified grimace. There was a slipper on the floor over by the big window. Its position suggested the force behind the older woman's tumble, although the sheepskin booty with a hole in the toe was so different from Estelle's usual Chanel uniform that a nervous, anxious giggle gathered in Mara's throat. As she glanced around again, she noticed the jagged edges of broken glass, and more spilled liquid under the staircase.

'Yes, I was drinking,' Estelle hissed with sudden vehemence. 'Make sure you tell them *that.*' There was a spiky anger in her voice now, as though Mara daring to take stock of the circumstances was presumptuous beyond belief. 'Scotch, if you must know. And yes, I urinated on myself. Make sure you include *all* the evidence in your witness statement.'

Mara opened her mouth, but didn't know how to respond.

Despite the obvious pain and discomfort of being entangled in the stairs, and the fact that Mara was helping her, something nasty filtered through the older woman's narrowed eyes. 'Enjoy your five minutes, *Mara with an M*. But I want the *slipper* in your story.' It was the most Estelle had said in one breath, and the effort left her winded and limp, as though she'd harnessed all the energy she had left to be bitter and angry. 'Is. That. Clear?'

It was a demand, not a question, and even though the woman lay prostrate and frail on the floor, Mara wanted to snap something snarky in return. Instead, she said, 'Okay.'

Not a moment too soon, an ambulance officer buzzed the door.

Mara kept out of the way while the officers did their thing, catching snippets of the conversation as they moved around their patient. Estelle was on heart medication and had been drinking; three Scotches sometime between ten pm and one am. She hadn't passed out before she fell, but thought she'd been knocked out when she landed. She remembered losing her slipper and hearing her leg snap. No, she did not want the young woman who found her to go with her in the ambulance.

Which was excellent news, because Mara was done being kind to Estelle Collings. She hoped she never had to see her again.

Part 2

The Patients

Coral

CORAL FOLDED THE last of Summer's washing, pressing tops and jeans flat with her hands because she didn't have time to iron. She put the laundry basket by the front door with the ever-growing mountain of things to be carried out to the car. In the kitchen, she wedged a casserole dish into a thermal bag beside a container of soup, Oliver's lunch box and a batch of his favourite muffins. If anyone else had asked Coral to bake banana-choc chip muffins at seven-thirty last night she would have laughed, but who could deny their three-year-old grandson?

Shoving towels in the dryer in between putting on make-up and doing her hair, she finally pushed her feet into ankle boots and dropped her watch and gold studs in her pocket to put on later. She checked that the windows were closed and there was a lipstick in her bag, pulled a face at the basket of her own unfolded laundry and made her first trip to the garage.

Forty minutes later, she pulled into Summer's driveway and grabbed the bags of groceries she'd picked up on the way, the laundry basket, the thermal bag and the wool Summer had asked for.

'It's me!' Coral called as she let herself in.

'Still in bed,' came the reply.

'I'll just bring everything in.' No need to find time for exercise;

all she had to do was keep moving everyone's stuff back and forth. When she was done, Coral put the kettle on, dropped Dan's breakfast things in the dishwasher and headed down the hallway.

'How is everyone today?' she asked, chest heaving a little as she leaned against the doorjamb and peered into the shadows of her daughter's bedroom.

'Still alive.' Summer was propped on pillows, one foot encased in a fluffy sock on top of the covers and Oliver wedged into her hip.

'Reg is sick too,' Oliver announced, his arm hooked tightly around the neck of a pint-sized panda.

'Oh dear, not Reg too?'

'We've got the pops.'

Coral raised an eyebrow at Summer for a translation.

'Hey Oliver,' Summer said, 'let's get Gan-Gan to take a look at those spots on your feet.'

'And Reg's feet.'

'Yes, Reg's too, but you first.' As Oliver hooked two little feet over the sheet, Summer waved Coral over. 'He was scratching at them during the night.' She ran a finger around the scattering of small red spots on the soles of both feet and lifted fretful eyes to Coral.

Summer had reason to be fretting: she was thirty-five weeks pregnant with a three-year-old, and had fallen down the back steps in the throes of a cold over the weekend and torn the tendons in her ankle. Summer and Dan had bought a printing business eighteen months ago, and she was currently managing the accounts and wages while Dan trained a new staff member and tried to get in as many hours as he could before the baby came. Alarm didn't even register to Coral, though, as she crossed the room to Oliver's side of the bed. Mozzie bites made him break out in nasty welts and he had an allergy to certain suncreams: it could be anything. Unhooking the prescription sunglasses from the front of her shirt, Coral squinted at his feet.

'Is it chicken pox?' Summer asked.

'No.' But the sight of the blisters made the knot of stress in Coral's gut tighten. She checked his hands, asked to look in his mouth.

'What?' Summer asked.

'I think it's hand, foot and mouth.'

'You sure?' Summer said, snatching her phone up.

'Pretty sure.'

A couple of seconds later, Summer compared her son's feet and a blister in his mouth to images she'd found online. Then she dropped her head back on the pillows and groaned.

Coral felt like joining her.

Summer read from her phone. 'Seven to ten days. Fever, cough, sore throat.' She ran a gentle hand over her son's hair. 'Highly contagious, so isolation for two weeks.' A pause to grimace. 'But only from other kids. And there's no danger to pregnant women.'

'That's good news.' Coral smiled over the alarm that was rising at the idea she could be home with a fever instead of on a plane to New York in a week.

'Even better,' Summer added, 'most adults already have immunity and it's rare to get more than mild symptoms.' She looked up at Coral with relief.

'Thank goodness.' New York was safe.

'I'll say. You can still look after us.'

'What about Reg?' Oliver asked, holding him out to Coral.

She made a show of inspecting the panda's paws. 'Yep, he's got it too.' Tucking the sheet around Oliver and Reg, she swept a hand across his forehead. A little hot. 'How about you stay here with Mummy while I go make her a cup of tea.' She reached across him to smooth a reassuring hand over Summer's long, blonde hair as her daughter quietly sobbed.

Something anxious buzzed in Coral's legs as she fumbled with a mug and teabags in the kitchen. Waiting for the kettle to boil, she stared out the window and thought about her own fretful days when the children were little: sickness, injuries, tantrums. The exhaustion, long nights and loneliness, and the well of patience that always seemed close to running dry.

She felt for Summer – and little Oliver – but the adrenaline tingling in her feet and knees was more than empathy. Oliver would need to be isolated for ten days and was likely to be miserable for some of that. Summer had to be off her foot for at least a week and Dan was focused on keeping their business running. They would all look to Coral for help. Not only them but also Val, the Stockholm clients and Jessica, who was still learning the ropes. She had to get them all sorted and reassured before she flew to New York in a week.

Because she was going to New York. It was her turn, her time. She had earned it.

'Did you remember the wool?' Summer asked, now propped up in bed like a duchess sipping her morning tea. When Coral handed over the large bag, her daughter gave her a disapproving frown. 'You brought all of it?'

'You asked for the wool.'

'I asked for the *baby* wool.'

Coral gritted her teeth. 'I didn't have time to sort through it. It'll be a good job for you and Oliver whiling away your hours here.'

'Hardly whiling away my hours, Mum,' she snapped.

More teeth clenching as Coral checked her watch. 'Do you want me to help you migrate to the lounge room before I go?'

'You're not staying longer? I thought Nana wouldn't be at the rehab place until lunchtime.'

Val had survived her fall with a broken ankle, nasty bruising and two stitches in her forehead – a surprisingly good outcome, considering. Twenty-four hours after being admitted, she was declared well enough to be discharged. Except Val was eighty-five, lived alone and wasn't considered strong or mobile enough to go home without risk of another fall. So now she was in limbo, waiting in a shared ward in a public hospital until a bed in a rehab facility could be found, which, according to the social worker, could take up to two weeks.

But Coral was an expert in getting packages delivered.

It had taken a lot of phoning and begging, and a crash course in the booking schedules of rehabilitation hospitals. The two that were the best chance of having a bed in time worked on a two-week program: patients were admitted on a Monday and reassessed two weeks later. Coral would be on a plane next Monday, and with her brother 'too busy' in Tasmania, her son Wade in London and Summer out of action, she'd needed to get Val into a program today. After repeated calls, cajoling, reminding and pleading, Coral had been told yesterday that there was a room and transport for her mum at Hepburn House Rehabilitation Hospital. After that news, she'd treated herself to a home-delivered pizza and two glasses of red wine.

'I've got to go into work,' Coral told Summer. 'I've got a client with a big rush job that has to be sorted before I leave on Monday.'

'You're going *this* Monday?'

'Sunday, actually. The flight's at six am so I'm staying overnight in Sydney. But yes, *this* Monday!' She grinned, resisting an urge to pump her fists in the air.

'God, Mum.' Summer swung her face away, alarm and trepidation in her voice.

Coral's chest tightened in guilt and empathy. Very pregnant, a sick toddler and confined to bed, and her mother couldn't wait to leave the country. It took her back to the month she'd been stuck at home with two fevered and spotty kids barely out of nappies. But as compassion shrank her excitement, the reminder of her own days as a young mum made a voice in her head snap, *Try doing it without any help.* 'I'm not leaving for a week yet, Summer. You'll all be feeling a lot better by then, and I'll be helping in the meantime. Which is all the more reason for me to get this job sorted out, so I can get back to sorting everything else that needs to be sorted before I leave.' Coral pushed an encouraging smile onto her lips, trying not to think about just how much sorting was involved.

The migration to the lounge room took another half an hour

of Coral's diminishing time, after Summer decided she needed a shower and Oliver wanted toast. Then one of Gan-Gan's muffins. Warmed.

'No-one move!' Coral cried from the front door. 'I can't handle any more disasters before I leave the country.'

That earned her a withering look from Summer. Oliver didn't glance up from the picture book he was pretending to read. Coral sighed.

☕

The Stockholm job had been postponed again, and Coral was delayed at the office by several phone calls with the client, potential couriers, and mapping out multiple new routes based on price, speed and urgency. All the while drumming into Jessica the need to check the progress at each step of the way.

'I'll be ready as soon as you are,' Coral told Rodney with a reassurance that was more practised than actual, wishing she'd had time for coffee. Pulling into the car park at the rehab hospital, she hauled Val's wheelie suitcase from the boot and frogmarched it along a pathway that meandered through the garden instead of taking a more efficient straight line to the front entrance.

She scanned the foyer for signs of a cafe, gave up and followed the arrow to her mother's ward. Val was sitting in a chair beside a window near her bed; her ankle was in a fat boot, a small plaster covered the stitches on her forehead and her white hair glowed like a halo in the sunlight. Coral considered telling her she looked saintly, but decided not to start that conversation.

'I thought you were going to be here when I arrived,' Val said.

'Sorry, I got held up at work.'

'I was worried they might have sent you away early.'

'Sent me away?'

'To . . . to' – a moment of hand circles as she searched for the right word – 'wherever it is you're going.'

'New York,' Coral said, a little unnerved by her mother's

confusion. On the cusp of explaining that going to New York wasn't being 'sent away', she changed her mind and made a show of inspecting the room instead. 'This is nice.'

It was: pretty pink bedcover and curtains, timber-look wardrobe and side table, ensuite bathroom, a glass-enclosed balcony that looked out on a lovely view. Considering the scramble to get Val into rehab, Coral was relieved her mother hadn't ended up in a four-bed ward in a converted aircraft hangar.

'Yes, it's quite fancy. I hope you're not paying extra for it,' she said, lips pursed with disapproval.

Note to self, Coral thought: thank Summer or Wade if they choose to spoil her in her dotage. Not that Coral was paying anything for the room. 'It's all covered by your health insurance.' Reaching for another change of subject, she added, 'I brought fresh clothes for you, thought you might like to wear something nice for the daily promenading in the corridors.'

Val sniffed. 'Is it still called promenading if it's with a walker?' She'd been horrified at needing the 'contraption', loath for someone she knew to see her moving with anything but 'vigour'.

'I don't know, but you'll never get back to walking without one if you don't use it.' Hefting the suitcase onto the bed, Coral added, 'I bought a couple of new things, since getting in and out of trousers is difficult with your broken ankle.'

After an hour of trying on hastily bought new-season fashions, Coral was repacking the suitcase with several rejections and yet another mountain of laundry. A commotion in the hallway gave Coral an excuse to take a breather and peer into the passageway. There were only three rooms at this junction of the corridor: Val's at the end and one on either side. Several staff members had gathered by the room on the left as someone inside kicked up a fuss.

'Someone's not happy about doing rehab in the pool,' she told Val, picking up a meal planner from the bed table. 'How about we go through the meal choices?'

'They said I had to decide what I want for the whole week.'

'Probably easier for the kitchen.' She flicked through the booklet. 'Looks like there are different options every day.'

'But how will I know?' Val said.

'It's right here.' Coral showed her.

'But how will I *know*?' Val said again.

'Know what?'

'What I want on *Thursday*.'

'Thursday?' Coral schooled her forehead not to frown. 'Why don't we start with tomorrow and see how it goes?'

'Is it Thursday tomorrow?'

'It's Tuesday tomorrow.'

'Will I be here on Thursday?'

Coral searched her memory for what her mother usually did on a Thursday. She'd been a regular at tai chi before last year's nasty fall. 'What's happening on Thursday?'

'Well, I don't know, do I, Coral? No-one's told me if I'll even be here on Thursday.'

Coral felt both the habitual bristling at her mother's tone and the futility of explaining the rehab program half a dozen times if Val wasn't going to listen. Until she remembered Val's worry that Coral had already left for New York, the repeated questions in hospital, the search for the sock in her pantry, the stack of sheets in the hallway.

Her throat suddenly tight, she said, 'It's okay, Mum. I can explain it again.' Val might remember with some prompting. The fall, the broken ankle, the bump to her head might have shaken things up, and it might take a while for everything to return to normal. At eighty-five, she couldn't be expected to regain her normal 'vigour' as quickly as she used to.

Coral sat on the edge of the bed in front of Val's chair, not sure how far back to start. 'You broke your ankle last week when you took a tumble in the driveway.' She paused to see if her mother would insist *I know all that*. When Val simply waited, Coral had a sudden longing to gather her mother into her arms and hold her tight. But if Val didn't remember, Coral didn't want to make her worry about forgetting. 'The doctor said you need to stay off it for a few weeks, so we got you in here for a stay in rehab. You're booked in for the next two weeks and you'll be assessed for going home after that.'

Andrew had agreed to fly up from Tasmania for some of the time Coral was away; he was equally ready to hotfoot it back south as soon as Coral got home from New York. He ran a bed-and-breakfast, and finding someone to cover him at short notice was near on impossible, apparently, and his husband Tim's stress levels were more important than Coral and her need for a decent night's sleep after a long-haul flight: bloody older brother. Not that Val needed to be confused by the sibling negotiations or the news that she was likely to be in rehab for a month. 'So you'll be here this Thursday and next Thursday and maybe some more after that,' she explained.

Val nodded, as though resigned to a trial. 'What about this?' She pointed at the moon boot strapped around her lower leg.

'It lets you use your foot a little while keeping your ankle in the right position.'

'I don't need that.'

Coral hesitated, not sure if Val doubted the explanation or was in denial about her injury. 'Well, you do for now. Let's look at what you're going to be eating for the rest of the week.'

The thought of having someone to prepare three meals a day made Coral want to move in with her mum. Val, however, frowned as though she'd never seen a menu. She was confused by all the different options; then annoyed at Coral for asking so many questions. In the end, Coral decided what her mother would be eating from Thursday through to Sunday, hoping Val was just tired from the journey to the rehab hospital.

When the lunch trays came around, Coral was desperate for a break from the circular conversation.

'I'm going to grab a coffee and a sandwich,' she told Val,

hitching her bag onto her shoulder. 'You get started on your roast chicken.'

'Will you be back today?'

'I'm just going to find something to eat.'

'When are you going to New York?'

'Monday.'

'Today's Monday.' It was said both with pride and as a rebuke: she knew the day, and how could Coral think she didn't?

'Yep, Monday all day today. I'm flying out *next* Monday.' She kissed her mother's forehead and headed for the door.

She stopped by the nurses' station to identify herself as Val's daughter – experience had taught her that it never hurt to let each link in the chain know there was someone ready to ask and answer questions. She also wanted to find out when the doctor would arrive to assess Val. Over the last week, her mother's accounts of various doctors' visits had ranged from praise at her astonishing recovery to reports of the doctor's dress sense and offspring. Coral needed a firsthand account.

'He'll be in to see her sometime today,' a nurse told her.

Coral took a moment to paste a smile over the frustration that shot through her. *Today* meant she hadn't missed the doctor – good news, she reminded herself. But *sometime* meant any time in the next five, possibly six hours, which blew a hole right through the good news. She'd spent most of last week trying to catch the *sometime today* arrival of the doctor, specialist or social worker.

This was a new hospital, Coral told herself; new doctor, new line of communication, and biting the head off a potential new ally wouldn't help – or get her back to the office any faster.

As nicely as she could, Coral asked, 'Any guesses at a more specific time?'

'He likes to see everyone on the day they arrive, but it can take a while to get to all the new patients.'

'Fair enough. So he's doing that now? Working his way through the new arrivals?'

A glance at his watch. 'He's probably on his lunch break.'

'Well, we've all got to eat. And then he'll head in which direction?' Coral pointed towards the corridor.

The nurse ran a blue-painted fingernail down a chart and pointed in the opposite direction to Val's room. 'He still has a couple of patients to see down there.'

'So I've got some time before he sees Mum?'

'Probably.'

Probably was Coral's pet hate. *Probably* didn't cut it in her job. She'd told Jessica to strike *probably* from her vocabulary. After a week of 'probably' and 'sometime', a large part of her wanted to lose her cool with the nurse, but Coral focused her energy on keeping her expression calm. 'Great, well, can you point me in the direction of the cafe?'

'Yeah, no.' He waggled a takeaway coffee cup. 'There's no cafe.'

No cafe? 'It's. A. Hospital.'

'Uh-huh. And the cafe's being renovated,' he said. 'Come back in a month and you might be lucky.'

Coral's caffeine-deprived self wanted to shriek, but the logistics expert in her had already moved on to practicalities. 'Where did you get your coffee then?'

'Coffee van guy. He's been coming during the renovation.'

'Where do I find him?'

'Out the front. But you've missed him. Usually done by sometime after eleven.'

'Nearest takeaway then?' When he'd given her directions to a place down the hill, she explained, 'I want to be here when the doctor sees Mum, but I really need a coffee and something to eat. So while he's on his lunch break, I'm going to duck out quickly. If it looks like he'll be there before I'm back, can you, I don't know, stall him?'

'I'll let him know you're not far away.'

Mara

Vaughn Collings was Estelle's cousin, managing partner of Collings Law Firm and the son of one of the brothers who'd started the business. Mara had known him since she was a kid. He'd owned some of the houses she and Patrick would play in after school when Mum was working late and Dad was still hammering away at renos. In the last year, she'd addressed invoices to Mr Collings, grateful he'd stayed with Dad when so many clients hadn't. Three months ago, she'd been grateful all over again as she'd sat in his office for a job interview. For many reasons, the last thing she wanted to do was disappoint him.

She'd tried hard to be accurate and detailed when he'd grilled her after Estelle had been taken away in an ambulance. And she'd spent hours working on the witness statement he'd asked her to write. Despite Estelle's spitefulness – or perhaps because of it – Mara had gone to pains not to be nasty. She'd made sure to include the slipper, as ordered, and even when pressed by Laura for the gory details, she'd left out the Scotch/urine and the *Mara with an M* comment. She'd decided to give Estelle the benefit of the doubt and assume the ungrateful old bat had been in shock. Who ever said *Enjoy your five minutes* couldn't mean taking the high ground?

Mara had handed her report in on Thursday; now it was Monday and she'd been called to his office again. What more could she tell

Vaughn Collings a full week after his cousin had been carted off to hospital that he hadn't already found out for himself?

'I thought you might be interested in an update on Estelle.'

Vaughn said it as though Mara and Estelle had formed a special bond during the fraught hour they'd spent together. The truth was that Mara would prefer not to be reminded about the bone sticking out of Estelle's leg. 'Yes, of course. How is she?'

The staff had been told Estelle had surgery to repair the damage to her leg and a badly dislocated shoulder. 'Her surgeon was happy enough with her progress for her to be transferred to a rehabilitation hospital today.'

'That's good news.'

He patted the air with his hand, a *let's not get ahead of ourselves.* 'Of course, it's just the first step in her recovery. At seventy-two, it will take considerable time for her to heal. She's starting that process with two weeks of inpatient rehabilitation, after which she'll be assessed to determine whether she can manage at home.' Another air pat. 'She may need more rehab before that can happen. And of course, it'll be some time, months probably, before she's able to return to the office, if she does at all. In the meantime, our work here can't stop because one of us slipped on a staircase.' His mouth turned up as though he was quite pleased with that turn of phrase, then he cleared his throat. 'My job is to think about our clients, which is why I've called you in today.'

Mara waited as he scanned several pages in a folder, no idea what a clerical assistant had to do with the greater good of the business.

'I'm told your work in the three months you've been here has been of a high quality,' he said. 'In particular, your report on the events of last week. You've shown some talent for dealing with,' he tilted his head, 'sensitive issues. It's a valuable skill and something we'd like you to develop.' He placed a hand on the pages in front of him. 'Estelle has a portfolio of her own clients that she keeps separate from our general accounts. Most of these are clients she has done work for over many years – almost fifty years in some cases. I believe you have already been introduced to her filing system?'

Mara nodded. It was well known that Estelle had clung to her old-school, paper-based records long after the rest of Collings had digitised, and that it was only tolerated because, at seventy-two, everyone figured it would only be for a few more years. Plus, Mara guessed, no-one wanted to teach her how to use a new system.

'I'm assigning you to assist in the transition of her files onto our digital system.'

Mara frowned. 'Scanning and data entry?'

'There will be some of that, but' – he hesitated for the briefest moment – 'you will be working as her Executive Assistant.'

Executive Assistant! That was a big step up, but . . . No, wait! There were three Executive Assistants at Collings and each one was stressed, worked long hours and put up with a lot of crap from their bosses. Mara didn't want to be an EA. She especially didn't want to be Estelle's EA. No-one wanted to be Estelle's EA: personnel gave up trying to find her one when none stayed longer than three months.

Perhaps seeing the alarm in her face, Vaughn added, 'The job will entail doing whatever is necessary to enable the rest of us to pick up her client load. Some tasks will be of a personal nature, I'm sure, but it's important for our clients and for Collings that there is no uncertainty or confusion in the handover process.'

'But I'm a clerical assistant.'

'Who has shown the skills we need to help this happen smoothly.'

She'd called an ambulance and written a report. Hardly advanced administrative skills, but Vaughn didn't look open to debate. 'When would this start?'

'Today. This morning.'

'Isn't she in hospital?'

'You will be working with her there.'

'At her . . . bedside?'

'I imagine that's how it will work.'

Mara tried not to grimace, but her face just wouldn't obey.

Vaughn held up a hand. 'I understand my cousin can be difficult, but under that exterior is a smart, savvy solicitor with a wealth of experience you can learn from. She is someone who cares deeply about . . . about her clients. She can be critical, but that comes from wanting the best outcome for the people she works with and for.'

That was one way of looking at it. 'I don't . . .'

'This will be a challenging assignment, but discussion with your manager and the fact you have a relationship of sorts with Estelle has convinced us you have the skills and temperament to deal with the role.'

'It's not . . . We're not . . . She was in a lot of pain and she . . . might be uncomfortable with me after . . .'

Vaughn nodded, but ignored her. 'As you'll be filling the role of EA to a senior partner, you'll be paid the appropriately higher wage. We can't put a timeframe on it, but I've estimated two months.'

'*Two months?*'

'That's not to say it will take that long. In fact, we're all hoping the transition will be completed as soon as possible. With that in mind, you'll start today and we'll assess your progress after Estelle's two weeks in rehab. When you've achieved all you can, you'll return to your old role, but the higher salary will continue for the remainder of the two months regardless.'

Good grief, it was danger money.

He closed the folder. 'This role will also aid with future promotion or positions you might be interested in. I know you were studying law in Canberra before you left due to personal reasons.'

Mara's heart thumped. No, he meant Dad's heart attack. Of course, Vaughn knew about that; his renovation had been set back months. 'Yes.'

'I'm sure you're aware of our undergraduate program; possibly it's one of the reasons you were interested in working here. The flexible work hours and study support for our law students is highly sought after. When you're interested in resuming your studies, this assignment will improve your chances of being considered.'

It was meant to be an inducement, but the mention of uni shot a sharp buzz of alarm through her veins. 'No.' She swallowed. 'I mean, no, thank you. I won't be applying for that.'

'Alright, well, there will be other opportunities we can consider you for. Any questions?'

Mara had taken the job at Collings as a first step in a new direction. She wasn't going to be a lawyer now, she'd come to terms with that, but she was still in the world of law. It was busy, the people were mostly nice and all she'd had to do for the last three months was finish the tasks set for her and hand them back. It was typing, compiling and filing, nothing emotionally charged or anxiety-laden, nothing that threatened to turn her world inside out. She wanted to tell Vaughn she didn't want a challenge, that she was just relieved to be given tasks that didn't make her want to cry. She was trying to work out how to explain that without sounding lack-lustre and unambitious when he jumped into her pause.

'On a personal note, Mara, your father was so proud of the way you looked after your mother during her illness, then again after his heart attack. He's told me on numerous occasions how grateful for and impressed he is by your patience and grit. You probably didn't think that experience and those qualities were what you would need in this job, but they are exactly what we, *I*, need right now, and I personally appreciate you taking on this role.'

Mara's insides were awash with emotions when he finished. There was no way she could ask to be left to do the easy stuff. She wasn't sure she could speak without bursting into tears, so she just gave a faltering smile.

'Alright, if there's nothing else, there are some documents that require Estelle's signature as soon as possible. And instructions for reporting back on your work. Make sure you see Isna on your way out.'

☕

It took an hour to hand over Mara's unfinished work and get instructions on the report she was to send in at the end of every day. She didn't know why she needed to account for her time, since it couldn't be billed to a client, but given she was about to spend two weeks at Estelle's bedside, a list of her daily activities seemed like the least of her worries.

Picking up a coffee on the way to the hospital, she searched for some bright sides. It'd be more money in her bank account, which was overburdened with uni debt and car repayments. Winding past the beaches and up over the headland, she pulled into a residential street high above the ocean and checked the address.

Hepburn House Rehabilitation Hospital looked like someone's home. A big, old, dark-bricked mansion surrounded by a bunch of huge, weepy trees and an old-fashioned garden. It reminded Mara of a hospice Mum's doctor had suggested. It had taken only thirty seconds parked at the kerb for her mum to decide she wanted to die at home. Mara hoped there were no terminal patients here; Estelle would be difficult enough without that memory too.

Inside, the building might have been a guesthouse if not for the unmistakable smell of antiseptic and overcooked meals. Mara stopped at an information board before turning right to East Wing. Checking door numbers along a wide corridor, she caught glimpses of sunny one- and two-bed rooms, distant views of the ocean and patients propped up against pillows or in chairs. Rounding a bend, she saw there were three more rooms arranged around the end of the hallway like clover leaves. Raised voices coming from one of them made Mara's feet slow.

Stopping outside the first door on the right, Mara saw a woman in a red jacket standing just inside the room and another in navy further in. Beyond them, two women wearing matching polo shirts, one about her own age, were engaged in a discussion with someone out of sight on the bed. Their words were indistinct but the third voice was louder, perfectly clear and made Mara flinch.

'You will *not* presume what I want,' Estelle enunciated with a vicious clarity. 'When I say I will *not* enter the pool, I mean I will *not*. *Enter*. *The*. *Pool*. Am I clear?'

'Perhaps we can discuss other . . .'

'We have discussed enough. You may leave.'

As the pair retreated, Mara spotted the word 'Physiotherapy' stitched across the younger woman's shirt. As she passed, Mara gave her a look of empathy; the woman returned it with a fist-pump of encouragement.

The two women ahead of her had stepped forward, as though queuing for an audience. Taking her place behind them inside the doorway, Mara pulled out the folder of documents that Estelle was to sign and watched warily as the next person was stared down.

Estelle looked better than she had the last time Mara had seen her, but was still a long way from the Chanel-clad woman who stalked the office. She was wearing a greying hospital gown with the frill of a floral nightie showing at the neck, one arm in a sling, the other hand bandaged. Her short hair was flattened on one side, her face pale, eyes smudged with tiredness. The lines around her lips, though, were tight and sharp with a snarky anger that seemed to have the room by the throat.

'I'll leave these with you then,' the woman in navy said, setting a raft of papers on the tray table before making a hasty exit.

'I'm Tori, the social worker here at Hepburn House,' the red-coated woman said as she stepped forward.

Estelle waved her bandaged hand. 'You can go away.'

'I'd like to discuss the services you'll need when you're discharged.'

'I've been here less than twenty-four hours.'

'Ms Collings. Can I call you Estelle?'

'No. You may leave your information and come back when I've had a chance to review my options. And send in whoever dispenses the painkillers.' Estelle swiped her hand through the air again and turned her face away to the glass-enclosed balcony beyond her window, ending any further discussion.

Mara reassured herself that Estelle was a workaholic, a control freak, and that she'd been in hospital for a week: surely she'd welcome some news from the office? Surely.

Pushing the corners of her mouth into a smile, Mara stepped around the end of the bed. *Do not get thrown out,* she told herself. But as she took a breath to begin, Estelle's gaze swung back and turned Mara to stone. The lined lips twitched in distaste, the tiredness under her eyes looked like dark holes in her face and the famous steely litigator's glare radiated a concoction of resentment, irritation and condescension.

Good grief, she was terrifying.

'Why are *you* here?' Estelle snapped.

'I . . . well, I, um . . .'

'Kindly go away until you remember.' Estelle's glare shouted disdain, impatience, superiority. How did she fit so many things into one expression?

'I have documents for you to sign.' Mara held out the folder, then remembered they'd shared an hour of pain and alarm. 'And of course, to see how you are.' She mustered a smile. 'How are you?'

Several more emotions slid across Estelle's face. Agitation, definitely; puzzlement, maybe; possibly curiosity. 'Who sent you?'

Mara had prepared for a brief, polite discussion about surgery and recovery, and hesitated over how to answer. 'Vaughn asked me to come, but of course, everyone at the office wanted me to pass on their best wishes.' Not really, but who didn't want best wishes when they were in hospital?

Estelle lifted her chin and squinted at her.

'Mara,' Mara prompted. 'With an M.'

As memory bloomed, the glint in Estelle's steely glare seemed to turn a little shiny. For a second, Mara felt sorry for her, that a junior employee sending best wishes from colleagues could bring a sheen to her eyes.

'You took time off work to come here?' It was a reprimand, not gratitude, and it took Mara another second to realign her empathy.

'No, I . . . have documents for you to sign.'

'I have not agreed to sign *anything*!' She spoke with such sudden vehemence and volume that Mara jumped. 'And how dare he send *you*.' As she raised a hand, Mara wanted to back away but the older woman snapped, 'Give me that.'

Mara passed the folder to Estelle and stepped out of reach.

Estelle's eyes narrowed as she skimmed the pages, the paper bending under the pressure of her finger as it ran down each page. Slapping the folder shut, she closed her eyes: nostrils flared, chest heaving as though the effort of reading had taken the breath out of her.

Mara spoke gently. 'He wanted you to sign it.'

'He can want all he likes. I'm *not* signing anything in a hospital bed!' With sudden ferocity, she picked up the folder and thrust it at Mara.

Not sure if Estelle was upset about the documents or about being in hospital, Mara took it and asked, 'What would you like me to tell him?'

'You can tell him he can shove his . . .' She stopped as a new thought took hold. 'No, I'll tell him myself.' She snatched it back, wedged one end of the folder under her sling and began tugging at the edges of the cardboard, wincing and hissing as her dislocated shoulder bit back.

'Wait, let me help.'

But Estelle batted Mara's hand away, pinning the file to her chest with her chin as though she'd decided to eat it.

Mara turned away to put her bag and coffee cup on the tray table and when she looked back, the pages had slipped out of the cardboard and fanned across the blanket. The woman hissed as she took out her fury on the empty folder and hurled it away. Or at least, she tried to. The folder whipped into the air before fluttering to the floor and skidding under the bed.

Mara dropped to her knees, reaching between the lowered bedrail bars. 'It must be hard with only one hand.'

'Oh, for god's sake.'

Dusting her trousers off and collecting the pages, Mara said, 'Would you like me to write the message for you?'

In an icy, even tone, Estelle said, 'I want you to tear them up.'

'But they're fine. They're not even creased.'

'I *don't care* what they look like. Tear. Them. Up.'

'But . . .'

'Put the pages in the damn folder and rip it in two.'

Mara closed the folder, lifted it and looked back at Estelle. 'Really?'

The older woman glared at her.

With a wince, Mara tore the file down the middle.

'Do it again,' Estelle ordered. 'Tear the bloody lot asunder!'

Mara ripped again and looked back at her. *Asunder enough?*

'Keep going. I want it sent back to him in pieces.'

Mara was going back to the office without a signature and the documents turned to confetti. Goodbye pay rise. Goodbye job.

'Do you feel that, Mara?'

'What?' *Defeated?*

'The satisfaction of tearing up someone else's expectations.'

Well, now that she mentioned it, yes, there was something gratifying about ripping up a wad of pages. Not that she was going to admit it. 'What should I tell Vaughn?'

'Absolutely nothing. You're to put those scraps in an envelope, label it "Private and Confidential", address it to Vaughn Collings, sender Estelle Collings, and leave it with Isna. And not one word from you. I believe that will make my position clear.'

'Coffee?'

Mara and Estelle both turned to a man at the end of the bed holding a cup and saucer.

'Is it the same as this morning?' Estelle snapped.

'It's the same every day.'

'Did we not have a conversation about this? I believe I told you that your coffee was no improvement on the other hospital. That if you could not improve on this *excuse* for—'

'I brought a coffee!' Mara grabbed her keep cup from the tray table. 'I forgot about it with all the tearing and stuff, but it's a thermal cup, it'll still be hot.' She held it out to Estelle. 'Cappuccino, no sugar.'

Estelle took it without question and drank like a desperado: long gulps, eyes closed, deep sigh. Mara exchanged a glance with the man. He passed her the cup and saucer.

'Do you know how long it's been since I've had a decent coffee?' Estelle frowned at her. 'And you just left this sitting on the tray table?'

You're welcome, my pleasure. Mara took a sip of the vile hospital coffee and fought to keep the grimace from her face.

'Why are you still here?' The tone was less agitated, but still.

'I'm your Executive Assistant.' The title sounded ridiculously pretentious: an hour ago Mara had been junior admin staff.

'According to whom?'

Mara frowned. 'Vaughn said you . . .'

'I haven't spoken to my cousin since last week.'

Last week? Maybe Estelle had forgotten: she'd bumped her head and was probably taking strong pain medication. Or maybe he'd emailed her: Estelle didn't look like she could check her inbox without help. Either way, Mara wasn't inclined to question her. 'Well, he's assigned me to work with you while you're in hospital.'

'Doing what, exactly?'

'Helping to transition your current client files to the digitised system.'

Estelle's eyes darkened with anger.

Mara licked her lips. 'For the other lawyers to access.'

Estelle did nothing for a long, still moment, her expression giving nothing away this time. Mara felt compelled to follow suit, and stood like a statue while she waited to be fired from her new job as assistant to the scariest person she'd ever met. *May it be fast and painless.*

'Will you be working for me or Vaughn?' Estelle finally asked.

Mara searched for something to say that wouldn't make Estelle shout at her. 'I work for Collings Law Firm. I guess that means both you and Vaughn.'

'Shrewd answer. Are you his spy?'

'I . . . What?' Was she? Isna had been firm about emailing every afternoon.

'Has he instructed you to report back to him?'

'Well, not directly to him but . . .' No-one had said she couldn't tell Estelle. 'I'm supposed to keep a record of the files you work on and any tasks I'm given.'

Estelle's gaze slipped to the panorama of ocean beyond her window, glistening under a cloudless sky. There were ships on the horizon, reminding Mara of the view in Estelle's apartment. But whatever the older woman saw there today made her lift a hand to her flattened hair and give it a fluff. When she turned back, there was a new edge to her steely glare. 'Alright,' she said. 'You'll do.'

Do? 'You want me to . . . stay?'

'I believe that is your assignment.'

'And make a record of the work?' She didn't want to lie about it.

'Of course. Although I imagine my cousin will get little joy from what he'll be reading.'

The small smile of satisfaction on the older woman's lips made Mara feel like a fly caught between the webs of two spiders. The kind that ate each other. She tried to keep the apprehension from her face, but Estelle didn't miss it.

'If the prospect of taking notes at my bedside doesn't appeal, you may leave now.'

Mara wanted to flee so badly that her eyes flickered towards the corridor. 'I . . . It's . . .'

'Don't start a sentence unless you intend to finish it.'

Mara wavered between staying and going. If she left, she would have failed the managing partner, her dad's best client, and she'd probably lose her job. He hadn't mentioned that she'd be some kind of double agent: spying for one partner and sending angry missives from the other. But if she told Estelle she was uncomfortable with conflict, the older woman might pile it on just for fun.

She had taken the job at Collings for a nice, easy, new start. She didn't want to fail at this too. Dragging in a fortifying breath, her cheeks heating, she said, 'I don't want to take sides in whatever the issue is between you and Vaughn.'

Estelle raised an eyebrow. 'That is a commendable position. I can assure you, Mara with an M, you will not be required to take a side. I will assign you work and you will be free to submit a record of said work, as requested by the managing partner. I will instruct the managing partner to direct any questions regarding said work to me, personally. Is that a workable arrangement for you?'

It took a moment for Mara to realise that Estelle wasn't being sarcastic. And that she was waiting for an answer.

'Oh.' Mara's face bloomed in a full blush. 'Yes, okay, that's workable.'

'Sensible choice. Find pen and paper.'

'I've got my phone.'

'You won't need that. Hurry up.'

Mara found a pen and a scrap of paper at the bottom of her bag. 'Sorry, I wasn't expecting to need stationary.'

'Write this down.' It was an address in a nearby suburb. 'Tell them I want my usual: tom yum, extra prawns and a side of rice.'

Mara glanced up in surprise.

'Is picking up lunch beneath you?'

'No, I just thought . . . we were going to . . . work.'

'We'll get to that. You're to come straight back. I can't face another hospital meal and I want that soup *hot*.'

Andie

CONSTABLE BESS PATERSON had called the night before to tell Andie that Benjamin Cameron was being moved to a rehab hospital today. His sister had said he'd be ready for visitors when he arrived.

'Want me to come with you?' Vivian had asked this morning.

'Thanks, but I need to do it myself.' She knew Viv would be focused on getting the thank you said and done so Andie could start moving on. She loved that Vivian was looking out for her, but she had to find her own way through this.

Andie had been at Hepburn House a year ago to pitch for a contract to recruit their new operations manager, and as she pulled into the car park she remembered the rabbit hole she'd fallen down when researching the hospital's background. The woman who'd grown up in the original home had become a doctor, then a surgeon, then a specialist in medical rehabilitation. When she'd inherited the mansion from her father, she turned it into a convalescent hospital which she'd run with her doctor husband. It was a beautiful old home with an inspiring story, and Andie had the same thought now that she'd had then: *Nice place to recuperate.*

She checked the dusting of make-up on her bruised cheek and russet freckles, smoothed a few wayward curls, straightened the sleeve of her jumper over the bandage on her elbow, then set off along the path that wound through the spring garden to the front entrance, wondering again what Benjamin Cameron might look like. She'd attempted to find him online, but there were endless Benjamin Camerons on social media. All she'd wanted to know was whether she'd recognise him and if she should brace herself for a wave of guilt at the sight of his injuries.

She followed the directions she was given at the front desk, passing serene-coloured rooms occupied by patients well enough to be sitting in chairs but clearly a long way from good health. Several seemed to be making a push for normal life: an elderly woman wearing make-up and jewellery, a middle-aged man dressed for a jog. Others seemed barely able to hold themselves upright, bundled in blankets despite the air-con. Rounding a bend and checking the room numbers at the end of the corridor, Andie wondered which part of the recovery curve Benjamin would be on.

She could see a wheelchair through his doorway, and a white hospital blanket draped over a bed frame that made the mattress beneath look like it was under sail. As she stepped inside, the silence sent a shudder through her. The still shape of a body under the covers set off a pulse of memory so forceful that she felt again the heat, the grief, the howling realisation. Waiting a beat for it to pass, she moved to the bed, looking at Benjamin Cameron's sleeping form.

The sheet was pulled to his chin, his face pale beneath a short mop of brown hair, a curve of lashes under his eyes and a fuzz of dark growth on his chin. The only sign of injury on his face was a strip of plaster bisecting one eyebrow and purple bruises around the socket and cheek. There was nothing familiar about him. He didn't look like swarthy Zack either, but the sight of him made Andie's heart thump.

Perhaps she made a sound, because his eyes opened. Of all the ways she'd thought this meeting might go, she hadn't imagined being caught staring at him while he slept. He blinked as though he was trying to focus, his irises a surprising flash of green.

Before she had a chance to speak, he said, 'Andie.'

It was a statement, not a question, and her mouth opened in surprise.

'Oh my god, Andie.' He rubbed a hand across his eyes. 'How are you? Are you okay?'

'I . . . um . . .'

'I heard you hurt your arm.' The green eyes dropped to her arm, then back to her face. 'And had a concussion.' A wince as he pushed himself up higher on his pillow. 'I imagined swelling, maybe a black eye, but you look,' one side of his mouth tipped upwards, 'great.'

She huffed a laugh at the compliment, the insanity of the moment. 'I was . . . I'm . . . Sorry, but . . . do I know you?'

His mouth took its time to widen into a smile. Then, as though lying down was bad manners, he hoisted himself all the way up to sitting, his face tightening in pain as he reached back to reposition the pillow.

'Can I . . .?' Andie took a faltering step.

'Would you . . .?' He leaned forward.

She rearranged the pillows at his back, smelling antiseptic on his pale skin, seeing more purple bruising on his upper arm where the sleeve of his T-shirt rode up. 'How's that?'

'Good, thanks.' But his face twitched again as he settled.

Andie stepped back, a thumb hooked through the strap of her shoulder bag. 'The police said your sister was happy for your information to be released. I wanted . . .'

'Did you get her message?'

'Your sister tried to contact me?'

He shook his head. 'She was meant to pass a message to the police, but there was a lot going on and it wasn't much of a message, really.'

'A message for me?'

'From me. Just, get well soon. Not much, like I said. And not exactly eloquent. But I hadn't been out of the coma for long.' He closed his eyes, smiled a moment. 'Looks like you did. Get well, I mean. Except for . . .' He waved a hand at his face, implying the bruises on her own, then dropped it back to the sheet.

His eyes stayed closed and Andie fiddled with her bag, not sure if he was drifting off again.

'Sorry.' He opened one eye briefly. 'Pain meds. Feels like I've got weights on my eyelashes. Still here though.'

'Okay, well.' Looked like she'd be doing the talking. She sat on the edge of the visitor's chair. 'Thanks for your message, especially since you're the one still in hospital. The thing is, I hit my head and I can't remember what happened. The whole night is gone and, well, we must have met but I don't remember.'

His eyes opened and he did that slow smile again. Perhaps with the drugs, he couldn't do it any faster, but there was something unconcerned about it, as though he'd already decided there was no point railing about something else the accident had messed up. 'We had dinner.'

'That night?'

'We split a bottle of red. Left the bar and got hit by a car.'

'Oh. Not a great night then.'

'No, it was fun.' Another lazy smile.

Andie hooked her good elbow on the arm of the chair, trying to understand how dinner had happened. 'I'd been waiting for someone.'

'Mitchell Michaels.'

'You know him?'

Ben shook his head. 'I sat beside you at the bar and you asked if I was Michael, then Mitchell. Like you were going through a list of likely names. So I said, "Starts with B, sounds like a hen."'

A tingle prickled across her scalp.

'You remember?' he asked.

'No, but the police officer who sat with me after the accident said I kept talking about a hen. It made no sense.'

'It didn't when I said it. But you looked cheesed off about

Mitchell Michaels and I thought your evening should end on a better note.'

Andie looked him over again, not sure what to make of him. 'Why were you there?'

'For a cider. I heard there was a good selection. Only you thought I was someone else. I said *Sounds like hen,* and you said Barry.'

A smile itched at the corner of her lips. 'Barry?'

He pulled both hands from under the covers and did a rolling motion with them. 'Warm, I said. Very warm.'

A chuckle started at the back of her throat, at what she must have been thinking, and because she used to love . . . Oh, charades. Bess Paterson said she'd talked about charades. 'Right, so I eventually guessed Ben and . . .?'

'I guessed your name.' He pointed at the side of his head. 'It was the hair. I said Nicole, then Kate, as in Kidman and Winslet. When I said Audrey, you said, "Sounds like first and last letters" and I guessed Andie.'

'As in McDowell?'

'You remember?'

'No. I just get that sometimes.' Same fat curls, but Andie's were copper coloured, not black. She raised an eyebrow. 'Why Audrey?'

'As in Hepburn. I know, I know, the pixie cut. But it was all about the hair with her too, right?'

She laughed. She couldn't help it. So much for the sober, earnest conversation she'd planned. 'Are you a hairdresser?'

'No, just a movie buff. And by the way, you already asked me that.'

It was all so bizarre, except trying to guess what he did was totally her and he knew about Mitchell Michaels. *Sounds like a hen* ticked a box, and *Barry,* well, she loved a daft conversation.

'I'm Ben, by the way.' He held out a hand.

She stepped forward and took it: warm, long-fingered, a slight tremor as she shook it. 'Andie. Only it seems you know that already.'

'It's nice to meet you again, Andie. I'm glad you're okay.'

'I'm so sorry you're not.' She dragged the chair closer and sat. 'And I'm sorry I came without calling ahead, it's just I've been wanting to meet you, to thank you.' She fell back on the words she'd rehearsed. 'I can't remember anything from that night but I won't forget what you did.' If Vivian had been there, that might have signalled the end of it, but Andie said, 'I thought we just happened to be standing on the kerb in that same random moment. I had no idea we'd met. I had no idea why I was even there so late on a Tuesday night. Just knowing that now is, well . . .' She pressed her lips together, whispered, 'Thank you.'

He edged a hand across the sheet towards her, as though he might have reached for hers if they'd known each other better. Or better than she remembered. 'Meeting you was the last thing that happened before my life flashed before my eyes,' he told her. 'Those two hours are seared into my memory.'

Her heart thumped with relief, gratitude. 'You poor thing. You must have wondered what was in your drip with that crazy conversation stuck in your head.'

'I meant in a good way. There are a lot worse things to be left to think about than a few laughs with a nice person.' He tilted his head towards his bedside table. 'Would you mind passing that cup of water?'

She watched him as he sipped, aware of the stiffness in his movements, the tired smudges under his eyes and the bed frame over the injuries to his lower body, and felt grateful it wasn't worse, impressed that his spirits were so good. When he'd passed the cup back, she said, 'How are you? I mean, obviously not great, but your injuries?'

He told her about the multiple fractures that had torn through the skin, the floating fragments of bone, the nerve damage that may not heal, the possibility of needing more surgery. And that was just his leg. He also had four broken ribs and a fractured collarbone. There'd been issues with breathing and pain management, but he was doing better now, he told her. He tipped his head back on the pillows, as though thinking about his long road to recovery had exhausted him.

It made Andie wish she could share the load; some of it should have been hers. 'I should let you sleep.'

'I'm okay for a while. It's nice you're here. You want the rest of the story?'

'Dinner that night?'

He adjusted his position with a grimace, waiting a beat before going on. 'I'd skipped lunch and had already finished a cider when you offered to buy me another one, so I asked if you were planning to eat. You said you'd planned to see if the conversation with Mitchell Michaels had enough steam to last through a risotto. I said, "What do you think about ours?" and you said, "Let's order a risotto."'

At his mention of risotto, something released its grip inside Andie's chest, not only because Ben remembered what she'd forgotten, but because his version of her night made her feel better about herself: that she hadn't been alone and sad in the hours before a car slammed into her. 'I sent a text to a friend about a risotto. So that explains that.'

He smiled, but it looked like an effort. 'I'm sorry, but I think I'm done now.'

'Of course. Thank you for talking to me.' Andie stood, picked up her bag, then had another thought. 'I'm guessing we were leaving when that car ran into us.'

'You were waiting for an Uber. I was waiting to make sure it turned up.'

'You were there because of me?'

'I thought that car was your ride. Then I thought the driver hadn't seen you on the kerb and I pushed you.' A tilt of his head. 'I remember thinking in that split second that I'd dislocated your shoulder.'

Guilt oozed in her veins but she lifted her bandaged arm.

'I broke my elbow when I landed, but it was better than being hit by that car.' She hesitated. 'I'm so sorry you were badly hurt.'

'Don't be sorry. It's not your fault. Or my fault.' He tipped his head back on the pillow, his eyes on her as something close to bliss settled onto his lips. 'We're alive, Andie,' he said. 'We made it. We got hit by a runaway car and we're still here. Absolutely nothing to be sorry about there.'

Andie wanted to share his euphoria, but the last time death had passed this close it had left her with grief and loneliness and a heartache that still clung to her like ivy. This time, death had pushed her as it passed. She'd stumbled, bewildered and frightened, to the brink of that dark, sad place and she wasn't sure that where she was now could be called survival; not yet. But she nodded, and because Ben deserved to feel the joy, she said, 'Yeah.'

'Andie.' He said it with insistence, like he wanted her to listen. 'We're alive. We're still breathing and our hearts are beating. We made it.'

He was right, she was alive. Screw death. She nodded, putting a little more energy into it. 'Yeah.'

He raised a fist in victory, then dropped it to the bed as though that was all he had the strength for. 'A little tired,' he said. 'But better than dead.'

She kept her smile in place for Ben's sake, but his words had opened a wound. She turned away, rearranging the strap of her handbag across her chest.

'Thanks for coming,' he said. 'I feel better for seeing you, and in better shape than I'd imagined.'

Fighting for composure, she took another glance around his room at the flowers beside his bed, a dressing gown slung over another chair, an overnight bag beside the wardrobe. Someone had brought him clothes, friends had sent get-well wishes and there was a sister keeping an eye on him. He was in pain, but in better spirits than Andie. She felt better for seeing that too.

'Closure for both of us,' she said. She could stop thinking about the accident now and move on.

'Andie?'

When she looked back, what little colour there'd been in his face had drained away.

'Can you see the buzzer for the nurse?'

'It's here.' She unhooked it from the bed rails.

'Hit the green button?' He pulled a sharp breath in, waited a second. 'Sorry, the pain just took off.'

A light on the buzzer had come on when she pressed it but she went to the corridor to check for a nurse anyway. 'Is your sister coming in later?' she asked over her shoulder, hoping someone better equipped to sit with him through the pain would be turning up.

His answer was through gritted teeth. 'She flew to Perth last night.'

'Did you need something?' a nurse asked from the hallway.

'His pain is bad,' Andie told her, then returning to Ben, told him, 'She's gone to get medication.'

His smile was brief, his forehead shiny with perspiration.

'Did you say your sister flew to Perth?'

'She had to get back to work. And her kids.' Pain made him wince.

'What about your parents?'

'Holiday in Scotland. Don't want them coming home.' He pulled in another sharp breath.

Andie had no idea how to help other than to try to distract him. 'Well of course, parents can be more trouble than they're worth. Better off on the other side of the world, sometimes. Friends, though, can't survive without them. Is someone coming in to see you later?'

He shook his head. 'I'll be okay. When the drugs get here.'

Andie stepped back as the nurse came in with a small dish and a syringe, hoping it was just pain and not something that would require bells and a crash cart.

The woman seemed unfazed by the sweating and teeth-gritting, murmuring to Ben as she slid the needle into his arm. 'Won't take long to kick in,' she told him. Checking his chart, she turned to Andie and lowered her voice. 'Don't stay long, he's tired from the transfer over.'

When she was gone, Andie picked up her bag again.

'Sorry, Andie. Can't keep my eyes open.'

'No. Of course. Can I get you anything before I go?'

'I'm good.'

He was a long way from good. 'I'll leave my mobile number,' she said, finding a pen and a scrap of paper in her bag. 'In case you think of anything.' She hoped he wouldn't need to call, hoped he had multiple people offering to bring whatever he wanted.

'*Titanic,*' he said, eyes still closed.

'Huh?'

'*Breakfast at Tiffany's.*'

Oh. He'd thought of Kate and Audrey. 'Um . . . *Dead Calm.*'

One side of his mouth turned up. 'Thanks for coming,' he murmured.

'Thanks for remembering.' She tucked her number under his water jug. 'Bye, Ben.'

She tiptoed to the door, glad he was lost to sleep. Walking back through the gardens, she was glad too that he was here. He deserved a nice place to recover. She was also glad for herself, that he'd remembered what she'd forgotten. Their meeting had been better than she'd dared imagine.

Still, she got in the car and burst into tears. Dropping her head to the steering wheel, she sobbed as though the experience had been awful. Concussion, she told herself. Relief, too, that she hadn't just imagined the *someone* she'd thought had been with her. That it hadn't been the ghost of Zack, but a nice person who'd wanted to make sure she got home okay. Who had given her the information she'd needed to close the door and move on.

Coral

THE NURSES' STATION was deserted when she got back with her lunch. Her mother was still by the window, her chair now at an angle where she could enjoy the distant view of the ocean beyond the hospital garden.

'Sorry that took so long,' Coral said, out of breath.

Watching as Coral shifted another chair across the room and joined her at the window, Val said, 'I thought you'd gone.'

'Just to get a sandwich. I want to catch the doctor.' Her head snapped up. 'He hasn't been in to see you, has he?'

'I don't think so.'

'You're not sure?'

'Some people came in. I don't know who they were.'

Glancing around the room as she took a long pull on her coffee, Coral noticed the meal tray was gone. She moved to the bed table and sifted through some brochures that hadn't been there before. 'Was it a social worker? There's information here about help at home.' And aged care facilities, although she wasn't broaching that subject yet.

Val folded her hands. 'I told her I was fine at home.'

Coral pocketed a business card. 'Anyone else?'

'Someone brought coffee and a slice of cake. Carrot, not as good as mine.' Val once won first prize in a competition for her carrot cake, and never let a slice of anyone else's get past her without a comparison.

'Of course not. Whose is?' Coral said with a sudden fondness for her mum. Val returned her smile with a mixture of pride, approval and just a hint of amusement. If her sense of humour was still there, maybe her memory wasn't too far away either.

'And I told him that,' Val said.

'The guy who brought the cake?'

'The doctor. He was here when I was eating it.'

'The doctor?'

'I told him I'd prove mine was better when he let me go home.'

'So you've seen the doctor?'

'Yes, Coral. I told you that.'

Coral clenched her teeth. 'What did he say?'

'That if I brought him a whole cake, he'd share it with the staff.'

'Not about the cake! About your rehab?' Coral heard the exasperation in her voice and saw the bewilderment in her mother's face before she, too, jumped to annoyance and turned to the window.

Great, I've made her feel stupid. She'd been gone thirty-five minutes: what happened to having some time before the doctor arrived? Damn the queue at the shop. Damn the . . . just damn! Downing the last of her coffee, she headed for the nurses' station again.

'Has the doctor been to see my mother?' Coral asked the nurse she'd spoken to earlier, now back behind the counter.

He checked a screen. 'Looks like it, yes. Must have happened during my break. You didn't see him?'

'No.' Coral rubbed her forehead with the heel of her hand, reminding herself not to berate him. 'Is he still seeing patients?'

'I know he had a meeting to go to when he was finished.' He shrugged. 'If you want to see him, you're best to catch him on rounds tomorrow.'

And waste another entire morning hoping to be in the right place at the right time? She'd been there, done that last week.

This week, time was sand running through her fingers. She was behind at work, there was an urgent job looming, her daughter was hobbled, her mother was hurt and possibly losing her mind, and Coral was going to New York in six days, seventeen hours and twenty-four minutes. She didn't have the time or the patience to try to catch the doctor tomorrow.

Gripping the edge of the counter, she forced a smile. 'On the chance he hasn't yet made it to the meeting, where do I look?'

The hospital was bigger than it appeared, with hallways angling off in numerous directions. Fifteen minutes later, she'd seen the entire place, including the hydro pool and the staff kitchen, and missed the doctor by two minutes. 'He's with a board member,' Jenny in Admin told her. 'He could be a couple of hours.'

Coral wandered despondently back to Val's room, wondering how long a dementia assessment took. She'd sat with her mother through several memory tests with her GP, but that was before this recent bout of forgetfulness. Could a more comprehensive test be done here? Before she flew to New York? Or would she need to schedule another test and another appointment, and a long, difficult discussion about the future?

Could Coral leave Val to negotiate the tests and medical professionals on her own? Her brother would be here, but his idea of taking their mother to appointments was to do the driving and wait in the car. The sooner Coral spoke to Val's doctor, the better it would be for everyone, especially Coral.

'I found the doctor,' Coral told Val, aiming for a positive approach. 'He's in a meeting, but Jenny in Admin is going to let him know that I missed him earlier, I'm going away and I'll wait all afternoon to see him.'

'Do you need to see him?'

'I'll feel better if I can, with going away next week.'

'You'll have to wait your turn.'

The frustration of the day, the week, got the better of her and she snapped, 'I'm busy too, Mum.'

'Well, you will go on holidays,' Val shot back.

'It's not a . . .' Coral held up a hand, reining in her words. 'It's fine. I'll wait. All afternoon, if need be.'

'We can have a natter then,' Val said, her irritation forgotten. 'It's been ages since we just had a chat.'

Dread and guilt prickled along Coral's spine and the screw on her stress tightened another notch. She had work to catch up on, emails to read, phone calls to make. She couldn't unclench her back teeth enough to natter.

'Mum, I . . . need to . . .' Her mobile rang. 'Take this call.'

She watched Val across the room as Jessica talked. If Coral could get an important package delivered to Stockholm on short notice, she could get herself on a plane to New York by Monday. She didn't need sleep, she didn't even need to pack much, so long as her gorgeous new suit made it into her luggage. What she did need was for her mum to be cared for and safe, her daughter ready to give birth and her assistant able to handle Stockholm.

To get there, though, she'd need caffeine, food, phone charger, stamina and persistence. She could do it, she told herself. It was what she was good at. Because she was going to New York. She deserved it, she'd earned it and she needed it.

The next two hours flew by: phone calls and emails, arranging underwear in drawers and pillows on the bed, setting up delivery schedules and chatting to Val. She was doing it, see?

'Coral?'

She looked up to see Jenny from Admin at the door. 'The doctor's here?'

'No, I'm sorry. His wife's been in a car accident and he had to go.'

'Oh my god, is she okay?'

'The car's a wreck but she's just shaken up, I think. He wants to make sure though.'

'Sure. Of course.' Coral smiled with as much empathy as she could muster, which wasn't a lot. She didn't resent the doctor needing to be with his wife, of course. But she wanted five minutes with him, she wanted to go home, she wanted her mum to be okay. She wanted to go to *New York*. 'So he'll be in tomorrow?'

'At this stage, that's the plan. If you still want to catch him, he starts rounds at eight am. Best to be here then.'

'Sure. Great. Well, I'll be here.'

Andie

ANDIE HAD TAKEN the long way home from the hospital, window down as she passed the beaches. She celebrated closure with lunch at a favourite cafe, texting with Vivian while she ate.

Viv had been in the middle of something at work and Andie kept the details succinct: meeting Ben at the bar, dinner, waiting for the Uber. The weird snippets of conversation that had made it through Andie's concussion would have to wait until she could tell Viv in person.

She whiled away the afternoon in the library, telling herself that Ben was in a safe place and in good spirits, despite his sister flying to Perth. There were nurses to care for him, physios to keep him busy and other patients to talk to. He wasn't alone.

Her phone pinged with a text message as she was unlocking the front door. She waited until the telly filled the silence of the townhouse before pulling her mobile from her bag.

Don't think I said goodbye. Sorry, wanted to. Thanks for visiting.

It pinged again while she read.

Ben sounds like hen, btw.

She smiled: *Hey Ben Sounds Like Hen, how's your pain? Did you sleep long?*

Then: *Nicole-Kate-Audrey-Andie here, btw.*

His answer came as she was heating curry in the microwave: *Pain's under control. Slept for three years.*

Andie: *Serious sleeping.*

Ben: *Thought I'd dreamed that you came until I saw your note.*

Andie: *Happy to have left evidence.*

Ben: *About your offer if I need anything? Maybe a text every now and then? Remind me the world outside is still there?*

She flashed back on the hours she'd spent alone: with Zack, without Zack. The weeks when alone was all she'd felt; the desperate need to not feel like an island in the ocean of her misery.

Ben: *Weather report. Movie review :)*

She pulled in a breath and refocused on Ben, feeling a twinge of guilt at making him wait. *Coffee photos? Useless but engaging information?*

Perfect!

She took a photo of her curry and sent it: *Dinner.*

Curry?

She typed: *Warm, very warm.* And hoped he got the reference. When he didn't reply, she added: *Butter chicken.*

All she got was three dots beside his number that disappeared a few seconds later. Andie took the phone and her dinner to the sofa. She'd just finished eating when the phone pinged.

Ben: *Sorry. Nurse with a needle.*

Andie: *More pain?*

Ben: *Not for long. Will be asleep soon.*

Ben again: *Night Andie.*

Then: *Glad I got that in.*

Andie: *Night, Ben.*

She didn't get a reply, and hoped that meant he would sleep until morning. Wakeful nights alone in a silent room were awful.

Mara

'It was a plate of sandwiches,' Mara told her dad as she served curry from the slow cooker. When she discovered there was no cafe at the hospital, Estelle had said, *We've wasted enough time. You can have my lunch. We'll work while we eat.* 'The lunch she thought was so awful that she sent me out to get her takeaway instead.' Mara rolled her eyes. 'At least it wasn't anyone's-guess casserole.'

'Or potato brick.'

They both smiled at the names they'd come up with for the hospital 'mystery meals' after Dad's heart attack.

It had been their version of Mum's silver lining. Even frail and grey at the end, her lips dry and cracked, Mum had always been able to find something to smile about.

Mara carried two plates to the table, sliding one in front of Dad. 'So I've got the sandwiches and my laptop on the edge of her bed, typing in client names between mouthfuls, while she's in her nightie calling out said names between slurps of soup. That's how she talks: said this and said that.'

'What did you do with the ripped-up document?' he asked as he forked up a mouthful.

'Well, she sent me back to the office to collect the files of the clients on the list. I had to ask someone for boxes to carry them, which started an inquisition about why I was removing files from the office and since when did I work for Estelle. So embarrassing, and that was before I let myself into her office to collect her laptop. She gave me the key, but by then I was clearly the office perp, so Vaughn was called out of a meeting and arrived at her office while I was searching the drawers for her chargers.'

'Not a good look,' said Patrick, who'd come home from soccer training and was dragging off socks and shin pads.

'Well, no.' She laughed, as though the memory of being discovered with her hands in Estelle's desk drawer wasn't making her sweat all over again. 'But all Vaughn asked was whether I'd brought back the document I'd ripped up.'

'Just asking for trouble, ripping up documents,' called Pat as he chucked dirty clothes through the laundry door.

Catching him up with the story so far as she dished up his dinner, she slid back into her seat, saying, 'So I was a coward and told him I'd given it to Isna.'

'Vaughn is a reasonable man,' Dad said. 'He won't blame you for ripping it up like that.'

'Yeah, let them fight it out.'

Mara shrugged. 'Maybe. No-one seemed to know I was working for Estelle, including Estelle. Someone said they thought I'd been fired, which didn't help when I let myself into her office. Estelle seems more interested in what she wants to eat than in doing any actual work.' She pushed her plate away and folded her arms on the table. 'After going back to the hospital with the files, she sent me out again to buy an ice-cream, a packet of fancy chips and a gin and tonic in a can.'

Her father covered Mara's hand with his own. 'You need to stick with it for a while, Maz.'

She bristled at his gentle rebuke. 'I know, Dad.'

'And Vaughn has been a good client for a long time. We don't want to let him down.'

'I know, Dad.'

He patted her hand and stood. 'You lot mind if I head off to the pub?'

'Go for it,' Pat said before Mara could ask, *Isn't darts on Tuesday?* She gave him a smile instead, saying nothing when he left his plate and glass on the table.

'Thanks for dinner, Maz,' he called on the way out. He needed to get out and enjoy life again, she told herself, as much as she needed to stick to something.

Helping himself to another spoonful of curry, Pat said, 'You're rocking the slow cooker, Maz.'

'I'm doubling the quantities now you're back. How was training after all that farm work?'

'I'm out of playing condition, but it was great running around with the boys again. How about you with this work thing?'

'It'll be okay.' She opened the dishwasher. 'It'll have to be.'

'Is it going to make you start crying again?'

She smiled at him across the benchtop. 'No, I'm okay these days. How about you?'

'I'm good.' He pushed his bowl across the counter. 'You know what would make me better?'

'What?'

'If you cleaned up so I can have a shower. I seriously stink.'

'You seriously do, and that's the only reason I'm letting you off the hook.' She'd always been an easy touch when it came to Pat and Dad.

She rinsed his bowl and stacked it in the dishwasher, telling herself it was good they were all getting on with their lives, even if that left her cleaning up. Even if, after a day with Estelle, Mara had been looking forward to a night in with her favourite people.

She scooped the remains of the curry into plastic containers and wiped down the table, thinking about how long it had been since they were all here doing normal family things like going out and begging off chores.

Four years since Mum's terminal diagnosis, eighteen months

since Dad's heart attack, nine months since Patrick had left to clear his head before he started his degree next year. Events that had taken Mara way off the track she'd been on.

Mara had wanted to be a lawyer since she'd watched *Erin Brockovich* at the age of thirteen. She was smart and she'd wanted to use her brains to help people, to fight for justice, sassy and undaunted. Getting into Law had been a dream come true, and working in a legal office in her gap year had only cemented her drive at uni. She hadn't thought twice about taking a step back for Mum, though. Or the second time, when Dad had his heart attack and lost the will to look after himself. Besides, she'd made a mess of her dream by then and had needed time to step back and reassess. Taking charge at home had helped her feel like she was achieving something, even if she'd ended up so far off course she wasn't sure where she was anymore. It had been for Dad and Pat: she loved them, and they loved her back.

Tonight, though, she was tired of helping other people get back on their feet. Of being stuck on a side road waiting for the traffic to clear. She'd used the detour metaphor to explain it to Dad when she told him she was going to start applying for jobs. *I don't know where I'm going, but I have to go somewhere before I end up sitting so long my battery goes flat.* He'd looked at her like she'd had too much coffee, but a week later, he came home all puffed up, saying Vaughn Collings was happy to talk to her about a job.

A law office wasn't her first choice, not when she'd had to accept that she'd never be a lawyer, but it was something, a change, and it didn't involve worrying about how anyone else was coping. Only now she was stuck on another detour helping someone else recover. It might be different if Estelle was even a smidgen grateful, but she was mean, rude and pissed off all the time. Mara was already exhausted by it. She wasn't sure she had enough compassion left to care for anyone else, let alone Estelle.

Dad was right, though. She needed to stick with it. She didn't want to be a quitter. Didn't want Dad to think she was.

Or Vaughn Collings, not when he'd placed his trust in her. Besides, if she left, what the hell would she do? She couldn't go back to working for Dad. *Find yourself, Maz,* her mum had said in the weeks before she died. *Don't just work for Dad. You'll end up marrying one of his builders and working for him too.*

Mara slumped on the sofa with a sigh. She needed her mum's silver linings. A bucketload of them.

Part 3

The Visitors

Coral

'YOO-HOO,' CORAL CALLED as she let herself into Summer's house.

'That you, Mum?'

Who else would let themselves in before seven am? 'It's me. I come bearing food and clean washing,' she called.

'Geez, you're early.'

Oh, how lovely might have been nice. 'Got a lot to squeeze in today.' She stood in the doorway of the darkened bedroom. 'How's the lump in the bed beside you this morning?'

Oliver poked his head above the covers. 'I've got more pops.'

Coral sat on the edge of the mattress, taking a closer look at the new blisters on his forehead and cheek as she made soothing noises while listening to Summer's recap of their bad night: fever, itching, bad dreams. 'Ah, the fun of parenting.'

Coral made a sweep of the detritus around the room, binning the germy stuff, bundling the medications and running antiseptic wipes over surfaces. Half an hour later, she'd put away the washing, organised breakfast for the two patients, taken Summer a cup of tea, given Oliver a quick bath and fresh PJs, and washed her hands a thousand times.

'Right, I'm off,' she said, hoping it wouldn't take too long for her shirt to dry after Oliver's splashing.

'Already?'

'Nana's doctor does his rounds between eight and eleven. Cross your fingers he doesn't turn up three minutes before eleven. Or when I'm in the loo.'

⬬

'How was breakfast?' Coral asked as she kissed her mum on the top of her head.

Val frowned. 'They gave me an egg.'

'That's what we ordered yesterday.'

More frowning.

'Was the egg okay?' Coral asked.

'Well, it was an egg.'

Coral frowned back, shook it off and said, 'Apparently the doctor's not starting until nine now, so I guess we've got an hour to' – *twiddle her thumbs* – 'fill in with all the natter you want.'

Again, Coral had hoped for *Oh, how lovely*, but Val shot her another frown. 'Aren't you meant to be at work?'

Yes. All day. A long day, because she would be away for ten days and there was a mountain she had to do before she went, not to mention the Stockholm job. But she smiled. 'Not until we see the doctor.'

It turned out Val was more interested in morning television than nattering, so while Val muttered about hair, clothing and the appropriateness of politics at breakfast time, Coral responded to emails, checked courier and flight details, and wrote to-do lists.

Coral had to-do lists and her To-Do List. The small to-dos covered individual facets of her life: kids, Val, clients, deliveries, shopping. The large To-Do was a master list of everything she needed to get done, encompassing all of life as Coral Rennick. She'd just written *Val's washing* when the phone rang. She checked the caller and clenched her teeth.

'I'm going to take a call on the balcony, Mum.'

'Is that work?'

'No.'

'I told you to go into work. You don't need to—'

'It's Richard, Mum.'

Val stopped mid-sentence, her face doing that thing it always did at the mention of Richard: a fond smile followed by pursed lips when memory kicked in. Twenty-odd years after he'd chosen the surf over Coral and their two small children, her mother's first response was still affection. It was the Richard Effect, and it never ceased to annoy Coral.

She closed the French doors behind her and stood at windows that looked down into the garden. 'Hi,' she answered, putting enough emphasis in her single word to make it clear she didn't have the time or patience for a chat.

'Hey, Coral. Summer said Val had a fall. How's she doing?'

Coral's back teeth loosened a little as she reminded herself Richard wasn't always an arse. He was hopeless at responsibility, but he was good at checking up on people. The fondness between him and Val had been a two-way street.

She filled him in on Val's injuries and the rush to get her a place in rehab before Coral headed overseas.

'On that note,' Richard said. 'I had a chat to Mum and Dad this morning and I'm a bit worried.' He paused, like he was hoping she'd offer to help.

And there was the Richard she knew: overlooking the pressure on Coral so he could add some more. *No*, Coral told herself.

'I called Summer, but she sprained her ankle.'

'Torn tendons. Yes, I'm aware. I'm the ham in that sandwich at the moment.'

'Oh babe, I'd never call you a ham.'

She tightened her lips. 'I meant I'm looking after both my ageing parent and my adult child. And don't call me babe.'

'It's just that Dad's had a fall and Mum's saying it's nothing to worry about.'

'Maybe it's nothing to worry about.'

'Dad was sounding confused and Mum was doing the, *All fine here, Seagull. Just a few cuts and bruises.*'

'Seagull?' she asked, avoiding the question he wasn't asking.

'Yeah, she's started calling me that again. Usually when she's trying to pull the wool over. Look, I wouldn't mind knowing what the cuts and bruises looked like. I asked Summer to drop in on them but she reckons with her ankle and Oliver contagious, she can't manage it.'

Coral felt a flicker of both pride and outrage – pride that Summer had said no to her father; outrage that she'd had to. 'Of course she can't do it.'

'Val's at Hepburn House, isn't she?'

'Yes.'

'I looked it up. Mum and Dad's place is pretty much on your way home. It'd only be a quick drop-in the next time you're visiting Val.' Like her role in Val's drama was merely to pop by the hospital every now and then.

Coral rolled her eyes. 'You're only three hours away. If you're worried, you should come down and check on your parents your-self.' *Like the rest of us do.*

'I would, but Harlow and I are flying to Bali on Thursday.' Harlow was his current partner, the one who ran a successful retail and online business and was happy, apparently, to be in charge of everything, including Richard.

'And I'm leaving for New York on Sunday.'

'Good for you. About time you pulled your finger out and got on a big plane.'

Coral's nostrils flared. She was not going to react. She was *not* going to remind him she'd brought up their children and paid off a mortgage while he'd done what he damn well pleased. Including eighteen months traipsing around the world in search of good surf.

'Richard, I'm supporting Mum in hospital as well as our daughter, who is seven months pregnant, hobbled and nursing a sick three-year-old. And I've still got a conference to prepare for.

I haven't got time to scratch myself.' She reined the irritation in, reminding herself that his idea of support had always looked a lot like obliviousness. 'Can't you ask a neighbour to check in?'

'I don't know any of their neighbours.'

'You're only three hours away,' she said again. 'You could drive down and back tomorrow.'

'Yeah.' He dragged the word out, dripping with reluctance. 'They haven't seen you since Mum had her knee done, what, two years ago? I thought they'd enjoy the catch-up.'

Did he think after all these years she didn't see through his guile? She rephrased her previous thought: he was good about checking up on people, hopeless at following through with anything remotely helpful. Hearing a voice from Val's room, she turned and saw a man in a white coat. 'I've got to go. And you're a shit son, Richard.'

☕

The doctor had been standing beside Val's bed for the last fifteen minutes, discussing her rehab plan over the next two weeks: twice-daily gym sessions plus walking up and down the corridors. He'd listened with patience and interest to Val's long-winded description of her health and her fall, and had predicted a full recovery, so long as Val followed through on her exercises once she left hospital.

Coral directed a pointed look at her mum: *You've got to do the exercises.* Val smiled back: *The lovely doctor thinks I'm doing great.*

'Val did a cognitive test during her stay in hospital last week,' the doctor said. He was still standing by the bed, a picture of the at-ease medical professional, but something in his tone made Coral hold her breath.

'Val's score was below the accepted range for normal cognitive function,' he told them. 'But not low enough to be considered dementia.'

'Does that mean I passed?' Val asked.

Coral reached for her mum's hand and tried to steel herself.

'There may have been a number of mitigating factors.' He counted them off on his fingers: 'Val suffered a trauma, she hit her head in the fall, she may or may not have blacked out, either before or as a result of the fall. There's no knowing at this point whether any of those factors will have a permanent effect. She is also on a number of medications that need to be considered.'

Coral glanced at the plaster still covering the stitches on Val's forehead. 'So what now?'

'It takes time and a range of tests to diagnose dementia,' he explained. 'While Val is with us, I'd like to begin that process to get a better picture of what's happening. If that's okay with you?' He looked at Val, who looked at Coral.

Coral felt a sudden urge to weep. 'Yes,' she said. Then, remembering it wasn't her decision, she smiled gently at Val. 'I think it's a good idea that we find out what's happening, don't you?'

'Oh, yes.' She said it as though the logic was obvious, but Coral recognised the tone: her mother didn't understand all the talk about scores and mitigating factors, but it was better to sound like she did than have people think she couldn't keep up.

Andie

ANDIE GOT UP like it was a work morning, like she had things to do and places to go. She walked along the harbour foreshore, stopping to chat with a friend heading into work, and to a client she spotted in a coffee queue. Concussion was bewildering, she told them both, and she'd be back at work as soon as the doctor decided her head wouldn't explode if she thought too much. It wasn't the same as going to work, but it made her feel more like the Andie she'd been before she got hit by a runaway car.

In a cafe, she snapped a photo of her cappuccino and sent it to Ben: *Good morning, have a coffee on me.*

His reply came moments later: *Ahhhh, caffeine. Hope that's a double shot!?*

Of course.

Enjoy.

Andie smiled and decided she could be more like herself on the phone too.

What brought you to Newcastle from Perth?

Job at the uni.

How long have you been here?

Three weeks.

She frowned. He'd been in hospital for two of them. *But you've got people here? Family, friends?*

Met someone but she doesn't remember.

Andie's hand rose to her chest.

Ben: *She likes butter chicken. Think you'd get on.*

Benjamin Cameron had saved Andie's life; he should have fifteen friends on a visitor rotation. People should be lining up at his door to pat him on the back.

Andie tapped a finger on her phone as she stared at his text. She should . . . *Move on.* It was Vivian's voice in her head, as though she'd reached out telepathically. Only moving on was easier said than done when the man who'd pushed you out of harm's way had been hurt in the process. Andie *did* need to move on though; at the very least, she needed to step well away from the dark place she'd been teetering on the edge of for two weeks. Her finger hung over the screen, unsure what to type. She decided to follow his jokey lead: *I know a lot of people, maybe I've met her.*

Then, seeing the bandage on her arm and thinking of his broken leg and ribs, she added: *Can I do anything to help?*

You have. You are.

She fingered the neckline of her top. He'd made her laugh when she'd been stood up, and again yesterday, when she'd felt like crying. He'd waited for her Uber to arrive and shoved her out of the way of the car. His presence that night had brought back fun memories of Zack.

Andie: *I'm so sorry you're there.*

Ben: *Better here than dead.*

It was the same phrase he'd used yesterday, as though he needed to keep reminding himself. But the bluntness brought a familiar surge of grief. Andie pressed fingers to her lips and tried not to think about *dead*. Because *dead* made her think of *alone*. And Ben Cameron was facing weeks alone in a hospital room.

She sent: *More photos coming soon then :)*

Just a text every now and then, he'd told her. She reminded herself it was an hour round trip to the hospital, that she should be resting, that Ben had a way of saying things that made her cry. What good would introducing her grief into his recovery do?

Except Andie remembered what it was like to be alone.

♨

Ben was in a recliner armchair beside the window, looking like he'd had a big night out: mop of brown hair sticking up, dark shadows under his eyes matching the stubble on his jaw, legs raised and shoulders slumped. Not great, but better than yesterday.

'Knock, knock,' Andie said from the doorway.

'Andie.' The word was infused with surprise, amusement, bewilderment. Maybe relief?

'Ben.' She attempted to copy his all-encompassing single syllable with *Surprise, it's me!* and *You're out of bed!* and *Hope you don't mind me dropping in again.*

'I didn't think I'd see you again. I thought we were destined to have just before and after moments. Like . . . like bookends around near-death.'

She reined in her alarm at his mention of death, holding up a cardboard tray as though it explained the change in their destiny. 'I brought coffee.'

'Come in. Please.'

Wheeling a tray table towards him, she noticed he was broader across the chest and shoulders than she'd first thought. The strip of tape was gone from above his eye, leaving a pink trail of skin through his brow, above eyes that, up close, looked like pieces of jade. 'I didn't know how you took your coffee so I brought a variety. And sugar. And a cookie.'

'God, you're a lifesaver. The coffee here is shit.' A wince tightened his face as he pushed himself higher. 'Thanks. For the coffee and for coming back.'

She explained the drinks selection and the newspapers she'd brought and lied that she'd been nearby and the hospital was on her way home. He took the flat white, she claimed the cappuccino and he insisted they split the cookie. Andie pulled over a chair, placing it at right angles to his recliner so they didn't have to talk across his broken leg.

'Can I tell you the rest of it now?' he asked.

'The rest?'

He sighed through a hit of caffeine. 'I had drug-induced dreams last night that I'd written down the rest of the story and tracked you around the world trying to email it to you. I actually checked my outbox this morning to make sure I hadn't done it.'

Andie wished her post-accident dreams were as uncomplicated. 'What story?'

'The night of the accident. I only got to tell you some of it yesterday, and I didn't want you thinking the last conversation you had before almost dying was with an idiot dude in a bar.'

She huffed a laugh. 'I was just happy to know I hadn't been drinking alone and feeling miserable. No idiot dude featured.'

'You weren't miserable. At least, you didn't seem to be.' He took a sip of coffee. 'You were my first non-work-related company since I'd been in Newcastle, and I don't think either of us was miserable when we sat down to dinner.'

Considering his current state and attitude, Andie wondered what would make him miserable. 'Had you been miserable?'

He tilted his head. 'I might have been verging on glum. To be honest, making a friend over dinner was exactly what I needed. So, thank you, Andie.' He raised his cup to her.

She smiled, feeling undeserving. 'So the job you started is at the uni?'

'A six-month secondment, replacing someone on study leave.'

Andie was good at working people out – understanding where they fit was her job and her uncanny talent. Maybe it was her concussion or Ben's post-accident euphoria, but so far, he was unfathomable: unruffled, unpredictable, fun with an undercurrent of serious. She'd crossed the Science and Medical faculties off her list, had Social Science and Education at the top. 'What do you do?'

'I'm a video and film editor. A camera operator too, but for the uni, it's the editing.'

Her eyebrows rose with interest.

'You did that the first time I told you,' he said. 'Like you were lining up the questions.'

'Did I ask a lot of questions?'

'Hammered me.'

She grimaced. 'Sorry, I can't help myself sometimes.'

'No, they were cool questions. *Why did you get into that? What do you love about it? What's your editing kryptonite?* I loved that last question. Have you used it before, or was that just for me?'

'I have, yes. Don't feel slighted, though. It's a great question. You get some interesting answers.'

He smiled at her, like they were on the same wavelength, and a chill rippled across her scalp. She glanced away, resisting the urge to ask all the same questions. She wanted to know, of course she did, but she didn't want to be on his wavelength.

'Well,' she made herself smile, 'I hope the rest of the story isn't just me hammering you with questions. Not sure I'd want my last conversation before almost dying to be an interrogation of someone.'

'It wasn't like that. I got to ask some questions. And I get your interest. You're in recruitment, you'd never met an editor and you love a good career story.'

'That's true.'

'You also love your job, you're learning tap dancing and you're in a hardcore walking group that meets super early and where you're fined if you don't show.'

She laughed.

'When you realised it was almost eleven, you were worried about sleeping in and breaking your streak.'

'Oh.' Andie sat back in her chair. 'The police officer who sat with me after the accident said I kept looking through my bag for five dollars. What else did I tell you?'

'That you'd just been to the wedding of two clients you'd introduced, you travelled the world for ten years, but you had a bad
experience and now you don't fly anymore. Your best friend Vivian
thought Mitchell Michaels was a date, and you pretended that was
funny.'

Andie folded her arms, wondering what else she might have
told him. She wouldn't have mentioned Zack – at least, she didn't
think she would – but Zack had been on her mind since she'd
woken up in hospital, and she wondered now if Ben was what
put him there. If a random encounter with someone who had no
opinion on her grief, who would go back to Perth in six months,
had made her feel safe enough to talk about the wound inside her.

'It's a little weird,' she said, keeping her tone light, playful,
'that you know things about me that I can't remember telling you.
I hope we didn't get all deep and meaningful. God knows what I
might have said.'

'Don't worry. We made a deal not to screw up a good start with
our depressing stories.'

Ben had a depressing story? She didn't want to think about
this upbeat man having other wounds. If he hadn't wanted to talk
about them then, she wasn't going to make him do it now. Wiping
her brow with mock relief, she said, 'Good to know the conversation was uplifting.'

'I'd want to know if I couldn't remember.'

There was more than a hint of seriousness to his voice, and
Andie wondered why it was important to him. She didn't ask
though, in case his answer was related to his depressing story; in
case it made her cry. 'Are you always positive?'

'Maybe a little more than usual right now.' He raised a victory
fist like he had yesterday. 'We survived, Andie. It's euphoric, right?
And yes, it's possible I'll come crashing down when the adrenaline
wears off, but for now, I'm holding on to it.'

His jubilance bewildered her. Where did it come from? Why
didn't she feel it?

As though she'd asked the question out loud, he said, 'It's my dad's fault. He always told us to be happy for every day we're above ground.'

Above ground. Heat raced to her eyes and she glanced away. She could have stayed, steered the conversation to other, safer topics, but her tears were too close to the surface now. Instead, she checked her watch and stood. 'I'm sorry, but I have to get going.'

'Sure. And hey, thanks again for coming. It's a relief to have told you some of the better parts of that night. There's more, if you ever feel like hearing it.'

He said it as though he didn't expect her back, and Andie was tempted to wish him well and move on. But as she turned to collect her bag, she felt the empty space of his room and knew this would be a lonely place when his euphoria came crashing down.

'How long will you be here?'

'Two weeks to start with, then, depending on improvement, I'll have some decisions to make.' His options, he explained, were to stay at Hepburn House for another two weeks, go back to the apartment in Newcastle in the hope of finishing his contract with the uni, or fly home to Perth to finish his rehab there. 'I'm not sure I want to do a month in here, but I'll need to be a lot better to manage on my own. I've got family and friends in Perth, it's where I'd prefer to be, but there's no direct flight from here and it'd be a long haul with all of this.' He indicated his leg, his ribs. 'Anyway, the social worker is investigating a transfer to a rehab place over there. Nothing will happen if I've got nowhere to go.'

Andie remembered being stranded a long way from home, in a different kind of pain. Waiting could be trauma in itself. 'I hope it gets worked out soon.'

He heaved a sigh. 'My parents need a break, and I don't want to be the problem that gets in the way of that.'

Andie didn't want to know why his parents needed a break, and she didn't have any advice about families; home was the last place she'd go for support. With nothing helpful to say, she just nodded.

'Recuperation will sort itself out. I'm not panicking yet,' he said. 'How about you? How's your recovery looking?'

Minor, compared to Ben's. It felt wrong to even mention it, but waving it off could seem overly dismissive of something they'd survived together. She told him about her elbow, the exercises for getting back full movement; the concussion, the brain fog and headaches, and the month off work.

'I was hoping to talk my boss into giving me something to do from home, but the brain fog,' she made light of it with a shrug. 'Not great for business, apparently.'

He watched her a moment, said, 'Don't rush back. Life's too short to go through it in a fog.'

It was kindness, but she knew all too well about life in a fog and she didn't want to go through it alone. She turned her face away, picked up her bag and said, 'I could drop in again in a couple of days, if you're up for more coffee?'

'Yeah, of course, if you're coming out this way. Sorry, I didn't ask, do you have to come far?'

'I'm about ten minutes from here,' she lied.

'I actually have no idea where I am. Near the coast, obviously.' He nodded towards the stunning ocean view beyond the window. 'But in relation to my apartment on the harbour, I've got no idea.'

'You're about twenty minutes' drive from there.'

'Is it anywhere near your place?'

'Kind of. Why?'

He hesitated. 'There are a few things I want from the apartment. Not much, but I'm desperate for my reading glasses and something decent to watch.'

'Oh my god, you haven't been able to read anything?'

'My sister picked up a pair of those magnifying glasses, but my eyes get blurry if I use them for too long. And I've got several hundred movies on a hard drive that I would love to get my hands on.'

'Several *hundred*?'

'Yeah, I wasn't kidding about being a movie buff. Also my dad's fault.' He did that quiet laugh again, as though thinking of his father reminded him of happy times. 'I just thought, if you're anywhere near there . . .'

'Of course, yeah. Can't have you going blind.'

Mara

IT WAS LATE morning by the time Mara drove into the car park at Hepburn House for the second time that day, already sick of being Estelle's EA. She'd just spent two hours clocking up an eye-watering tab for clothes and toiletries, going to specialist food stores, buying alcohol and appropriate glassware to drink it from. Now, she had to lug it all inside.

She loaded her arms with packages and bags, redistributing weight so she didn't drop anything she couldn't afford to replace, which was basically all of it. Leaving a couple of fingers free for her keys, she beeped the lock and headed along the path through the garden to the front entrance.

'Hey, wait up!' someone called from behind her.

As she turned, a large package wedged under her arm began to slip, and she froze.

'Want a hand?'

The voice behind her was female and friendly. Not game to move, Mara said, 'Can you grab that parcel on my hip?' There was a rustle of bags and the weight of the box lifted away. 'Thanks. That was close.'

'I think we're attached.'

She looked down to see her rescuer's hand trapped between the tangle of handles on her arm. Looking up, she saw it was the physiotherapist who'd given her the fist-pump of encouragement yesterday. 'Sorry, I've got a thousand things here. Hang on.'

Mara lowered the bags over her other arm only to discover that hand was trapped too. When she bent to put everything on the ground, she took the physiotherapist with her and their heads came together with a crack.

Her eyes swam.

The physio staggered back a step, then laughed and said, 'You okay?'

'Be better if I could rub my head.' Mara smiled, but she was mortified, and still attached to the stupid bags. 'Sorry, my hands are stuck.'

'Hang about.' The physio squatted to pick at the straps. 'How's that?'

'A little embarrassing,' Mara said, straightening.

'Thought you might need this.' The woman handed her the thermal cup Mara had bought. 'Good grief, did I drop it?'

'You left it on the roof of your car.'

She rolled her eyes. 'Thank you. Again.'

Tucking short, jet-black hair behind her ears, the woman said, 'You taking all that inside?'

'Thought I could do it in one trip, but I might have overestimated.'

'I'll give you a hand. We're going the same way.' Scooping up several bags, she waited until Mara had gathered the rest then started down the path with her. She was tall and robust, with a glossy, China doll haircut and a silver nose stud. Mara felt plain and child-sized beside her. 'You were outside Estelle Collings' room yesterday, weren't you?'

'That was me. You're one of the physios?'

'Yes. Are you her granddaughter?'

'God, no. I work for her.'

'Like, an aide?'

'Executive Assistant, for the moment. I work at her law firm.

I'm meant to be assisting her with clients' files, but she keeps sending me out shopping. Hence the bags.'

Mara had said it light-heartedly, but the physio frowned. 'That's a bit rough, expecting her to work while she's in rehab. Especially at her age.'

A twinge of guilt warmed the back of Mara's neck; she hadn't even thought of that. 'Well, yes, but it's so other people can take over her workload.'

'Still, her fall was only a week ago. No wonder she's agitated.'

'You mean the ordering people around thing?'

'It can happen after a fall like hers.'

'Actually, she's always like that.' Mara had to tilt her face up to look at her. 'Sorry, that's probably not good news for you.'

Amusement edged into her expression. 'Part of the job, really.'

'I can take it from here.' Mara stopped as Estelle's room came into sight, not wanting the physio to trigger Estelle's irritation about the hydrotherapy pool. 'You've been a big help, thanks so much. And good luck.'

She did the fist-pump thing again. Mara would have returned it if she'd had a free hand.

Estelle was asleep when Mara walked in and she hesitated at the end of the bed, not sure what to do next. Waking her was a bad idea, so she set the parcels down as quietly as she could, figuring she'd make a start on the client files. But as she stepped towards the document boxes, her foot caught in the handle of a shopping bag and she did a tiptoeing recovery dance, trying not to fall or make a sound. Okay, clearing the trip hazards was the first job.

She'd separated the clothes from the rest of the parcels when Estelle's bark shattered the silence. 'What on earth are you doing?'

Mara jumped, snatching her hand away from the wardrobe door. 'I . . . I was trying not to wake you.'

'Doing what?'

'Putting some of the shopping away.'

'Turn on a light.'

Mara found a switch and braced herself for a lecture about making noise and going through her closet. Instead, she got: 'Clothes! Thank god. Bring them here.'

Mara tried to explain that the shop had agreed she could return anything Estelle didn't want, but by then Estelle was only interested in the contents of the bags and Mara was as good as invisible. Not unhappy to be forgotten, she watched from a safe distance and searched for a silver lining. She'd been given a pay rise to go shopping and stand around. Except she'd been fine with documents and memos.

Waving at a mound of clothes as she reached for another bag, Estelle said, 'You can put those away.'

'Which ones are you keeping?'

'All of them.'

Wow, everything. Glancing over the storage space, Mara said, 'Have you got your other things somewhere else?'

'If I had other *things*, as you say, I wouldn't have needed you to pick up these.'

'But there's only a nightie and some underwear in here.'

Estelle sat back against the pillows, two fingers flicking at the frilled neckline of her nightie. 'My ex-husband bought this dreadful item and whatever else is in there.'

Mara frowned. 'Couldn't someone pick up clothes for you?'

'Isn't that what you've just done?'

'Your own clothes. From home.'

'I gave my housekeeper time off until I need the apartment ready,' she said, starting on another bag.

'What about family?'

'I don't have children.'

'The rest of your family?'

Estelle's face stiffened as she slid a tissue-wrapped package from the bag. 'I would not expect family members to be involved in my hospital care.'

Not close to family then. Except . . . 'What about Vaughn?'

Estelle lifted a pale blue jumper from the tissue, eyes moving over it with appreciation. But her voice, when she spoke, was hard. 'Vaughn has not been to my apartment for twenty years. I see no reason to send him there now.'

Twenty years? Okay, Estelle was a difficult person and Mara could see why Vaughn might not be a regular visitor. But twenty years? It wasn't like they didn't talk, they worked together every day. 'But Vaughn came to see you in the hospital.'

Estelle's gaze sharpened on Mara. 'Who told you that?'

'I, well, . . . he said . . .'

'What did Vaughn say?'

Nothing, now that Mara thought about it. He'd talked about her injuries and care, and Mara had imagined visits with flowers and to drop in essentials. 'Well, I assumed he'd been in to see you.'

'Never make assumptions, Mara.'

Good grief. Estelle was old and injured. She'd been in hospital for a week and her only visitor had been her ex-husband. Was that even family? Talk about tragic. Her new boss was bitter and scary, and was arguably lying in a bed she'd made for herself with her bitter-scary attitude, but again: Estelle was old and injured. She'd been in hospital a week and was looking at two more. At least.

Thinking of Mum and her silver linings, Mara smiled and said, 'At least you've got clean knickers.'

Mara hadn't expected a reply – after all, it was Estelle, and bright sides clearly weren't her thing. So she was surprised to see a touch of amusement cross Estelle's face as she held up yet more knitwear. It wasn't a smile, not even a tremor of her lips. More an upward rearrangement of the lines on her face.

Mentally high-fiving herself, Mara began hanging and folding the clothes.

'I see you took the opportunity to do some shopping for yourself.' There was an accusation in Estelle's tone that made Mara turn.

'Oh no, that's for you.'

One pale eyebrow slid upwards.

'It's a keep cup,' Mara said. 'Thermal lined. I've got one too. They keep coffee hot for ages.'

Estelle sat the box on the tray table without interest. 'A cup will not improve the coffee here.'

'No, but if I pick up a couple of cappuccinos in these on my way in each day, they'll still be hot when I get here, and at least we can start the day off with the good stuff.'

'I see.'

See what? That Mara could think for herself? That she could be trusted with a simple shopping task? Mara sighed. 'I can take it back, it's no problem. I'll do it on the way home.'

'Set up an account at a cafe for two coffees every morning and provide me with the payment details.'

'You want two coffees in the morning?'

'One for each of us. I presume you will want one for yourself.'

'Yes, I just wasn't expecting . . .' *You to do anything nice.*

'I've seen you making use of the machine in the office. You can consider this the same.' Oh, not nice, just a business expense. 'And Mara?'

'Yes.'

'Good work.'

Well, she'd take that, Mara thought, her face lifting with a smile. No wonder Estelle had so many lines; being in her company was like being sucked down by gravity. 'The cup I bought has an orange poppy on it.' She took it out of the box to show her.

'Yes, I see that.'

'Like getting coffee and a fresh flower every morning.'

'Are you always so . . . peppy?'

'I try to be.'

'Don't try so hard.'

Coral

A MOBILE COFFEE van was at the front entrance of the hospital when Coral was leaving and the smell of fresh grounds wafted to her like a calm breeze in the middle of her cyclone. She stood for a moment in the shade of the van's raised window and pulled in a deep breath. 'Where were you when I needed you yesterday?'

The guy in the van shot her an understanding grin over the top of an espresso machine. 'I'm here around ten-thirty for an hour every weekday. At least until the cafe renos are finished.'

She checked her watch. 'Just made it. And here I was thinking I'd need to buy a coffee machine.'

One side of his mouth slid up in a lopsided grin. 'What are you having?'

'Double shot flat white, extra hot, thanks. And a slice of whatever that is.' She pointed at a moist, iced bar of cake under a plastic dome on the counter.

'Date loaf.'

'Lunch, depending on how the rest of my day pans out.'

Up close, Coral saw that his dark hair was flecked with grey, with curls that looked like a seventies shag cut. As he got to work, she glanced into the van, admiring the cleverly organised workspace. She loved an efficient, streamlined, labour-saving system. 'Where's your next stop?'

'I'm done after this.'

'Nice. How do you get a job like that?'

'Took the payout and bought the van.' He looked up from the milk he was steaming and grinned like he'd never had a moment of regret.

'Is it as good as it looks?'

'How does it look?'

'Like you get to drink coffee and chat all day.'

'That's pretty much it. Although I don't drink coffee all day. After the first one, the fumes are enough to keep me going.' He set her coffee on the counter. 'Start at five, done by lunch and I get time for a surf in the afternoon.'

'Oh, you surf.' She said it like it was the downside.

'Among other things.'

What things did a person do with six or seven free hours in a day? Every day. Could she really retire? 'Five am, that's an early start.'

'The heart-starter is free though.' He flashed her another lop-sided grin as he slid her cake across the counter and rested his elbows on the stainless-steel surface to chat. Perhaps relaxed was something that came with all that spare time. She might be hopeless at retirement.

'Your day's really over by lunchtime?'

'Nah, it's only just starting.' He grinned.

She nodded, trying to remember the last time she'd had six hours with nothing to do. The last time she'd been without a To-Do List. 'I'm going to be in and out of here this week. Do you take phone orders?'

He handed her a card. 'Shoot me a text if I don't answer. I'm Alby.' He shook her hand across the counter.

Alby. Of course he was. Too cool to be David or Phillip or Peter. 'I'm Coral, and thanks.'

'Hey, Coral,' he called as she started to walk away, 'there's only one slice of the date loaf left. You want to make it dinner? Half price for leftovers.'

'Not sure I should have two meals of cake in a day, but I reckon I can find someone to enjoy it.'

⬤

She should go straight to the office, she told herself as she steered out of the car park, but the early start, Richard's call, the meeting with the doctor had unsettled her. Bloody hell, dementia. A nugget of hot, anxious alarm had lodged itself in her chest. She pressed a hand to the spot between her breasts, the . . .? What was that bone called? Nope, it was gone. Maybe she had dementia too.

No, she didn't have time for dementia. Especially if Val had dementia. When Summer was about to have another baby, and she hadn't seen Wade in more than a year. With her life slipping away on other people's needs.

She stopped at a T-junction, her composure starting to twitch at the thought of time slipping away. She didn't have time to panic, either. *Pull yourself together, Coral.* She glanced in her rear-view to confirm there was no-one waiting for her to move off, then took a sip of her coffee, lukewarm now, but she was used to that. Broke a corner off one of the slices of date loaf and moaned at the sugar hit. Comfort food, there was always time for that.

Glancing around, she realised she was only two streets from Richard's parents' house. Damn him for asking. Damn them for always being good to her. They'd barely batted their eyes back when Richard broke the news that she was pregnant. She'd been just shy of twenty-one, halfway through an arts degree, and their son was too busy surfing to get a proper job.

Coral and Richard had been together since they were fifteen, it wasn't as though they weren't expected to get married at some point. But Helen and Graham could have been difficult; they could have piled on the guilt like Coral's parents. Instead, they just got on with it, handing over the keys to the caravan in their backyard and helping arrange the hastily planned, self-catered wedding at the surf club.

Six years and a second child later, Richard packed his boards for another trip up the coast, leaving Coral to more weeks of trying to reach him, of *When are you coming back?* and *I can't do this on my own.* This time though, she told him if the surf was more important than his family, he shouldn't bother coming back. She'd meant it as a challenge, a reminder of what was important, but he'd heard it as something else, thought she'd called him on his true feelings and was giving him permission to leave. So he did.

Helen and Graham were upset for Coral and the kids, disappointed in their son, but he was their only child, a treasured son who'd arrived when they'd almost given up hope. They'd always excused his selfishness. They just wanted him to be happy, whatever the cost to anyone else. They'd been good grandparents, though, babysitting when Coral got work, Helen whipping around with the vacuum cleaner and leaving a casserole in the oven; Graham fixing doors and fences, her car once or twice, turning up at the kids' soccer matches and tennis games. Never judgemental of her parenting or coping skills. There for the kids, because Richard wasn't.

He really was a shit son, and Coral was a sucker. She flicked her indicator on, pulling up outside their house two minutes later.

It wasn't the house with the caravan in the yard anymore; they'd sold up and bought a villa ten years ago. It had a small, neat yard front and back, enough garden for Helen's flowers and a big enough lawn for Graham to justify keeping his lawnmower. There were no early spring seedlings in, Coral noticed. The lawn needed a cut, too; the shaggy bits growing over the pathway would have horrified Graham five years ago.

There was a crash inside after Coral rang the bell, a struggle with the locks, then Helen appeared, looking alarmingly like a bewildered old lady. Coral talked her way inside, not sure Helen recognised her until she'd steered her to the living room with updates on Summer and Wade.

'His planned three years in the UK is almost up,' Coral was

telling her when Graham trundled in from the back bathroom. He had half a dozen white plasters stuck in random places, as though he'd nicked himself while doing a full-body shave.

'And what have you done to yourself?' Coral asked, remembering his hearing and raising her voice as she gave him a kiss and helped him ease into a chair at the kitchen table.

He was thin and his skin hung off him like wet paper. A plaster on his shin covered only about a third of a nasty, wet-looking graze that made Coral wince.

'I thought that sounded like Coral's voice,' he said, patting her hand. 'How are you, love? Is Summer's baby here yet? Don't you remember bringing her back to the caravan from the hospital? Gee, we missed you when you were gone.' A dribble of saliva ran from the corner of his mouth, joining a wet patch on his collar.

'It's Coral, Graham,' Helen said, loud enough for the neighbours to hear. 'She dropped in on her way home from the hospital up the hill. Val's having a stay in there. She had a fall.'

'Maybe she can lend me a few of these.' He fingered a plaster on the heel of his hand and heaved out a wheezing chuckle.

'Don't be ridiculous, Graham,' Helen shouted from the other side of the kitchen.

Coral pushed her mouth into a smile and held up her package of date loaf. 'I thought you might like a treat. Can I put on the kettle?'

Richard's idea of a 'drop-in' ended up taking an hour and a half – time Coral didn't have. Battling for composure through several complicated accounts of Graham's fall/trip/turn, she finally convinced Helen his grazes needed proper dressings and made them a doctor's appointment for that afternoon. Helen assured her their home care package included taxi fares for appointments, which was just as well, because if Coral had had to take them herself, she would then have had to drive three hours up the coast to Richard's place to kill him. Instead, she booked the cab to make sure they actually went.

After that, it was standard procedure. She checked the fridge, the pantry, the dishwasher, the bin, the loo and the washing machine. Folded a few towels, made the two beds they now slept in, all as quickly and unobtrusively as she did at Val's, so they wouldn't think she was checking up on them. Which she was, of course – and Richard would get a full report, not the *We're fine, don't worry about us*, that Coral suspected he happily accepted as truth. Heaven forbid they ask Richard to help. Or that Richard put himself out for anyone but himself.

Coral gripped the steering wheel with a chokehold as she drove away from the house, let out a scream through gritted teeth as she rounded the corner, then called Richard.

'I threw out two-week old ham and something growing fur at the back of the vegetable drawer. They've got enough teabags to survive a six-year lockdown and pretty much nothing else. They need more help. They need shopping and cleaning, and possibly incontinence support for Graham; he smelled like old man wee.'

'You'd have some contacts for all that, after sorting out Val, wouldn't you?' he asked.

'I have contacts for Mum's service provider. You need to sort your own out.'

'Can you shoot me the website details then?'

'It's a website, google it. By the way, the wound on Graham's shin looked nasty, he'll probably need the new dressing changed in a couple of days. You should get in touch with the doctor's surgery to see if they can arrange that.'

'Have you got a number?'

'No, Richard, I don't.' Actually, she did, she remembered. 'You need to talk to your mum about their doctor's appointments and medications. You should come down tomorrow and make sure they're following up on your dad. I'm not sure it was just a fall. They both mentioned a turn.'

'What kind of a turn?'

'I don't know, Richard. What *is* a turn? Try googling it. Or, I know, ask your mother.'

'Ease up, babe. I'm just trying to get to the bottom of this.'

'Don't *ease up* me. And don't call me babe. If you want to get to the bottom of it, get in the car and come see for yourself.'

'Yeah, it's a bit late for that now. Harlow and I are flying out tomorrow.'

'You said Thursday.'

'We're flying out of Brisbane, got to head up there tomorrow. I'll do some ringing around, see if I can get something started while I'm away.'

Coral scrubbed a hand across her face. It wouldn't happen, it didn't work like that; it was a long and complicated process that relied on family and friends to keep the person afloat until the assessments, interviews, forms and signatures were all ticked off and uploaded. Helen and Graham shouldn't have to wait that long.

'Look,' she bashed her forehead with the heel of her hand, appalled at what she was about to say, 'I'll organise some food for them while you're away, but you get on the phone today and start talking to people about this. And come down to see them as soon as you're back from Bali. And don't let Helen tell you everything's fine.'

'Babe, you're a champion.'

'Don't call me babe.'

He chuckled in her ear.

'Fuck off, Richard.' But he already had.

Mara

MARA HAD BEEN relegated to the balcony to eat her lunch. She'd only caught glimpses of it previously, but now, as she stepped through the French doors, she realised that what had once been an open verandah had been closed in with glass and filled with fat-cushioned cane furniture and glossy green foliage.

She'd also assumed the balcony was Estelle's private domain, but it continued past her boss's windows and beyond the end of the East Wing. Mara walked to the corner, then around the next one, where the balcony came to a dead end outside the room across the hall from Estelle. The garden outside also wrapped itself around this end of the building, and all three rooms had French doors that led to their own lovely outdoor room.

Definite upside, she told herself as she settled into a deep armchair and unwrapped her sandwich. Dad would know what all the decorative bits in the ceiling and brickwork were called. Mum would have loved the view of the garden. There were some early spring flowers out, their heads swaying in the breeze. Out on the ocean, two ships were balanced like tightrope performers on the horizon. She couldn't tell which direction they were facing, and they didn't appear to move the whole time she ate. They just sat, going nowhere. Like her.

Estelle was asleep when Mara finished her lunch. The remains of her smelly cheese and fancy crackers were on the tray table in front of her, as though she'd dropped off the moment she'd set her knife down. Crossing the room to roll the table away, Mara stopped, telling herself she wasn't there to tend to Estelle's every need. Her primary function was to ensure the smooth handover of Estelle's client workload, and sitting around waiting for Estelle to send her off on another shopping spree wasn't going to get that done.

Moving the document boxes to the balcony side of the room where she could clear some space, Mara flicked through a few random files: 1981 here, 1972 there, no indication of whether they'd been digitised already.

'What are you up to?' Estelle's voice snapped like a whip.

Back turned, Mara rolled her eyes. Did she think Mara was memorising confidential information? 'I'm alphabetising,' she said. 'I grabbed them out of order yesterday and I wanted to be organised when we got started this afternoon.'

'I see.' Grudging consent. 'You can get off the floor, we won't need the files today.'

'But I thought we were—'

'I have another task for you. Get this table out of my way first.'

Mara corrected her earlier thought: She wasn't here to tend to Estelle's *unspoken* needs.

The task was to send a letter to each of Estelle's private clients. Actual letters. On paper with a signature and stuffed into envelopes. Around ninety of them. Had she not heard of email? There was a brief debate about dictation: no, Mara didn't take shorthand; of course, Estelle would *do it herself* if her hand wasn't bandaged; no, Mara didn't need pen and paper, she had a phone with a recording app and a laptop for notes.

'I was once proficient at every aspect of running the office.' The statement seemed to be both bragging and bitter. 'A woman didn't simply get a law degree and *practise law.*'

Mara wasn't sure if Estelle wanted respect or was on the verge of a *You young women have no idea* rant. Either way, Mara just wanted to make a start on the client files so she could get back to working from the office. She opened her laptop and manufactured an expression that she hoped said *Ready to be instructed by the expert in the room.*

Mara had assumed the letter would be a formal notification to Estelle's clients that their cases would be, for an indefinite period, in the hands of other solicitors. She was wrong.

It was wordy and long-winded; Estelle did mention taking 'a couple of weeks' to recover from a fall, but emphasised that she would be overseeing all work carried out on her behalf. The rest . . . well, the gist was that everyone should ignore anything they heard or read to indicate she was stepping back from her role at Collings. That anyone suggesting, implying or otherwise assuming she was about to retire was lying. Okay, Estelle didn't actually use the word *lying*, but the hostility in the wording made Mara's fingers grow damp on her keyboard. The final paragraph requested that said clients dismiss any information regarding her role at Collings unless it came directly from her. Or her Executive Assistant.

That made Mara's head pop up.

'Insert your full name there,' Estelle said.

'*My* name?'

'You are my EA, are you not?'

'Yes, but . . .' The job description had not included: *Accessory to ignoring Vaughn's instructions.*

'Finish your sentence,' Estelle snapped.

She took a hasty breath. 'Yes, but only temporarily.'

'For the duration of my recovery.'

'And . . . But . . .' She searched for the right . . .

'Sentences, Mara!'

Terrifying. 'Vaughn wanted me to assist with the handover of your client files and this isn't . . . that.'

Estelle's face did another one of its multi-response expressions: aghast, displeased, condescending, with a hint of wheels turning somewhere deep and nasty in her mind. Then she let it all go, leaned against her pillows and in a tone that seemed way too casual, said, 'My father was called Mr Collings until he retired at the age of eighty.'

'He retired at eighty?'

'My *point* is that he was referred to by all staff as Mr Collings. Even I was required to use his honorific in the office. It was a sign of respect and seniority. There was none of this first-name basis unless invited to do so.'

Mara wanted to laugh at the idea of calling her dad Mr Ellsworth, but there was something pointed in Estelle's words that wiped all amusement from her face. Mara couldn't tell if the older woman wanted her to call Vaughn 'Mr Collings', or she was accusing her of not showing enough respect. 'Vaughn asked me to call him by his first name when I was fourteen.'

A micro raise of an eyebrow. 'Ah yes. Your father is the builder.'

'Yes.'

'The assumption then is that it was a favour to your father to find you a position at Collings when you'd dropped out of university not once, but twice.'

'I . . .' Mara's heart thumped. 'How did you . . .?' A blush heated her cheeks.

'How did I know he'd found a convenient vacancy in the admin staff for you?'

'No, I didn't mean that, and that's not what happened.' *Was it?*

'And *there* is the disadvantage of not finishing your sentences. Try again, Mara. How did I . . .?' She raised her eyebrows.

It was like being in front of the school principal. Mortifying, shameful and nowhere to run. 'How did you know I'd . . . How did you know about uni?'

'I am more than capable of looking up staff resumes on our system. Yours was hardly inspiring.'

Mara's pulse drummed in her throat. *No, don't cry.* That would make her weak and snivelling as well as uninspiring. She pressed her lips together, swallowed hard. 'I...I...' – *finish the damn sentence, Mara* – 'met the qualifications for the position and I... I've found the challenges in the role within my capabilities.'

'We'll see.' Estelle looked unconvinced. 'You can work on the balcony.' The customary sweep of her hand in dismissal caused a spasm that twisted one side of Estelle's face. 'And go and find the nurse with my pain relief.'

Andie

ANDIE USED THE keys Ben had given her to let herself into his apartment, glad to have something else to fill her afternoon. He said he'd rented it furnished for six months: it was a white, minimalist one-bedroom space with a great view of the harbour.

Andie had once thought about going into real estate, mostly for the chance to be nosy about how other people lived. She'd ended up in a job where she picked their brains instead, but the urge to poke about was still there. She glanced into the bedroom and its small walk-in robe, peeked into the bathroom and opened a storage cupboard in the hallway.

Andie thought about clients who'd come to Newcastle on short-term contracts to decide if they liked the city enough to stay. They brought enough stuff to make it feel like home without packing up their entire lives, in case it didn't work out. By comparison, Ben looked like a tourist in an Airbnb. There were, possibly, half a dozen changes of clothes, two pairs of shoes, a couple of towels, nothing in the kitchen that looked well used and one photo on the shelves in the lounge room.

She bent closer to study it. A black and white image in a plain glass frame; arty yet sweetly candid. A family grouping, if the physical likenesses were anything to go by: Mum and Dad at the centre, Ben and presumably his sister on either side, all four with their arms around each other. Something had happened in the moment before the picture was snapped, and only the father was looking into the lens. Mum had turned her face to one side and appeared to be resting her cheek on the dad's chest. Ben's sister was leaning forward, turning towards the others, a strand of hair blown across her smile. Ben, the tallest, watched on with a gentle, joyful expression. It made Andie wonder again about other people's families, struck as she often was by the foreignness of all that happy togetherness. Why had Ben chosen this image to bring? Was it the best moment of his family life, or had the family been defined by a thousand moments just like this? Did the answer explain his upbeat attitude? Had his life been so lovely, he couldn't imagine a dark side?

Running a finger across the few books on the shelves, she wondered if his sister had taken some of his belongings back to Perth or whether he just didn't have much stuff. Maybe he was environmentally conscious and tried to leave a small footprint. Maybe he'd been waiting on a load of personal things. Not that it had anything to do with her. She'd drop his stuff off tomorrow, find a reason to visit next week, and let him get on with his life . . . so she could get back to hers.

☕

Andie: *I have your hard drive and glasses. Also picked up your mail and a pot plant that was looking sad.*

Ben: *Thank you!*

Ben: *Feel free to give the plant away, if plants aren't your thing.*

Andie glanced at his Devil's Ivy. She'd once nursed one from a single leaf; winding and tying the long stem, cleaning the leaves and hosing it off every now and then. Zack had called it her pet plant, had joked about leaving it a bowl of kibble. She'd had a bunch of plants back then: a temperamental Boston fern, a Giant Peace Lily, a family of little succulents, and an African violet that flowered hot pink for six months of the year. A neighbour had kept them watered while she and Zack had been travelling and during the weeks she'd spent in her black hole at Vivian's place, and she'd come home to find the plants thriving. The sight had made Andie's chest tighten with dread; at the thought of tending them, of seeing new growth or finding a bud easing between the leaves. Of feeling anything for them. She didn't want to be responsible for them. She didn't want to care what happened to them.

She'd given them all away.

Andie: *I'll see how we go.*

Ben: *Hardy as, that guy. But hey, I'd only just bought it, not like we're soulmates.*

Andie: *Good to know.*

Mara

MARA BROKE TOAST into her soup as she told Dad and Pat about her afternoon. 'I went back to the office, printed out ninety-three copies of said client letter and sat at a table to sign them. Which was when Vaughn came out, read it and started shouting, "When did she write this?" and "Who's seen it?" and "Why didn't you email me a copy?" Like, right there in the middle of the office.'

'He was shouting?' Dad frowned.

'Not shouting but, you know, loud enough to be embarrassing. That was when I realised that the steely glare must be a Collings family trait.'

'What'd you do?' Pat grinned like it was hilarious.

The first thing she'd done was apologise, because that seemed like the best thing to do when being pierced with laser eyes. 'I said I was following Estelle's instructions, which was what he'd told me to do, and I suggested he talk to Estelle about the letter.' Not as concisely as that, but at least Vaughn hadn't chastised her for not finishing her sentences.

'In the end, he took the pile of letters and the report of the work I'd done and told me to do nothing until further notice.'

Patrick hooted while Dad reached for more toast. 'I hope you were polite about it. Vaughn has been very good to us.'

A favour to your father. Hardly inspiring. Mara winced again at Estelle's words. She almost asked her dad if the job had been a favour, but decided she didn't want to know.

Coral

THERE WAS AN email from Wade in Coral's inbox when she checked her phone in bed on Wednesday morning. They'd been texting regularly over the last couple of weeks with updates on Val and Summer, but it had been ages since he'd emailed. She rubbed the blur of a restless night from her eyes, looking forward to a happy, wordy update on his latest from the UK. Only for her hopes to be dashed with his opening line.

> *Hey Mum, just a quickie. A pipe burst in the apartment above mine and apparently there's a fair bit of water damage. The tenant reckons he'll need to move out. Can you go over and have a look? Take some pics? I'm trying to get an insurance assessor out there but the time zones are all wrong for getting someone on the phone. Sorry about the timing. Hope Nana's doing okay. Love ya, Wade XX*

Coral closed her eyes, rested her head against the wall behind the bed and allowed herself a moment to sigh and roll her eyes at Wade's *Won't need a rental manager, Mum, the bloke's a mate of a mate, he'll look after the place.* Then, because it was easier to get a thing done if she didn't let it piss her off, she gathered her thoughts, visualised the To-Do List and looked for a hole in her schedule large enough for the thirty-five-minute round trip to Wade's apartment. Then she was out of bed and heaving washing into the dryer before hitting the shower.

⚱

The appointment with the hospital social worker was set for late morning, which gave Coral enough time to check in on Summer, bath Oliver and explain about Helen and Graham.

'If you can order their groceries online this morning,' Coral told Summer, 'I can pick them up and drop them off this afternoon.'

She got petrol on her way to Wade's apartment, a single-bedroom unit, walking distance from a shopping strip and on the bus route to the city and beach. He'd bought it during the Covid lockdowns, despairing he'd never get overseas, then put his hand up for a transfer with his accounting firm as soon as the world got vaccinated.

There were watermarks on the mat outside the front door, like a warning of the damp, grungy smell that hit Coral as she stepped inside. She squelched down the carpeted hallway, threw open the doors to the small balcony and braced herself for the damage.

Skirting boards, chair legs and the kickboards under the kitchen cupboards were all waterlogged and swollen; there was an ugly stain in the bathroom where the leak had run down the wall, and a sludgy puddle across the floor tiles. The carpet would need to be replaced, and possibly the floorboards underneath.

'Fuck,' she hissed, thinking about the mammoth task to get it all fixed. It was an insurance job, but that in itself would be a minefield of assessors, builders and quotes, all of which required someone to be here to let them into the ruined apartment. It wasn't like Summer or Richard would be available to do it anytime soon. 'Fuck.'

She took photos, videoed a walk-through and emailed it all to Wade, hoping his insurance was up to date. She checked the time. '*Fuck*,' she hissed again.

⚱

Coral was ten minutes late for the meeting with the social worker, who hadn't turned up anyway, according to Val. She was in the building, a nurse assured her. And yes, there was probably time to grab a coffee from the van if she was quick.

'Make it a double shot,' Coral told the guy. 'Thanks, Alby.'

'How's your day going?' he asked as he worked the coffee grinder.

She tried for a word to describe it, but only managed an exhausted laugh.

'That good?'

'I've just been squelching through my son's flooded apartment. He's in London, I'm on photo duty.'

'Burst pipe?'

'The apartment upstairs. I've no idea what that place looks like but it can't be worse than Wade's.'

'My parents' place was flooded in the *Pasha Bulker* storm,' Alby said. 'The water rose up through the floorboards. The insurer ended up having to put in underfloor fans to dry the place out. Took six months to get Mum and Dad back in.'

Coral winced. 'That long?'

'It wasn't fun, but my folks ended up with a new kitchen and carpets.'

'Nice to get a silver lining.'

He slid her coffee across the counter, fixed his deep blue eyes on hers. 'It can take a while to see the shine though.'

She nodded, his grasp on her situation making her throat unexpectedly tight.

He tilted his head towards the tubs lined up on his counter. 'You look like you could do with some fortification.' He dropped a coconut-covered ball into a paper bag and handed it to her.

'Oh.' She'd already paid for the coffee and fumbled for her phone.

131

'On me,' he said. 'Flood buddy to flood buddy.'

'Are you sure?'

He looked at her with a twinkle in his eye and Coral smiled. Possibly for the first time in days.

Mara

MARA HAD ARRIVED at Hepburn House with two takeaway coffees and an explanation of her encounter with Vaughn. But Estelle had sent her straight back out without giving her a chance to start work.

It was Wednesday and the client files were still untouched, but Mara felt a thrill of victory that Estelle had asked her to pick up some things from her apartment.

The housekeeper Lynette led her into the living area. 'How's Estelle?'

Mara realised she didn't really know. Estelle's recovery hadn't come up in conversation and Mara hadn't been game to ask. 'Okay, I think. Improving.' She'd been moved to rehab, so that had to be an improvement.

'She sounded tired when I spoke to her yesterday.'

'She had a physio session in the afternoon. Maybe it was after that.'

'Typical Estelle, she didn't want to talk about it,' Lynette said, as though it was unheard of for Estelle to want attention. 'Here, I've started collecting the things she asked for.'

Mara had been stopped in her tracks again by the view of the harbour through those double-storey windows.

'Amazing view, isn't it?' Lynette said. 'One of the perks of working for Estelle.'

She said it in the same brisk way she said everything, but Mara figured it had to be sarcasm and glanced at her, ready to share an empathetic eye roll. Lynette, though, had turned to the items arranged on the table. When she'd run through a list, she checked her watch and said, 'If you don't mind, I'll leave the rest for you to get. It's all in her bedroom, just turn right at the top of the stairs. I'm off as soon as I've finished back here.' She gestured for Mara to follow her, leading the way to the kitchen.

Mara stopped in the doorway, taking in the pale marble, the glossy white cupboards and sheen of stainless steel. Good grief, she'd be frightened to make a cup of tea in here, in case she left fingerprints.

'Since she's going to be gone a while, I've stripped the fridge back.' Lynette opened one side of an enormous fridge-freezer. 'Have a look, see if there's anything you can make use of.'

'Me?'

'Estelle prefers me to take whatever I want whenever she goes away. And those big hampers she gets from clients at Christmas? Always gives them away. My family love them. Here,' she shuffled the last few items around, 'there's half a dozen eggs and a round of brie. Jar of olives and stuffed vine leaves. Help yourself.'

The apartment felt huge and quiet when Lynette had left. Extravagant and daunting, like Estelle. Everything was sumptuous and sophisticated. Mara could sprawl on the furniture, make a coffee, flip through the books or fire up the discreetly mounted flatscreen telly, but the thought of security cameras and Estelle's fury kept her on task.

She found Estelle's bedroom at the end of the upstairs hallway: it had another startling view and was large enough to accommodate a *chaise longue*. Clothes had been lined up along it and there was a suitcase on the floor. Mara packed them into it and was about to leave when she took a moment to imagine waking up here instead of the small demountable she lived in. It had been an old site office that Dad got cheap after a job; he'd used it as a home office until he cleaned it out for Mara last year. It was a step up from her small bedroom in the house, and had its own bathroom – one she could barely turn around in, but at least she didn't have to share with Dad and Pat. A kitchenette had been converted to wardrobe space because, as Dad had said, why would you need to cook in there when the kitchen he'd built for Mum was a dream?

Unable to resist a peek into Estelle's walk-in robe, Mara's mouth dropped open. There were display shelves and a padded seat, forty or fifty of the suits Estelle wore at the office, plus satiny evening wear, racks of knitwear, shoes and handbags. She snapped a photo for Dad's ideas file, collected the eggs and cheese she'd nabbed from the fridge, and had one final look around.

The place reminded her of a woman her dad worked with sometimes who styled homes for sale. She'd told Mara once that the job wasn't just about making a place look better, but making it look generic: removing all trace of the owners so a buyer could imagine their own life there. That's what Estelle's place looked like. There were no stray lipsticks or earrings in the bedroom. No cards on display, no notepad and pen, no keys lying around. Maybe Lynette had cleaned up after Estelle went into hospital, but it wasn't just the lack of *things*. There were no photos with people, no smiling groups, weddings or babies, no sepia images of men in uniform or women in long dresses. No evidence Estelle had memories she looked back on with fondness.

Maybe that was what happened when you were mean to everyone.

🍵

Pulling Estelle's suitcase through the foyer of Hepburn House, Mara rounded the corner and almost walked into the physiotherapist she'd bumped heads with the day before.

The physio stepped back with a start, her face breaking into a smile when she recognised Mara. 'Oh hey, you've got wheels today.'

'Easier than bags. Although still a hazard, apparently.'

'More shopping?' she asked.

'No, this stuff's from Estelle's apartment.'

'Wow, looks like she's moving in.'

'Let's hope not because I'd have about a thousand more trips.'

Estelle was tapping on her laptop with the index finger of her bandaged hand and ignored Mara as she walked in. She obviously wasn't interested in pleasantries, so Mara went straight to the conversation she'd rehearsed. 'I didn't send the letters yesterday.'

'I know,' Estelle said without looking away from the screen.

'I printed them out and was putting them into envelopes when Vaughn—'

'Yes.'

'He said I was to wait before sending them and told me—'

'I've spoken to Vaughn.'

Mara sighed. How could she finish a sentence if Estelle kept interrupting?

'He claims you said I instructed you not to tell anyone what you were doing.'

'He . . . What?' The accusation in Estelle's tone made Mara rewind through the conversation with Vaughn. 'I was putting them . . . and he saw me . . . read one of . . .'

'Sentences, Mara,' she snapped. 'Is that what you told him?'

'No. Why would I?' Mara winced at her curtness.

Estelle turned her laptop towards Mara. 'You're to pick up one of these.'

'A printer?'

'We'll be doing our printing here from now on. Something small but with scanning capability, I think. You're capable of setting one up?'

'I, well, sure, if there are instructions. But I don't mind going back to the office.' She might actually get some work done, which would give her something to put in the report that made it look like she was earning her money.

'I *will not* have Vaughn overseeing my communications with clients.'

Andie

ANDIE HAD MADE a list: walking group, breakfast somewhere, appointment with an elbow therapist, hospital visit; lunch somewhere else, library, supermarket, German class (if her brain could think past *Guten Morgen*). Andie was pretty sure filling every hour of her day wasn't the recommended recovery approach for concussion, but it was her recovery and she had no intention of spending it at home alone. Even if that meant the threat of tears when she delivered Ben's glasses.

He was in a wheelchair when she arrived, sitting by the window. His hair was still mussed up – maybe it was always that way – but he'd had a shave, and aside from the bruises on his cheek and his elevated leg, he looked relatively healthy . . . until he pushed himself upright and grimaced with the pain.

'How is . . . everything?' she asked, setting down the coffee she'd bought at the van out the front.

'Yeah.' It was a sentence in itself. 'Just back from physio, still on the *oh my god, the pain has stopped* high. It's pretty good while it lasts.'

'How long will it last?'

'Going on my two days of experience, anywhere from half an hour to five minutes. You got here just in time. I'm desperate for a coffee.'

She carried a visitor's chair over to his wheelchair and sat down as she gave him his cup. He raised it in a toast. 'Good to see you, Andie. Did you get to your walking group this morning or do you need a loan?'

'You remembered I was walking today?'

'Plenty of time to remember stuff.'

Something she tried to avoid. 'Your hard drive and glasses,' she said, pulling them from her handbag.

He inspected them like they were treasured possessions. 'I didn't think you'd be back for a couple of days. I really appreciate this, thank you.' There was something solemn in his voice that made her wonder how his euphoria was going.

'No problem.'

He tapped the hard drive. 'What kind of movies do you like?'

The kind that wouldn't make her feel too much. 'Travel documentaries. Comedies. Katharine Hepburn being a feminist. What about you?'

'Good storytelling, great images.'

'That's a genre?'

'It is in my head.' He grinned with a kind of nerdy pride.

She grinned back; she loved other people's nerdy passions. Then feeling a buzz of connection, she turned away. 'Oh hey, the view from that balcony looks amazing. Can you go out there?'

'I assume I'm allowed out there. I mean, I've heard people out there. But can I get there? No.'

He was in a wheelchair, she could help him with that, and going for a walk might mean fewer opportunities for him to make her cry. 'Want to check it out?'

'Like a caper?'

'Caper?'

'A lark, an adventure, an escapade.'

Right, he did say caper. 'Okay, sure, it could be a caper.'

She pushed the French doors open and went back for Ben. It was harder than she expected to get the chair moving, over the threshold and angled around so they were looking along the balcony. 'Nice,' she said, finally taking in the expanse of glass and comfy furniture, the indoor and outdoor gardens with their stunning ocean view. 'Shall we sit over there by the wall?'

'Andie.'

'What?'

'It's a caper.'

'Uh-huh.'

'First rule: be reckless and bold.'

There were rules? 'Okay, well,' she glanced around, 'how about I park you at that window and you can think about tipping yourself into the garden?'

She caught his smile in the glass, felt one of her own starting. 'There's a corner,' he said. 'We should go around it.'

The balcony continued around the three rooms at this end of the corridor, like a message to patients and their visitors that recovery wasn't only about physio.

They went all the way to the other side, stopping twice to peer down at the garden, another time to point out Andie's car, then turning back, the distant ocean filling their view like wallpaper.

'Had enough capering?' she asked when they got back to his door.

'Not yet.'

Something in his voice made her glance at his reflection in the glass. His elbows were hooked over the armrests, his face turned to the horizon, something blissful in his expression. She turned the chair so he was facing the window and backed it up to the wall.

'My new rehab goal is to get out here under my own steam,' he said.

'What was your old one?'

'Go to the toilet on my own.'

'Also worth striving for.'

'Would you mind if we sat here for a bit? I'm going to have to lie down soon, but this is too good to leave just yet.' His voice was soft and contemplative and it made her worry about the topics he'd reach for in this mood. But how could she say no, when this place could heal parts of him that the physio didn't reach?

She sat on the sofa beside him and took a moment to soak in the view with him. Something about the giant expanse of blue stretching to the horizon felt like . . . yearning. For something she'd once had, that was now locked away. She shook her head, turned to Ben and found something else for both of them to think about. 'I saw the photo of your family in your apartment.'

'Oh yeah, love that shot. It was Dad's sixty-eighth birthday and we were celebrating another survival.'

Survival? Oh no.

But before she could change the subject, Ben said, 'I haven't spoken to them since . . .' He waved a hand towards his injured leg, something remorseful in the downturn of his mouth.

Andie avoided talking to her mother about anything personal, and even she hadn't been able to dodge the conversation about being hit by a car. She was probably the wrong person for Ben to confide in about family, but she couldn't help wondering why he hadn't spoken to them when they were clearly close. 'Do they know about the accident?'

'My sister told them.' He rubbed a hand over his mop of hair as if the topic had given him a headache. 'I didn't want her to, but we compromised with I'm doing fine, no need to come home.'

Andie nodded. 'My friend Vivian felt compelled to ring my mother when I went into surgery. I had to tell Mum not to come down from Brisbane – I'd need to recover from that too.'

'It's not that. Mum and Dad are great. I just don't want them to come home because I was injured.'

Andie frowned. 'But aren't they in Scotland? It's not like they're interstate.' It wouldn't cross her mother's mind.

'They'd be on the first plane if they knew I'd had surgery. While in an induced coma. For multiple breaks.' He rubbed his head again. 'My dad finished a third chemo treatment in April. It was hard going and they really need to have some fun, not come back to more medical drama.'

Something tightened in Andie's chest. The appropriate response was probably to ask how his father was now, but three lots of chemo sounded bad, and she didn't want to hear the answer. 'I'm sorry,' she said instead, hoping he'd feel her empathy and change the subject.

Ben, though, seemed to take her comment as an invitation to explain. 'Dad's had non-Hodgkin's lymphoma for years. He almost died when I was in high school.' Ben rubbed at the stubble on his chin. 'It wasn't picked up until it was already advanced and basically everywhere. The doctors threw everything at it for about a year, and he spent months on the sofa between treatment cycles and when he was recovering. That's when he got me hooked on movies. Watching them was something we could do together.' One side of his mouth slid up into a smile. 'He was great after that for ten years and then bam, it was back. More scary diagnoses, more chemo, more recovery.' He lifted his gaze to the view, as though taking a moment to let the memories run.

Andie watched his profile, a soulful slackness taking over his face that did nothing to ease the alarm growing in her chest. It didn't sound good and she didn't want to know. So she redirected his thoughts to better memories. 'More movies together?'

He shot her a smile, perhaps grateful to be brought back. 'Yeah. He started writing online reviews, used to joke he'd be letting readers down if he died.' Then he paused again, green eyes on the ocean, Adam's apple lurching as though his dad's bravado had made his throat thicken.

Like Andie's was now.

'Then two years ago, it was back. More chemo, then clear scans, then another relapse last year, only six months after he'd finished the last lot of chemo.' He pulled in a long breath, rubbed a hand over his hair again.

Her heart thumped and her teeth clenched. *Please, Ben, don't tell me how long he has left or how he's spending his final days. Please, don't say any more.*

'He got onto a trial for a new drug last time and now he's in full remission. They're talking long-term with this drug. As in years.' Ben's voice slid higher. 'It's why I took the six-month contract here. It was a break for all of us, short-term but enough time to get some teaching experience. Dad's a bit worse for wear after the chemo this time, but he's doing great.'

He gave the smile he always had when talking about his dad, only this time, now that she knew the story, Andie saw that it wasn't just fondness, but hope too. And it was that, more than the surprise ending, that made Andie's eyes fill with tears. She wanted to say something positive, but she knew if she opened her mouth, all she'd manage was a sob – one abraded by a grief that didn't belong with Ben's hope.

Why had she thought she'd be good company for Ben? He had enough going on, he didn't need her angst. She didn't either. She was a recruiter, for god's sake, she could recruit volunteers to look in on him; and surely she was resourceful enough to find other ways to fill her days until she could get back to work. Things that didn't make her sob. That didn't make her feel like life just . . . hurt.

She cleared her throat, smoothed her hair and turned back to Ben. 'I'm really glad he's doing okay, but I'm sorry. I have to get going.'

'Sure.' He hesitated, as though he might have said the wrong thing. 'Do you mind taking me back in?'

'What kind of a caper would it be if I left you stranded?' She made it sound funnier than it was, annoyed with herself as she wheeled him back, for making Ben feel like he was at fault, for not being able to explain that it was her problem, not his.

As she collected her bag, Ben said, 'That was a damn fine caper, Andie.'

She glanced up to see if he was joking, but he looked like being wheeled around a hospital balcony with a busted leg had been a truly joyful experience.

'My first for a while,' she said. Quite a while.

'If you're out this way again, maybe we could try the garden.'

'Sure.' She smiled. 'Let me know if there's anything you need. I don't mind dropping in.'

'Just the company.'

Her heart thumped. She knew all about needing company.

'Don't get me wrong,' he added, 'the coffee has been great and the balcony adventure was a blast. But the company is . . .' His eyes found hers for a moment, something lonely and despondent in them before they bounced away again. 'Well, something to break up the day, you know?'

It was the first crack she'd seen in his fortitude and it made her waver.

'I'd see you to the door if I thought I could get back on my own,' he said, covering the moment with a smile.

'You could add that to your list of rehab goals.' She pulled her bag over her shoulder and walked to the door, telling herself he'd be fine. There were nurses and physios and other patients; he wasn't alone. Not really. Only . . .

She looked back at him, good sense and impulse warring inside her. 'The thing is . . .' she said, and stopped.

She had no idea how long she stood there. Long enough for bewilderment to creep into Ben's expression. Him and his bloody caper. Telling her to be reckless and bold. She didn't do that kind of thing anymore, but she walked back in anyway.

'The thing is,' she tried again, debating how to spin it so it didn't sound like pity, 'I'm really bad at recovery. All that resting makes me a bit nuts.'

'Okay,' he said.

'And the thing is . . .'

'Is this the same thing or another thing?'

'Let's call it part two of the same thing.'

'Okay.'

She got to the point. 'Look, you need some company and I need something to do, and it just feels like we could help each other through the next couple of weeks.'

'We could?'

'We could have coffee every day,' she said. 'Have a chat, discuss the news, do a crossword, whatever. Something to break up both of our days. Every day.'

His expression said, *Don't want to put you out. Don't want to be pitied.*

'We could have a caper,' she said. 'Several capers. A caper-a-thon.'

A corner of his mouth edged up.

'That's settled then.' She turned to leave, not sure she hadn't lost her mind.

'You don't have to do this,' Ben said.

'I know.'

'It's not your fault I'm here.'

'I know.'

'If something else comes up . . .'

'I'll shoot you a text.'

'Or if it's just a hassle.'

She looked back at him from the door. 'See you tomorrow, Ben.'

In the corridor, Andie nodded at the young blonde woman lugging a huge printer box, walked through the garden, got into her car and burst into tears. Because she could spend the next two weeks going to the supermarket and the library, emailing and texting, having coffee in a hundred cafes, but she knew it was marking time. It was pretend. It was pointless.

She'd done that before, after Zack died, and the life they'd just started together had died with him. And everything she'd been left with was pointless. She'd worked hard to live again without him; she couldn't let concussion drag her back to that place.

Ben was a purpose. He would be her purpose for the next week and a half.

She'd just have to work on the crying.

☕

Andie cleared her throat of her crying jag before answering Vivian's call. 'Hey.'

'You in the car?'

'Coming back from Hepburn House.'

There was a pause. 'You saw Ben Cameron again?'

'He asked me to pick up some things from his apartment yesterday.'

'He found your phone number then.'

Andie hadn't spoken to Viv since she'd given her the blow-by-blow of the first visit. 'Yeah, we've had a couple of text conversations. The poor guy has only been in Newcastle for a couple of weeks and doesn't know anyone. He has literally no-one to visit him while he's in rehab. And, well . . .'

'He asked you to come back.'

'No, I just couldn't stand the idea of him being all alone in there.'

Something cautious crept into Viv's voice. 'Alone is okay for some people, Andie.'

Defensiveness flared in Andie's reply. 'So I went back and asked if he needed anything. He didn't have his own glasses. Apparently alone can be bad for some people's eyesight.'

'Yeah, okay. I didn't mean . . . Just, you need to take care of yourself too. You wanted to move on from this. And you're supposed to be resting.'

'I'm not good at resting, and this is something to do.' She was about to tell her she'd be going to see Ben daily, but changed her mind. 'It's what I need to do right now.'

Coral

WHEN VAL'S LUNCH tray arrived, Coral went in search of the missing social worker, retracing the route she'd taken in search of the doctor on Monday. She eventually found her emerging from a staff kitchen. Coral ordered herself to be patient, not to bail the woman up with remonstrations about missed meetings and hours wasted.

It turned out Tori had been in to see Val much earlier this morning. They'd discussed her situation at home and Val was adamant she was doing fine, managing well, didn't need assistance, wasn't experiencing loneliness and was not interested in aged care; she just wanted to go home. Coral wasn't entirely patient then, briskly suggesting Tori might ask a family member what *fine* and *managing* really looked like and that Val's upcoming cognitive tests should be considered. In reply, Tori explained rather sharply that, as Val was able to speak for herself, her preferences would be taken into account ahead of the motivations of her family.

Coral rocked back on her heels. Did Tori think she was pushing for aged care because she was sick of looking after Val? They settled on a review of her care assessment and a conference to discuss what extra services Val might qualify for.

Coral made her way back to her mother's room, guilt itching at the back of her mind. Was she just another version of Richard and only thinking of herself?

146

What she wanted was for her mother to be comfortable and healthy in the last years of her life. Happy, not anxious about how her linen was folded or whether the pantry was organised. Pausing outside Val's room, she felt her chest tighten at the prospect of another round of explaining and being patient. Yes, she wanted her mum to be happy – but she didn't want to die from the stress of making that happen.

'Are you going already?' Val asked after Coral had explained her 'meeting' with the social worker as simply as she could.

'Well, I . . .' She checked her watch. 'I haven't been into the office yet.'

'Have you had lunch?'

'I grabbed a sandwich from the coffee van,' she lied, then hesitated, her skin heating as she thought about dementia and Tori's insinuations. 'I've got another couple of minutes,' she lied again. 'I didn't get to tell you about the flood at Wade's apartment.'

☕

'Did Richard organise this?' Helen asked as Coral dumped four bags of groceries on the kitchen bench.

'I got Summer to do it, actually. She tore tendons in her ankle and is laid up for a couple of weeks. She's dying of boredom, so ordering your shopping was a welcome distraction.' Coral checked the dressing on Graham's leg to make sure they'd made it to the GP. 'She'd be happy to do it for you again next week.'

'She's a trick, isn't she?' Graham said from the kitchen table.

As Coral unpacked the shopping, she asked about a nurse to redress the wound (done, at the surgery), when they last had a care assessment (not sure they ever had) and whether Richard had spoken to them about another one (oh yes, he mentioned something).

'Seagull's off to Bali again tomorrow,' Graham said, as though this was brilliant news. 'That girlfriend of his, what's her name?'

'Harlow,' supplied Helen.

'What?'

'*Harlow.*'

'That's it. She's a go-getter, isn't she? Running some fancy retreat over there so Seagull can do some surfing.' As though the purpose of the retreat was to accommodate Richard's passion for the sport.

Perhaps it was, Coral thought, looking for somewhere to put tins of soup and cartons of long-life milk and trying not to feel like the partner who'd held their Seagull back.

Her decisions back then – or lack thereof – had shaped the rest of her life. Not that she'd take it all back: it had given her Summer and Wade. But she'd be happy to pass up the bits where she'd been lumped with Richard's stupid decisions.

Once upon a time, just like a fairytale, Coral had aspirations of being a surfing photographer. Admittedly, it had been on the back of Richard's dream to follow in the footsteps of Newcastle surfing icon Mark Richards. Nicknamed the Wounded Seagull for his long, lanky arms that would unfold like a bird's wings, Richards had won his first world championship when Richard was just a thirteen-year-old grommet. The teenager had been tall and lanky too, so he got the abridged nickname Seagull.

Their ocean-themed names were the reason he'd noticed her in the first place: Seagull and Coral, like they were drawn together. Yes, eye-rolling stuff. He'd been set on continuing the ocean theme with the kids, hence Summer and Wade; at least Coral had talked him down from Neptune and Gidget.

In the end, neither of them had enough ambition to see their dreams through. Richard lost the drive to compete once he discovered it involved hard work, and Coral's burgeoning photography career took a back seat to life as a single mum with two kids, and an ex who lived three hours away.

She'd never parted with her SLR camera and its fancy lenses, though. They were still gathering dust in the Black Cupboard – Summer and Wade's name for the space she'd tried to turn into a darkroom, which had ended up storing bike helmets, beach gear and gardening tools. There had been times when she could have done with the money she might have got for the camera, but the thought of selling it had felt like giving away the last part of someone she'd once been. Or could have been, or nearly was.

'That's the shopping put away then,' Coral said, straightening her shirt and glancing around. 'What have you got lined up for dinner tonight?'

'We'll make do with a bit of toast,' Helen said, as though the stress of having Coral arrange her cupboards had exhausted her.

'Why don't I heat up a pot of that soup before I go?'

What was another ten minutes?

Mara

MARA HAD PICKED up a printer, a folding table and office supplies and set it all up in the corner of Estelle's room. It was mid-afternoon by the time she was done and Mara still hadn't had lunch or opened a file, but she threw up her hands in victory when the printer finally whirred into action.

Her boss peered over the top of her glasses, looking unimpressed.

'My computer is talking to the printer, the printer is printing. All is right with the world.' Mara grinned.

Estelle's expression remained deadpan.

'It's taken me an hour!' She raised a fist in victory, and Estelle looked back down at her laptop. Talk about sucking the joy out of things. 'Okay, what are we printing?'

'My client letter.'

'I ran them off yesterday. I thought you talked to Vaughn about them.'

'We had a *discussion.*' Estelle took a moment to haul back on the emotion that had coloured her last word. 'About several issues arising from my letter. One of which was his attempt to interfere with my client correspondence. To protect my clients and ensure that doesn't happen again, we will start the process again from here.'

'What about the letters in the office?' Mara had co-signed all ninety-three of them and stuffed almost half of them into envelopes. 'I can pick them up and finish them off here?'

'No, you cannot.'

'I don't understand.'

'You don't understand my instructions?'

It wasn't her job to understand, but . . . 'I thought Vaughn was trying to support your clients while you recover.'

Estelle's laugh was a bitter bark. 'Oh yes, that's Vaughn being supportive. That's what he claims he's doing, and he uses it against me.'

'I don't think he meant—'

'You have no idea what he means.'

It also wasn't Mara's job to defend Vaughn, but Estelle was suddenly rigid with anger over something Mara thought she had misunderstood. 'I'm sure it's not what you think. I mean, he's your cousin.'

'My *cousin*,' Estelle started, then turned her face to the window, jaw tight. When she spoke again, her voice had dropped an octave. 'My cousin is a snake.'

Mara shifted in her seat.

'My *cousin*,' she pushed the word through gritted teeth, her glare fixed on the window, 'is attempting to *force* me into retirement. He's wanted me gone for years and now he thinks this place, my fall, the surgery is the perfect excuse to push me out.'

A bad fall could affect your mental health, hadn't Mara read that somewhere? People got depression or anxiety from the pain and the loss of independence. Maybe paranoia, too. 'I suppose it might feel like that when you're stuck here,' Mara said, hoping to sound reasonable and reassuring. 'But Vaughn didn't say anything about retirement to me.' Okay, he'd raised the possibility that Estelle might not go back to work, but she was seventy-two, who wouldn't think that was an option? 'He said he assigned me to work with you because he was thinking of your clients. That it's what you'd expect in the circumstances. You know, putting the clients first.'

Estelle looked back at Mara. 'My cousin came to the hospital to *tell* me I was retiring. He wanted to make an announcement. He made it sound as though he was doing me a favour.'

'I'm sure he didn't visit you just to tell you that.'

Estelle's lips twisted in scorn. 'His first words to me the morning after my surgery were, "You won't be coming back from this."'

'My mum was completely out of it after her surgery,' Mara said. 'I took her a rug from home and she remembered that, but not my brother Patrick, who was there for hours. Maybe you can only remember the bit that upset you.'

'Oh yes, Vaughn brought something for me too. Documents to sign, authorising his administration of my client files. As if I'd be stupid enough to sign anything from my hospital bed. As if that would be legally binding. I told him to go to hell. And don't give me that sceptical look. I've had to fight for everything in that business, and clearly I'll have to fight to leave when I choose. I won't be pushed out, not by my snake of a cousin. I survived his father. I survived my own father. And I plan to leave on my own terms.' She stabbed a finger in the air. 'I will not be told by another Collings male what I am or am not capable of.'

Estelle's voice had risen in volume and pitch until she was almost shouting, as though years of pent-up anger had found a vent to release its head of steam. When she was finished, she glared at Mara like she expected her to tell her to calm down. As if, in the eye of her steely glare, Mara would be game to do that.

Still, Mara couldn't leave it at that. She couldn't sit with all that anger in the room, couldn't bear for Estelle to be stewing in all that fury. So she said the first thing that came to mind. 'When my mum was sick, she said it helped to find an upside to things.'

'An upside.'

'Sometimes it's just the smallest thing.'

'Perhaps that's your problem, Mara. When *things* get hard, you find something easier to do. You give up. Is that why you gave up on university, not once but twice? Did it get too *hard* for you, Mara?'

Mara sat back as though she'd been punched.

'Or are you not clever enough?' Estelle went on. 'You seem relatively bright, but it takes more than intelligence. Were the lectures too boring or the exams too hard? Are you typical of your generation, do you just want life to be fun and easy?'

'No, that's not what—'

'Was it easier to work for your father than to try hard?'

'He was . . . he had a heart attack and—'

'Are you working for lawyers because you're too lazy to be one?'

Mara's heart thumped. 'I wanted to . . . I don't know what—'

'You get nothing from taking the easy way, Mara. You get—'

'Ms Collings.' It was the physio with the cool bob haircut, standing in the doorway with a wheelchair, smiling with enthusiasm – until the mood of the room reached her.

Estelle turned her steely glare in her direction. 'Yes?'

'I've come to take you to your session in the gym.'

'Not now, thank you.'

She came in anyway. 'Three pm is your allotted time, Ms Collings. It's now or miss out. And as you say, you get nothing from taking the easy way.' She stopped the wheelchair beside the bed. 'Do you need a hand getting in?'

Mara watched Estelle digest the physio's words, weigh up her response then fling her covers aside, beaten by her own reprimand. Settling Estelle in the wheelchair, the younger woman lifted her eyes over the top of Estelle's head and met Mara's gaze. How much had she heard? Enough to hear the reproach in Estelle's voice, surely. Enough to wonder what Mara had done to deserve it?

'I'd like those letters printed by the time I return,' Estelle said as she was wheeled towards the door.

The physio winked as she passed, like it was all in a day's work on the ward. Mara smiled back out of politeness, but was mortified.

☕

Mara shoved letterhead paper into the tray of the printer. It was none of Estelle's business why Mara had left uni. She didn't have to explain herself. But Estelle's words had cut her like a knife. Uni had got hard and Mara had screwed it up. She could have gone back, but she didn't. Because she just didn't have what it took to become a lawyer. And Estelle could see that.

The printing was almost done when Estelle was returned by an orderly. Mara kept working, her back to her boss, glad to be busy. Before the orderly left, Estelle asked him to open the suitcase Mara had brought. It was several minutes before she addressed Mara.

'Why is this here?'

Mara turned around, annoyed now that she'd bothered to bring Estelle the cosy blanket. 'I thought you might like some colour from home in here.'

'Where did you find it?' she snapped, as though Mara had searched her rooms.

'In your bedroom, near the clothes Lynette left out.'

Estelle pulled in a breath but stopped before saying anything. She put the blanket on the bed, ran a hand across the soft mohair, lifted her chin. 'How is your father now?'

Mara blinked, surprised that Estelle had heard anything she'd said while the woman had been steamrolling her lazy arse.

'I didn't know he'd had a heart attack,' Estelle said. 'How is he?'

Was she asking because Mara had brought her a blanket? Was this her version of *Thanks, I suppose I could try to be pleasant in return*? Mara allowed a little snappishness into her tone. 'He's doing well, thank you.'

'How long was he in hospital?'

Did she think asking for the details would cancel out what she'd said? Mara would have ignored her if she was brave enough. 'Four weeks. Almost a week in intensive care, the last two in rehab.'

Her boss nodded. 'You can go home when the printing is finished.'

'It's only four-fifteen and I haven't finished the envelopes.' Or the daily report.

'You can do them first thing in the morning.' As though the printer had heard, it whirred to a stop. Estelle waved a regal hand. 'Off you go. I need to get some rest.'

Not really an early mark then. Still, leaving early was a bright side; and all the brighter after that tongue-lashing about giving up and being lazy. As she neared the nurses' station, the physio with the black bob looked up and came over. Mara cringed inside.

'How's it going in there?'

Did Mara want to explain? 'It's okay. It's fine. I got an early mark.' She raised a fist like she'd won, when really, she felt like she'd taken a beating.

'Nice.'

'And I set up a new printer.' Two upsides.

'I'm impressed. Maybe you could give some advice to our tech people. The printers are always playing up.'

Mara huffed a laugh. 'How did Estelle's gym session go?'

'Not bad, considering.'

'Considering what?'

'She's got a lot of pain. Her age. Her level of fitness.'

Mara nodded, feeling bad now for wanting to throw something at Estelle. Pain would make her irritable. On top of her normal level of irritable. 'Did you come out of her session unscathed?'

'Pretty much. I've had worse. I'm Rylee, by the way.'

Mara pointed at the badge on her shirt. 'I saw your name tag.'

''Course.' She looked at her a moment.

'Oh, I'm Mara.' *Idiot.*

'M*ara*?'

'Yes. Thanks for asking. Most people get it wrong.'

'I get Kylie, Miley, Raleigh and Haylee. And don't even get me started on the spelling. Good to get it right if we're going to keep running into each other.' She smiled like she meant it. 'Anyway, I'll see you round.'

Mara smiled to herself as she continued down the hall. Maybe she'd have someone to chat to while she was here: three upsides.

Coral

THE STOCKHOLM JOB was in trouble. Coral didn't understand the technicalities, only that the diamond-tipped drill heads were meant to leave by today – mid-afternoon at the latest – if the shipment was going to reach its destination by Monday, Swedish time. And it wasn't going to be ready.

Coral had been managing complicated deliveries for Rodney for more than ten years. Every so often, she volunteered to be the courier on one of the fun door-to-door jobs: she loved the relay of flights that could end up on a six-seater plane to the middle of nowhere. By comparison, the delivery to Stockholm was far less complex, but with a very specific deadline. If that deadline wasn't met, it would cost Rodney's client a lot of money, and hence Rodney too.

She had a good relationship with Rodney: easy communication, personal chitchat, invitations to each other's Christmas drinks. He'd never rung her at five-thirty in the morning, and she'd never heard him sound panicked.

The ins and outs of why the project was delayed made no difference to Coral, but she sat in her nightie in the light of her bedside lamp and let Rodney talk, because a) he sounded like he needed to, and Coral had always considered reassuring her clients to be part of her job; and b) she wasn't sure she could have stopped him. Besides, the drama of one of his engineers almost cutting off a finger had been quite gripping, especially delivered by this usually unflappable fifty-three-year-old man of few words, who was clearly having a meltdown.

When he'd finally run out of reasons for the disaster, Coral suggested they both needed coffee, trying to talk him down as they boiled their kettles. She finally managed to narrow him down to a new timeframe, including all the likely, possible, wishful thinking and worst-case scenario versions.

Coral took a shower to wash off the panic Rodney had transferred to her, letting the warm water calm her enough to do a mental reshuffle of the To-Do List. Summer, Wade and Mum had to be relegated to numbers two, three and four, while she worked up the delivery options for each of Rodney's scenarios. Best case was he'd get a week's grace from Stockholm, the team would finish today and the diamond-tipped drill heads would sail into Swedish hands with time to spare. But Rodney wasn't hopeful, so Coral needed to be prepared for every contingency, including someone running through an airport shouting, *Urgent package!*

She'd done that a few times: hair-raising in the moment, hilarious in hindsight. Actually, a big thrill to beat the odds, or fate, or the giant storm cell that had been the obstacle in her path, turning up dishevelled and panting with minutes to spare. Not that she'd be volunteering for this one. She liked Rodney and didn't want him to lose thousands of dollars on the contract, but she didn't have the energy or enthusiasm to run through an airport, unless it was to get her to the conference in New York.

It was mid-morning by the time she'd worked through enough delivery options to take a break. She dropped in on Summer, who looked tired, pale and fed up. She was still in pyjamas but out of bed, bad foot and XL baby bump beached on the sofa, watching as a listless Oliver built and knocked down towers of noisy blocks. Coral didn't have time, but after putting a casserole in the fridge and filling her daughter in on Helen and Graham, she washed a few dishes, put on a load of washing, got Summer a coffee, and checked Oliver's spots.

'Can you give your grandparents a call today?' Coral asked as she picked up her bag to leave, which seemed to be the signal for Oliver to start a tantrum. Coral produced a notebook and several stray colouring pencils from her handbag, which kept him entertained, at least until she was out the door.

The next stop was Val's place, where she checked phone messages, watered plants and picked up an armful of the frozen meals she'd previously packed into the freezer. She then dropped those off at Helen and Graham's, stopping only long enough to give reheating instructions and check Graham's grazes, which thankfully looked less red and angry than the day before.

'Double shot?' Alby asked as Coral approached the coffee van.

'Yes, please. A small cappuccino as well and,' she took a moment to peruse the options, 'do you have any more of the date loaf?'

'It's fig and walnut today.'

Tempting, but she really needed something more sustaining. 'Sandwiches?'

'Not usually, but you can order ahead for tomorrow.'

Coral's gaze slipped sideways as she tried to remember what she was doing tomorrow.

'Shoot me a text if you decide you want one,' Alby said, handing her another of his business cards. 'It's better for me that way. I tend to lose bits of paper in here.' Starting on her order, he asked, 'Are you working here this week?'

'My mum's in for rehab.'

They chatted as the smell of fresh coffee rose. She told him about Val's fall and, for no other reason than he'd asked and seemed to be listening, she explained about the cognitive tests, her mum's search of the pantry for a sock, the confusion over the hospital menu. Val's insistence that she was doing fine, managing well.

'Ah, denial,' he said, fitting a lid to the top of her cup. 'I mean, I get it, who wants to accept they can't do what they've always done?

Hard to be the one dealing with it though, and trying not to crush their spirit.'

'Oh god, yeah, exactly,' Coral said, relieved to have found someone with the words to express how she felt. 'You've been through it?'

'My dad. I got him a place in aged care. Nice place, his own room, keen to go. I moved him in and when I was leaving, he asked how long until he went home. So I explained it all again, he said he understood and he'd see me in a week. When I turned up, he was waiting outside with his suitcase packed.'

Coral's chest tightened. 'What did you do?'

'I moved him in with me, looked after him until he died.'

'Oh, I'm so sorry.'

'It was a year and it's not for everyone, but I've got a medical background, I had the time to spend with him and I'm glad I was able to do it.' He set a paper bag beside her coffee order. 'You look like you need something to eat. There's one in there for your mum, too.'

Her throat thickened at the unexpected kindness. 'Thank you,' she said, tapping her phone on his card reader, feeling better for talking to someone; someone who understood.

In Val's room, she opened the bag to show her the slices of fig and walnut log before she pulled her phone out and realised Alby hadn't charged her for the cake.

Mara

'My answer remains the same, and it is extremely irritating to be asked the same question every morning.'

Mara watched as Rylee fielded Estelle's morning irritation. 'I understand,' she said. 'And I remain extremely hopeful that you will change your mind about the pool.'

Estelle huffed her annoyance. Rylee held up crossed fingers at Mara and winked as she wheeled Estelle out.

Left in peace to finish the client letters, Mara was done by the time Estelle was returned, her red non-slip hospital socks an amusing accessory to her very expensive new knitwear.

'I can pop out to the post office now, if you need a rest after your session,' Mara told her.

'I do not need a rest. Take down these names.'

Clients, Mara assumed, not game to interrupt as the first three or four rolled off Estelle's tongue as though she'd been making a list in the gym. After that, Estelle paused between each, frowning, searching the ceiling, once examining the palms of both hands before the name came to her. When there were twenty on Mara's list, Estelle said, 'That will do for now.' Her head dropped to the back of her armchair as though the mental exercise had exhausted her more than the gym.

Glad to be finally getting to the job she was meant to be

doing, Mara said, 'I'll get started on their files.'

'You will do no such thing.'

Instead, Mara was instructed to fill in a spreadsheet with their details. Estelle wanted employment, country of origin, names of spouse and children. 'And any other fact of interest you come across.' Was it a test? Mara wondered as she worked in the sanctuary of the balcony. A time waster? Something to baffle Vaughn when Mara reported back on how she'd spent her day? Whatever it was, it involved searching through the oldest files in the document boxes, one dating back to the early 1960s. Still, once Estelle had nodded off and Mara was actually working with client records, the job felt like a reprieve.

An hour later, Mara lifted her head at the sound of a sweet, older voice from the room beside Estelle's. 'Ooh, I'd love a cuppa, thanks.' Several minutes later, Estelle shouted, 'Mara!'

Sighing, she stood at the French doors and waited for instruction.

'Go and buy a coffee machine.'

'*Buy* a coffee machine?'

'A small one that uses pods. We can do without a milk steamer.'

'Oh, you're serious.'

'Of course I'm serious. You can go to the post office while you're about it.'

⚰

'More shopping?' Rylee asked when Mara passed the nurses' station with a huge bag from an electrical store.

'Coffee machine.'

She raised an eyebrow. 'That's a first.'

When Mara attempted to explain her purchase choice to Estelle, the response was, 'I don't care, just get it working.'

She set it up on the work table, and when the first wafts of freshly brewed coffee drifted into the air, it was like smoke signals, summoning people from near and far. A nurse arrived to check it out, and one of the other physios appeared in the doorway taking deep breaths. Even Estelle perked up.

'How is it?' Mara asked when her boss had completed a connoisseur's inspection of her first cup.

'An excellent first result from a machine of that type. Help yourself.'

So Mara did, adding milk to a long black. She lifted her cup in a toast. 'Cheers.'

'I believe it is traditional to toast with a glass.'

'We've only got cups.'

'To what are we proposing a toast?'

'The new machine.' Of course.

Estelle lifted her coffee. 'To our espresso machine. May it provide us many a decent and reviving cup.'

It was so formal and unexpected that Mara let out a chirrup of laughter.

Then, surprisingly, Estelle followed suit. And as she did, something strange happened to her face. It was as though all the flinty angles were pulled up and back, smoothing the deep lines between her brows and around her mouth to form an expression of delight. And surprise at being delighted.

It looked really nice on her, Mara thought, as if a smiling, friendly person was hiding inside her. Without a thought to her own safety, Mara gave Nice Estelle a little encouragement. 'Did you know bees love coffee?'

'I suppose they make good partners.'

'And people who drink coffee are less likely to get depression or Alzheimer's.'

'I will dictate a harshly worded letter to the hospital on that very subject.'

'Beethoven loved coffee, and Bach wrote an opera about it.'

Estelle's laugh was throaty and spontaneous. Mara felt like she'd coaxed a nervous animal out of its hole.

'How much coffee will I need to drink to write an opera before I die?' Estelle asked.

Good grief, was that a *joke*?

'I might have to limit *your* intake,' Estelle added, 'if it means you'll be even more chirpy.'

'Perhaps if you drink up, you'll be out of here sooner.'

'One can only hope.' The older woman patted her hair down, as though that was enough of that. 'Is coffee your only field of speciality knowledge or am I to expect this kind of entertainment during every coffee break?'

Mara shrugged. 'When my mum was sick, I'd sit with her for hours sometimes and google stuff to keep her entertained. Things that didn't take too much effort to think about. I still remember a lot of it.'

Estelle set her empty cup down. 'Yes, well, it's time to get back to more important . . . *stuff*, as you call it.'

If Mara had worked for Estelle for longer, she might have recognised the shift in her tone and responded differently. But as she took their cups to rinse in the ensuite, she corrected herself. '*Trivia* then.'

'You can't do your job if your mind is focused on *trivia*.' The tap was running, and Mara assumed Estelle had raised her voice to be heard over the water. Only it stayed that way when Mara turned it off. 'Which means not getting carried away with amusing facts when there is work to be done.'

'Were we carried away?' Mara had meant to say it under her breath, but the tiled bathroom amplified her words.

'You will *never* finish what you start if you can't discipline yourself to stay on task.'

When Mara stepped back into the room, Estelle's face was pinched and the steely glare back, as though she was purging herself of the light-hearted humour. 'You need to get back to work even when work is not as riveting as the *trivialities* your mother enjoyed.'

Mara froze with a mug in each hand, bewilderment and alarm setting her legs like cement. Where had the anger come from?

Estelle took Mara's pose as intent to stay for the full lecture. 'Is it any wonder you couldn't finish a degree with your brain full of facts that have nothing to do with your education? Perhaps if you put as much effort into your future as you do into remembering these *trivialities*, you might not be the one left to set up coffee machines in hospital rooms.'

Mara stiffened in shock, her cheeks burning as though they'd been slapped. But even stuck in a freeze response to the sudden assault, something protective rose inside her. She didn't remember the trivia because it was entertaining. It was a beautiful memory from her Mum's last days, that she didn't want to forget. And she wasn't about to explain that to her nasty boss, who thirty seconds ago had been amused by said trivialities.

'When I was your age, I worked fifty hours a week to prove myself,' Estelle castigated her. 'To my managers, to my *father*. That's what I had to do to get where I wanted, what *women* had to do. There was no working my way up just by doing my job. Not when I had breasts and a uterus. Not when I wasn't a *son*.' The word was issued with a hiss of venom that seeped into her next ones. 'I've had to prove myself every single step of the way. I'm *still* proving myself. To a man who is ten years my junior.' She threw up a hand like it was a full stop and turned to glare at the gorgeous view.

Mara released a breath, relieved it was over, horrified that her mum's beloved sense of humour had been dragged into Estelle's resentment.

Andie

BEN'S ROOM WAS dim when Andie looked in and it took her a moment to see him on the recliner. His face was turned to the windows, which were half covered by a curtain, and she wasn't sure if he was awake. She rapped quietly on the doorframe, and a weak smile lifted the corners of his mouth as he turned.

'Hey,' he said, tiredness in his tone, his eyes a duller green.

'I can come back if you're resting.'

He shuffled upwards a little. 'No, come in.'

She went through the routine of depositing the coffee, moving the tray table so he could reach it and pulling up a chair for herself. Up close, his skin was sallow. There were dark rings under his eyes and a troubled look in their depths.

'Are you okay?'

He took a sip of coffee as though he needed the hit before he could answer. 'Had a bad night.'

'Pain or dreams?'

'Pain.' He scrubbed his face with a hand, his palm scratching over the stubble on his jaw. 'And dreams. Couldn't get comfortable.'

'Can you miss your physio session this morning?'

'I've already done it.' A grim smile. 'Knackered now.'

'I don't have to stay.'

'No,' he said when she made to leave, 'you're good for me. Good company,' he corrected. 'If you can put up with a boring visit.'

'You mean, no five-k walk and a Pilates class?'

He smiled, shifting a little higher in his chair. 'Also, I've got a favour to ask.'

'Okay.'

'How are you at lying?'

'I, well – you want me to lie to someone?'

'My parents.' He rubbed a hand over his hair, the troubled look returning to his eyes. 'They're calling this morning. We set it up last night when I was feeling okay, but now, I'll get three words out and they'll be on the next flight home.'

'So you want me to lie to them?'

'Yeah.' A sheepish smile.

'When are they calling?'

A glance at the clock. 'In about ten minutes.'

Andie had no problem lying to her mother – *I'm fine; you don't look your age; gotta rush* – and she'd told half-truths to clients to be kind – *they're looking for someone with more experience/a degree/a car.* But she didn't understand the dynamics of other people's families. 'What do you want me to tell them?'

'That I'm asleep and I'll call them back tomorrow, their time.'

'But it's,' Andie did a quick calculation, 'midnight-ish in Scotland? Wouldn't they expect you to be woken when they call?'

'Not if I was sick.'

'Which you don't want them thinking.'

'Good point.' Another head rub. 'Tell them I got called to a physio session.'

'Sounds plausible. Okay, I should be able to pull that off.'

Exactly ten minutes later, the phone rang and two smiling parents appeared on the screen.

Ben put it on speaker and passed it to Andie. 'This is Ben's phone,' she said.

'Hello? Who's this?' His mother's voice was full of cheer and expectation.

'We're after Ben. Ben Cameron.' His father was less chirpy, but still keen.

Andie was stumped for a second. When had her mum ever answered with anything less than a demand for attention? 'Hello, yes. Ben got called to a session with the physiotherapist. He said if he missed you, he'd call back in a few hours. Morning, your time.' Brief, to the point, ready to hang up.

'Oh no, oh dear.' His mum. 'We keep missing him. How is he?'

Andie looked at Ben, who made a rolling motion with his hands.

'He's good.' More rolling from Ben. 'Doing well.' *More.* 'Much better than he was.'

Ben scrunched up his face. *What?* Andie mouthed.

'How bad *was* he?' his dad asked.

With Andie's mother, a few quick, emphatic reassurances would have done the job. But thirty seconds on the phone with Ben's parents told Andie that *He's fine, don't worry,* wasn't going to cut it.

'He was dealing with . . . some pain, after the,' *coma* was what she was going to say before Ben started shaking his head, 'ah, accident. But that seems to be under control now.' She raised her eyebrows.

Ben gave a thumbs up.

'But how *is* he?' his mother asked. 'In himself.'

Up and down, dealing with a lot, not sleeping well. All the wrong answers.

'I mean,' Ben's mum added, 'we googled the accident and the pictures are . . .' Her voice trailed off.

'Not great,' his dad finished. 'We're a long way away and obviously, we're concerned about him. We'd be grateful for anything you can tell us.' This from the man who'd had a tough year.

Andie looked at Ben; he dropped his gaze to the floor. She felt a pang of empathy for them all. And just a tinge of envy.

'I know it must be really hard for you guys over there.' Ben's head snapped up, but Andie held up a hand. 'But he's doing okay. Really. I mean, he's injured and he's in rehab and not his best self right now, but – and I'm not a medical professional – I think he's got this, you know?'

Ben's mother made a sound, a mix of relief and heartache.

His dad said, not unkindly, 'Who are you?'

'I'm Andie. I'm a . . .' Friend? Acquaintance? The woman he pushed out of the way? 'A visitor.'

'A visitor,' his mum whispered, sounding curious now.

'From the uni?' Dad asked.

Andie glanced at Ben, who rolled his eyes. She raised her eyebrows in a question; he turned his palms downwards. *Don't give too much away.* So she told them she was helping out while he was in hospital, visiting and bringing him things, coffee and papers and crinkle-cut chips. That last one made them laugh, like it was proof he was alive and well.

Ben was silently laughing and shaking his head with fondness. It made a lump form in Andie's throat. Then Ben twirled a finger in the air: *wrap it up.*

Such a pity, she was enjoying their family time. 'I'll make sure he knows you guys called,' she said. 'I know he's keen to talk to you.' He should be.

'God, they're great,' she told Ben when she'd hung up.

'Yeah, they are.'

'Anytime you want someone to lie to them, I'm your girl.'

Coral

VAL WAS DUE to be taken through a round of cognitive testing *sometime* on Thursday afternoon, and Coral was hoping to quiz whoever did the testing. She arrived as the lunch trays were being collected, and spent the next couple of hours going back and forth to the balcony to tap out emails, notes for Jessica, and another courier route for Rodney's drill heads. In between, she maintained a commentary of the latest family anecdotes for Val, to avoid having to explain again about rehab, meals or assessments. Because today had already presented Coral with more than enough to be stressed about.

'Poor Summer,' Coral said when she'd finished recounting Oliver's tantrum this morning.

'Summer will be fine,' Val said with confidence. 'She's like me, too strong to let it stop her.'

Unlike me? Coral thought, but moved on, explaining about Wade's latest email. He'd finally admitted he needed a rental manager for the apartment and asked Coral if she could collect some things he'd stored there. 'Some boxes he was worried would be damaged if left on the wet carpet. Of course, the whole lot will have to come up.'

'That apartment of his was a good buy, though,' Val said with a fond smile. It was a comment she'd repeated numerous times after her grandson had once sat down with her to explain the ins and outs of his first home-buying adventure. 'He's always been clever with his money.' It was something Val took particular pride in, having faced near financial ruin after Coral's father had passed away at the age of fifty-two.

Coral then filled her in on Helen and Graham's drama, how a once-robust Graham now seemed frail, and Coral's guesstimate of a hundred boxes of teabags in Helen's pantry.

'They were very good to you when I wasn't able to do much after your father passed.' Val said it as though Coral was being unkind about them.

Coral sighed. 'I didn't think you'd mind if I gave them some of the meals I left in your freezer. I can replenish your supply when you go home.'

'Oh, it's just that soup you make. They can have it.'

Coral bit down on her irritation. 'There was also chicken curry and the spaghetti sauce you like.'

'You'll make more.' There a loftiness about the way she said it that seemed to belittle Coral's time and effort. 'And how's Richard?' Val asked. 'He must be worried about his parents coping.'

'Not too worried. He flew out to Bali today.'

'Well, I suppose he has things to do.'

'He's surfing.'

Val's eyebrows shifted, as if that was only to be expected. 'At least he's kept it up all these years.'

'What do you mean?'

'You didn't do anything with the camera you spent all that money on years ago.'

'Two entirely different things.'

'They broke up your marriage.'

'Richard broke up our marriage. He left us to surf.'

'You told him not to come back, Coral.'

'I told him ... He was meant to ...' She stopped, heart thumping, realising she'd walked into a conversation she wasn't willing to have. She stood, tried for words and failed; held a hand in the air like a stop sign before retreating through the French doors.

Glaring at the garden below the balcony, Coral tried to loosen her jaw, slow her breathing. Why was everyone else strong and clever, good and busy, when the only quality Val saw in Coral was her usefulness as a large-batch soup maker?

She shook her head, straightened her shoulders. There was a reason she and Val didn't normally see each other every day; there was only so much disappointment either of them could bear.

The young woman who, according to Val, was working for the cranky woman in the room next door looked up from her laptop as Coral turned to go back in. Coral said hello, thinking *Poor thing.* Imagine being subjected to full days on hospital duty and not even being related to the patient.

Coral never managed to meet whoever was doing the cognitive testing. Fifteen minutes later, she left, out of time and patience for any more family discussions. In the hallway, she passed the curly-haired woman who visited Ben, the man in the room next to Val's. Coral had seen them on the balcony together, had heard they'd both been injured in that car accident down at the harbour. Coral smiled at her, but it was an effort. Did it make Coral a bad person to be jealous that even in a bad situation, those two were able to laugh?

Mara

BEWILDERED AND A little shaken by Estelle's outburst, Mara had been grateful for an escape to the balcony and that she'd been given a 'task' to 'focus on' before her boss had her brain explosion. She sent files to the printer on a regular basis so Estelle didn't mistake her silence as 'undisciplined'. When Estelle was at her second gym session, Mara left several pages of the spreadsheet on her tray table: only half of the client list, but proof Mara was capable of working efficiently even when it wasn't 'riveting'.

Mara kept an ear tuned to Estelle's room when her boss returned, hearing her ask someone else for coffee, her phone, to fetch a damp washer, a warm top, painkillers. The balcony was a whole world of upsides.

Finding the spreadsheet, Estelle started making phone calls. Mara recognised the name from the top of the list, but not the voice her boss used: friendly, charming, empathetic. Not the same as Nice Estelle, more like an Affable Estelle, who must only be allowed out to talk to clients. *Some* clients. Mara had heard her talk to others and her tone had been very different. This version of Estelle was so unlikely that Mara really *couldn't* focus, lifting her head every time her boss made a new call. Then one came in from the Collings office and that ended the conviviality.

'I have *not* seen that . . . It was that scatty girl with . . .

Correct . . . Incorrect . . .' It was the usual abruptness. Mara didn't bother listening after that.

The charm returned when Estelle rang another client, then the office called back, and the next hour or so became a seesaw of Affable and Obnoxious Estelles. Mara tried hard to concentrate, but the bizarreness was riveting.

There were other distractions, too. The man from across the hall appeared, his wheelchair being pushed by a woman with a mass of curly chestnut hair. Mara had heard they'd been in the car accident at the harbour, and it was hard not to shudder at the fading bruises on their faces.

'How's your day going?' he called to Mara.

'It's fine,' she said. Better than being hit by a runaway car.

'We're on a caper,' he said.

Mara looked to his companion for a clue. *Caper?*

'Apparently the first rule of a caper is to be reckless and bold,' the curly-haired woman explained.

There was something light-hearted under the sensible explanation and Mara felt the tension in her mouth start to loosen.

'Anything interesting at your end?' the man asked.

She stood and pointed into the garden. 'There are spring bulbs starting to come up.'

The three of them gathered at the windows to look.

'What colour will the flowers be?' the man asked.

'You can't tell until they come up.'

'The printer, Mara!' Estelle's bark made her shoulders drop.

'Your mum?' the woman asked.

'My boss.'

'I'm Andie. This is Ben. He's in the room across the hall.' She said it as though it might come in handy as an escape hatch.

'I'm Mara.' She smiled, grateful for their cheerful interruption. 'I'd better go. Nice to meet you.' Collecting her laptop, she turned back and said, 'Enjoy your caper.'

'Enjoy your garden,' Ben said.

As Mara stepped through the French doors, she heard Ben say, 'Second rule of a caper, brighten someone's day.' Well, they'd done that.

Later, back on the balcony, Mara's head snapped up from her laptop when a door opened with a clatter. Mara saw the daughter of the old woman next door stalk onto the balcony and stand at the window, hands clamped to her hips, staring at the distant ocean like she'd been turned to stone.

Mara turned to the view too, eyes skimming across spring flowers and then the expanse of deep blue sea, hoping the woman at the other end of the balcony got a hit of the tranquillity.

'Coming, Mum!' The woman slumped her head in defeat or exhaustion or despair. Maybe it was all three. When she straightened, she noticed Mara, saying, 'Good spot to work?'

'Feels like I've got an office in a garden.'

'I could do with one of them. I'm Coral.' She cocked her head towards the room. 'That's my mum, Val.'

'I'm Mara.' Hooking a thumb. 'I work for Estelle.'

'You here for the two weeks?'

'Uh-huh. You?'

'I have to fly to New York on Monday.' She gave a brief, strained smile, then turned to her mother's room, pulled in a breath and straightened her shoulders before going in.

Mara felt a pang of empathy: she knew that need to escape, breathe and then brace for more. At least she was being paid to put up with Estelle.

Sometime later, another voice interrupted her concentration. 'Thought you might be out here.'

Mara looked up to see Rylee at the corner of the balcony.

'How's it going?' the physio asked.

'Not bad.' Conscious of how sound travelled, Mara stood and dropped her voice as she walked closer.

'She was . . .' Rylee tilted her head, 'out of sorts in her session this afternoon.'

'She was . . .' Mara dipped hers back, 'upset earlier. Sorry about that.'

'Did you upset her?'

'Yes. Probably. I've no idea, really. She just went off.' Mara made a guilty face. 'Should I be trying to keep her calm?'

'Could you?'

'Well, I suppose I could be . . .' *Invisible? More slave-like?*

Rylee nudged her with an elbow. 'I meant, is keeping her calm even possible?'

'Oh, right.' She blushed, embarrassed she'd misunderstood. 'Probably not.'

A brief frown. 'I came to see if you were okay.'

'Oh. Sure. Yeah, I mean, she was difficult today. But no more than yesterday. Well, maybe a little more, but it's like you said, she's in pain and frustrated.'

'Actually, I think it's like you said and she's just like that.'

There was reassurance in her eyes, her smile, and grateful, Mara took a breath to thank her. Then she wondered if Rylee had meant to be kind or if Mara was just desperate for someone to be nice to her. So instead, she said, 'Is Estelle improving?'

'It's slow progress. How long will you be working with her?'

'Two weeks to two months, depending on how quickly we get through her work.' She shrugged, wanting to mirror Rylee's caring and sensible expression, but her *Kill me now* grimace had a life of its own.

Rylee gave Mara's elbow a quick squeeze of empathy. It was surprisingly firm, professional yet personal, kind and friendly. It made Mara pleased to have her around, and uncertain whether to trust it. Rylee was a physiotherapist, that reassuring thing was probably standard in her line of work. The gesture, the whole conversation, had felt like something friends might do, only Mara hadn't got that right for a while. She smiled, though, because it was a long time since anyone had thought to ease her turmoil. If that was Rylee's job, she was really good at it.

After she left, Mara stared into the garden, wondering what she was doing here. Was Estelle right? Was Mara too undisciplined to finish anything she started?

Maybe she'd never wanted something enough to stick with it?

Did it even matter what she wanted, when other people could die or have heart attacks or break bones at any second? Her life might be better spent caring for people she loved, who loved her back, who needed her, instead of working for bitter, nasty people who were just mean.

Coral

IT WAS AFTER seven when Coral got home. She was bone tired, but knew she needed to get Wade's things in tonight.

While one of her mass-produced meals heated in the microwave, she brought in her son's boxes, lining up collections of records, old trophies and unused glassware with Summer's casserole dishes and discarded wool. Coral was dying to curl up on the lounge with a glass of wine and her bowl of spag-bol, but she had more work to do, and the mess would add to her stress if she didn't sort it out now.

Padding around in stockings and slippers, she dropped the wool into the spare room, saw her half-packed suitcase on the bed and gave a despondent sigh. She'd been looking forward to the fun of packing, but now it just felt like another job she had to do, and New York another thing adding stress to her life. Without warning, her chin wobbled and her eyes filled with a hot flood of . . . what? Self-pity? Misery? Resentment?

'Fuck,' she hissed for what felt like the fiftieth time that day. She wouldn't get to New York if she wallowed. And she needed to get there, because in New York, she'd be off the hook. For ten glorious days. Of course, she'd call and see how everyone was, be comforting and sympathetic, and yet guiltily happy to be useless in every functional way. In New York, she'd be strong and clever.

She'd drink champagne and be appreciated, and no-one would have any idea how many single-serve meals she could produce in a weekend.

Part 4

The Trauma

Coral

THERE WERE NO emails from Rodney when Coral checked at six am. His team had missed the deadline last night without a word, and Coral hoped the silence meant they were focusing on what needed to be done, not panicking about the next pick-up option.

Whatever it was, Coral couldn't do anything to influence it, she was just the cog in the middle keeping as many delivery channels open as she could, for as long as she could. Theoretically, she'd done everything possible before the package left, so she should be able to relax. Except it was nerve-racking waiting for Rodney's go-ahead, knowing she'd have to make a call on the fastest delivery. And the longer Rodney took, the fewer the options available. If it wasn't on its way tonight, they'd be talking emergency contingencies.

Summer looked terrible when Coral let herself in. Busying Oliver with a few things to carry, she saw that her daughter's long blonde hair was dirty and dull, barely contained in a slipping claw clip. She was wearing a stained and crumpled sweatshirt of Dan's over pyjama bottoms, a half-eaten piece of toast stuck to the leg. She must be so sick of herself. When she turned her face, Coral could tell she'd been crying.

'How are you, honey?' Coral asked as she dropped a kiss on her head.

'Oliver, get *down* from there. I'm fine. We're *fine*.' The words were terse as she shrugged off the arm Coral attempted to slip around her shoulders.

Coral gave her daughter some space, picking up an unfinished bowl of soggy cereal and peeling the toast from Summer's leg. 'Come on, Oliver, you can help me in the kitchen.'

He seemed a little better today. At least well enough to use a voice loud enough to be heard from the other end of the house. 'Come on, Mummy!'

Summer flinched.

'Inside voice,' Coral said, taking his hand. 'Let's give Mummy some time on her own.'

It was the wrong tactic, she realised two seconds later as Oliver wailed, 'But I want Mummy to come to the kitchen!'

They were both in a mood. It was a few minutes before Coral could entice her grandson away. By then Summer's chin was wobbling and her eyes welling.

Coral closed the lounge room door, checked her watch, squared her shoulders and set about finding something to keep Oliver occupied long enough to clean and sort what looked like the remains of several meals, hasty ironing and Oliver's latest attempt at a Picasso. She kept up a commentary, like she had with Val: 'Good helping! Fabulous jumping! Can you whisper like the trees? Gan-Gan spills her milk sometimes too.'

Forty minutes later, Oliver was bathed and dressed, the dishwasher and washing machines running. The kitchen was clean and there was a selection of lunch options for Summer and Oliver. Coral handed her daughter a cup of coffee and a muffin and said, 'Right, I think that's all I can do for now.'

'Can you stay for a while?'

'I'm sorry, honey. I've got an urgent job on and I'm hoping to catch up with Nana's doctor and/or social worker before I leave for New York.'

Summer's face was pinched. 'I spoke to Nana yesterday and she sounded really confused.'

'It's only sometimes.'

'Granny and Popsy were upset about their shopping bill. They didn't think they needed everything on your list. And they were upset that they didn't have the cash to pay you back.'

Coral hesitated, taking in her daughter's tone, her expression, and realised Summer was chastising her. Perhaps Summer was just ticked off with everything today.

Coral softened her voice. 'I'll give Helen a ring and sort it out.'

Summer crossed her arms and turned her face away, as though Coral had said something even more annoying.

'What?' Coral asked.

'I can't believe you're still intending to go to New York on Sunday.'

Coral blinked: at her daughter's tone, at the suggestion that she might not go. She let it sit for a beat, desperately willing the slow burn of guilt to go away. 'It's work, Summer.'

'You could get out of it.'

She didn't want to get out of it! 'It's a conference and I'm delivering a paper.'

'I've been to those' – Summer made finger quotes – '"conferences". They're just a big get-together where everyone pats each other on the back over a piss-up.'

It was a long time since Coral had wanted to swear at her daughter. She rolled her lips together, working hard to contain her anger. This was Summer under stress, Coral told herself. She'd done this when she was a teenager, railing at the things that frustrated her instead of doing something about them. At seventeen, she'd shouted at her mother instead of cleaning up her room or buckling down and finishing an assignment. Now, at thirty-seven, she was pregnant and hobbled with a sick toddler, and her mother was the closest target. Perhaps her only target.

Coral had been pregnant and scared once too, and she'd had little sympathy from Val. It was one of the reasons Coral was determined not to leave her daughter to sink or swim. It didn't take the sting out of Summer's words, though, or the guilt of leaving her and Oliver, Val and now Helen and Graham to fend for themselves.

She didn't want to repeat her mother's dismissiveness, but Coral's current stress just wouldn't withstand Summer's angst.

Holding up a hand, she searched for a response that wasn't a swear word or a snarky retort or sympathy that, at this moment, she couldn't carry off with sincerity. In the end, all she managed was a composed, steady, 'Your washing is on and your lunches are in the fridge. I'll talk to you later.'

She dropped into the office on her way to the hospital and found Jessica frowning at her computer screen. It set off a buzz of alarm. 'What's wrong?'

'Oh hey.' Jessica held up a coffee cup. 'Just about to make a cuppa. Want one?'

'No, I'm not staying. What are you frowning about?'

'Oh.' Eye roll. 'Mother-of-the-groom outfits.'

Coral blinked, trying to unscramble Jessica's answer.

'Brandon's mum wants to talk styles when we have brunch on Sunday.'

Coral fought to hold back a wave of fury that rose like a tsunami: slow and monstrous.

'I'm more interested in colours,' Jessica went on, apparently taking Coral's silence for fascination. 'Don't want her clashing with my bridesmaids.'

Coral's heartbeat thumped in her ears. She felt an overpowering urge to shout at Jessica about the many and varied reasons why anything bridal was beyond her today. But the voice of experience, the calm one she'd used with Summer just fifteen minutes ago, reminded her that losing her cool would waste time and break her focus.

She waited a beat, ignored Jessica's comment and said, 'Have you got your head around Rodney's new delivery schedules?'

'Oh yeah, sure.' She scooped up a wad of pages. 'I did a printout.'

'But have you got your head around it?'

'Yep.'

Coral eyed her for a moment. 'Next pick-up option's at one, right?'

She checked her printout. 'Yes.'

'What was the last you heard from Rodney?'

Jessica checked her inbox. 'Nothing since his email this morning.'

'Right. I spoke to him in the car, doesn't sound like they're going to make this one but he's going to text me in an hour to confirm. Can you be ready to cancel the pick-up and put everyone else on standby? I've got to go to the hospital.'

'No worries.'

No worries! There were more worries than Coral could count. She collected notes off her desk, dropped pens back in holders, straightened her keyboard, checked her external hard drive was working. 'Did you get your passport up to date, like I asked?'

'Yes.' Hopeful smile. 'Am I going somewhere?'

'You're an emergency contingency. Don't get your hopes up.' Could she trust Jessica to stop thinking about the wedding long enough to get on the right plane? 'And try googling something more useful than outfits for your mother-in-law, like the flight schedules to Stockholm.'

Mara

'I SUPPOSE YOU went travelling after you dropped out of Canberra University,' Estelle said after her first sip of her morning cappuccino.

It was Friday: one day left of this horrible week. Mara was drinking a double shot, determined to face Estelle with a smile. She didn't deserve it, and the assumption that Mara had simply gone travelling made her jaw clench, but her tone had suggested Estelle was also trying to leave yesterday's anger behind. 'I dropped out because Dad had a heart attack.'

'Did you intend to go back?'

'I didn't have a plan. My dad and brother needed me so I came home.'

'You have a brother?'

'Patrick. Four years younger. He was in his final year at school.'

'Yes, younger brothers are important.'

The way she said it made Mara bristle. 'It wasn't like that; his education wasn't more important than mine. Dad was in hospital, and Pat couldn't deal with that and exams on his own.'

'Where was your mother?'

She thought Estelle knew. 'Mum died nineteen months before Dad's heart attack.'

Something flickered in the older woman's eyes. 'When you said she'd been unwell, I didn't realise . . . I understand why you were called home.'

'I wasn't *called* home. I came home.'

'Yes, I see there's a difference.' Another sip. 'And how did your father feel when you didn't return to your studies?'

'We didn't really talk about it.'

Estelle's expression twitched with, *Well, that explains it.*

'He was sick,' Mara countered. 'And not coping well with being sick. I said I was staying and he didn't argue.'

One fine eyebrow arched with disdain. 'I broke my collarbone when I was at boarding school and needed surgery to pin it. My father wouldn't allow me to return home until after the exams were finished.'

'Was it close to exam time?'

'It was only four weeks into term.'

Mara couldn't tell if that story was meant to make her feel good or bad about her dad's reaction. It didn't say much about the old Mr Collings, though. 'That was mean.'

'I was ordered back to university the day after my brother's funeral.'

'Oh my god.' Mara put a hand to her heart. 'I'm so sorry.' About her brother and her horrible father.

'It was a long time ago.'

'But still. That kind of thing . . .'

Estelle swiped a hand as though it was over and done with. 'My father was a hard man. I had to learn to be hard to earn his respect.'

It was said as though her father's respect had been a worthy prize, but what about his love and kindness? What about learning not to need his respect? There was so much wrong with Estelle's reasoning, but it seemed to explain a lot. 'You should write a book.'

'Oh yes, the history of Collings. Some family members think it would be an appropriate retirement project for me. I suppose Vaughn put you up to suggesting that.'

The comment was tinged with more resentment, and the thought of provoking Estelle's fury again made Mara panic. 'The history of Collings! Who'd read that?' Then, remembering she was talking to a Collings, she added, 'Sorry, I meant a book about you – your memories, your father, the business. You know, a memoir.'

'Don't be absurd. Who would read *that*?'

'I would. No, seriously. The things you had to put up with. You, your generation of women, what it meant to push back. And you hung in there anyway. You were a trailblazer, Estelle.'

Her boss let out a bark of laughter, possibly intended to make Mara feel ridiculous. But it didn't mask her pleasure in the compliment, or stop her chin from lifting in pride, or her eyes from glistening with something that looked a lot like validation. It was possible, Mara thought, that for all Estelle's money and arrogance, validation was probably a rare thing in her life. Knowing about her father and brother, it felt pretty good to be able to give her that. So Mara ignored the scorn and said, 'Go you, Estelle.'

'Yes, well,' Estelle patted her hair, 'I think we've lingered long enough. And look, young Rylee is here to take me to my torture session.'

Mara and Rylee exchanged a surprised glance at Estelle's playful tone. With any luck, Mara might have given them both an easier day.

Laura at the office wasn't so hopeful: *Can you accidentally on purpose throw a bomb at Estelle's phone today? Or just at Estelle?*

Mara: *I wish! Was she yelling at you yesterday?*

Laura: *Still in recovery. How have you not killed her yet? It's a hospital! Drugs. Poisons. Scalpels.*

Laura: *Those electric shock paddle things. Wheelchairs/stairs.*

Mara: *Already fell down stairs.*

Laura: *Proof she's undead! Keep your head down! Hide her phone!*

Estelle's good humour didn't last. Once she was back in her recliner, she barked, 'What are you printing?'

Mara took the sheets from the printer and handed one set to Estelle. 'This one is as you requested.'

Estelle did a quick flip through the pages and held out her hand for the other.

'In this one, I've given you some room to write. I noticed you were making some notes after your calls yesterday, and I thought this might be easier.' When there was no comment, Mara added, 'You also have some messages from the office.'

'I will deal with these first.'

The messages had sounded urgent though, so Mara tapped her phone to read the last one. 'Isna is asking—'

'Mara!'

Her eyes snapped up.

'Did you not hear me?'

Sure, yes, but Isna had texted three times. The blue eyes had turned flinty, though, and Mara wanted to finish the week without quaking through another episode of her boss's resentment. 'Sorry. Let me know when you're ready.'

A few minutes later, Estelle was asleep, the pages dropped on her lap. She could have just said she was tired.

Mara rolled her eyes as she started a text to Isna: *She's back in her room but sleeping now.*

Isna: *Did you tell her it was about the amendments to the statement of claim?*

Mara: *I tried but she didn't want her messages.*

Isna: *Your job is to keep her informed.*

Mara sighed.

Andie

BEN'S MOBILE WAS ringing when Andie wandered in. It was on his tray table, his parents' faces lighting up the screen.

'Ben?' She did a quick check of the bathroom and balcony, hesitating only a moment as she thought of his dad's cancer, their long-distance stress and her own desperate hours longing for the sound of home. She wasn't their *home*, but she could be reassuring.

'Hello, it's Andie,' she said.

'Andie, it's Stuart, Ben's dad. Is he there?' It sounded like he was holding the phone close and keeping his voice down.

'I'm sorry, but you've missed him again. I've just arrived, I think he's in a physio session.'

She heard disappointment in the breath he let out. 'Yeah. Okay.'

'Do you want him to call back?'

'No, it's late here.' Another breath, some shuffling, as though he'd moved into another room. 'I was awake and thought, hoped, I might catch him.'

She imagined him pacing a Scottish lounge room as he pushed a hand through sleep-dishevelled hair. 'Do you want me to pass on a message?'

'It's okay.'

'Alright, well . . .' The next step was *Goodbye*, but the poor man had called in the middle of his night, he deserved a second to process.

'It's eleven-thirty here,' he said. 'I should have called earlier but we're on a tour now. It's great, but I'd love to get hold of Ben.'

'It must be frustrating.'

'How is he?'

In pain yesterday, not fabulous the day before. 'He's doing okay.' Ben might prefer she left it at that, but Andie knew what it was like to long for a connection from the other side of the world. 'Pretty tired after the physio sessions, but not complaining.'

'That's Ben.' There was both pride and concern in his tone. 'How's his pain?'

How much did Stuart know? Was Ben running with *It's a simple break, nothing to worry about* or *Multiple breaks but healing well*? 'I'm sorry, I can't give you those details.'

'Sure, I understand. Worth a try, though. It's good of you to be keeping an eye on Ben. Are you with a service?'

'Service?'

'A visitor service. For patients with no support.'

She didn't know Ben well enough to guess the story he'd want to spin, or whether he'd mention saving her life, but she figured a fellow survivor of the same accident would be more reassuring than a colleague he'd only just met.

'No, we were both in the accident,' she said.

'Oh, I'm sorry. Were you injured too?'

'A broken elbow and concussion,' she told him. 'Only a couple of days in hospital and then I stayed with friends for a week, so I'm doing okay.'

'I'm glad to hear it,' he said. 'It must have been frightening.'

'I don't remember most of it. The upside of concussion, I guess.'

There was a pause, then, 'Were you with Ben?'

The question was tentative, the emphasis on *with*, and Andie smiled at his hesitance to ask about his son's love life. She remembered Ben hadn't wanted her to give much away yesterday, which was fine because Andie's rule of thumb was *say nothing to a parent or sibling until necessary.*

'We were both just standing on the kerb when the car ran out of control,' she told him, then gave a potted explanation for the rest: she'd wanted to meet the person who'd shared that moment, discovered he'd only just moved to Newcastle and couldn't stand him having no visitors. 'So I drop by every day with coffee and the papers and we shoot the breeze for a while.'

'That's very kind of you, Andie. I'm sure Ben appreciates it. And speaking for myself and my wife, because I know she'll feel the same way, we very much appreciate it too.'

Andie blinked at his sincerity. 'I'm still on sick leave, so it's giving me something to do too.'

'That may be, but . . . well, thank you. And don't forget you've had a nasty shock too. Make sure you're taking care of yourself.'

She pressed her lips together, cleared her throat. 'Thank you. I will. And Stuart, if you can't get hold of Ben, I'm happy for you to call me.' Not that she'd tell him anything Ben didn't want, but some occasional reassurance might help keep them in Scotland.

Ben arrived only seconds after Stuart had hung up.

'I told you she'd wait,' said the nurse pushing his wheelchair.

It was the same nurse who'd given him the pain relief that first day. Forty-something with an aura of no-nonsense hustle. The nod she gave Andie spoke a combination of, *Good you're back* and *We're both looking out for this guy.*

Andie smiled in return, saying to Ben, 'You just missed your dad. He was up late and thought he might catch you.'

Ben pushed a hand through his mop of hair, guilt in his frown.

'Don't worry, I maintained the lie,' she added.

'The one to keep your parents in Scotland?' the nurse asked, lifting the foot rests on Ben's wheelchair so he could stand.

'Yep,' he said, his face set in grim focus as he prepared to take the three paces from the wheelchair to the recliner. 'Don't stop,' Ben said.

The nurse looked at Andie. 'He means you. Keep talking.'

So while he made his way from wheelchair to recliner, Andie gave a word-for-word account of the conversation with Stuart, hoping Ben's guilt and perhaps his progress, too, might be eased by her retelling.

Finally seated again, he said, 'Fiona, this is Andie. Andie, Fiona.'

'Ben gave me the gist,' Fiona said. 'How's your arm?'

'It's fine, thanks.'

'Good to hear. Right, Ben, we're done here.'

When she'd left, Ben asked, 'How did Dad sound?'

Tired and worried. Andie hesitated, not sure if the lying was meant to go both ways. Would Ben be worried if she told him that? Would Stuart want Ben not to worry? She only had her mother to go by, and worrying other people wasn't something she shied away from. Ben and his parents had something else going on, though, and whether it was the right thing to do or not, she said, 'He seemed okay. Reassured, I think, to get some information. Maybe a little more when he realised I wasn't just dropping by for a chat because it was my job.'

A huffed laugh. 'Thanks, Andie.'

'My pleasure.' More than she'd expected. 'Will you call him later?'

She'd asked out of curiosity, but he seemed chastised. 'Yeah.'

'We could swap parents? You could ignore my mum all you like.'

'Not easy?'

'That's an understatement.'

'What about your dad?'

'He's never been in the picture.'

'I'm sorry.'

'Don't be. He was an arse to my mum, and I have multiple half- and step-siblings who are happy to share her emotional chaos.'

She shrugged – *that's life.* But he watched her a moment, maybe imagining what it was like to be in her family. Perhaps he was thinking about his own, or seeing something new in Andie's face. Whatever it was, she wanted to hold his gaze, and to look away from it and, for some stupid reason, to burst into tears. She didn't do any of those things, though. Because one side of his mouth kicked up with an idea and, like it was on a string, hers did the same.

'I'm thinking the hydrotherapy pool,' he said.

'What about the hydrotherapy pool?'

'Caper?'

Coral

ALBY HAD CORAL'S double shot underway by the time she reached his van.

'You look frazzled,' he said.

'That's a relief. I thought I might look worse.'

'Is it your mum?'

'Mum. Work. Adult kids. Life.'

He gestured to a sweet, syrupy-looking cake, raising an eyebrow in question. 'Or a sandwich? I've got a couple in the fridge.'

'I thought you didn't do sandwiches.'

'Not usually.'

She managed to relax enough to return his smile. 'In that case, you'd better give me a sandwich and a couple of slices of cake. And you didn't charge me for the fig and walnut yesterday.'

'No,' he said with finality. 'How was it?'

'Thank you, it was delicious. Mum enjoyed hers too.'

'What work are you in?'

'Logistics. I've got a client with a rush delivery due in Stockholm on Monday and it's at the nail-biting stage.'

A nod. 'And kids?'

'My son's in the UK, so I'm handling the fallout from his flooded apartment. My daughter's baby is due in five weeks and she's limping about on crutches and has a sick toddler.' Why was she telling him all this?

'Ouch.'

That was why: empathy. She smiled again as she took the cup he passed her. 'Your coffee has been a daily lifesaver this week. What will I do over the weekend?'

'I'll have the van at Nobbys Beach tomorrow morning, if you need a hit.'

For a moment, Coral was struck by the sudden, dizzying possibilities of life in a parallel universe. One where she had time to stroll along a beach and chat to a nice, older guy who'd make her a coffee and say *Ouch* in the right places. A soft chuckle rolled from her lips. 'Yeah, right, okay. Unlikely, but I'll keep it in mind.'

She sat with Val for an hour, explaining again that if she didn't spend Sunday night at an airport hotel in Sydney, she wouldn't make her six am flight to New York. That yes, her suit for the presentation would get crushed in her luggage but there'd be an iron at the hotel; that she didn't know if there were stairs to the podium but she wasn't worried about breaking an ankle in her new heels. Then she lied and said she was already packed and Summer was doing great.

Rodney called while she was there to say he wouldn't make his one pm deadline, and neither the social worker nor the doctor arrived before Coral had to head back to work.

Mara

ESTELLE'S MOOD DID another about-face, and when she called Mara in from the balcony, it was for coffee, not another reprimand.

'Make one for yourself,' she said, rearranging herself on the recliner. 'What are you working on now?'

Mara braced herself before explaining she was digitising the files from the spreadsheet, hastily adding it wasn't for the Collings system but so it would be easier for Estelle to work with. To Mara's surprise, Estelle simply nodded and moved on.

'What took your mother?' Estelle's tone was mild, but the question landed with a jolt. Mara didn't want to discuss her lovely mum with her mean-spirited boss, but she wasn't brave enough to refuse to answer, so she kept it brief. 'Breast cancer.'

'A terrible disease. It has claimed two very dear friends of mine.'

Doubting Estelle had very dear friends, Mara said, 'The wife of your client?' It was one of the details she'd added to the spreadsheet, and unexpectedly useful for diverting focus away from her own story.

'Cynthia Della Porta. That was ten years ago, but yes, she was also taken.'

'Taken,' Mara repeated.

'Passed away is quite popular these days.'

'Actually, taken feels . . . right. I always thought passed away sounded too gentle.'

'The truth is rarely gentle.'

'No, it's not.' Mara took a sip of her coffee as that thought settled between them.

'What did your mother do with her life?' Estelle asked.

'She was a high school maths teacher, although she ended up working with Dad. Mum started out doing his accounts and when the business grew, she just kept going until . . . Well, she used to say she did everything but the building.'

All this drew from Estelle was a nod.

'She loved it,' Mara said in her mother's defence. 'She always said she was her own boss, she worked when it suited her, she was there when we got home from school and she had time to do the afternoon sport run.'

'Is that your goal too? To be home for children?'

She had no goals now, unless she counted, *Find something to interest her*. The job at Collings had been the first step towards that, and look how that was turning out. Not that she would explain any of that to Estelle.

'I haven't thought about children yet.' She finished her coffee and stood. 'I should get to work.' Picking up Estelle's handwritten notes, she turned for the balcony and then stopped. 'Oh, your messages. It's actually one message, several times. Isna needs to speak with you about a statement of claim.'

In the couple of minutes it took for Mara to settle into an armchair and open her laptop, Estelle had gone from civil to shouting into her phone.

Coral

THE SOCIAL WORKER rang while Coral was in the office working up routes for emergency contingencies, including having Rodney's drill heads picked up and delivered to Stockholm by a single escort. Expensive, but they were running out of options.

'I'd like to sit down with you and Val on Monday to discuss her home care options,' Tori said.

Coral's stress started to bubble like water in a kettle. 'I'll be on a plane to New York,' she snapped, then hoped it didn't sound like her mother's care was just a hassle.

'Is there another family member who can attend?'

Coral's brother still hadn't committed to what day he was arriving from Tasmania. 'Does it have to be Monday?'

'It would be best for Val to get something in place before she leaves rehab, and I'm on a course on Tuesday, Wednesday, Thursday.'

'I'll need to get back to you.'

'Can you let me know today? I've got other patients to book in.'

Coral sent her brother an email:

To: Andrew
From: Coral

The social worker wants a meeting next week and Mum needs someone with her who'll understand what's being said. Can you let me know when you'll be here? I'm flying to New York on Monday, and losing my mind trying to cover everything. Please? Asap? Hoping you get this before close of business!

Coral

She sent a similar message by text too. It was early afternoon, but she wasn't hopeful of an answer before the day was out.

An hour later, Rodney rang. 'Good news!'

Coral stood up from her desk, ready to give Jessica instructions to set Option Three in motion.

'We've got two days' grace,' he said. 'We can get it there on Wednesday.'

'Oh.' She sat down. 'That's great, Rodney.' And her stress just got an extension. 'When do you estimate you'll be ready for pick-up?'

'Sunday night at the earliest. Most likely Monday. Can you give me best-case and worst-case options?'

Coral dropped her head to the desk. 'Sure. I'll get them to you this afternoon.' She'd be on a plane when his package was ready, and would have to trust wedding-obsessed Jessica to manage the complicated, urgent delivery. Fuck.

Despite the extension, a sense of urgency swarmed like bees across Coral's shoulders as she went through the motions of yet another delivery schedule. When her mobile rang she snatched it up without looking at the screen, thinking it was one of her airline contacts. 'Tell me something good,' she said.

It was the hospital, calling to arrange a conference with Val's doctor to discuss her latest cognitive tests and the next steps. 'He's slotted you in for Tuesday morning.'

Part of Coral's mind reared up in anger at the assumption she could present herself at the hospital when she was told. But after twenty-three years in logistics, another part of her brain automatically shifted into whiteboard mode, visualising the time slots of her life and finding the gaps where she could squeeze things in. The bullet points representing her next five days pulsed like warning lights.

And in that moment she knew.

She wasn't going to make that flight to New York.

Her heart thumped. 'Okay. Alright. I'll be there.' She hung up and for twenty, maybe thirty seconds, she gripped the edge of her desk and listened to the pounding of blood through her veins. Then she pulled in a long, deep breath and got down to what she did best: shuffling and reshuffling all the pieces in the schedule.

The conference started on Tuesday, New York time, but she wasn't delivering her paper until Friday afternoon. She found a flight leaving Sydney on Thursday afternoon that got her into New York on Friday morning: praise the lord for time zones. It would give her enough time to check in to her hotel, shower, change and cross her fingers her speech didn't sound like jet-lagged gibberish.

It wasn't great, and it meant she'd only have six days in New York, but it gave her three more days to meet with Val's social worker and doctor, help Summer, get an insurance assessor into Wade's apartment, check on Helen and Graham and make sure Rodney's drill heads got to Stockholm on time. There might even be time to eat and sleep.

Mara

'I SUPPOSE YOU think I should be *nicer.*' Estelle glared at Mara as though the concept was an insult.

Mara hadn't said a word as she'd come through the French doors, but she'd been on the sidelines of Estelle's extended tantrum for three hours, fielding Laura's pissed-off texts and Isna's instructions for documents to be printed and for Estelle to read them properly before complaining. As though Mara had any control over how much her volcano of a boss read before erupting. If she did, she wouldn't have spent the afternoon feeling like she was trapped in a ring with a rampaging bull, hoping it didn't notice her.

Ten minutes ago, Laura had stormed out of the office, Isna had called Vaughn into the situation and Mara had considered warning a nurse that a blood vessel in Estelle's brain might explode at any minute.

Nic*er* was impossible, Mara thought now. Not that Estelle's question was even a question, more a *Fuck off with your* nice *bullshit.* But since it was hanging there between them, Mara wondered in a fleeting, middle-of-a-catastrophe moment of clarity whether anyone had ever suggested to Estelle that *nice* might get a better result.

'It wouldn't *hurt* to be nice,' Mara said, and immediately wished she hadn't.

Estelle looked her up and down as though Mara was something she might see in a bedpan. 'Of course you would say that, you stupid girl!'

Mara glared back. It wasn't boldness or stubbornness or some overblown belief that if she made a stand Estelle might back down. Sure, the disgust on Estelle's face and her belittling were offensive and cruel. But who was the stupid one?

Estelle's fury storm had been going on for hours. She'd pissed off everyone she'd come in contact with – the people who were actually trying to assist her – and she was still unhappy with the changes she wanted made to the document. Mara was exhausted from listening and tending to the victims and worrying about getting caught in the crossfire. She was sticky from anxiety sweating, her blood felt like it was pumping too hard and it just seemed so fucking pointless to get mad at the people who were trying to fix the problem.

Mara was suddenly, overwhelmingly fed up with being berated by this clueless woman.

Gathering as much calm as she could muster in the circumstances, Mara said, 'People work better when they're not being yelled at, and it takes nothing away from you to show some kindness.'

Estelle's nostrils flared. 'I know how everyone at the office feels about me. Being *nice* or *kind* won't change a thing. Do you think I could have been a trailblazer if *nice* was my objective? Do you think *nice* has anything to do with being a good litigator? My father taught me from an early age that *nice* is weak.' She narrowed her eyes at Mara. 'Nice won't get you anywhere, Mara. You might be halfway through a university degree if you weren't so *nice*. If nice is what you want, you would be better served looking for a *nice* man to father some *nice* children, so you can follow in your mother's footsteps and do *nice*, unchallenging work and be at home for your *nice* children.'

Estelle's lips were pinched tight when she finished, as though she'd said her piece and the conversation was over. But her rant had tripped something hot and loud in Mara's mind, and even the part of her brain that was capable of clarity was saying that this bitter old woman should not get away with insulting Mara's family.

'You. Know. *Nothing* about me.' Mara's voice was sure, strong, determined. She hardly recognised it. 'You've twisted the few facts you have about my family into something so banal and prosaic that it's beneath you. Your father might have given you money and a job, but mine gave me love, protection and decency. You're the one who should be ashamed of their family's choices.'

Estelle's eyes flared. 'How dare you speak to me like that!'

'How dare you speak about my mother! How dare you tell me I should have gone back to uni instead of looking after my father. How dare you tell me how to live when you're in hospital with no-one to visit you.' She paused to catch her breath, the aghast expression on Estelle's face doing nothing to quell her fury. 'You don't have a single family member who cares enough to bring you a fresh set of pyjamas. The only people who do things for you are the ones you pay. The only time you show any respect is when you speak to a select few clients who aren't even on your books anymore. All you can think about is getting back to work so you can keep yelling at people who don't like you.'

'I don't go to work to be liked,' Estelle snapped.

'No, you're trying to prove you can last as long in the job as your father did. The same father who expected you to earn his love, who sent you away after your brother died, who treated you like you didn't deserve to be part of the family, let alone the business. Why would you want to be like him?'

There was a brief hesitation in Estelle's eyes. 'You know *nothing*. You've *finished* nothing. All you've managed to do is give up. Of course you would think I should retire too.'

'I couldn't care less whether you retire or die at your bloody desk. But I have no idea why you'd want to spend your final years in the office shouting at people.'

'Sloppy work remains sloppy until it is completed to an acceptable standard.'

'But you're not improving standards, you're perpetuating bad behaviour. You're bitter about the way you were treated for being a woman, and instead of doing anything about it, you treat everyone the same way you were treated. You've been senior partner for twenty-something years, you could have stopped it or changed things or set a better example. You could have done *nothing* and it would have been better. And now, at seventy-two and recovering from surgery, you're ranting from your hospital bed about sloppy work.' She hesitated, surprised at what had fallen out of her mouth, not sure *Trailblazer, my arse* was the best note to finish on. Then she remembered what Mum used to say when she was telling war stories from her teaching days. *If someone needs knocking off their perch, they're more likely to listen if you give them a ladder to climb back up.* Not that Estelle was likely to listen to anything else she had to say, but that didn't mean Mara couldn't try to be constructive.

'You could be thinking about leaving your business in a better state,' Mara added. 'About your legacy when you do retire.'

'What do *you* know about legacy? You're a child.'

'I know people think you're an icon of the legal profession in this town. But hey, if you want to be remembered as a bitter and twisted bully, you're doing great.'

'I suppose you think I should retire quietly and without a fuss? How very ageist of you.'

'What I think is that you've got more options than having a tantrum about sloppy work and getting back at your snake of a cousin. Instead of breaking the spirits of the women trying to follow in your footsteps, you could be sharing your knowledge. You could be a mentor. You could write a book about your most interesting cases. You could tell the world how shit it was being a lawyer in the seventies. You could do work that made you happy.'

Estelle had had a rejoinder for everything until then. Now, she just stared at Mara with an unreadable expression. It didn't look like fury, but it could have been simmering outrage. Or exasperation, bewilderment or mystification. Because, well, happiness? Her father probably thought that was weak too.

Mara stood her ground for several moments, heart thumping, braced for another nasty retort. When all she got was silence, she decided she was sick of trying to decipher Estelle's expressions and worrying about how she'd react. She turned for the French doors, shoved her laptop in her bag, collected her coffee cup and lunch container and took a glance around the balcony. Best thing about this whole stupid job.

'Where are you going?' Estelle demanded as Mara walked through the room.

Mara turned at the door. Adrenaline was pulsing through her veins, her legs trembling, her heart hammering. But she wanted to be calm, didn't want Estelle to think she'd won. 'I've turned up every day because I wanted to prove I could finish the job I was given. And because I felt sorry for you. But I don't have to put up with rude and ungrateful behaviour to prove I can work hard or follow through. I deserve as much respect as the next human being. I don't know what you deserve, but it's not my care and concern. Good luck in your recovery. I won't be back.'

Mara was shaking as she walked to her car. She got into the driver's seat and gulped water from her bottle, her tear ducts tingling, a smile forming on her mouth.

That. Was. Insane.

She was insane. What had she done? When had she ever been so . . . articulate? Undaunted? Brazen? Stupid?

Vaughn would not be impressed. Dad would be disappointed. Mara, though, felt like she'd just cut the head off a dragon. Her muscles were zinging and depleted from the effort. It was probably the adrenaline and exhaustion, but it felt great.

Sure, the dragon's head would probably grow back by morning and spew fire at someone else.

But not at Mara.

Andie

'HEY, CAMILLE,' ANDIE called as she hoisted grocery bags onto Vivian and Theo's kitchen counter.

'Hey Andie,' the twelve-year-old replied without moving her eyes from the TV.

'Getting lots of homework done there?'

'Yep. Got a Netflix quiz on Monday.'

Andie cooked dinner at their place a couple of times a month. She loved their five-burner stove, and it was easier to transplant one person than three. Well, that was the story they all went with when Andie texted, *My night to cook!* The truth was, they all knew Andie didn't want to be left with the sudden silence at her place after they all went home.

Today, she was doing pizza on ready-made bases. She was too tired for anything that needed more brain function; she probably should have rested more this week. Today, faced with going home at three pm on a Friday to stare at the walls all night, she'd dragged herself to the supermarket so she could hang out at Viv and Theo's instead.

They weren't home yet, so she sat at the bench to check the text that had pinged as she arrived, eyebrows rising at the essay-length message.

Hi Andie, it's Carmel, Ben Cameron's mum. Stuart gave me your number, I hope you don't mind me texting you.

We didn't know you'd been in the accident with Ben and wanted to send you a big hug for everything you must be going through right now. Of course, you'll have your own family and friends looking out for you, but we know what it's like to be going through a tough time and sometimes the smallest thing can make you feel a whole lot better. So from us in Scotland to you, we hope you're recovering well and your arm and concussion continue to do all the right things. We think you're very brave to be up and about so soon, and so very, very generous to be helping Ben at such a time. There's not much we can do from here to help you, except tell you how much we appreciate you looking out for Ben and taking the time to reassure us over the phone. Ben is adamant that we don't come home early from our holiday and we want to respect his wishes – he may not have told you that our trip was an anniversary gift from him, and we adore him for it. Needless to say, we feel a long, long way from him and your time and care are worth more than I can say. 😘

Who were these sweet people? The last conversation Andie had with her mother had been terse because Andie hadn't offered to fly her mum down from Brisbane for the 'nursing' that neither of them wanted her to do. Andie was thinking about how to reply to Carmel when Vivian came in.

'I've got wine and chocolate 'cos I've had a shit day. You grab the glasses and I'll pour.'

They took their glasses into the bedroom while Viv got changed. She'd just said, 'Heard any more from Ben Cameron?' when Theo arrived, and the subject was forgotten until the four of them were sitting around the dining table.

'How's recovery?' Theo asked.

Andie gave them an update on her elbow: getting a bit more movement; and the brain fog: still lifting, but her recall was better.

'Heard any more about the Pusher?' Theo asked. 'What's his name?'

'Pusher?' Camille perked up, as though the conversation had just got interesting.

'Ben,' Andie said to Theo. 'He pushed me out of the way of a speeding car,' she told Camille.

'Oh, that guy.' Camille did big eyes at her mother, as though there'd been a separate conversation about him.

'He's doing much better,' Andie said. And, guessing what Vivian might have said to provoke the big eyes, she added, 'I've been taking him coffee and the papers, we have a chat and go on a caper.'

Camille frowned. 'What's a caper?'

'A bit of fun, an escapade,' Andie explained. 'You know, like a caper movie.'

'A caper?' Viv's puzzled amusement seemed a little forced.

Theo looked between her and Andie, something French about his bewilderment. 'Is caper a real word?'

'Nobody really uses it in conversation,' Viv said.

Andie pointed at her with a slice of pizza. 'Except Ben, apparently.'

There was a brief flicker of a frown. 'So what happens on a caper?'

'I push him about in his wheelchair. He's got a balcony off his room, so we mostly go along there. We went in search of the hydro-therapy pool today, and we're planning to check out the garden.'

'No-one's going to make a movie of that,' Camille said.

Andie aimed a pointed look at Vivian. 'No, but it breaks up a boring day.'

After dinner, Andie and Viv took their wine into the courtyard, leaving Camille and Theo with the cleaning up.

'What's the story with Ben?' Viv asked.

Andie shrugged. 'I just decided he shouldn't be alone in hospital.'

'It's not your fault he's there.'

'I know.'

'You don't owe him anything.'

'That's not why I'm visiting him.'

Vivian's face looked doubtful.

'I know what it's like to be alone,' Andie said. 'And you know why.' Viv knew more than anyone about the moments of aloneness that were burned into Andie's psyche. She'd never heard the whole story of Zack's death, not from beginning to end. She'd offered to listen, but Andie had never been able to make herself relive it: each part on its own was bad enough. 'And waiting to recover from these,' Andie lifted her elbow, tapped her head, 'is like grieving all over again. I need to do something, Viv, and visiting Ben has been . . .' Surprisingly fun. And had involved a lot of tears. Although Vivian was unlikely to think that was helpful. 'A focus. Busyness. Distracting.'

Viv nodded as though giving it some thought. 'It's just,' she reached across to take Andie's hand, 'I'm worried about you.'

Vivian had been there through the aftermath of Zack's death, and Andie knew her despair must have been hard to watch. She squeezed her friend's fingers. 'I've been worried about me too, but visiting Ben is helping.'

Andie's phone pinged and she pulled it from her pocket like it signalled the end of that topic.

Carmel: *Hi Andie, Carmel again. I hope you don't mind me asking for advice. I want to order some things for Ben online and I can't figure out how to arrange for a delivery to him at the hospital. Any ideas on how to manage the Hepburn House end?*

Big hugs, Carmel X

Andie smiled as she got to the end. *Big hugs* from someone else's mother: who wouldn't like that?

Viv smiled too, liked she wanted in on something nice. 'What?'

'A text from Ben's mum.'

'You're texting with his mother?'

'She texted me. I haven't answered yet.' When Vivian just looked at her, Andie said, 'Kind of a weird situation.'

She explained about Ben's parents being in Scotland, and the lie that turned into a longer conversation, and then another with his dad. 'Carmel texted before to thank me for helping Ben in their absence, and now she's asking about getting a parcel to him.'

'Do they know you were injured in the accident, too?'

'Yeah, they've been really sweet about it.'

'And then asked you to deliver packages to the hospital?'

'She was asking how to get one to the hospital. I'll tell her to send it to me.'

Vivian nodded, lips pressed together as though determined not to say anything more. But then she did. 'You're not responsible for his injuries.'

'I know.'

'You don't owe him anything.'

'Viv. I know.'

Andie looked her in the eye as she said it. Vivian looked right back, and for a long, silent moment, they held a battle of wills over who knew best. Andie got it: Viv had shouldered Andie's burden twice in two years; she was invested.

But Andie wasn't looking for advice, and didn't have the energy to talk about it. She tipped her head towards the door and called, 'Hey Theo, it's Friday night, you need to join us.'

Part 5

Recovery Assessment

Coral

CORAL WOKE ON Saturday morning with an eerie sense of calm. The urgency of the last week had passed, and the next few days were as organised as they could be. She could have read a book, listened to a podcast or just watched the garden from the bedroom windows, but she sat in bed with her laptop, running through the To-Do List again: timeframes, pitstops, room for Summer and Val. She'd shop on Sunday, cook Monday and Tuesday, finalise her packing on Wednesday.

Satisfied she could keep calm and carry on, she checked her watch and considered visiting Val. There was no rush; she had all day to get there. Summer didn't need her either, because Dan was home to fetch and carry.

Well, gee, a morning to herself.

She tried to enjoy it, she really did. She opened a novel, the first in . . . she couldn't remember. Only she couldn't sit still long enough to finish the first chapter. Her three-bedroom, constantly-in-need-of-repair house hadn't had much love in a while, and the idea of time to do more than a quick tidy was appealing, but Coral whizzed through the housework as though her only speed was overdrive. After that, she considered all the repairing/sanding/painting jobs, deciding they were all too big to start before she went away – or to come back to unfinished. Wandering outside, she pulled a couple of weeds in the garden, looked at how many more there were and gave up on that idea.

Rodney had said he and his crew would be working all weekend. This morning, she decided it was time to see the objects that she would, at some time in the next few days, be responsible for getting to Stockholm. She stopped at a bakery on the drive out of Newcastle, arriving thirty minutes later with a hug for Rodney, and sausage rolls and cake for the small, hungry team who'd been there since six am.

'Let me show you our babies,' Rodney said, leading Coral through the workshop.

She listened through an explanation of specialised diamond cutting surfaces that worked under extremely high temperatures and pressure, the rare materials required for the extended life their client had wanted, and issues with a supplier and last-minute machining.

'They'll look like this.' He lifted the lid of a padded case holding a prototype.

'Wow,' Coral said, hiding her disappointment. She'd lost sleep, had probably killed brain cells with stress and postponed a flight to New York for what looked like two fat, shiny arrowheads. Diamond-tipped had sounded so much prettier.

'What do you think?'

'I think it's time we talked about a fully escorted door-to-door delivery.'

They'd discussed it at the start, but only as a last resort. Now he said, 'How soon can you get me prices?'

☕

The sense of urgency that had powered Coral yesterday returned as she drove back to Newcastle, her thumbs tapping on the steering wheel with the need to get on to her laptop. There was a hold-up in the traffic ahead, so she took a detour around the harbour and as she waited at a pedestrian crossing, she caught sight of the lighthouse up ahead and decided she didn't need to go home to work up the prices for Rodney. She could do with a coffee, too – and maybe a pit stop in a parallel universe.

Coral did a loop of the road around the beaches, looking for Alby's van while assessing whether she felt like an idiot now that she was here and hunting him down. He was set up under some trees in a stretch of harbourside parkland and, pulling into a parking slot, she started across the grass with her laptop and handbag. The weather was *stunning*, she realised. A high blue sky and a touch of heat that held the promise of summer. Had it been like this all week? When was the last time she'd noticed?

Watching as Alby's focus moved between customers and the coffee machine, she wondered if he'd recognise her away from the hospital. If he told all his customers where he parked his van on weekends.

'You made it,' he said. It sounded like, *Good for you.*

'I dropped in on a client, was going home this way and,' she shrugged, 'I needed a coffee.'

One side of his mouth turned up. 'You having the usual or have you got a weekend go-to?'

Wanting him to think she might actually spend weekends sipping fancy orders in cafes, she said, 'Better stick to the usual. I've got some work to do.'

He wrote her name on the side of a cardboard cup – without asking her to remind him what it was – and set it in place on the coffee machine. 'Hard to keep up with the day job when there are hospital visits?'

'And the rest.'

'You getting any downtime?'

'This is it.'

'Oh yeah?' He aimed a nod at the laptop.

She conceded with a tilt of her head. 'It feels better to be on top of things.'

He gave a nod, aimed his chin towards a stand of trees. 'There's a table in the shade over there.'

Coral took his suggestion, and some time later, was tapping out an email to Rodney when a shadow fell over her laptop.

'You still going?' Alby asked.

She lifted a finger like a mini stop sign, attached her quote and hit Send. Shutting her laptop, she sat back with a sigh and frowned at the plate he slid onto the table. 'What's this?'

'Thought you could help me with my leftovers.' It was an assortment of healthy and not-so healthy cake, slice and one large green jelly snake.

'No-one bought the snake?'

'A travesty, I know.'

She glanced at his van across the park. 'Have you got someone helping out in the van?'

'Nope, I'm finished for the day. All packed up. What about you?' He tapped her laptop. 'You got someone helping you out?'

Coral was about to tell him she'd finished her work too, but hesitated a moment as his question landed. Then for another moment as it set off a sudden heat behind her eyes. 'If I had someone to help, I wouldn't be here doing this.' She laughed, making it a joke, hoping he didn't see just how depressing it was. 'Anyway, I'm finished now.'

He nodded, like it was about time. 'What's on for the rest of your day?'

'I'll head up to the hospital to see Mum soon.'

Picking up a slice of cake, he said, 'Hard work being the visitor sometimes. Doing the round trip every day, keeping up the conversation, making it upbeat and entertaining.'

'While trying not to think about the to-do lists backing up while you're there.'

He huffed a laugh. 'How's your daughter doing?'

He remembered? 'Not having much fun, that's for sure. I'll probably drop in later to see how they're all doing.'

He pushed the plate towards her. 'I think you need the snake.'

She took it, bit off its head. 'I was meant to be flying to New York on Monday.' She tilted her head, like it was another thing she was juggling, intending to explain that she had everything under control, to insist that she wasn't disappointed. But the way he said nothing and the way that seemed to say something, somehow prompted her to tell him the whole story. As she talked, her gaze shifted between the beach, Alby's leftovers and his face, wondering at times if he was as interested as he seemed, or if he was just being kind to the frazzled woman who kept turning up for his coffee and cakes. She wondered, too, what he'd done before he bought his van, if listening had once been his job. Whatever it was, he ended up getting the full story of Coral's stress storm.

There was only a slice of nut bar left by the time she finished. She sat back, glanced away, suddenly embarrassed about downloading on someone she barely knew. 'Anyway, the pressure is off now that I've got a few extra days before I leave.' She swiped the air, pushing it all away. 'It'll be a breeze,' she laughed.

'Take it easy,' he said.

She smiled at his kindness, biting down on a sudden neediness. 'I should go.'

He tilted the plate towards her. 'Last piece?'

'No, but thank you. The comfort food helped.' She stood to leave.

'See you Monday, then. I'll have your double shot waiting.'

As she left, she couldn't help wondering why a virtual stranger was the only person who showed any interest in how she was doing?

Andie

ANDIE FOUND BEN on the balcony, looking like the scruffy bloke between two well-dressed older ladies, all three with their arms akimbo as they blew out a gust of air.

'Breathing exercises,' said Fiona, who was standing in front of them in the same pose.

'Everyone, this is Andie,' Ben called, before introducing his room neighbours, Val and Estelle.

'One more round,' Fiona called.

'The physios have got time off for good behaviour,' Ben said between breaths. 'So Nurse Hardcore here is running the gym over the weekend.'

Fiona grinned. 'Slow breath in.'

'Look what she makes us do,' Ben said.

Fiona and Val chuckled. Estelle gave a discreet eye roll.

'Well, it's bad news from the outside,' Andie said. 'No coffee van. Guess the coffee guy gets a weekend too.'

'Every weekend,' Fiona moaned.

Ben looked horrified.

'My daughter Coral brings me a cappuccino from the van every time she visits,' Val said. 'It's really very nice.'

'These ladies need a decent coffee if they're to continue breathing,' Ben said.

Val said, 'I wouldn't mind . . .'

Andie: 'I could . . .'

Fiona: 'There's a list of cafes . . .'

'*I've* got a coffee machine,' Estelle said. 'I had my assistant buy one.' Her expression suggested she expected admiration, but the loaded silence that followed seem to make her falter. 'I, well . . . Of course, you're welcome to use it.'

'I'll get cups,' said Fiona, the breathing session over.

Reconvening in Estelle's room with wheelchairs and walkers, Fiona made the coffees while Andie joined Ben and Val in looking around.

Val: 'There's no printer in my room.'

Ben: 'We could have a movie night in here with that screen.'

Andie: 'The blanket on your bed is a thoughtful touch.'

'My assistant brought it in,' Estelle said. 'Mara. I believe you've met her.'

'I suppose she gets a weekend too,' Ben said.

It was meant as a joke, but Estelle's lips turned down. 'If she comes back.'

'Where's she gone?' he asked.

'We had a . . . disagreement.' Estelle waved a hand as if it was of no consequence, and Andie suddenly recognised her.

'We've met before.' Andie explained how years ago, she'd been on the committee of a women's networking group. They'd sent Estelle Collings multiple invitations to speak at their monthly lunch event. When she eventually accepted, there'd been a full house, half of the audience keen to hear what she had to say, the other half taking notes in case they were defamed: at least, that was the joke. Not that Andie mentioned that part, or Estelle's reputation for being either loved or hated. But it made her feel sorry for Mara.

'Not easy working from a hospital room,' Andie said, 'for a boss who's not in the best of spirits.'

The older woman lifted her chin. 'I imagine so.' Arrogant yet contrite.

'I find an apology is always a good place to start.'

'I like a good apology,' Val said, as though she'd been offered a cappuccino.

'Yes, well,' Estelle started, then found nowhere to go. 'How are the coffees coming along?'

While Estelle elected to enjoy hers in her room, Andie and Ben followed Fiona and Val back to the balcony. Leaving them to continue on to his room, Andie parked his chair beside a sofa, handed him a newspaper and took the other for herself, sipping as they read. Who said visiting the injured had to involve conversation? Or tears?

☕

'It's Saturday, right?' Ben asked sometime later.

'All day.'

'So hard to keep track when it's just one thrill after another in here.'

'Must be exhausting.'

'More than you'd expect.' He closed his paper and folded it, took off his glasses and said, 'I'm thinking: movie matinee.' Before she could reply, Ben added, 'I know watching a movie on a laptop probably doesn't rate as an exciting alternative to whatever you have planned for the weekend. But I can offer a half-decent sandwich and a single-serve tub of ice-cream. Vanilla, if it's a selling point. Possibly jelly and fruit too. I've also got an extensive library of movies that might be some compensation for the lacklustre menu. If a movie matinee in a hospital room was something you might consider.'

'What would we watch?' Andie asked, as though it might make a difference.

'I've prepared a list of suggested viewing for you.'

'For me?'

'Like I said, one thrill after another in here.'

'So you're not compiling movie lists for every person you know?'

'I didn't say that.' He made a face like he'd been caught out. 'So your list consists of comedies, travel and Katharine Hepburn being a feminist.'

'You remembered!'

He smiled, pleased she was pleased. 'What do you think: a matinee then?'

'If I can have the jelly.'

Lunch was as good as Ben had described it, improved by the knowledge she wasn't leaving him to a lonely Saturday afternoon. As they ate, he talked her through his curated movie list, explaining the reasons for each choice. She couldn't decide if he was trying to make up for the drawbacks of lunch and the laptop, or if he was excited about the extended visitor time, but it was sweet that he was so invested in her movie choice.

They agreed on *50 First Dates* after Ben said, 'You might relate to the concept of forgetting that you met someone. Not that we're Drew Barrymore and Adam Sandler, but they deal with a whole lot worse, which might be comforting.'

Drew Barrymore's memory loss was cuter than Andie's, and Adam Sandler wasn't bruised and broken like Ben. Andie enjoyed it more than she'd expected: the set-ups, the goofiness, even the jokes that ran too long. Right up until the ending. The final scene was so unexpectedly touching that before she realised where it was going, it had reached into her chest and squeezed her broken heart.

Then her eyes were overflowing and a sob had wedged in her throat like a lump of stale bread. She tried to keep it to herself, swallowing hard, surreptitiously wiping her cheeks with her sleeve. But a hitch in her breath caught Ben's attention, his eyebrows lifting briefly above his glasses before coming together in a frown. Andie shot to her feet and paced away.

'Andie?' His voice was gentle, surprised, uncertain.

'It's meant to be a comedy,' she snapped, swiping at her cheeks, her back to him.

'I know. It's a sweet ending.'

'You might have warned me.'

'I didn't realise . . .'

Andie closed her eyes, annoyed she'd lost control so quickly, that her wounds were still so goddamn close to the surface. 'It's fine.' She gave her face another wipe as she turned around. 'I'm fine, don't worry.' She checked her watch, like she was keeping track of the time. 'I should go.'

'Not like this,' he said. 'Stay, take a breath.'

For half a second, she thought about it. He had no-one, she told herself. It was lonely; she was lonely. He thought it was just the movie that had undone her, that in another five minutes she'd be normal Andie again. But the emotion that had risen to the surface was like a submarine coming up from her depths; the pain pulsing through her veins was like tiny shards of glass.

She needed to get it under control. 'It's fine. I'm fine.' She collected her bag, slung him a smile. 'See you, Ben.'

Not waiting for his response, she strode into the corridor, head down. She sucked in lungfuls of fresh air as she walked to the car park, ordering herself not to let a stupid movie open her stupid wounds. She got behind the wheel, not waiting for it to subside. She could drive and cry. She was fine.

Coral

FOR THE FIRST time since Val had been in Hepburn House, Coral pulled into the car park without feeling like she was on limited time. Val too seemed more relaxed, despite the fact she thought Coral had already left for New York.

They did some rehab together, walking the full length of the corridor twice, then stood at the windows on the balcony gazing at the garden. After the long and complicated conversation trying to explain her flight changes, Coral was amazed at how many plants her mum could name, as though they were in easier reach in her brain.

Coral called Summer as she was pulling out of the car park. 'Just leaving the hospital, thought I'd check in.'

'It's been so nice having Dan home all day.' Summer's voice sounded twenty kilos lighter than yesterday as she gave a rundown of their activities: sleep-in, pancakes, an hour to herself when Dan took Oliver outside to help him in the garden. 'I even painted my nails,' she laughed.

'I'm glad. You sound more like yourself. By the way, I've postponed my flight to New York. I'm not leaving until Thursday now.'

There was a pause. 'Because of what I said?'

'You and Nana and work. A few more days takes the pressure off.'

'Will it give you enough time?'

'I'll be checking into the hotel only a couple of hours before my presentation. I can sleep when it's all over,' she laughed.

'Right. Great. And enough time to sort out everything for Nana?'

Coral sighed, feeling again the guilt at leaving Val, the irritation that no-one recognised what New York meant to her. 'I think so. Andrew will be here sometime next week so he can cover anything else.'

'Okay.' A beat. 'Sorry I went off at you. It's been a shit week and you've been great, and I'm sure your conference won't just be a piss-up.'

A lump filled Coral's throat, along with a chuckle. 'Thanks.'

'Thanks, Mum. Want to come round for an easy dinner?'

'That'd be lovely.'

'You still in the car?'

'Almost home. Will I head over now?'

'That'd be great, we can have a proper chat while Dan's bathing Oliver.'

Coral smiled. 'Sounds perfect.'

'Can you grab a couple of pizza bases and a bag of salad at the supermarket on the way?'

Coral rolled her eyes. 'Want wine too?'

Clearly missing the sarcasm, Summer said, 'That'd be great. See you soon.'

Mara

'COME ON, MAZ,' Pat said as Mara looked for a place to stop.

The invitation to join him for a drink while he waited for a couple of old schoolmates was tempting, but she'd stepped out of the shower fifteen minutes ago and was dressed for a night in with her feet up.

She'd woken this morning with an energy surge: cleaning and baking as though twenty guests were coming to stay for a week. She couldn't decide if it was a celebration at being free of Estelle or anxiety that she hadn't told Dad or Pat she'd screwed up her job. She'd even made a cheesecake and had dinner ready to go in the oven, hoping a meal together might create an opportunity, but for the first time in an age, Dad had plans. So did Pat; Mara's only option was to be taxi driver.

Pulling into the kerb, she ran a hand over her still-damp hair.

'You look fine,' Pat said.

She glanced at the old jeans and flannel shirt she'd thrown over a T-shirt.

'And it's not like you've got anyone else to hang out with.'

She made a face at him but eyed off the pub anyway. She'd been there before; there was nothing dressy about the place, and it was a chance to tell Pat she'd chucked in her job. 'Okay, one drink.'

She found a table in the beer garden while Pat went to the bar. The last time she'd been out socially with her brother was before he left for his farm job. Not that he was making an effort now, she thought, watching him stop to talk to someone. Pulling out her phone so she didn't look like she had no friends, she heard her name and glanced up.

'It *is* you.' Rylee was grinning as she stopped by Mara's table. 'I wasn't sure, with your head down.' She had bright red lips, long, dangly earrings and a half-full glass of beer.

Mara smiled back, aware her hair was wet, she had no make-up on and the collar of her shirt was frayed. 'Oh, um,' – at least she'd swapped her ugg boots for lace-ups – 'what are you doing here?'

'Same thing you're doing, I guess. Only I've got a drink. You want one?'

'Thanks, but I've got one coming.' When Rylee looked like she was in no hurry to leave, Mara said, 'Want to sit down?'

Sliding in opposite, Rylee said, 'I heard you had a big blow-up with your boss yesterday.'

Mara winced. 'Was everyone talking about it?'

Rylee shook her head. 'Estelle was in a weird mood in her afternoon session, so I asked around. Someone said there'd been shouting and you'd stormed out.'

'Oh, hey there.' It was Pat with Mara's drink, sliding it onto the table but keeping his eyes on Rylee, a big, stupid smile on his face. 'Patrick,' he said, with an upward lift of his chin, like he was trying to do casual.

Rylee tucked her hair behind an ear before holding her hand out for Patrick to shake. 'Rylee.'

Oh, sidelined already. Not friends then, not really. Mara had been there before. 'My little brother,' she said, stressing the *little* as she looked back at Pat. 'Rylee's Estelle's physio.'

'Sharing war stories?' he asked.

'Mara's the hero in that scenario,' Rylee said. 'I'd kill Estelle if I had Mara's job. Your sister's awesome.'

Mara's eyebrows slid up. Patrick glanced between them, as though he suspected there was a joke he was missing. 'Okay, right.' He glanced up and waved at someone he knew across the beer garden. 'Leave you to it then.' And took off again.

Mara wondered if Rylee would leave now there was an opening; she seemed like the kind of person who might aim for a crowd and talk to anyone who looked interesting. But she grinned back at Mara. 'Little brothers: so easy to mess with their heads.'

Mara laughed. 'You've got brothers?'

'Three. And two sisters. I'm the second oldest, first to leave Wagga.' She held up a fist. 'Striking a new path for others to follow.' She grinned again, making Mara feel a little daunted. 'Anyway. Estelle. Was it bad?'

'I think bad is understating it.'

'She just went through the motions in the gym. Didn't even berate me. I couldn't tell if she was pissed off or upset.'

'Probably still fuming. Or plotting my destruction.' Mara made a face. She wished she'd been able to talk to Dad or Pat, but she hadn't wanted to explain how Estelle had insulted them all, or admit that she'd ended up shouting at a seventy-two-year-old woman in a hospital bed. She hadn't been ready to see Dad's disappointment either, or listen to Pat's jokes.

But that didn't mean the argument wasn't still burning under her skin. Or that she couldn't unburden it with someone else, she thought as she looked back at Rylee. Someone who understood about Estelle; someone who thought Mara was awesome.

It was a relief to finally explain Estelle's marathon of fury, the shouting over the phone, the demands for Mara to print, scan, make coffee, call for painkillers. 'It was insane.'

'So you decided to leave?'

'That would have been the sensible thing to do.'

'Oh.'

'Yeah.'

As Mara took a long sip of her drink, she saw Pat across the beer garden giving her a thumbs up and felt a rare flash of anger at her brother. Did he think by coaxing her into a pub he'd sorted out her social life? Like he'd been back home for five minutes and knew what she needed? *Like he had any idea?* The thought was sudden and vehement, as though her outrage at Estelle had been extended to her brother: the unfairness of their assumptions, their relegation of her to *Girl who can do better.*

She was tempted to just leave, before catching the way Rylee was waiting for the rest of the story, the way she'd listened to the first half as though she was ticked off too. And suddenly Mara wanted to tell someone who might actually hear her.

'She called me a stupid girl,' Mara said. 'She insulted my family. She thinks I know nothing because all I've done is give up.' She drew a breath to go on, then just as suddenly, Rylee's intent listening made Mara reluctant to explain about all the ways she'd screwed up.

'Anyway,' she cleared her throat, 'I told her she was in no position to discuss my family when her own family was horrible.'

Rylee's eyebrows slid up a good three centimetres. It looked a lot like admiration, and then Mara couldn't resist telling her the best stuff, finally laughing as she said, 'Once I'd started, I couldn't stop. It just kept falling out of my mouth.'

Rylee sat back and grinned. 'And she chucked you out?'

'I chucked myself out. Told her she didn't deserve my care and concern, and said I wouldn't be back.'

Rylee said nothing for a long moment, smiling at Mara like she was insane and cool and brave. She raised her glass in a toast. 'Will you go back into the office to work?'

'I'm not sure I'll be asked back.'

'Hey, Rylee!' a girl called. 'We're heading off for pizza now.'

Rylee acknowledged her with a wave. 'One of my flatmates,' she told Mara. 'Hey, you want to come?'

'Oh,' Mara said, surprised and uneasy. She glanced at the group of nicely dressed people waiting for Rylee. 'Actually, I'm only here because I was dropping off my brother. Not really dressed for anything else.'

'Are you heading out later?'

'Oh, um, no.' Would Rylee think she was a Nigel no friends? 'Having a night in with a movie.'

'Oh yeah, what are you watching?'

'After this week, it'll either be a tear-jerker or kick-arse.'

'Go the kick-arse. You deserve it.'

'Rylee!'

'Coming,' she called, turning back to Mara. 'I won't see you at work now.'

'Not unless I get a degree in physiotherapy over the weekend.'

'Don't attempt that!' Rylee pulled a phone from her back pocket. 'Want to swap numbers? I can fill you in on Estelle's tantrums.'

'Like I need that,' Mara laughed, but held out her phone, feeling a wary tremor of joy at being asked.

A deeper, louder voice called, 'Rylee! Pizza Roma.'

This time, she stood. 'No idea where that is so I better go. Don't beat yourself up about Estelle. She's hard work.'

'Thanks.'

Then she was gone, and Mara told herself not to expect a call.

Mara

'Are you going to answer that?' Dad asked.

Mara's eyes snapped up from the name on her buzzing phone. 'No,' she said, flipping it face down on the kitchen counter. She did not want to speak to Estelle.

Dad raised his eyebrows. Now was the perfect time, Mara told herself. Tell him about walking out on her job while he was puttering about with breakfast cereal. Only, if he told her to go back and apologise? She didn't want to have that conversation. She was still recovering from the argument with Estelle.

'What have you got on today?' he said, clicking the kettle on.

'Might do the groceries, maybe wash the car.' No rush with all the free time on her hands.

'Can you take a minute to have a look at my orders?'

'What's the problem?'

'Just got a bit behind the last couple of weeks.'

She frowned. 'So you don't want me to just *look*.'

'If you've got a spare couple of hours.'

She sighed. It wasn't the first time he'd asked since she'd started at Collings; this time, she skipped the discussion about putting on someone to replace her. 'You've been out most nights this week, Dad. Of course you're going to get behind.'

'But you're so much faster at it than me, Maz.' He gave her

his best smile: *Go on, love. Help your old man out.*

She sighed again. 'I'll see.'

He glanced up from his muesli. 'Everything alright, Maz?'

Like a reminder, her phone pinged a notification that her caller had left a message. *Now,* she told herself. Explain to him how the argument had shaken her, how her future felt so uncertain. But she wasn't sure her dad could be reassuring without telling her what to do. 'Yeah, fine,' she said instead.

She waited until he'd taken his breakfast outside before checking her phone. Estelle had left a voice message that was three minutes and eighteen seconds long. Good grief, how long did it take to tell an underling to go screw themselves? Mara's finger hovered over the delete button, remembering Estelle was a litigation lawyer. Could she sue? For defamation? Elder abuse?

She listened to the message twice, and was still staring open-mouthed at her phone when Pat said from the fridge, 'Secret rehab business?'

Mara killed the screen and frowned at him. 'What?'

'That physio at the pub.' He raised his eyebrows. 'Saw you exchanging numbers.'

Her phone pinged again and, checking the screen to avoid Pat's gaze, her face heated. It was Rylee, and Mara was embarrassed at how hopeful that made her feel. Remembering Rylee's *easy to mess with their heads,* Mara said to Patrick, 'Don't be an arse.' She stuffed her phone in her pocket and took her coffee with her.

☕

Rylee: *How was your night in? What did you watch?*

Mara: *The Brave One. Jodie Foster being a vigilante. Made me feel okay about not killing Estelle* ☺ *How was your night out?*

Rylee: *Good movie choice. Not too big a night. What are you doing with your morning?*

It was a relief to tell someone: *Staring at my phone in shock. Just got a voice message from Estelle. She asked me to come back!!*

Wha . . .?

I know!!

What are you going to do?

Stare at my phone some more. Hope your morning's going better?

Been for a swim. Omg freezing! I'm up for a coffee if you want to vent.

Did she? With a new, maybe friend? Who might brush her off if she got angsty. Mara didn't want to like Rylee too much, just in case.

She started to tap *Thanks but no thanks* and stopped. There had been too many things she hadn't talked about since Mum died, that she hadn't been able to share without unloading everything, without upsetting someone else. She could tell Rylee about this, though. She'd experienced Estelle's sharp tongue. She could listen to the voice message and commiserate, discuss, have a laugh – perhaps all three – without needing to know everything. And Mara really needed Estelle's voice to stop going round and round in her head.

Mara: *Which beach?*

Andie

ANDIE SLOWED HER walking pace to answer Vivian's call.

'I'm dropping Camille at the beach with some friends,' Viv said. 'Meet you there for a coffee?'

'Thanks, but I'll pass.'

'You passed on the Saturday morning coffee crowd yesterday too. Everything okay?'

Not really, not after the movie. 'Yeah, I'm fine.'

There was a hesitation. 'It's Sunday, Andie. There are lots of things to do and people to keep you busy.' It was concern. And with reason, since filling the weekend with company was usually Andie's first priority.

'I'm going up to the hospital.'

'Andie.' It was low and uneasy.

'Viv, I'm fine.'

'Okay, well . . . you could do both. Have coffee at the beach on your way to the hospital.' There was a smile in her tone. *Come on, we love doing coffee on the weekend!*

It was true, they did, but Andie had spent the night being mad at Ben for talking her into that movie, then mad at herself for falling apart, and at the concussion for shaking everything loose in her brain. By early morning, she just wanted to clear the air so she could keep visiting without the fear of crying or questions.

And she didn't want to discuss any of that with Vivian. They'd been friends for a thousand years and, like the natural way of things, they would end up talking about it, and Viv was already concerned about Andie visiting Ben.

'Not today,' Andie said.

'Did something happen?' Of course Vivian would pick that up; and she would only worry if Andie pretended otherwise.

'We watched a movie yesterday and I got upset at the ending.'

'Andie.' Low and uneasy again.

'It's fine, I'm fine. But Ben's having a rough time and I don't want him feeling bad because I was upset.'

'You need to look after yourself.'

'That's why I'm going to talk to Ben.'

'You're not responsible for him.'

'Viv.'

'It's just . . . You keep going back there.'

'It won't be for long. He'll be going back to Perth in a couple of weeks.'

'You said you wanted to move on from the accident, not have it going round and round in your head.'

'It's not.' Okay, the movie incident had, but not like after Zack. Last night, there'd been a kind of need to make peace with it. 'Not like that.'

'Okay, but I'm worried about you.'

Andie's gaze flicked upwards with sudden impatience. 'I'm fine. Really. Enjoy the beach. Talk to you later.'

☕

'I wasn't sure you'd come today,' Ben said when Andie had pulled up a chair beside his recliner.

'Sorry about yesterday.' She concentrated on stowing her sunglasses in their case. 'The movie caught me off guard.'

He nodded, tapped a thumb on the bundle of Sunday papers she'd brought. 'It's your business, and I'm not sure it was just the movie, but whatever it is, I don't want to be making it worse.'

'You're not.'

'I feel like I keep treading on something that upsets you.'

'It's not you, it's me.'

'That old line.'

She smiled, glad he wasn't asking, but uncomfortable about the way he was watching her, like he wanted to understand. 'I think the accident, the bump on my head, kind of shook a bunch of things up for me. But I'm okay. Just . . . dealing with some old stuff.'

He nodded again, but seemed unconvinced.

Before he could say any more, Andie said, 'Caper?'

'Sure.'

'Garden?'

It was Sunday, the nursing staff was minimal and Ben didn't want to wait for someone to help him into his wheelchair, so Andie followed his instructions on where to place it and how to help. She hovered beside him, close enough to feel the heat of his effort, his hand grazing hers as he searched for the armrest; his faltering, painstaking progress reminding her how far from recovery he was. How the last thing he needed was to feel responsible for her wounds.

Outside, Ben tipped back his head. 'Ahhhh, fresh air.'

Pushing his chair across the forecourt of the hospital, Andie said, 'It's going to be warm today.'

'Bring on summer.'

'Do you go to the beach in Perth?'

'It's my natural habitat. I grew up near Cottesloe Beach. My parents still live there.'

Andie slowed as they reached the garden, and as they ambled along the path, Ben talked about growing up in the waves, waiting for the Fremantle Doctor to blow in and doing the Rottnest Channel Swim. 'The beaches were a big drawcard for the Newcastle Uni job,' he said. 'I got in one swim before the accident, possibly that's all I'll get while I'm here.'

'Staying in Newcastle isn't an option now?'

'I've already missed the first month of my uni contract and at this point, I've no idea when I'll be able to get around campus or how much of my job I can do remotely. I think it's fairer on everyone to let them find someone else.'

She'd expected that, not the small tug of disappointment in her stomach. 'Makes sense. When will you go?'

'It's complicated.' He pointed her towards another bend in the path. 'It comes down to when the doctor will clear me to fly, whether I can get a place at a rehab hospital in Perth and how I'll manage the long flight and connections.'

'Will you stay at Hepburn House until you leave?'

'It depends on how quickly my ribs heal so I can get onto crutches, and how long insurance will cover in-patient treatment.'

'It must be frustrating.'

'Yeah, although . . .' He didn't finish the thought.

'It could be worse?' she suggested.

Standing behind him, Andie saw the tilt of his head. 'Your company has taken the sting out of it.'

'Except when I burst into tears and bolt.'

'Even then.' Ben pointed. 'That's our balcony,' he said, as though it was Andie's room too.

'Your room is around the other side.' She followed the arc of the path, ducking under the drooping foliage of a weeping gum, the strappy leaves of agapanthus slap-slapping against the spokes of Ben's wheels.

'There's Val.' Ben lifted an arm to wave. 'And there's Estelle's coffee machine.' Andie stopped below the French doors to Ben's room.

'Is that a bench seat over there?' He pointed into the foliage.

'Yep, among the daffodils.'

'We need to hack a path.'

'We do?'

'Caper rules: hack a path to somewhere amazing.'

'Like a bench?' she said doubtfully.

'Like a bench!'

It turned out there was a bark-covered track and Andie could push Ben right up to the seat. 'How's this?'

Glancing at the daffodils surrounding them, he said, 'Feels like we've been absorbed into the garden.'

'It does a bit.' Andie tucked her hands under her thighs, taking in the garden and the breeze that sighed through the trees.

'Is it about your husband?'

Ben's tone was gentle and thoughtful, and she turned to him with the beginnings of a smile before his words hit like a jolt of electricity. 'My . . . what?'

'You told me about him the night we had dinner.'

Andie turned away.

'You said he died suddenly. That you'd only been married a few months.'

She frowned back at him. 'I said that?'

'It's not true?'

'No, it is. I just . . . don't talk about it.'

'I guess it's not something you'd normally launch into with someone you've just met.'

'No, I mean I never talk about it.' How much had she told him? Why had she told him anything?

'To anyone?' Ben asked.

She studied him a moment, looking for judgement, advice, concern. But his question only seemed to be clarification. Her answer needed to close the subject. 'No.'

'Because it's upsetting?'

Andie looked away again, wanting to close the door he'd cracked open. Only, here among the dappled shade and the daffodils, and the realisation that she must have trusted him once to talk about Zack, leaving it open didn't feel so awful right now.

'It's . . . It – *he*,' Andie swallowed hard on the name she didn't say, 'feels like a short, intense and intensely painful chapter in my life that will get easier to live with if I leave it alone.'

Ben nodded, like it made sense, like it was her life and what would he know? Then some more, like he had a thought he wanted to share. *Not advice*, Andie silently begged. *Don't ruin it with that.*

'Some chapters are really fucked up, right?' he said.

A grateful smile started on her lips.

'If it helps,' he said, 'you weren't upset when you told me about him.'

She looked at Ben, sensing the truth in what he said, that their conversation had been safe and uncomplicated. 'What were we talking about?'

'Life. Leaving home and coming home. Starting new chapters. I was starting one in Newcastle, you said you were too, kind of.' He picked up a leaf that had dropped onto his thigh. 'You said your husband died two years ago, that it was sudden, that it had been hard starting again. But you were. He would want you to. You would want yourself to, if you could go back to a time before it had hurt so much.'

Andie's throat tightened at the words that sounded like hers. It felt like Ben had listened, not judged, not told her to be strong or to have hope or visualise a brighter future. 'Is that when we agreed not to talk about our sad stories?'

'Sometime around then.'

'What was your sad line?'

A nod, like he understood she didn't want to be the only one. 'That I'd had to make difficult decisions for my family, that my choices had hurt people. A relationship, my career. We agreed that we were fine and everyone was comfortable with fine, but fine could be a bit shit, really.'

She smiled. He smiled back. Maybe they did it like that the first time, too.

Ben said, 'I've no idea what you're going through, Andie, and I'm sorry that you are. You are a lovely person and I wish all good things for you; stuff like strength and sass and good socks and excellent movies and buckets of ice-cream, if those things float your boat.'

'Good socks?'

'Shorthand for something cosy.'

She smiled again, glad he'd wanted to bestow comfort, not the promise of happy things to come.

'For what it's worth,' Ben said, 'you know my dad has all these theories on life and death?'

She nodded, willing him not to try to cheer her up.

'I can hear Dad's voice in my head right now.' Ben held up a hand to her, seeing her alarm about where he was going with this. 'I don't know what you're going through or what your husband was like, and this isn't advice of any kind, just the words of someone who's been facing death for a long time and doesn't mind telling other people how to deal with it.' Ben did his sweet, fond smile. 'I wish I could do it in his voice, because he manages this funny, poignant, don't-fuck-it-up kind of thing. Anyway, he's like, *Blubber like idiots if you have to, just don't leave me out of the conversation. You know that's really going to piss me off.'*

Ben made a face, then looked away. Andie wasn't sure if he was leaving her with his dad's thought or giving himself a moment, but his father's words settled on her skin like a lotion, cool and soothing where it touched. *Don't leave me out of the conversation.*

Zack. His name came to her with a smile. His smile. His eyes, his laughter, his love. And she felt it not as a knife slicing open her soul, but a hot, deep ache of memory.

'Is that a frog?'

Andie blinked. Cleared her throat. 'What?'

'A frog.' He pointed at the daffodils beside his chair.

She leaned closer, spotted the patch of lime green he'd seen and pulled in a surprised breath. Careful not to scare it away, she gently shifted a leaf aside to reveal a shiny, bright . . .

They laughed in stereo.

'Yep, that's a frog,' Ben said.

Andie picked it up and turned it over. 'Made in China.'

'Fell off someone's mantlepiece?' Ben suggested.

'Looking for Miss Piggy?'

Andie set it on Ben's open palm and he examined it like it might hop off at any moment. 'A treasure from our caper.'

Mara

'I CAN'T BELIEVE you went for a swim in September,' Mara said, setting two coffees on a table under the Nobbys Beach pavilion. 'It has to be twenty-five degrees before I go in.'

Rylee clutched her coffee like she needed the warmth. She had a beanie on and was rugged up in a fleece-lined jacket. 'No beaches in Wagga. I feel like it's my duty to swim. Even if I get hypothermia.'

'How long have you been in Newcastle?'

'Three months. I moved here when I got the job at Hepburn. How about you?'

'We moved here from Armidale when I was sixteen.' Almost nine years ago, not that Mara felt like a local. She didn't want Rylee asking about the friends she didn't have, so she added, 'I was in Canberra for a while too, then working for my dad when I came back. I started the job at Collings three months ago too; I still feel like I'm settling in.'

'I thought I'd meet a bunch of people through my flatmates, but they're both nurses and we're all working different shifts, so I hardly know anyone. It's been nice meeting you. Hope you don't mind a needy new friend wanting to hang out.'

It sounded genuine, Mara wanted it to be, but she'd been burned before. Deciding it was better not to leap to a conclusion either way, she waved it off with a hand, trying to look nonchalant. Pulling her phone out, she changed the subject. 'Sure you want to listen to this?'

'Absolutely!' Rylee took Mara's mobile, listened to Estelle's voicemail, then said, 'That's a serious apology. Do you think she wrote a script?'

'That's just how Estelle speaks.'

Rylee frowned for a second. 'Oh yeah, good point.'

They shared a knowing look that made them both laugh out loud.

'I think something different every time I listen to it,' Mara said.

'Well, she packed a lot into it. I think I was too stunned to hear much after the first bit.'

'Want to hear it again?'

'Let's put it on speaker.'

Setting the phone on the table, they both leaned on their forearms, heads close as it played. It felt like teamwork.

☕

This is Estelle Collings. I'm ringing regarding our heated discussion on Friday. I've . . . I would like to apologise. My comments were unjustified and cruel. I have a tendency to lash out. That's no excuse, but I would like you to know I regret having lashed out at you so callously. If it's any consolation, I rarely apologise and am only leaving this evidence on your phone as I assume you will not answer a call from me.

So there you are, proof of my failure to whomever you choose to share this with.

I congratulate you on your impressive eloquence in expressing your thoughts about me. You are entirely within your rights to refuse to return. I, however, having considered our time together, can say that I enjoyed your company. And your ideas. And yes, your kindnesses.

I expect a change of heart is unlikely, but if you were to accept my apology, I will commit to being respectful. At least, as you put it, within the limits of my flawed upbringing. I say that whether you return to work or simply to visit a bitter older woman now contemplating her legacy.

If our paths don't cross again, I think you would make an excellent lawyer, if you can find a way to finish. I wish you the best.

☕

'What do you think this time?' Rylee asked.

Mara slid her hands into the warmth of her pockets. 'I think the apology is genuine, but the rest . . . I can't decide if she's mocking me or saying I had a point.'

'She sounds sincere when she says you'd make a good lawyer.'

Mara sat back, reluctant to feel any satisfaction in Estelle's attempt at a compliment.

'Were you studying law?' Rylee asked. When Mara nodded, she said, 'What does "find a way to finish" mean?'

'I dropped out. Twice.'

'Glutton for punishment?'

'Something like that.' Mara made light of it before realising she didn't want Rylee making assumptions too. Rylee was a physio, she must have worked hard at uni, and Mara *hadn't* just given up. 'Actually, no. I was doing Arts Law at Newcastle the first time and . . .' She tucked back a strand of her blonde hair. 'Then International Law at Canberra Uni and . . .' Her gaze drifted away as she searched for a simple explanation. 'Every time I started, life dropped a bomb in front of me.' Maybe that sounded like an excuse too.

'How much time have you got?' Rylee asked.

Mara hesitated, her face starting to heat. 'Do you need to leave?' Was she bored already?

'No, I've got an hour and a half before a video call with my dad. It's his Sunday afternoon thing since I've been away.'

'That's nice.'

'I know.' She grinned, like he was the best. Cocking her head towards the path to the next beach, Rylee said, 'It's good to walk and talk, and I love the view round that headland. We can warm up with some hot chips.'

Mara waited at the handrail above the sand while Rylee bought the chips, trying to remember if she'd ever had a video call with her dad.

Rylee returned with two cups of steaming chips. The tide was in and the rocks below the walkway were dark shapes beneath the water. Several walkers had stopped to point towards the horizon and Mara and Rylee joined them, looking for the telltale splash of whales on their migration south for the summer.

'These bombs that dropped while you were at uni,' Rylee said as they started walking again. 'Are you okay now?'

It was nice that was her first question; Mara had suspected the suggestion to walk was an excuse to change the subject. Perhaps that was why she shared more than she'd planned. 'My mum got breast cancer when I was in second year at Newcastle Uni.'

The look that Rylee sent her seemed filled with both compassion and respect. Maybe it was something she'd learned in her job, but it made Mara keep talking.

'She'd had it before. It's why we moved to Newcastle, so she could be closer to treatment. It wasn't as though Mum and Dad had never thought about coming here, and it seemed positive, planning Dad's new business and a house they were going to do up.'

Mara had left all her friends a five-hour train ride away. She'd wanted to do law even then, and getting the marks she needed while she helped Mum through treatment had taken priority over socialising. Several life-changing events later, she'd lost contact with those friends and never figured out how to make up the shortfall.

'Anyway, Mum had chemo and surgery and was fine for two years. The second time, the chemo was awful and Dad was trying to keep the business afloat, so I left uni to look after her. When she got the terminal diagnosis, I didn't go back.'

'You nursed her?'

'Yeah.' Mara kept her eyes on the beautiful old ocean baths ahead of them. 'We hired all the equipment, and except for a few trips to hospital, she managed to stay at home until, well . . .'

She didn't finish, but Rylee got the gist, glancing briefly at her but saying nothing, as though the moment needed space.

They stayed on the path beside the beach, dodging Sunday bike riders and family groups. When the walkway widened again, Rylee said, 'When did you go to Canberra?'

Too soon. 'When we all thought Mum was going to get better, I told her I'd been thinking about International Law. When we knew she was dying, I started talking about staying home to help Dad and Pat, but she didn't want me to put my life on hold. She got really adamant about not wanting her disease to hold me back from my dreams. That's how she used to put it.'

'She sounds amazing.'

'She was.'

As they reached Newcastle Beach, they stopped at the handrail, forearms on the crossbar as they looked out at the waves. 'Mum passed away in the May and I started in July for the second semester.' Mara closed her eyes, remembering the darkness she'd felt back then. 'I didn't understand about grief and how it could hang about, letting you get on with your life until you just couldn't.'

She'd only meant to give the facts, not how they'd hurt her, and she shot Rylee an uneasy glance, not sure how she'd react. Rylee looked back at her, nodding as though she was okay with whatever Mara needed to say.

'It was like a slow-motion slide,' Mara said. 'Because I started late, I never felt like I fitted in. I came home for Christmas and pretended it was great, feeling guilty for leaving Dad and Pat for something I wasn't even enjoying. My grades were pretty good, then they were average, then it was just a struggle.'

Rylee gave her a soft nudge, as though she was saying it was okay and shit and understandable. *That* felt like friendship.

'The next semester started better. I got to know some of the first-year students in my dorm, got close to one in particular. We were just friends, but good friends. Soulmates, I thought. Then . . .' Mara pushed her hands into her pockets. 'He left.

Dropped out and went overseas without even saying goodbye.' She glanced away, not wanting to think about it again. 'By then I was failing. Then Dad had a heart attack, so I came home.' She shrugged as though it was as simple as that. 'Pat was doing the HSC so I stayed to help them both. Then I stayed to help Dad in the business, and then I just stayed. I got the job at Collings and ended up with Estelle.'

Neither of them spoke for a while, both watching the waves barrel onto the shore.

'How's your dad?' Rylee finally asked.

'He's good. Pat took a gap year, like me. He's starting uni next semester. And I'm deciding what to do next, otherwise known as unemployed.'

'You could go back to uni.'

The thought made Mara's stomach twist. She pushed away from the railing, started walking again. 'Uni got pretty dark towards the end. I . . . wasn't great and . . . it was just really tough.'

'Are you okay?'

No-one had ever asked her that. No-one had ever known to ask, she reminded herself. 'Yeah, I am. Thanks.' Although giving up on her dream still felt like another version of grief. 'But going back to uni? It just feels like asking for trouble.'

'As in, waiting for another bomb to drop?'

'Exactly.'

'You know it doesn't work that way?'

'Yeah, but still.'

'So what will you do tomorrow?'

Now they were back to that. 'Estelle kept going on about dropping out twice. She said I was undisciplined, that I'd never get anywhere because I was too nice. I don't think she's right; I feel as though everything I've started has been cut short. I *want* to finish something. I wanted to see out the two weeks or however long with Estelle. She's a nightmare and it's not what I want to be doing, but I kind of need to prove to myself that I can see something through to the end.' Mara huffed a frustrated sigh. 'I haven't finished anything since I left school.'

'You nursed your mum until the end,' Rylee reminded her.

'Yeah, I did.' Mara was proud of that. 'Only, Mum would be disappointed if that was all I achieved. *I'm* disappointed. And my resume is starting to look like a long list of excuses.'

'So you want to go back tomorrow?'

Mara shrugged. 'Part of me wants to make a point and finish what I started. Another part of me wants to make a different point and refuse to go back to someone who treated me badly.'

'Pros and cons?'

She'd been hoping for: *Oh yeah, you need to finish something* or *God, you can't go back to that situation.* It's what Dad or Pat would have done. That was why she hadn't talked to them, Mara reminded herself.

'If I go back tomorrow, will Estelle think she's won? That I'm a pushover? That she can treat me like shit and just apologise if I get upset? I mean, I don't need to finish badly enough to go through another week of insults and arguments.'

'And if you don't go back?'

'My dad feels like he's got a stake in my job at Collings. Vaughn Collings has been a longtime client, and if I just walk away, Dad'll feel like it reflects on him.'

'Does he know about last week?'

'Some of it. I think he thinks I'm overreacting and I should just stick it out. If I don't go back, he'll end up wanting me to do his books again. Hard to say no when I've got nothing else to go to.'

Stepping apart to let some runners through, they were passing the rocks under the tide again before Rylee said, 'I reckon it comes down to what you need to do for yourself. And when you've decided that, it's how you manage other people's expectations.'

Mara frowned at Rylee, not sure what she meant.

'You could tell Estelle you won't stay if she can't treat you with respect. Or tell your dad you can't work for him because you need to find something that'll give you a career.'

'Oh right. Easy,' Mara laughed. Terrifying in Estelle's case, emotionally harrowing when it came to her dad.

'Nah, you'll be great. Apparently, you're impressively eloquent.'

Mara laughed again, then turned to face the ocean.

What did *she* need to do?

When had she ever asked herself that?

Part 6

Pain Management

Coral

CORAL WAS EXHAUSTED. She could feel it like a weight on top of her before she'd even rolled over and checked the time. It felt like a hangover, but she hadn't had a drink last night. Or dinner, unless Vegemite toast and a cup of tea counted.

It was all she'd been capable of making after she'd taken Oliver home and cleaned up the mess of a day with a still-isolated three-year-old. She could have done without another layer of tiredness, but she hadn't been able to resist the lure of time spent with her grandson, especially when it also gave Summer a day with her husband – because when had Coral ever been given that luxury? This morning, though, as Coral swung herself to the edge of the bed, her back and knees complained, and her head hurt where she'd bumped it half a dozen times. When had dining-table cubby houses got so small?

How had she had enough energy to bring up two kids on her own? More to the point, where had all that energy gone?

She opened her laptop but she was onto her second coffee before she could make sense of the changes she'd made to the To-Do List late last night. After her day with Oliver she'd been too tired to start cooking or packing, so she'd recalculated some of her time-frames, pinching and squeezing to fit in a casserole here or a slow cooker prep there. Looking at it now, she wondered when Wonder Woman would be turning up.

Still in her dressing gown, she sat at the kitchen bench and worked the list over again, her stomach churning and her shoulders tight as she checked she had included everything, and in a workable order. She went over it again in the shower, conjuring the whiteboard in her head and having a moment of panic when she couldn't remember what she was meant to be doing after the meeting with the social worker this morning. Surely she couldn't have left an hour free.

'Of course not,' she said out loud when she checked the list again and saw she was making a stop at Summer's on the way to the office.

Fast and edgy seemed to be her default pace today, and she speed-walked the pathway to the hospital entrance, gasping when the coffee van wasn't there. It was too early for Alby, she realised, chastising herself for not grabbing a coffee on her way in.

'What's wrong?' Val asked when Coral arrived out of breath.

'Nothing. Why?'

'You look like you're in a flap.'

'I'm not in a flap, I'm busy,' she snapped. She took a breath and put her hands on her hips, heart pounding. 'Sorry, I've been rushing.' She dumped her bag, pulled up a chair and pushed a smile onto her face as she sat. 'Okay, I'm here, I can relax now.'

Except Val was confused about why Coral had arrived so early, who they were meeting and when Summer was having her baby. Coral explained and recapped, moving about the room as she talked, tidying the bed, folding a blanket, fluffing pillows, inspecting the wardrobe for clothes that needed washing and the bedside table for things that needed replenishing. Then, caught on a treadmill of conversation, filling time before the social worker came and agitated about her overcrowded To-Do List, words just kept flowing out of her mouth. About building cubby houses and making cookies, tea and toast for dinner, dinner at Summer's that she'd had to buy on the way, Jessica and her bridal angst, Rodney and his drill heads.

'You can't just give it to Australia Post to sort out?' Val asked, as though the sensible thing would be to hand the job to someone who knew what to do.

'What, pop it in the mail and see if a postie can get it to Stockholm?' Hearing her voice loaded with sarcasm, she slid into a chair beside Val, smiling in an attempt to take the sting out of it. 'It's my job to manage complicated deliveries.'

'Well, you did take that job.'

'I needed that job.'

'If you'd put more effort into supporting Richard, it might never have come to that.'

Coral sat back in her chair and blinked. What was she thinking, being so unguarded with her mother?

'You know *I* didn't need to work until after your father died,' Val said.

'No, and you never had your own money. And when he died, he left you in debt.' A string of bad investments, loans at stupid rates, purchases he didn't need.

'Your father *tried*, Coral.'

'Did he though?'

'He wasn't an easy man to live with, but we managed to muck along alright in the end.'

Coral's father had cultivated a hearty good nature that was camouflage for an undercurrent of self-importance, alcohol and black moods. Coral remembered him as overbearing and insensitive; a terrible husband and a dismissive father. These days, there were terms like domestic violence and coercive control. Coral didn't think he fit those definitions, but there were lots of ways to hurt your family. 'That's how you see it now?'

'We got *on* with things, Coral. I expected you would have learned something from that.'

She said it like it was sage advice. As though it was better to put up than be alone. As though Val hadn't just rewritten her own history, then turned it into a criticism of her daughter. Coral's heart thumped so hard she felt light-headed.

'Sorry I'm late.' It was Tori. 'I got chatting with another patient and his wife. Such a lovely couple, they've been married fifty years next year.'

Coral stood as the young woman came in, but she only had words for herself. *Take a breath*, she instructed. *Don't let your head explode in front of the social worker.*

'Right, well.' Tori cleared her throat. 'Val, how are you?'

If Coral hadn't cancelled a flight to New York to be here for this meeting and didn't have a thousand other things waiting for her attention, she might have enjoyed the fifteen minutes of pleasantries. But a vein in her neck kept pulsing and her legs felt like jelly as she paced about, and she broke into a sweat at Val's recap of a happy marriage and a life well lived that Coral didn't even recognise.

Turning to Coral, Tori asked. 'And what's the situation with your holiday to New York?'

'It's a *work* trip.'

Tara made a note in her file. 'Are you often away on work trips?'

'Two or three times a year.'

Another scribble that made Coral wonder if she was getting a black mark against her name. 'And you were able to cancel this one?'

'No, I changed my flights.' Then, not wanting to sound like the callous daughter, she added, 'I'm going to miss the first few days of a conference, but will get there in time for my presentation.'

'Oh, you're a speaker.' Tori perked up, like Coral might be the source of another fun client story. 'What field are you in?'

'Logistics. Complex and sensitive deliveries.'

'Oh.'

It's thrilling for some people!

'Okay, well,' Tori checked her notes, 'I see Val has been booked for a second round of rehab.'

'She has?' Coral said. When had that assessment been done?

'She has,' Tori confirmed. She turned to Val. 'So you'll be with us for a while longer.' Then to Coral, 'Less worry for you while you're away.'

Val lifted her chin as though she was an honoured guest. Coral felt bad that worrying hadn't been part of her travel plan. Tori closed her file.

'Wait,' Coral said, 'what about the review of her home assistance package? We're meant to be doing that today.'

Two minutes later, Coral gathered Val's washing into a bag, her heart thumping and nausea sitting in the pit of her stomach like gravel. She brushed her lips across her mother's cheek and hitched her handbag to her shoulder. It wasn't Val's fault the meeting had been a complete waste of time. She sent a wave from the door and turned into the corridor, pausing out of sight to pull in a deep, seething breath.

It also wasn't Tori's fault that she wasn't the person responsible for doing the review of Val's home assistance. Or that her role in it was only to pass the information on to someone else. Or that her best guess for when an assessment might happen was *sometime next week, probably.* Coral's teeth were clenched tight as she passed the nurses' station. It was a good thing, Coral tried to tell herself, that Val was the social worker's first priority, and that she'd made Val feel seen and heard in the discussion. Coral appreciated that, she *did.* But she'd *changed* her flight to *New York.* For a meeting that provided no new information *at all.* That could have been done *over the phone.* That had cost Coral fifty-thousand brain cells *in stress.*

She turned into the hospital foyer and stopped to breathe, suddenly desperately thirsty. And hot. She stepped to one side, set down the bag of Val's laundry and sucked in some more air, hearing the social worker's voice in her head once again.

'Your mum has told me how much she appreciates the cooking you do for her. I hear you make a mean pumpkin soup.'

Accept the compliment, Coral coached herself. Be grateful Val remembered the soup. But it was too hard today. Today, all she could think was, *Why couldn't Mum tell me she appreciated the bloody soup herself?* A single, casual mention of her 'mean pumpkin soup' and Coral might not have minded losing half a million brain cells over a pointless bloody meeting. Or changing her flights. Or not being halfway to New York by now.

She couldn't breathe in here.

Urgency carried her out the front entrance. The sight of the coffee van made her heart pound.

Alby had three cups on the go when she got there, but he lifted his chin at her. 'Your regular?'

'Yes, please.' Now. Quickly. Before she imploded.

No, she was fine, she told herself. She was standing in the pleasant shade of a van that produced excellent coffee. She was taking deep breathes, she was rocking back and forth on her heels, she was waiting patiently and she wasn't losing her cool.

She checked her watch, and as her mind did an involuntary calculation of where she might have been right now – somewhere over the Pacific – a rush of nausea swept through her.

The next instant her heart was pounding and she felt like she was breathing through a straw. She took a few wobbly steps to the side of the van, flattening a hand against it as sweat broke out across her scalp and under her arms and in the valley between her breasts.

Another customer collected his order, giving her a sideways glance as she used her sleeve to mop perspiration from her throat.

She heard Alby call, 'You right there?'

She was bending forward, braced by his van, wondering if she was going to throw up. She wanted to nod, she wanted to be fine, but her lips were tingling and her legs were shaking. She couldn't get enough air to fill her lungs and if she didn't sit down she was going to fall.

There was a tight, hot pain in her chest and she was suddenly very, very scared.

'Coral.' She could tell it was Alby by the waft of coffee aroma. His voice was calm, gentle and close to her ear. 'Breathe, Coral.'

'I just need to sit down,' she whispered, too scared to suggest a crash cart.

'Can you make it to the gutter with me?'

She moved like a marathon runner who'd finished the course without drinking enough fluids. Fingers were pressed into the pulse in her neck. There were voices and feet around her, sweat in her hair and her insides were trembling. Alby said in his calm, gentle voice, 'Deep breaths, Coral. That's it. Have you got pain? In the chest? Anywhere else? What else is going on? Deep breaths, that's it.'

Alby was a barista, not a doctor, but right now, she didn't care. Was it a heart attack? A stroke?

Not now, not here, not with so much to do. Not before she got to New York.

Not there either.

'There's a doctor coming.' The woman with the curly hair from across the hall was sitting on the kerb beside her now. 'Handy to be in the car park of a hospital when this happened,' she said, rubbing Coral's back.

Blood pressure cuff. More fingers on her pulse. Someone asked what she'd been doing. Was she on medication? Was the pain easing?

She managed to walk to a wheelchair. She hadn't peed her pants. She didn't want to die.

Mara

WHEN MARA WALKED through the door on Monday morning, Estelle looked over from her recliner, opened her mouth to speak and said nothing. Mara thought she saw surprise and relief, although it was the hint of satisfaction in her expression that made the anxiety in Mara's stomach tighten. But she was determined not to fill the silence with mundane pleasantries.

She passed Estelle her coffee without a word, set her handbag on the bed, straightened her jacket and tucked her hair behind her ears. 'Firstly, I want to say something.' There was a nervous quaver in her voice, so she took a quick sip of coffee before going on. 'I didn't come back because I thought I should or because I'm kind or because I felt sorry for you. I came back for myself. Because I want to finish this assignment in a way that doesn't disadvantage my prospects for another job. And because I need to finish something. You were right about that, but it wasn't a new concept. I needed to do it for myself well before you told me.'

'I see,' said Estelle.

'I appreciate the message you left me yesterday. For my own part, I apologise for shouting, but I won't apologise for what I said.'

'I would be disappointed if you did.'

'I . . .' *Disappointed?* 'Oh.' She hesitated. 'Well, I, um . . .'

260

Estelle's lips pursed in irritation, presumably because Mara still couldn't finish a sentence. But her eyebrows were raised in not unkind anticipation, an odd mixture for Estelle, although Mara wasn't sure if it was a good or bad omen.

'I haven't come back to continue where we left off. I accept that my work at times needs correction, but I won't stay if you are rude or insulting. I also won't accept personal criticism of me or my family. If you have nothing positive to say about my family, I request that you don't say anything at all.'

'Is that all?'

Mara pulled back her shoulders. 'Yes.'

'Then I accept your conditions.'

'Oh.' That was . . . easy. 'Thank you.'

'Now for my condition.'

Perhaps too easy.

'I request that you continue to speak your mind. I am not interested in having a mouse for an assistant. You have proved yourself capable of roaring and I expect you to continue. Is that clear?'

'Oh, I . . . yes?'

'You have something to say?'

'Well, I . . . You want me to argue with you?'

'I'd prefer you didn't shout, although I am aware I have a tendency to do so myself, but, in a sense, yes. I'd rather a discussion than talking to a wall. There are any number of people who can be walls, it's not a skill to aspire to. There is a time and place for acquiescence, which I believe you capable of discerning. The rest of the time, I require you to think, ask questions and speak up.'

'And finish my sentences?'

Estelle's pursed lips twitched. 'That also. Now go away and look busy before I'm tempted to be amused.'

Huddled over her laptop on the balcony, Mara's shoulders heaved with silent laughter.

☕

'I can't find any invoicing records for the list of clients I've been working on.' Mara stood at the French doors, her laptop balanced on her forearm.

Estelle's cheeks were red after her gym session, but there were dark smudges under her eyes, and annoyance in her voice. 'Why are you looking for invoices?'

Not a mouse. 'I thought, since I was organising the case files, I'd make sure the records were complete.' It was make-work until Estelle gave her something else to do. 'There are time sheets but no invoicing details. I can't even find reference numbers.'

'That's right.'

'Would the invoicing be on the Collings database or did you have your own back then?'

'Those clients were never billed.'

She frowned. 'As in, pro bono work?'

'Exactly.'

'Oh, wow.' She remembered the many hours involved in most of the cases. 'I didn't know Collings did that.'

'They don't generally. My father never approved. I was required to record my hours, in case my billable hours dropped because of it. Of course, I made sure all but the unavoidable was done in personal time.'

'Oh, wow,' she said again, with a different kind of awe. 'That's a lot of personal time.'

'We won every case. Which was a thorn in my father's side.' Both statements were said with pride.

'Go you, Estelle.'

'Yes, well.' She fluffed her hair. 'Some very interesting cases among that group.'

'I read through some of them. The doctor from Iran, the man in the train accident, and that woman with the bent toes.' The kind of cases she'd once dreamed about working on.

Estelle glanced at her watch. 'Perhaps we could have some coffee now.'

'Why is the coffee machine on the balcony, by the way?'

'I had it moved there over the weekend so Val and Ben could help themselves.'

Mara's eyebrows lifted, but she held back the *Go you* this time, not sure Estelle was ready for her kindness to be cheered.

Mara had thought that was the end of the pro bono discussion, but while Mara was filling their cups, Estelle began the story of the patient who'd had the toes of both feet straightened by separate doctors in a simultaneous procedure. One foot was great, the other was so badly damaged she would never get full use of it again. Estelle had met her through a paying client, who had asked advice for a friend who had no resources for a lawyer.

It was fascinating: the dual surgery, the doctor and his insurer, the patient and, as it turned out, other patients who'd also been subjected to the surgeon's incompetency. Estelle's telling of the case was peppered with her own brilliance, but Mara figured it was possible she deserved it, since the client got a payout that well and truly covered her pain and distress. Since Estelle had told Mara to ask questions, she did; politely breaking into the monologue to confirm specifics and legal issues, engrossed by the details. They could have had three coffees by the time Estelle reached the bit about attending the woman's seventieth birthday party a few years later.

Despite her enthusiasm as she recounted the case, Estelle was pasty-faced by the time she finished. Picking up their cups, Mara thanked Estelle for telling her the story. 'About my work,' Mara said before heading back to the balcony. 'Is there anything for me to upload to the Collings system?'

'Absolutely not.'

'So I should continue to report that you have no files to be uploaded?'

'Thank you, yes,' she said, as though Mara was writing the reports for Vaughn on Estelle's behalf.

'Now that I'm not looking for invoice records, the files on your pro bono cases are all up to date.'

'Thank you.'

Mara stood for a moment. 'I could go through the rest of the files I brought from the office. Update, reorganise, hunt down anything that's missing.' She said it like a question, wondering if she'd be recalled to the office if there was nothing else to do, not sure how she felt about that today.

Estelle raised a hand, a *yes, thank you, off you go* gesture. More tired than dismissive. Mara was pretty sure Vaughn wouldn't feel the same way.

☕

Mara was called to Estelle's room when the lunch tray had been delivered. Expecting instructions, she took her laptop to make notes, only to be sent back for her sandwich so they could discuss another pro bono case while they ate.

Estelle had represented a man who'd been injured when a suitcase fell on his head in a train: also fascinating, and not just for the damage an overnight bag could do to an eye socket. Estelle's recall of the details was impressive, her resolve to help the man inspiring, and the personal relationship that had developed between them bewildering. Estelle had been a guest at his wedding and, twelve years later, she'd written a reference for his step-daughter that had helped earn the girl a university scholarship.

For someone who was so hated in the office, Estelle's friendships with her clients seemed out of character. As her boss pushed away her lunch tray and adjusted her sling, Mara wondered if the relationships were real, or if they'd been manufactured for the sake of business. Or to impress her father, and now Vaughn.

'Do you form a personal relationship with all of your clients?'

'Certainly not. There are some I wouldn't waste a second of unbillable time on. But,' her gaze slid towards the window, 'there are others who . . . strike a chord, shall we say. The personal injuries, the genuine ones. They have so much to lose, so much they've already lost. Not just them but their family, often for the generation that follows. Fighting injustice can be a unifying experience.'

The conversation made Mara yearn for more, but as she went back to her 'office' on the balcony, she thought about Estelle being hated at the office, about her attitude that *kindness is weakness* and about the pro bono work. Estelle Collings was a lot of things, not the least of which was complicated.

Andie

'MATCHING MUGS,' ANDIE said, picking up the two tartan coffee cups that had been nestled among the gifts Ben's mum had sent.

Claiming one, Ben pointed at the red, green and yellow tartan design. 'Clan Cameron. Mum said the other one is for you. And I'm to make sure you get some of the shortbread.'

Andie inspected her new mug, even more fond of Ben's mum now. 'That's so nice. We could text her a selfie of us with our mugs, so she can see you're doing okay.'

Breaking into a Scottish brogue, Ben said, 'Then we need coffee to christen our *quaichs*.'

'Whatever that means.'

Andie had been late this morning. Firstly, held up waiting for the courier with Ben's parcel, then when she'd found Val's daughter Coral in the throes of a medical episode. Afterwards, none of the bystanders had been inclined to ask Alby to start frothing milk, so Andie had arrived without cappuccinos just as the lunch trays were being collected. The timing was perfect to fill their new tartan *quaichs* at Estelle's coffee machine, now set up on the balcony.

'Mara must have returned,' Ben said, pointing out a laptop on the sofa at the far end of the balcony.

Taking their mugs back to the stretch of balcony outside Ben's room, Andie took a selfie and sent it to Carmel, then settled into a comfortable silence as they sipped. A week ago, Andie had worried over what they might talk about, but today the quiet between them felt comfortable, companionable.

Safe, she thought. Safe enough to make her say, 'My husband's name was Zack.'

'Zack,' Ben said without surprise, his eyes still on the view. 'You said his name when we had dinner, but I couldn't remember.'

'I think he would have liked your dad's philosophy on not being left out of the conversation.'

Ben turned to look at her, something in his gaze making her push that door a little further.

'I stopped talking about him,' she said. 'Because I couldn't do it without tears and people are uncomfortable with the crying.' She cupped her hands around the warm mug. 'My friends have seen me through a lot, Vivian especially. She, they, want me to move on from the black hole I was in, and I guess crying looks a lot like I'm still teetering on the edge of it. I want to move on too, but . . .' She shook her head. 'The loss. The memory of it. It's hard.'

Ben's eyes didn't move from her face, and if it had been anyone else, Andie would have felt watched for signs of falling apart. But it was Ben, and it felt like space: to think, to breathe, to cry or not. So she turned her face to the distant view and watched the shift and heave of the ocean.

After a while, Ben asked, 'How did you guys meet?'

She smiled at the memory of their meet-cute. 'At a work function. He threw a glass of red wine at me and we both howled with laughter.'

Zack had been carrying a drink to a woman whose business he was trying to win, tripped over his own feet in front of Andie and upended both glasses down the front of her dress. She'd loved his reaction, he'd loved hers and that's all it had taken for them to fall in love. He'd lived in Sydney then, but that hadn't slowed the progress of their relationship. Three months later, he moved to Newcastle; four months after that, they were married above the beach with a handful of friends watching on and the energy of a huge ocean swell like a promise of the future that lay ahead of them.

'Had you been waiting for him to come into your life?' Ben asked.

'God, no. I'd never wanted to be married or have kids. I was consciously and happily single, independent, childless and career-focused, and had planned to stay that way until I was old and doddery.' She tucked a wayward curl behind her ear. 'My family is a hot mess. Mum had me at seventeen and my father, according to family lore, hung around just long enough to hold a crying baby and decide there was more to life than that.' She shrugged. 'She's provided step-fathers, boyfriends and arseholes, as well as four half-siblings and varying numbers of step-siblings. It's emotionally complicated, always competitive and thrives on conflict. I decided at an early age that family life was safer if I could stand back and watch.'

'And Zack?' Ben asked.

'He was my polar opposite. He lost both his parents in a car accident when he was nineteen and he had only happy memories of them. Even the arguments and hard times, he remembered with fondness.' She glanced at Ben, wondering if he recognised that in himself. 'He was forty when I met him, and his dream of having a joyful, boisterous family was still part of his plan.'

'Only . . .'

'Poor thing fell in love with me.' The joke felt good on her lips again. 'And I fell in love with him.' It was a relief to say that too. 'He thought we could create our own model of family life, that the future was what we made it, not what our past dictated.'

'I think my dad would like your Zack's philosophy too.'

Your Zack. For the first time since Andie had been talking, tears heated her eyes. Beside her, Ben simply waited for her to continue, or not.

'He painted this dream future of married life. House, kids, dog, caravan in the yard. Pretty much in that order. Noisy teenagers, grandkids, old age. Love, always love. He was very convincing. And I was sold on it all: a future that had never been on my radar, that I had never even imagined. I felt like a barista being offered a job as a brain surgeon.' She smiled, even as the pressure of what was to come began pushing up from her chest. 'But there was a life I wanted to show him first. So he'd understand that part of me, so we'd have that to share as well. So we set off to explore the world. We gave ourselves a year, going wherever the wind took us, and agreed that wherever we were in twelve months' time, we'd come home and start the rest of our lives.' She turned her gaze to that heaving, breathing ocean that had been there at the beginning and the end. 'We had two months.'

She stopped then, not sure she was ready to say the last part. Wanting and not wanting Ben to change the subject, to move on when she couldn't. But he didn't. He just sat in her silence, leaving it be, letting her be.

'He didn't get his dream,' she finally said. 'He died in the Solomon Islands and I came home without him.' She swallowed hard. 'I was with him and it was awful and the experience over-shadowed the grief. It still does. Sometimes I can't separate the two things. Sometimes I'm not sure which part I'm crying about.' She wiped at a tear that had found its way to her cheek. 'And some-times the worst of it is that that future with Zack, the kids and old age and togetherness, died with him. It was about him, it didn't exist without him. It was imaginary and just a dream really, but it's gone.'

'It was a good life,' Ben said.

She let out a breath, relieved he hadn't tried to tell her there were all sorts of lives to be had. 'Like another dimension. That's how it feels, like I spent a year in another dimension.' She cocked her head. 'Well, that's one of my analogies to explain how it feels.'

'Why do you need to explain it?'

'Because I . . .' She stopped, started again. 'Because people,

people I love, think . . . Well, it's hard to make them understand why grieving isn't . . . Why I can't see where to . . .' She closed her eyes, pulled in a breath. God, she couldn't even explain why she couldn't explain.

'Try me,' Ben said.

'Try you?'

'With an analogy.'

Was he making fun of her?

He hooked a thumb towards his room. 'I've got a couple of hundred movies on a hard drive in there. I love an analogy.' He raised his brows, said again, 'Try me.'

She hesitated, not sure she wanted to lay bare her experience, but there was something appealing in his objectivity. Giving him a cautious sideways glance, she said, 'Well, there's this one: I was abducted by really lovely aliens, shown how great life could be, then dropped back to earth a year later, where nothing had changed and there was no way back to the spaceship.'

Ben lifted his gaze to the ceiling. 'I like that.' He nodded. 'It's got a nice kind of imagery. A *Close Encounters*, *E.T.* feel to it. Might be good for a friend who doesn't mind a bit of sci-fi.'

Andie's lips twitched with amusement. Then, as a new perspective dawned. 'You mean, tailor the analogy for the person I'm explaining it to?'

'Why not?' He smiled, like they'd started a project. 'Got another one?'

'How about: a chunk of my life has been chopped out and I'm supposed to somehow join the two ends together.'

'I was always going to like that one. Let's call it edited out and the two ends spliced together with a jump cut.'

Andie laughed. 'Yeah, okay. Good revision, thanks.'

'My pleasure. Got any more?'

'About a thousand.'

It was unexpectedly liberating to discuss the explanations without the pain, without needing him to understand. She talked through other analogies that attempted to describe how she felt about that extraordinary, impassioned, life-changing year with Zack. Ben listened with the focus of a consultant hired to improve her commentary; reviewing, critiquing, reworking, occasionally rejecting. When Andie said looking back on that year made her feel like she'd been time travelling, Ben shook his head.

'It would be time travel if you'd used science to visit another time. So unless you've got a time machine, you're talking about time slip: accidentally travelling to another time via some kind of paranormal event.' He pointed at her. 'Good for fans of *Outlander*.'

'My book club read it before it was a TV series.'

'Perfect for those guys.'

She stayed for far longer than she'd planned. Their conversation was affirming, and strangely fun. Andie found herself laughing at the images she'd needed to express the burden of her truth. Not once did Ben tell her to be more positive or look for hope or be strong. Which, in its own strange way, made her feel more resilient than she had in a long, long time.

When they finally ran out of analogies, the conversation fell to another round of silent contemplation. The garden below the balcony was full of light and shade in the afternoon sun, and the ocean filled the horizon with its ever-present glitter. Ben's voice was gentle when he broke the peace. 'What happened in the Solomon Islands?'

Memory rose like panic. 'I don't talk about . . .' Andie wrapped her arms across her chest, hands in fists. 'I can't . . .' She squeezed her eyes.

'I'm sorry.'

God, it wasn't his fault. 'No, don't be.' She managed a tight smile. 'Today has been . . .' She shook her head, no words to describe it. 'Thanks for not telling me to be more positive.'

'I don't think you need to be more anything.'

'More resilient. I could be more of that.'

'I think you're being too hard on yourself.'

'I've been a mess since that car hit us.'

'Give yourself a break, Andie. You survived a random accident, lost your memory, broke your elbow, and now you're spending your recovery time keeping me company. That doesn't sound like needing more resilience.'

'I cry in the car every time I leave here.'

'And I thought it was just me crying every time you go.'

She pulled in a horrified breath. She was meant to be helping him.

He grinned, sweet and gentle. 'A few years back, after my dad's cancer flared up again, he was worried about how much he was crying. He figured he'd been through it before so he should be able to get on with things without needing a daily sob. So he consulted Dr Google and discovered the health benefits of a good cry. Apparently ordinary tears, like when our eyes water, are pretty much just water. But scientists found the tears when we're having an emotional cry are flushing out toxins and stress hormones while also releasing feel-good things like oxytocin and endorphins. After that, whenever Dad had a cry, he'd say he was having a feel-good cry.'

One side of Andie's mouth edged up, at the story, at Ben's dad, at Ben's way of steering her to new thoughts.

'He asked me the other night if I was getting my daily dose,' Ben said.

'Are you?'

'Sure. We survived a near-death experience, I figure tears are part of the deal.'

'Do you really cry every time I leave?'

'Not *every* time.' Joking, sheepish. 'It's not because you've left. More because you were here, although not in the way that sounds. It's relief, I think. Like . . . pain meds. Like you're a big syringe full of . . . reality.'

She frowned, not understanding.

'Everyone in here is sensible and professional,' he explained. 'They're great, but I'm their job. And you're . . . just you. Kind, generous, funny.' His expression softened. 'Injured. Sad. Trying to find your way through complicated emotions. And you're really great at it all.'

'Great? I don't think so.'

'God, yeah. Your laugh is . . . like funny just can't be contained. You cry like your soul has cracked open. You listen like you're fascinated, you say things you've reached deep for. And when you leave, I'm just . . . It's just,' he shrugged, 'a relief that someone else is feeling things.'

Andie had felt wrong for so long that Ben's description left her speechless, and as she stared at him, she had the sense of some big, slow cog in her brain inching incrementally forwards. Or backwards. Perhaps it didn't matter which direction, only that some unnamed element inside her had shifted.

Then, as though her silence had meant she thought Ben was nuts, he added, 'If that makes any sense.'

She reached a hand towards his. 'Yeah, it does. It's a relief for me too. That you're okay with feeling things. With me feeling all my . . . feelings. To know it's not just me feeling a bunch of stuff.'

He took her hand in his: it was warm, it felt like solidarity. Andie smiled, and he smiled right back, and in that moment, she felt less wrong than she had in two years. 'Thanks, Ben.'

'Thank you.' He rested his head against the wall behind him, as though the effort of feeling had zapped his energy.

'I should go,' she said, standing before he could try to change her mind.

When she'd helped him into his recliner, he said, 'See you tomorrow?'

'Of course.'

'Enjoy your cry.'

'Enjoy yours.'

And Andie did cry when she got back to the car, but without the angst this time. This time, she cried like it was what she was meant to be doing.

Mara

WHILE ESTELLE SLEPT, Mara tiptoed out to the garden for some fresh air. A breeze had come up, teasing her hair as she wound her way along the path, slowing to breathe in wafts of gardenia and lavender. As she headed back across the hospital forecourt, Rylee was coming towards her.

'I saw you earlier, but it's been flat out today.' She dropped her voice. 'How's it going with Estelle?'

'Surprisingly good. I took your advice and gave her my "terms",' Mara put air quotes around the word, 'and she just said, "I accept your conditions."'

'Oh yeah?'

'Amazing, right?'

'Impressively eloquent must be your thing now.'

Mara laughed.

'So you're here for the week then?'

'Looks that way.'

'Want a coffee sometime?'

'Sure.'

Rylee grinned, calling as she walked away, 'Shoot you a text if I get a break.'

'Are you interested in personal injury or pro bono work?' Estelle was upright and alert in her chair when Mara returned.

'The details of the cases are really interesting.' It wasn't like she had anything urgent to do today. 'Like Dr Hassan?'

'Ah, yes. That was complex.'

'The Iran–Iraq war?'

Estelle looked at the ceiling for a moment. 'Nineteen eighty-six. I went to his home for the first meeting. He'd been a surgeon in Iran and he was working as a taxi driver.' She detailed the man's escape from Iran with his family, the subsequent problems in providing the necessary documents to prove his qualifications before he could work in his field in Australia. In the meantime, he was supporting four young kids and a wife who spoke no English. Estelle had worked on his case for almost ten years. He was now a professor, and two of his children were doctors.

'You should put that in the book,' Mara said.

'This book you've mentioned,' she said, then trailed off, as though she wasn't sure what she wanted to know. Or how to ask.

'Stories from your legal career,' Mara suggested. 'Or the story *of* your legal career.'

There was some shifting in the lines of Estelle's face as she thought about it, perhaps a struggle between interest and not wanting to appear interested. Finally, she said, 'How would one approach such a project?'

'Oh, well, I guess you'd just write it.' Which, once Estelle had raised a dubious eyebrow, seemed like a stupid answer. 'I mean, I think you have to write it before you can sell it to a publisher. And I suppose you'd have to know you could before you committed to it. You wouldn't want to get halfway through and realise you hated writing about yourself.'

'Of course, it couldn't be all about me.'

'Clients and cases and, I suppose, your family and Collings.'

Estelle stared out the window, giving nothing away about what she was thinking. When Mara went back to the balcony, she felt as though there was something closer to a rapport between them. Perhaps that was stretching things, but something cordial, at least. Genial and less frosty. A thaw, maybe.

Coral

It was a rehab hospital, it didn't have an emergency department. Although, as it turned out, it wasn't an emergency. It wasn't Coral's heart; she'd had an anxiety attack.

The doctor who checked her over explained all the reasons he was confident it wasn't her heart. The fact that the pain in her chest disappeared when she lay down was, apparently, the big giveaway. He asked if there was anything stressful happening in her life and she burst into tears. He assured her that Val wouldn't be told, suggested she see her GP for a check-up, and that she needed to reduce her stress and deal with her anxiety.

Much later, when she walked back into the sunshine, she felt like she'd been hit by a truck. She was relieved she wasn't going to die, embarrassed it had happened so publicly, grateful she hadn't peed her pants. A reason to persevere with pelvic floor exercises, if ever there was one.

Alby's van was still parked in the driveway, and Alby was sitting sideways in the front passenger seat reading something on his phone. 'Oh, hey there,' he said, standing as she neared.

'Were you waiting for me?'

'I thought you might need a ride. Or something to eat. How are you feeling?'

'Better than I was. You didn't need to wait, but thank you.' She ran a hand over her hair. 'It was an anxiety attack.'

He lifted his chin in a nod.

'A little embarrassing, sorry about the drama.'

'No need to apologise. They can be pretty scary.'

She took a longer look at him, wondering if he'd had one too.

'I used to be a paramedic,' he explained. 'It can feel like a heart attack.'

'I can attest to that.' She flattened a palm to her chest at the memory, grateful for Alby's calm, gentle voice in her ear.

'So, sandwich? Cool drink? Maybe skip the coffee for now?'

'Is that paramedic advice?'

He smiled. 'Just trying to get rid of my leftovers.'

Exhausted now, she took his spot on the passenger seat while he disappeared into the van. He wouldn't let her pay for the sandwich and drink, and he carried Val's laundry bag as he walked her to the car park, the meandering path through the lush garden helping to ease her tension.

'What's all that?' he asked when she opened the boot.

'My daughter's clean washing and some frozen meals for my ex-husband's parents.'

One eyebrow slid up, but he said nothing. 'You should eat something before you drive.'

She glanced across the gardens, making sure Val couldn't see her from here. 'I need to sit for a while anyway.'

'How are you doing?'

'Shaken up.' It may not have been a heart attack, but it was some serious pushback from the stress she'd been under.

'You want some company?'

God, yes. She was overwhelmed and uneasy, and frightened about having another anxiety attack in the car. But she looked across the roof at him as she opened the driver's door. 'You don't have to stay. You've done more than enough already.'

He opened her passenger door anyway, bending to look in as she slid behind the wheel. 'Got nothing else to do.'

His throwaway line was laced with kindness. He earned a point for not accepting her exit option, and another for not just getting in. She didn't think she could match his no-drama-either-way tone, so she just cocked her head: *Come on, get in.*

He slid the seat back as she opened the bottle of water, saying nothing while she sipped and took a bite of the sandwich, suddenly starving.

Finally, he asked, 'Did something happen this morning?'

Coral sighed. 'Literally *nothing* happened this morning.' Tightening a hand around the steering wheel, she said, 'I rescheduled my life to be here for a meeting that achieved nothing.' She clenched her teeth. 'And Mum . . .' No, she didn't need to tell him what Val thought about her. 'I . . . It's . . .' She almost said, *Fine*. But clearly it wasn't.

'You've got a lot going on,' he said.

She took another bite of the sandwich and he waited in silence as she chewed. 'I thought I'd be okay once I got on the plane,' she told him. He shifted in his seat to look at her. There was no judgement in his face, just a calm patience as he waited for her to finish that thought. 'Only I didn't get that far, did I?' She tried to make it light, but her throat thickened. 'And that, what happened out there, really bloody scared me.' A tear welled and she blinked it away, taking another sip of water. 'I thought rescheduling the flight would take the pressure off but I think I just proved that theory wrong.'

'You're in logistics, aren't you?'

'Yeah.'

'Can't you organise your way out of some of the stuff you've got going on?'

She pushed a hand through her hair. 'Sometimes it's just easier to do it myself.'

'Until you're doing everything.'

'It got out of control. Basically, a firestorm of other people's shit hitting fans.'

'You can't help other people if you're on the ground gripping your chest.'

She sighed.

'And actually, it's not literally a firestorm. No-one will die if you say, "No, I can't do that today."'

She nodded, but it wasn't as simple as that.

As though reading her mind, he looked at her with that calm patience again. She didn't have to explain, and she didn't think he expected her to, but it had been a long time since anyone had bothered to question it.

'I didn't get much support when I was going through what my kids are dealing with now. I know they're adults, but I remember what it was like. I was young and pregnant, then a single mum with two little kids. It was hard. And lonely. Mum pretty much decided I'd made my own bed and I should lie in it. I never wanted it to be like that for my kids, I want them to know they can count on me. And I'm good at getting things done.' It was what she did, what she was known for, what she'd always prided herself on. When her father died and Val needed to sell her house and find somewhere to live, it had fallen to Coral. When she fell pregnant, she'd made the decisions; when Richard left and she needed the security of a house, she'd made it work. Friends and colleagues turned to her because whenever anything happened, she could always see how to get things done, how to make sure the right things happened. She didn't do it for everyone who asked. But for family . . . she'd been doing it for them so long, it felt like instinct. Like it was how she loved them. Because just being there and being Coral had never seemed to be enough.

She pulled in a breath and shook her head. She was definitely not going to admit that to this kind, generous man. It was bad enough that she'd had a fake heart attack in front of him. 'Getting stuff done is my superpower, so why not use it for my kids?'

'Superpower?'

'Yeah. Cool right?'

'Very cool. Will it work if you're sitting in a corner rocking?'

She heaved another sigh. 'No.'

'Oh, so you *can* say no.'

She huffed a laugh.

'Hard to say it to people you care about,' he said.

'Not sure I know how. "Yes" feels like it's hardwired into me.'

'No!' he said with mock firmness. 'Say it with me now, Coral. *No.*'

She laughed, but said it. '*No.*' Shook her head, but the humour felt good, and the word felt like it had promise. 'Maybe I should say no to New York.'

'Not if it means you'll keep saying yes to everything else.'

She inclined her head.

'I reckon it's just like you thought, you'll be fine once you get on the plane. You just need to give yourself a break between now and then.'

She looked at him again – lean, tanned, a little jaded – and realised Alby was the only person who actually wanted her to get to New York.

Coral felt recovered enough to drive, but the experience had left her shattered. It wasn't just the pain in her chest and the panic of thinking she'd been about to die; it was the thought of what she'd done to herself, the realisation that trying to make sure everyone else was okay had literally toppled her. All she wanted now was to sit quietly and let everything she'd been carrying slide off her shoulders and back off for a while. Except that Summer was expecting her to drop in.

After a debate with herself about how much to tell her daughter, she texted Summer: *Been held up at the hospital, run out of time to drop in.*

It wasn't *No, I can't be there today*, but it was close enough for now. She didn't have the energy to explain or reassure, to deal with Summer's alarm or another conversation about not going to New York.

She rang Jessica from home, told her she wasn't feeling well and that the only call she wanted was the one to tell her Rodney's drill heads were ready to go.

Then she slept. For hours.

Mara

MARA HAD CALLED a family dinner for Monday. At the time, she hadn't decided if she was going back to the hospital or what would happen if she did, but she'd wanted an opportunity to explain the situation that didn't involve catching Dad and Pat between social events.

It had been a week since they'd all sat down together and it was good that their lives were busy now, but Mum had always said spending time over a meal was important too. She'd be pleased they were still doing it.

Pat looked between Mara and Dad. 'Are we waiting for someone to make a speech?'

'We-ell,' Dad's face snapped to serious and Mara stiffened in alarm. 'Nah, just kidding.'

Mara glared at them both. 'What's so funny? It's a family dinner.'

'You're right, Maz, honey. Thank you for organising us.'

'This is good.' Pat pointed at his meal as he chewed.

'Mum's baked pork chops. She made them for my birthday dinner when I was twelve.' Everyone got their choice of dinner on their birthday. And Mara got Mum's cookbook when she passed away.

'And you've done a good job of them,' Dad said, like Mara was still twelve years old and hadn't kept his business afloat when he was a mess.

She pushed aside a twinge of irritation and pressed on to her news. She wanted her dad to be proud of how Estelle had accepted her 'terms'. Once she'd started, though, it was difficult to explain Friday's argument without insulting him or making Estelle sound like the monster Mara had agreed to go back to.

When she mentioned Vaughn, Dad jumped in as though she'd given him an opening to change the subject. 'I was talking to Vaughn today,' he said. 'Reckons you've got a bit of a cushy job over there at the hospital.'

'Cushy?' she frowned. 'Not with Estelle.'

'You should get that physio onto her,' Pat said. 'Get her to work a little harder on that broken leg of hers and it might keep her quiet.'

Mara looked back and forth between them, disappointment making her shake her head. 'Vaughn hasn't been to see her since she came out of surgery,' she told her father, then turned to Pat. 'She's seventy-two and the bone went through her leg. I wouldn't wish more pain on anyone who'd been through that.'

There was an exchange of glances between father and son, and Mara was pleased to have made her point. But it had punctured the mood of their dinner so when Dad brought up the footy, she tried to shrug off her pique, and by the time she served up the cheese-cake, their easy conversation was back in full swing.

Pat stacked the dishwasher without being asked, before collecting his keys and heading out. Dad washed up the baking dishes while Mara packed away leftovers and made sandwiches for their lunches tomorrow.

Drying his hands, her dad said, 'What are you up to now?'

'Bit of telly?'

'Sounds good.'

'Maybe the next episode of that crime series we've been watching.' She was putting the lunches in the fridge as she talked, and didn't see until she straightened up that he'd grabbed his keys from the bowl on the hall table.

'You're going out too?'

'Yeah.'

'Got all your orders done then.'

Her tone seemed to make him hesitate. He jiggled the keys on his palm, glancing in the direction of the door. 'I'm just . . . Got to get something from the car.'

Mara watched him disappear into the garage, wondering where he'd planned to go. And later as they watched TV, about the texts that kept lighting up his phone.

'Who are you texting?' she finally asked as they got up to make a cup of tea.

'The boys.' His term for the beefy blokes who worked for him. 'One of them needs a lift in the morning.'

'That took six texts?' Mara's dad was notorious for his yes/no answers.

'They put me on WhatsApp. Everyone's gotta make a comment.' He rolled his eyes as he dropped teabags into mugs. 'What's your schedule tomorrow?'

'Go to work, come home.' It was snappish, but the texting had annoyed her. The whole night had.

'What time have you been heading off in the mornings?' He was usually gone before she left.

'Seven-thirty-ish.'

'That early?'

If he was trying to make up for the texting, she should try to come halfway. 'It doesn't take long to get to the hospital, but parking can be a pain when I stop to pick up the coffees.'

'Sounds like you've got a system.'

She went to her granny flat after the episode finished, even though it was still early. She was tired from worrying about Estelle and unemployment, and annoyed with her family. She must need a good night's sleep.

Mara

MARA PUTTERED INTO the kitchen in her dressing gown, put on the kettle, emptied the dishwasher, packed her lunch, set the slow cooker going and took her breakfast back to her granny flat to eat while she got ready for work. After drying her hair, she headed to the garage to deposit her work stuff in her car so she wasn't juggling it with her jacket and handbag later.

Dad's truck was still there, which was odd. She hoped he'd taken the morning off to finish his orders, but in case he'd slept in, she hit the button for the electric door; its screech and rumble was the standard wake-up call in the Ellsworth household.

Twenty minutes later, she collected the keep cups for the coffee run and headed through the house again on her way to the car. She was thinking about checking the slow cooker when she looked up to see a woman in the kitchen.

Mara stopped halfway across the lounge room, a frown creasing her forehead as her brain tried to make sense of why this woman was there. Filling the kettle. In a silky robe. Sleep-messed dark hair. Looking back at Mara like she'd been caught out.

'Oh.' The woman glanced towards the hallway.

Fifty-ish, Mara thought. When had Pat developed a thing for cougars? She was debating whether to start with *I'm Pat's sister* or make a joke about the walk of shame when she heard her father's voice.

'Hey, lover, how's the coffee coming?'

Mara turned to stone. A moment later, Dad waltzed into the kitchen with a grin, saw his daughter and mirrored her frozen pose. 'Mara.'

In that instant, last night replayed through her mind: the fake announcement at the table, the keys in his hand before he decided to stay, the text messages, the questions about what time she was leaving in the morning. She licked her lips but no words came, just her eyes flicking back and forth between her dad and the silky-robed woman.

'I thought you'd left,' he said.

'I haven't.'

'I heard the garage door.' Almost an accusation, as though it was Mara's fault he'd let a woman loose in the kitchen.

'I thought you'd slept in.' Mara clenched her teeth. 'Apparently you did.' She remembered his texting: Was this woman a . . . a sex worker? Did he miss Mum like *that*?

Before she had a chance to get her head around it, Dad shot a glance at the woman. She looked back at him, and something passed between them. Mara couldn't read the exchange, but the intimacy of it made anger flare. Not a one-night stand, not an escort. Dad knew this woman well enough to have a silent conversation across a room. Like he and Mum used to.

Not just that. He'd hidden her in his bedroom like a teenager. Like Mara was his mother, not his daughter. Like her job was to cook and clean and do his books while he shagged a woman who was free to wander the house in a silky robe when his kids weren't home. Her dad gathered himself to say something more, but Mara got in first.

'I'm *Mara*,' she ground out in the direction of the silky robe. 'Enjoy the *coffee*.' Turning on her dad, she laced her voice with sarcasm. 'Good job on the introduction, Dad.'

She slammed the door as she left.

Mara gave Estelle her coffee and went straight to the balcony. She dropped her handbag, and the contents clattered across the floor. She bumped her head as she picked up her lipstick from under a chair, then spilt her cappuccino. When she'd finished mopping up the mess, Estelle called out to her.

Mara stood at the balcony door. 'I haven't stained anything.'

'I'm not concerned about the furniture. Come and sit down.'

Mara did as she was told, perching on the edge of the seat beside the recliner and waiting in stony silence for the reprimand.

Estelle's eyes raked over Mara's surly expression. 'What on earth has happened?'

Her tone was both demanding and concerned, and so uncharacteristically Estelle that Mara swung her face away, embarrassed, angry at herself.

'This is not right.' Estelle's exclamation was terse and firm, as though she was incensed on Mara's behalf. The moment gave Mara an inkling of what it must be like to have Estelle fighting on your side. 'Mara, please. Take a tissue.' She waved at the box on the tray table. 'And . . . and . . . some deep breaths.' Estelle mimed scooping air into her lungs.

Mara chuckled as she wiped her eyes.

'You mustn't let this fester. Go and make a phone call, or find your friend Rylee. Or you can tell me. I've been told my uncompromising personality is quite the thing for railing against the wind.'

'It's . . . I . . .' She almost said *nothing*. But she didn't want to run to Rylee with another drama, and railing sounded pretty appealing. 'My dad. He . . . I . . .' How did she explain?

'Is he unwell again?'

'He's fine.' The anger swelled. 'Apparently having a fine time too. He . . . There was a woman in the kitchen this morning.' It sounded stupid now, but Estelle didn't blink. 'With a silky robe and messed-up hair and smudged bloody mascara.' Mara rubbed a hand across her face. 'I thought he, we, all of us . . . I was trying to hold him together, and the business. All of us together and . . .' He thought I'd left for work this morning, said it like it was my fault the three of us were standing there like, like . . .' She threw up her hands and glanced at Estelle, expecting to see irritation at the unfinished sentences. Instead, something stoic in her face spurred Mara on. 'It's not that he slept with someone. I'm an adult, I've had sex, it's not *Pride and Prejudice*. And she wasn't a hooker. They were . . . together.'

'You didn't know he had a friend?'

'They're more than friends. They're . . . close. I could see it.' She pulled in a breath. 'He should have *told* me. Been a grown-up. Treated me like I'm a grown-up. Not pretended he was still pining for Mum. That he couldn't cope without her.' Mara scrubbed her forehead with the heel of a palm. 'I cooked Mum's pork chops and cheesecake last night. And six hours later he was . . . was . . .' Mara waved an arm about, searching for . . .

'Fucking someone else,' Estelle said.

'Exactly!'

A second later, Estelle's choice of words hit home. Mara's eyes snapped to Estelle, who arched a single brow.

'Exactly.' Mara laughed.

'My father never managed to remain celibate for long,' the older woman said. 'He remarried six months after my mother died. Eventually gave me three step-mothers.' Leaning forward, she patted the armrest beside Mara's hand. It felt like permission for Mara to rail.

So Mara did. 'It's not *just* the silky-robed woman. I'm mad at Dad but I get it. I'll only ever have one mum but she was his wife, he can have other relationships. And I want him to, I do, but . . .' Her eyes drifted to the view beyond the balcony. 'It's . . . every-thing. Since Mum died. Since his heart attack. Everything *I've* done. And not done. Everything I've . . .' She squeezed her eyes shut, her voice breaking as a fresh swell of emotion snagged in her throat. '. . . lost.'

'You have given a lot for your family. More than most.'

Estelle meant her university degree; perhaps also her time, money and career. That was all she needed to know, all Mara wanted to tell. All she was prepared to think about.

'Now,' Estelle's voice was sharp and brusque again, 'the cure for heartache is to pour your energies into being productive, using your intelligence to make yourself strong. So off you go.' She waved a hand towards her ensuite bathroom. 'Fix your face and get back to work.'

Mara stood, the idea not unappealing.

'Fetch your laptop when you're done. You can assist me with a review of my draft advice for a defamation case.'

'*Your* legal advice?'

'Indeed. You, Mara,' her boss aimed a steely gaze at her, 'are to ask questions before offering an opinion on any issues you consider relevant.'

Coral

WHEN RODNEY RANG at seven last night to say his drill heads were ready, there'd still been time to organise a next-flight delivery through their usual channels, but the thought of mustering the urgency to make it happen had Coral pressing a hand to her chest in fear.

Jessica squealed when Coral phoned to tell her to be ready to fly to Stockholm. Last night, Coral's plan had been to let Jess handle the pick-up, while she went for a walk and visited her GP before meeting Val's doctor in the afternoon to discuss the cognitive testing.

This morning, though, Coral woke before dawn with the whiteboard in her head and an eraser in her imaginary hand, wrestling with what she could drop. Eventually, she'd emailed Wade to tell him she wouldn't get to his apartment before she left for New York and he should start looking for that rental manager. She texted her brother to remind him she was leaving on Thursday, and Alby, to thank him for his kindness yesterday. Then the restless, can't-stop-yet energy that she'd carried around for weeks wouldn't let her stay still.

She drove Jessica to Rodney's plant, gave Rodney a hug before they left and Jessica a pep talk on the drive to Newcastle Airport. At the check-in counter, they cheered the package on its way to the luggage hold. Coral could have left then, but she stayed for a coffee with Jess while they waited for the flight to be called for the first leg to Stockholm, telling war stories about other urgent packages, like she hadn't been tripped up by her own stress yesterday.

Standing at the big windows overlooking the tarmac, Coral watched Jessica walk to the stairs with an overwhelming desire to charge the gate and take the younger woman's place. To do a job that was simple and easy, that would take three days, most of which would be spent watching in-flight movies or driving through Sweden in the summer solstice.

As she started back through the airport, Coral waited for relief to descend. *Woohoo, one job down!* But all she thought was: she could do with a summer solstice. She could do with getting on a plane and being transported to somewhere else; a parallel universe, perhaps, where she wasn't responsible for so much. Where sometimes, just sometimes, it was her turn.

Retirement, she thought. Only when she saw that particular whiteboard in her head, it was already full of other people: Summer and her growing family, Val and her care needs. And if she rubbed it all out with her imaginary eraser, all that was left was a great, big expanse of scary nothing.

Because the truth was she'd been doing stuff for other people for so damn long, she had nothing else.

Andie

'ARE YOU UP for another movie?' Ben asked as Andie arrived.

'Only if it's not a tear-jerker.'

'I was thinking *The African Queen,* classic Katharine Hepburn getting down and dirty.'

It ran surprisingly long for an old black-and-white, and Ben fell asleep around the time Katharine Hepburn and Humphrey Bogart were reaching the end of their journey down the Ulanga River. Andie turned to share another grin and saw Ben's head tipped back on his recliner, his glasses still on, face angled towards her as though he'd dropped off waiting for her next remark.

She was about to turn back to the movie when something in the sleeping softness of his expression made her pause. She cast her eyes over the dark curve of his lashes and the laugh lines that looked like parentheses, as though his mouth was an essential part of the equation of his face. The hint of a smile stirred something inside her. Not attraction, although at another time in her life that might have been what she felt. Now, though, what oozed through her was . . . fondness, loneliness, yearning. For uncomplicated togetherness. For the moments like these with Zack, when she'd turn to find him ready with a smile or to reach for her hand, stroke her cheek, wind a finger through a corkscrew of her hair. An intimacy that wasn't about sex, that came from knowing, understanding, seeing, caring. She missed that, and the missing felt like a lead weight on her lungs.

Her breath caught on the sob that rose like an eruption. She tried to focus on Katharine Hepburn, but the actor's bedraggled image only made it worse, and Andie wept silent tears for the on-screen lovers as the scenes of their voyage out to sea brought back memories of her final journey with Zack.

As the music reached a crescendo, she felt Ben's hand on her shoulder. He didn't say anything, just held the warm, gentle connection: *Whatever you need to do.*

What she needed to do was cry, so she dropped her head to his armrest and sobbed. She had no idea how long it went on, only that Ben let her be. His hand slipped from her shoulder to move the tissue box closer, turning the movie off when it finished and starting a playlist that washed over her: The Beatles, Adele, Elton, Ed. Then Freddie Mercury busted out: 'I Want to Break Free'.

She looked up with a laugh. Wiped her eyes, pushed the curls off her face.

'*African Queen* really gets you where it hurts, right?' he said.

More than he knew.

'Do we need chocolate?' he asked.

'There's chocolate?'

He pointed to his bedside table. 'Top drawer. Fiona did a trip to the snack machine for me.'

Andie broke up a block of caramel-filled squares, took a piece and said, 'We were two hours by boat from the mainland when Zack died.'

She didn't look at Ben as she said it, anchoring her gaze on the view outside his room, her heart thumping. Ben shifted the chocolate to the arm of the chair between them.

She told him about the crazy trip out to the remote island resort, although 'resort' was an overstatement. Six thatched huts suspended over clear, blue water, a stone's throw from thick tropical jungle that grew to the edge of the sand. It had taken two hours in a small speedboat to get there. Choppy seas had turned rough and they'd hung on tight as the boat rode the waves like a roller-coaster. It had been fun until Andie turned green with seasickness. She'd puked over the side with Zack holding on to the back of her shorts so she didn't tip into the ocean.

They saw only a handful of people in their week at the resort: another couple who stayed two nights; four men on a fishing trip who were gone all day, sunburnt and drinking at night. Andie and Zack had walked through the jungle to the single village on the island, bought coconuts and handwoven mats, passed the school and a small medical centre – staffed by a single nurse, Andie learned later. The distance and disconnection had seemed like paradise.

On their last day, they'd visited a neighbouring island, swimming and snorkelling, fishing on the way back, their catch served up for dinner. The sunset was stunning, the air balmy, the wine cool and light; the staff that night reduced to just the owner, who joined them for coffee.

Andie paused for a piece of chocolate, as though the sugar might sustain her through the rest of the story. 'He died of a brain aneurysm in the middle of the night.' She said it quickly, before she lost her nerve. 'He sat up in bed and it woke me. He didn't say anything, just sat there with a hand to his head.' She pressed the heel of her palm to the cavity of her eye, like Zack had done. 'I said, "What?" and he looked at me as though he wasn't sure I was really there. Then he whispered, "Andie."'

She swallowed hard on the memory. The chill it had sent down her spine, the adrenaline that had pushed her upright, the thundering of the blood in her ears as he'd stared wordlessly. She told Ben how she'd helped him lie down, told him to breathe, just breathe. She'd wanted to run for help but he'd held on to her hand, pulling her down to him. If she'd known they were his last moments, she wouldn't have struggled so hard to pull away, to shout for help.

'You wanted to save him,' Ben said. It was matter-of-fact, and she nodded in agreement.

Zack's eyes had caught on hers one more time. There'd been an urgency in the way his gaze had clung to her, as though he'd known he didn't have long. In her memory, it felt like a moment locked in eternity, a message passing between them like a physical connection. His love, their life, the choices they'd made together. Fulfilment, joy, trust, desire.

Andie pulled a tissue from the box and mopped the tears on her face, only then realising she was holding Ben's hand. A white-knuckle grip, as though tethering her to the present while she disappeared into the past. She didn't know if she'd reached for Ben or if he'd understood she'd needed the lifeline, but she was glad of it. Of his silent, wordless support, his well-timed chocolate offerings.

'We can buzz for another snack-machine run if we need to,' he said when they were down to the last two pieces.

'We might need something stronger,' she said, because Zack's death was the start of another chapter.

She'd had to leave Zack's body to find help, negotiating the narrow pier linking the huts in the dark, calling for someone to come. The fishermen were drunk; the resort owner had been sound asleep. He roused someone from the village to get the nurse, who trekked through the jungle to examine Zack and declared him dead, cause unknown. It took hours and a thousand phone calls to confirm the death with medical authorities; to arrange for an appropriately sized boat to transport a body back to the mainland. Andie spent that time numb with shock, confused and pleading, exhausted and wired. She refused to leave Zack alone in their hut above the water, afraid of a high tide, a tsunami; of anything that might take him away before she was ready. Because she knew, even in shock and fear, that once he was gone, she'd never see him again.

The trip to the mainland was a nightmare. The boat was

barely bigger than the one they'd arrived on and she sat under a canopy in front of the driver, boxed in by the hastily packed luggage and the mound of Zack's body. The ocean was a heaving mass and she was seasick from the moment she stepped aboard, her stomach spasming as she clung to the bag that held Zack, planning to tie herself to it if the boat capsized so she'd sink to the bottom with him.

When they arrived, there were delays at every step: at the port, on the roads, in the hospital, with Immigration and the embassy; doctors, police, food, phone calls. She was alone through all of it: for hours and hours with his body, then in the hospital, the morgue, waiting rooms, the police station, the embassy, a hotel room. Andie struggled to make herself understood in English or Pidgin; struggled to understand their explanation of the aneurysm discovered on a CT scan. She couldn't sit still, couldn't eat, explain, remember.

Andie's mother, when she'd called, said, *Well, you would go somewhere so remote.* Vivian sounded light-years away on the phone. Andie told her not to fly over because she was expecting to make the trip home with Zack the next day. Only there were delays and more delays, confusion, numbness, tears and an unbearable aloneness for a long week before she landed in Sydney.

She was a mess when Viv and Theo met her, the three of them forming a sobbing huddle in Arrivals. There were more details and delays before they got back to Newcastle, where Viv and Theo finally took over for her. It felt like breathing again, but that sense of being alone clung like a yawning hole in her chest, filled with the memories that shook her awake at night. She slept on their sofa for a week before she could bear the bedroom at the end of the hallway. She wouldn't stay in the house when they were out, wouldn't drive anywhere without a passenger.

She pressed a hand to her chest. 'I can feel it here still,' she said. 'As though the experience left a scar.'

'Fuck, Andie.' They were the first words Ben had spoken in

twenty minutes. 'I mean . . . bloody hell, life is fucking traumatic sometimes.'

It was said without sympathy or concern: an unadorned appreciation of her nightmare. And it made her eyes well again. 'Thank you for not trying to find something positive.'

'I don't think I could.'

'People do. Thank goodness you got home. That you had travel insurance. You had Viv and Theo, the embassy, spare cash, a home to come back to. That I never need to get on a plane again. As though it's wrong to not find something to be grateful for. I am grateful for all those things, but that doesn't change the fact that I was utterly shattered by it.'

'Or that Zack was dead.'

She nodded, grateful for the bluntness.

'I still don't like to be alone for long. And two weeks on my own to recover from concussion?' She shook her head. 'I came back to see you because I couldn't handle knowing you were alone here.'

'I hate to say it, but there's the positive. For me, not you. You came here and I'm seriously grateful for that.'

'I really just needed a good night's sleep.'

'Then I'm grateful you couldn't sleep.'

She smiled. 'That's the first time I've told that story from beginning to end. After all the confused, exhausted-and-in-shock versions I gave at every step along the way, I couldn't bear going through it again. Remembering what happened is difficult enough. I thought saying it out loud would tear the wound right open.'

'Are you okay?'

'I feel like I've taken off a backpack filled with house bricks. Like maybe each brick was a moment in the story and I was taking them out one by one.'

'And now you don't need the backpack?'

'I don't know yet. I only know I really needed to say it.'

☕

'You've never told me the whole story.' Vivian sounded indignant.

Andie braked behind a queue of traffic and rubbed a hand across her forehead. She'd called Viv to explain how talking to Ben the last couple of days had felt like moving on. At least from some things. It was meant to be reassurance, that Vivian's concerns about her visiting Ben were unnecessary. 'I never wanted to relive it. But today, it felt right.'

'I would have thought if you were going to tell someone, it'd be me.'

Andie frowned. 'I didn't plan it.'

'I mean, I've been there for you through all of it and you've only known Ben for, what? Not even two weeks.'

Was she hurt or jealous? 'Viv, come on.'

'We've been friends forever, Andie.'

'Exactly.'

'The point is that I know the real you, the best you. After everything we've done together, everything you've been through, I probably know you better than you know yourself. I'm glad you feel good about finally talking about what happened, but I know how you are, and you're not going to move on by talking to someone who doesn't know those things about you.'

Andie shoved the car into gear. 'Okay, well, I wasn't asking for advice. I'll talk to you later,' she told her and hung up.

Part 7

Range of Movement

Mara

WORKING WITH ESTELLE had been a roller-coaster but today, Mara was looking forward to it. Dad had already left and Pat was sleeping in when she went through to the kitchen, and she enjoyed the quiet, and the extra time not filling the slow cooker. The silky-robed woman may have done Mara a favour, helping her realise her father was capable of managing his own life and meals.

As she stopped to get the morning coffees, Mara realised she wasn't scared of Estelle anymore. There were boundaries now, and already they'd proven more beneficial to Mara than she'd imagined. Yesterday's session reviewing Estelle's draft advice had been brilliant.

'Morning,' Mara said as she dropped her bag, shed her jacket and pulled a chair up beside Estelle's recliner.

Her boss looked ready for her morning gym session with runners and a slash of red lipstick. She took the cup Mara passed her and said, 'I think you'd be an excellent candidate for the Collings undergraduate program.'

Mara froze on the edge of her chair.

'It's not a guarantee, of course, but I would add my own recommendation to your application.'

The suddenness of the subject, the assumption that Mara was

on board, left her stumbling for words. 'No. Thank you, but I . . . Vaughn already . . . I said I wasn't interested.'

'Of course, there are other schemes and scholarships available. I would be happy to write a reference; my name does carry some weight in a number of institutions.'

'No.' It was louder and firmer than Mara had intended, but anxiety was stirring in the pit of her stomach and it needed to be shut down. 'I'm not going back to uni.'

Estelle's lips tightened. 'You are an intelligent, curious young woman, Mara. You have far more potential than you realise. It would be a waste to settle for less than what you are capable of.' It was a reprimand. Flattering and generous by Estelle's standards, but still a reprimand.

Mara tried hard to make her anger rise in response. *It's not up to her. It's none of her business.* But the compliment had touched something inside her and suddenly, there it was: the idea of a legal career, independence, respect. Things Mara had aimed for, dreamed of; things she'd thought were within her reach, that she was worthy of. Things she couldn't achieve without a university degree.

University.

Mara's stomach buckled whenever she thought of it. The idea had seemed so golden, but the reality had made her realise not everything within her reach was hers to take. She took a gulp of coffee, breathed hard to fight down her alarm. 'I don't want to go back to uni.'

Estelle's eyes narrowed. 'I don't believe you've lost your interest in the law.'

God, no. Not after yesterday. 'It makes no difference.'

'Mara . . .'

'No.' She stood so swiftly her chair almost toppled. 'I'm not going back to uni.'

'Mara!'

The older woman's voice was sharp, but it was shock and

concern, not anger, and Mara's eyes tingled with the threat of tears. But she wouldn't be upset about this in front of Estelle; she couldn't cry over spilt milk to the woman who'd stomped through litres of it. It was a relief when the anger finally came.

'Don't tell me what I should do!' she snapped. 'Everyone tells me what I should do. Everyone *thinks* they know what I should do. But *no-one* knows. Not about . . . *this*.'

She took a step back, then forward, her anger swelling into fury. 'I don't care how smart you think I am or what my bloody potential is. I won't do uni again. I . . . *can't*.'

Estelle's mouth was ajar, shock in her eyes, a little wariness in her posture.

'Okay, Ms Collings, you're up!' An orderly had arrived to escort Estelle to the gym.

Estelle shot him a steely glare. Mara turned and stormed out to the balcony.

Andie

'OH, SORRY.' ANDIE stopped at Ben's door when she saw a woman at his bedside.

'No, come in,' Ben called. 'I think we're done here, aren't we?'

The woman was wearing the navy blue jacket of hospital staff and nodded as she stood. 'I'll keep you updated. Enjoy your morning tea.'

'You making official complaints again?' Andie joked as she handed Ben his coffee.

'I've been cleared to fly home.' Something eased in his eyes as he said it. 'She can start talking dates with rehab hospitals in Perth now.'

'That's great.' It was, but Andie had to work on her smile. 'How soon will it happen?'

'I got the impression it could be a couple of weeks before something becomes available.'

She nodded, keeping her relief to herself. 'You might be off the big walker by then.' Andie cocked her head at the oversized device he'd just started to use, with high forearm rests to kept the pressure off his ribs.

'I wouldn't manage the flight connections and the six-hour trip on my own with that.' He shrugged but it seemed forced.

'You want to go sooner,' Andie guessed.

A tilt of his head. 'Mum and Dad are on their way home now and I'd really like to see them. So they can see I'm okay, and not get ideas about flying over here to see me.'

'Yeah, of course.'

'And my sister has taken time off work for my dad, and now me,' he went on, as though he owed her an explanation. 'She's got two kids and a husband and I just feel like being over there will be easier on us all.'

Andie turned away to finish her coffee, not wanting Ben to read her thoughts on her face. Of course he had to leave, she'd always known that, but she wanted all the rehab beds in Perth to be booked out for . . . well, until she was ready to say goodbye. Especially after the last few days. He'd been everything she needed, she hadn't had to be fine for him, and she finally felt as though her emotional wounds had started to heal.

'Of course, the visitor service won't be as good over in Perth.' Ben grinned, but something in his eyes made her think he was also reluctant to finish what had started between them.

She didn't know exactly what that was, but with a thump in her pulse, she saw that what she felt was more than she'd realised. More than gratitude, more than simple friendship. Something that might tear open the wound in her heart, if she let it.

'You reckon?' She smiled. 'Carmel will be there with coffee and homemade cake every day. And Stuart will have a daily philosophy.'

He watched her a moment. 'What about you?' he asked. 'What will you do?'

'I should be cleared to go back to work in a week or so.'

'I don't mean work.'

She glanced away and shrugged. 'I guess I'll go back to what I was doing.'

'Coming up with analogies?'

She wanted to tell him what she told Vivian, what she told anyone who asked – that she was fine. But she'd already told him everything else. 'Marking time, I guess. Pretending to be Andie Kellett until . . . I am.'

'You're not Andie Kellett?'

'I don't know who I am. I know who I used to be, but . . .' She rested her forearms on his bed. 'I used to be so together. I knew who I was and I was proud of it. Single, career-focused, travelling the world. Then I met Zack and I was just as sure about being his partner, the mother of our children. But when he died, that version of me died with him. That Andie doesn't exist anymore. But the single, happily childless Andie doesn't either. Now I don't know who I am or what I want.'

'Which Andie are you pretending to be?'

'Confident, friendly, got-myself-together Andie.'

'Why pretend to have it all together?'

'Because it's easier if friends don't worry about me. Because not being strong or positive feels like failing. Because being happy makes me sad. Because I once loved travelling the world, but now the idea of getting on a plane scares the hell out of me. Because I'm goal-oriented, and faking it till I make it is better than feeling lost.'

He took her hand. It was warm and gentle and made her throat tighten. 'I like the Andie who doesn't know what she's doing.'

He said it as though anyone who thought different was nuts. She huffed a laugh, pressing trembling lips together.

He took a breath to say more but stopped.

'What?' she asked.

'It's just . . . We survived, Andie.' It was what he'd said the first day she'd visited. 'We might be dead if one of a thousand small things had happened differently. If our lives were movies, we just got bonus scenes, or an unexpected twist. I don't know what you should do with yours, I don't even know what I'm going to do with mine, but I'd hate you to miss a really great caper because you were busy pretending to be someone else.' He fixed his eyes on hers and said, 'I think the real Andie Kellett deserves a lifetime of brilliant capers.'

She nodded. She wanted to tell him she'd had enough capers, only the sincerity in his face, his earnest wish for her life, had made her heart thump with possibility.

Mara

MARA ALWAYS HAD the balcony to herself at this time of the morning, so she stood at the window watching a ship on the horizon until her anxiety and anger had dulled and the heat in her eyes had gone.

Wanting to look busy when Estelle returned, she opened her laptop and tried to focus. Eventually, she heard Estelle murmuring to a staff member, something about a jacket and her wheelchair. A minute later, a nurse wheeled Estelle onto the balcony.

She didn't acknowledge Mara until they were alone. Mara braced herself for what Estelle had to say.

'You don't have to tell me what happened,' Estelle finally said. Her voice was firm and gentle, her eyes their usual piercing blue. 'But I want to know you're okay.'

She *was* okay, she'd made herself okay. She'd had to be okay. For Mum, for Dad, and Pat. For herself. She'd been okay out here on the balcony with the garden and the ocean. Only, when she opened her mouth to say so, her face crumpled.

'Oh, dear girl,' Estelle murmured. A moment later, she slipped a tissue onto Mara's lap.

For several minutes, neither of them spoke. There was just the sound of Mara's hitching breath. She was stunned by the cresting of emotion, longed to let herself cry, but instead she wiped her cheeks and fought for composure, because Estelle was still there, still waiting to be told . . . something.

'I was okay until you asked.' She tried a smile. 'Not that the crying was your fault. I don't really know what that was.'

'University is my guess.' It wasn't a question, but Mara nodded anyway. 'Have you spoken to someone about it?'

'No.'

'Has the university been made aware of your situation?'

Mara huffed a humourless laugh. 'They were aware of my grades. It was pretty obvious where that was going.'

'You earned distinctions in your first semester, and high distinctions at Newcastle Uni before that.'

'You were right, I was undisciplined.'

'I think something happened.'

Mara dropped her face.

'There are well-documented avenues for female students to report . . . incidents. But it's not an easy path to take.' She said no more, as though she'd opened a door and it was up to Mara whether she went through it.

Mara glanced up at her.

'Victims can be made to feel responsible,' Estelle said.

'It's not . . . what you think.' There was no-one to blame but herself.

'Perhaps if you spoke about it, we could decide between us what it is.'

The gentle insistence, the offer of solidarity, the simple fact that Estelle hadn't let it go, that this older, short-tempered, demanding woman wanted to understand, made tears well in Mara's eyes as she nodded. Because there'd never been anyone to tell, and Mara didn't think she could push it all down now that it had resurfaced.

She started at the point things had got hard: how the grief of her mother's death had tricked her into thinking she'd been okay, then quietly eaten away at her until she lost all sense of who she'd been before. She was outgoing then reclusive, ate everything in sight then felt sick at the thought of food, slept for days then was wired for a week. She couldn't concentrate, couldn't remember anything. She felt dumb, as though her intellect had gone to the grave with her mum, and guilty for leaving Dad and Pat, for not making the most of Canberra, for screwing up. For being sad when Mum had wanted her to love life.

'That's a lot to feel guilty for,' Estelle said.

Mara had managed to keep her tears in check as she'd talked, but Estelle's words broke the dry spell and she bent her head to sob again. A moment later, another voice told her they weren't alone on the balcony.

'Is everything okay?' It was Andie, her tone cautiously assertive: *Checking to see if you need an escape route.*

Mara had expected Estelle to wave a hand in dismissal, but instead she waited for Mara, who gave Andie a tearful nod.

'Perhaps a coffee for Mara?' Estelle suggested.

Andie glanced between them. 'You also, Estelle?'

'Thank you, yes.'

Mara watched the exchange, impressed and grateful for Andie's silent yet undaunted evaluation of Estelle.

There was small talk as Andie made the coffees, offered biscuits from a container on the table now considered the 'Balcony Coffee Station'. Handing each of them a mug, Andie dropped a hand onto Mara's shoulder for a moment, then left them to it.

'You were vulnerable,' Estelle said after a sip of her coffee. 'And there are people who will take advantage of that.' Like before, she left the question of what had happened unsaid.

'It wasn't like that. I was lonely and he was . . .' Mara pulled in a breath and blew it out.

'Take your time.'

'He was a friend, we were in the same dorm. He had some mental health issues, depression, anxiety. And I was sad. It was a connection.' She explained how they'd both kept a low profile on campus; their sleep hours were off kilter, he had a dark sense of humour that, in her sadness, had made Mara laugh. He'd felt like an anchor, and she'd given practical advice when he couldn't make sense of the world. It made her feel better about herself, reminded her of who she was, what she was good at. Made her like him in a way he didn't like her.

'The week before mid-semester break, we slept together,' Mara said.

'Was it consensual?' Estelle asked.

'Yes. Definitely.' She wanted Estelle to understand, but she averted her eyes as she told her. 'Unexpected but great, actually. We both laughed afterwards, a bit shocked by the sudden . . . passion, I guess. I thought, this is it: the moment when things get great. I stayed the night, and in the morning, he said he didn't want to be in a relationship.' Her face heated at the memory. 'He said he was worried about screwing up the friendship, so we just agreed to pretend it hadn't happened.'

Mara, though, had been overwhelmed with regret; mortified she'd misunderstood the situation and angry for setting herself up for more heartbreak. But she knew she couldn't let one night ruin the single friendship she'd made. When she went back after the semester break, she was determined to repair things. Only he didn't go back. She spent two weeks trying to track him down, worried their night together had triggered his mental health issues, concerned about what he'd do to himself, that it would be her fault.

I'm in Prague! he'd laughed when she finally got hold of him. He'd dropped out of uni on a whim, rolled a dice for a destination and was super glad it hadn't been Kazakhstan. He thought it was hilarious. After that, he took days to answer her texts, sending only photos of him looking like every other drunk or hungover young tourist.

Mara was stupid and naïve enough to take another two weeks to realise she was nothing to him. She felt used and alone. Someone else she cared about had been cut from her life, and it made grief spiral through her, blowing apart any remaining sense of herself.

She became the weird, sad girl in her dorm. People avoided her, and she slept and slept, missing lectures and deadlines.

One night, the resident assistant knocked on her door, refusing to leave until Mara answered. No-one had seen her for days, he said; her neighbour had been alarmed when she couldn't hear Mara crying anymore. When Mara peered out, a group had assembled in the hallway as though expecting to find a body. Mara convinced the RA she wasn't self-harming, she didn't want to kill herself, she just didn't want to talk to anyone. He told her to get extensions for all her work and take a week off. The next day, Dad had his heart attack.

Estelle made a noise in her throat: a smothered jolt of shock, possibly contrition, too. Mara might have been gratified to hear it, if the memory of those next few days wasn't burning in her chest.

'I got on a plane, went straight to the hospital, found Pat and Dad and just . . .' She shrugged. 'Dad kept apologising for almost dying, saying how he'd promised Mum he'd be there for us. And Pat was freaked out by the tubes and machines and thinking he was about to be an orphan. So I . . . I . . .' She pressed fingers to her lips.

'Pushed it all down.'

'I didn't want to give them anything else to worry about.' Mara squeezed her eyes shut. 'I was . . .' She shook her head. 'It was such a relief to be away from uni that I was almost happy Dad had a heart attack. I felt bad about that. Guilty and upset and relieved and ashamed of myself. Of how I messed everything up.'

'You were clearly in the throes of depression,' Estelle said. 'Still grieving, and not just your mother.'

Mara nodded slowly. In eighteen months, she'd lost her mother and her best friend, faced her father's near death and screwed up her dream of becoming a lawyer. She could have gone back to uni, she could have started again somewhere else, or done it online. But university had crushed her, and the thought of risking that again, of being sucked into that frightening vortex again, filled her with dread. So she gave up her degree and her independence so she could feel safe and loved. So she could be herself.

'You dealt with so much alone.'

Estelle's words felt like a pardon, one Mara hadn't realised she needed. It brought tears again, but of relief and acceptance this time and she let them spill out into the silence of the balcony. A long moment passed before she felt the touch of a hand on her hair. A single pat, followed by the tentative weight of Estelle's palm, the soft caress of her fingers.

'You are a strong, brave young woman, Mara.' It was a statement, a declaration, pure Estelle. And her words, the matter-of-factness of her voice, the warmth of her hand, the tender, unexpected connection between them loosened something inside Mara, allowing her to be still and quiet and let someone else hold her pain for a while.

Coral

'WHEN ARE YOU back?' Alby asked.

'Next Thursday.' Coral tapped her phone to pay for her order.

'Will your mum still be here?'

'Yep. She's got another two-week program after this one ends on Friday.'

'I'll write your name on another two weeks' worth of cups then.' He slid two across the counter and set a bag of coffee next to them. 'For your trip.'

'Coffee beans?'

'You don't want to risk the stuff they serve over there. Pack a coffee plunger and make it in your room.' He nodded at the beans. 'My blend, ground this morning.'

Something tightened in her chest. A good something. 'God, thank you. You're . . .' She'd find him a gift. A giant American cookie or a Statue of Liberty hat or . . . 'the best barista ever.'

Coral gave Val the latest on Jessica's door-to-door delivery, announcing that she was about to touch down in Stockholm as though it was breaking news. As though Val had never doubted Coral could get the job done.

There was a coffee station on the balcony now, the origins of which were still unclear. According to Val, Estelle next door, varyingly named Esme and Elsie, had donated an espresso machine to the patients and visitors on the balcony. Since Coral was about to leave her mother with these people, she had taken inspiration from the generosity and brought cookies as an advance thank you.

Stepping onto the balcony, she saw Mara at the far end sobbing while her boss muttered quietly. Remembering the raised voices she'd heard from that room, something bristled in Coral. She wanted to march over and tell the old bag to lay off. Setting down the container, she looked back just as Estelle glanced over the head of the weeping girl. The older woman smiled: a grim, troubled expression that changed Coral's mind about intruding. Instead, she nodded, an acknowledgement of the moment and of the pain of being young and fragile.

A while later, an orderly told Val and Coral that lunch was being served on the balcony, where they discovered tray tables set up and the other patients and their visitors arriving.

When Coral had helped Val into a chair, Andie drew her aside. 'How are you now?'

'I'm okay, thanks. And thanks for sitting with me in the gutter.'

'Any time.' She gave Coral's arm a gentle squeeze, leaving to have a similar quiet conversation with Mara, slipping her a business card before joining the lunch gathering.

'Is this the girl who was doing the crying?' Val asked in a too-loud voice.

Mara had the blonde hair and porcelain skin of an English rose, and a blush stained her pale cheeks.

'Mum!' Coral said. Then, aiming a gentle smile at Mara, 'What she means is, we hope you're feeling better.'

'I am, thank you.' She glanced at Estelle, who nodded.

'You can't get to my age and not know about needing a good cry, love,' Val said. 'Isn't that right, Elsie.'

'It turns out Val and I share some history,' Estelle said, ignoring the slip and changing the subject. 'We discovered in the gym that we were both debs at Newcastle Town Hall, albeit a few years apart.'

'Ten years, let's not be shy about it,' Val cackled. 'And we both went to The Palais. We probably danced past one another once or twice. I met my husband at the Palais. Did I tell you that story?'

'Indeed you did,' Estelle said. 'We've both enjoyed the reminiscing,' she told the group, with a smile that dared anyone to say otherwise.

The talk moved on to the garden, the gym sessions and Coral's trip to New York. Everyone but Val made enthusiastic comments. Andie had been there a couple of times and offered some advice. When she mentioned bagels in Central Park, Val scoffed. 'Why do you need to go so far for a bagel? We've got perfectly good bread here.'

Andie and Mara had both smiled at Coral with a kind of camaraderie that made Coral wish she'd had more time over the last week to talk to them. Maybe they'd still be visiting Hepburn House when Coral got back. Maybe she could get one of Andie's cards before she left tomorrow.

On a whim, Coral said, 'Would anyone be interested in morning tea on the balcony tomorrow? I'm stopping in on my way to the airport and it would be lovely to throw Val a little party before I leave.'

Everyone seemed keen to be there, deciding it should be BYO mug and agreeing they were lucky to have the balcony. Maybe Coral could create a cosy balcony like this, if she ever got around to fixing up her stupid, falling-down house.

Mara

MARA HAD EXPECTED Estelle to go back to her recliner after lunch, and was surprised when she asked Mara to assist her into one of the cane armchairs.

'I hope you don't mind me joining you for a while longer; I've been wanting to sit in one of these since I first came out here. I have fond memories of curling up with a book as a child in a sunroom not unlike this.'

It was the start of a long, quiet conversation that lasted all afternoon. Later, Mara couldn't remember if Estelle had steered the discussion in the direction it had gone or whether Mara's revelations – and perhaps Val's memories – had opened a Pandora's box that Estelle couldn't close.

Four weeks after Estelle started law at Sydney Uni, her younger brother, considered since birth to be the heir to the Collings legal business, hung himself in the garage of the family home. On the morning of the funeral, her father told Estelle that he was grateful his sixteen-year-old son had resolved his situation before his family was stained by his homosexuality. That all their lives would have been better if Estelle had been a boy.

Estelle's grief had also been complicated, she told Mara. She bore the guilt of her brother's suicide, for leaving him in Newcastle with their father, believing he'd given up because she wasn't there to protect him. She fell into a relationship with a law professor. It was 1969, the attitude and rules around sexual misconduct were different, and when someone reported him, he simply broke it off and continued on with his life. Estelle, though, was devastated; three weeks later, she miscarried a child she hadn't known she was carrying. Admitted to hospital, she too had fallen apart. She had refused her father's demands to go home, to leave uni, to stop speaking her brother's name. He later claimed her 'hysterics' were proof that she was a liability in the business, and that her two miscarriages during her subsequent marriage were the result of her earlier disgrace.

Needing somewhere to stay, Estelle had contacted one of her father's ex-wives, not because they'd ever been close but because the woman hated him as much as Estelle did by then. She told Estelle the men in her family would spend their lives walking all over her if she didn't pull herself together and stand up to them.

She took the advice. 'The experience hardened me,' Estelle said. 'Made me perversely obsessed with shaming my father for his complete miscalculation of his offspring.'

The older woman recounted the experience with her usual hard-edged tone, but her words brought tears to Mara's eyes. Several times, Estelle herself had needed a tissue, too. Those hours on the balcony weren't all heartbreak, though. They also discussed what Estelle might include in a memoir, the research needed and how the chapters might be arranged; whether Estelle could write them without the tediousness of a legal document.

'And what about you, Mara?' she eventually said. 'What do you want for yourself now?'

Mara shrugged, comfortable being honest with Estelle now. 'Stepping away from Dad's business was meant to be a first step to figuring out what else I could do.'

'Is the law out of the question?'

Another shrug. 'Maybe not entirely.'

'Do you have aspirations of being a legal secretary?'

'It might be interesting, but I don't want to do admin forever.'

'A paralegal?'

'Maybe.'

'Or do you still dream of a law degree?'

Mara pulled in a breath and blew it out, shutting down her automatic alarm.

'If,' Estelle qualified, 'dreams could be plucked from the air.'

'Sure, yeah, why not? But life isn't like that. I don't think I've got what it takes to try again.'

'You had no support, Mara. Anyone would struggle under the circumstances you faced.'

'You got through.'

'And look how I turned out.' She made a cynical, amused face and Mara laughed. 'You would not end up like me. There are people in your life who would make sure that didn't happen.'

'Perhaps,' Mara said. 'But I think I'm too scared to try again.'

They did no work that day, and at four pm, Estelle told Mara to go home and do something nice for herself.

Mara didn't bother with a report, spending the drive home thinking about everything they'd discussed. Someone else might have assumed Estelle's recount of her experiences was an older woman crowing about how hard life could be, and that Mara had nothing to complain about. A week ago, Mara might have thought so too. But it wasn't that. Those stories were to show that Estelle understood Mara's pain in a way others would not: the loneliness of grief, the spiralling of emotions, the need to shut it down. That she was there to support, to listen, in her steely-eyed, no-nonsense way, if that was what Mara needed.

Something had happened between them that day. Mara wasn't sure she could call them friends exactly, but it felt pretty great to know someone as fearsome as Estelle had her back.

Mara

'You're to start back in the office on Monday,' Vaughn said when Mara had settled in the chair on the other side of his desk, his tone far less affable than the last time she'd sat there.

'Oh . . . I . . .' She'd thought the meeting she'd been called in to might be about the reports. 'Why?'

'Estelle will be going home over the weekend and intends to formally announce her retirement next week. Clearly, your role is no longer required.'

Mara sat back in shock. Estelle was leaving rehab? Had she known that when they'd talked yesterday?

Vaughn held up a hand before she had a chance to respond. 'While I had moments of doubt, it's clear you are more than capable in an Executive Assistant role. So, in appreciation of your efforts, you're to return in a new role, working as EA to our two junior partners. Continuing, of course, on the higher rate of pay you received with Estelle.'

'I . . . I'm . . .' Two partners? Mara glanced out into the main office, trying to imagine herself orchestrating the lives of two busy people. 'Okay, well, thank you, I guess. It's just . . .' Damn Estelle for making her think about what else she wanted. 'I'm not sure my future is as an Executive Assistant.'

'Of course, if you've changed your mind about the

undergraduate program, your work with Estelle would be taken into consideration.'

The familiar dread tightened in her gut. 'Well, no, but . . . Can I think about the new role?'

'Perhaps I haven't been clear, Mara,' he said with an edge to his tone. 'This role is the only one being offered to you. While the last two weeks may have been difficult, Collings expects a certain level of aspiration in its staff. You need to decide if you want to be part of our team.' He checked his watch and pushed his chair back. 'You have until close of business tomorrow to let me know your decision.'

☕

There was a text from Estelle when Mara got to her car, asking her to pick up some things from the apartment. A suitcase for all her stuff?

Why hadn't Estelle told her she was going home? Had she asked Vaughn to recall her to the office? Was yesterday's long conversation meant to mark the end of their association? Because obviously that's all it was: she'd been stupid to think they were almost friends.

'Estelle will move into the downstairs guest rooms for now,' Lynette explained as she headed through the apartment with an armful of linen. She opened a door on the other side of the staircase that Mara hadn't noticed before, leading her through a sitting room and kitchen into a bedroom, where she deposited the bedding.

'This was originally a separate one-bedroom apartment,' Lynette said on the way back out. 'Estelle put in the connecting door.' Pointing to a large artwork, she added, 'The last scholarship student painted that for her.'

'Scholarship student?'

'She billets one every now and then. Masters and PhDs, mostly. A couple of foreign exchange students. Friends visiting from overseas when there's no-one in.'

Following the housekeeper up the stairs, Mara asked, 'When did Estelle tell you she was coming home?'

'Yesterday afternoon. It's all happened quite fast, but that's Estelle for you. Once she decides, it's all systems go. She's already organised daily physio and a live-in nurse for a few weeks. An adjustable bed is arriving tomorrow.'

Mara trailed her through an upstairs guest room and library before they made their way to Estelle's quarters. Mara left with a suitcase and a change of clothes for Estelle, reminding herself she'd want to go home too if she lived there; it was gorgeous. Although if Mara had an assistant, she would have told them they were no longer needed before they got the news from someone else. Especially if they had bared their souls together.

Don't be upset about it, Mara scolded herself as she pulled into the hospital car park. But she felt cast aside. It wasn't the first time she'd been down that path and it hurt to be back, feeling like the stupid girl let down by someone she'd thought was a friend. Someone she'd trusted when she should have known better.

Mara paused outside Estelle's room to straighten her shoulders. If she'd learned anything from her boss, it was to be direct when she was ticked off. 'Good morning,' she said, handing Estelle her coffee. 'So you're going home on the weekend.'

Irritation tightened Estelle's face. 'I suppose Vaughn told you that.' At Mara's nod, the older woman paused for a moment before lifting her chin. 'I have something to discuss with you. Please sit down.'

The gravity in her tone made alarm buzz in Mara's veins. Was she . . . going home to die? Pulling a chair to Estelle's recliner, she tried to hold back the fear that another person she cared about was going to suffer.

Estelle took her time, absorbed by the keep cup between her palms before finally chuffing a small laugh as she looked up. 'It's your fault, Mara. I'd still be here shouting down the phone if you hadn't told me how ridiculous I was.'

'I . . . I . . .' *What?*

'Don't worry. I agree with you. There are far more productive ways I can spend my time; apparently I just needed you to put me in my place.'

'I—'

Estelle held up a hand. 'Well done, Mara. It takes a lot to impress me.'

'But . . .'

'I have quite a lot to get through, so you might as well hear me out without any more of those unfinished sentences.'

'Wait. You're not dying?'

'Good lord, no. I haven't got time for that rubbish.'

Mara grinned with relief, and stayed silent while Estelle explained that she hadn't made a decision until their conversation on the balcony yesterday, and that telling Mara to go home had been an excuse to start making calls. Which took several hours and a few more this morning; she'd wanted to get as much in place as possible before Mara arrived.

'Vaughn doesn't know the details,' Estelle said. 'But he was the first to be told I won't be going back to the office. He can have that point. I'm more interested in what happens next.'

Point? Was Mara the pawn in whatever end game Estelle was playing with her cousin? She took a breath to say she didn't want to be part of it when Estelle said, 'I'm going to write that book you talked me into.'

'I didn't—'

'I know,' she interrupted. 'But it does feel better to blame someone else for my rare bout of enthusiasm.' Smiling, she began detailing her plans for the book that would be scheduled around guest lecturing opportunities that she was discussing with university contacts, potential board positions and ideas for mentoring.

'I can focus on rehabilitation while in the planning and organising phase and gradually increase my workload as I get stronger.'

'You've got it all worked out then.' Mara shifted to the edge of her chair, hoping Estelle would take the hint. She didn't want to hear any more about the plans that had left Mara with the choice of a job she didn't want or no job at all.

'Not all, Mara. I have something to discuss with you. An offer, with several parts. I know it's taken some time to get to the point, but again, please hear me out.'

Mara sighed and sat back in the chair.

'I'd like you to be my research assistant.'

Mara's mouth dropped open.

'It's not a full-time position, and would include some work around the other paths I'm exploring. Three days per week, if you are interested in the rest of my offer. If not, we can discuss alternatives. Now,' she clasped her hands on her lap, 'I'd like to preface this next part by explaining that, in many ways, it comes from my own selfish desire to see someone else achieve her dream. Someone who I might have been, who reminds me of myself.' She took a breath and looked . . . uneasy. 'I would like to support you through the rest of your law degree.'

Mara's spine stiffened. 'I . . . You want to pay my . . .?' Fees, a scholarship, some pocket money? After everything they'd discussed yesterday, Estelle actually thought money would entice Mara back to uni?

'Let me explain.' Estelle told her it wasn't a financial offer, except for the salary as research assistant. But there would be opportunities to discuss cases as they worked on the book, plus a more formal mentoring arrangement that would include weekly tutoring and exam preparation.

'I trust Lynette showed you through the apartment?' Estelle asked.

Mara was still waiting for *tutoring* to sink in and needed a second to catch up before she nodded.

'When I bought the apartment next door, I was thinking long-term and planning live-in aged care assistance in my distant future. But I have several friends who live overseas, and it's been a bonus to give them somewhere to stay. Of course, from next week

I'll be using the downstairs rooms. While I'm there, I've allotted the spare room next to my office for overnight nursing staff. The upstairs quarters are yours, if you'd like them.'

Mara cast her mind back to the guest room and library. 'For the research work?'

'I mean for you to move into. Forgive me if I've misinterpreted the situation, but at your age, I assumed you must be itching to have your own space. It would only be until I'm able to get up the stairs. Then the downstairs rooms would be yours, as per the arrangement with other students I've billeted. Rent-free until your last exam as part of . . . well, let's call it my support package.'

Estelle's plan had been delivered in her standard clipped tone, and when she finished, Mara had a sudden urge to laugh. Her brain had stopped working, and the idea of uni, the whole intricate plan, all seemed . . . indecipherable. She wanted to say *Are you insane?* and *I don't want uni* and *Your apartment!* But when she opened her mouth, she managed to say . . . nothing.

'You don't need to decide now,' Estelle told her. 'In fact, I don't want an answer until you've had a chance to really consider it. Of course, there would be an employment contract and residency agreement, to protect us both, and some thought to filling your two free days until the semester starts. But you should talk to some people, your family; think about whether you can put up with me for the next two to three years. Decide if you still dream of studying the law and whether you're game to try again. It's no small thing, I understand that. And if you decide not to pursue your degree, the position of research assistant will still be there for you, if a part-time job works with whatever your future holds.'

Estelle completed her proposal by reaching for Mara's hand and giving it a brief, warm clasp. 'That's enough for now.'

'I don't know what to say.'

'Nothing yet. We'll talk more later.' She tilted her head to the window. 'That sounds like Val's morning tea on the balcony. Fetch me those crutches and my wrap, will you?'

Coral

'WHY WASN'T I told about the impressive coffee cups down this end of the corridor?' Coral said as she set paper cups from the visitors' lounge beside two tartan mugs and a couple of fancy keep cups.

'The mugs are ours,' said Ben, tilting his head towards Andie on the sofa beside his wheelchair. As he explained about his parents over in Scotland, Coral wondered again about those two. She'd heard they hadn't met until the accident at the harbour, and that Andie was keeping Ben company until he could get back to Perth. And sure, it was lovely for Andie to do that, but the long, quiet conversations, the laughter: there was definitely something between those two.

Coral passed around the slabs of carrot cake she'd organised with Alby, glad she'd decided to throw the morning tea. Now that she was packed and she'd picked up the hire car for the trip to the airport, it was nice to say goodbye to Val in a relaxed moment, and the company of others would avoid any more emotionally charged conversations before she got on the plane.

'Mara is responsible for our thermal cups,' Estelle said. 'Not the only impressive suggestion she has made while we've been here.'

Something between those two as well, Coral thought. No sign of yesterday's grim concern from Estelle or the jumpy tension she'd seen in Mara at times.

The conversation ambled along to New York and back to the hospital garden and Val's award-winning carrot cake.

'I've got to get going soon,' Coral finally announced, 'but I wanted to thank everyone for coming and for being the nice crowd at the end of the corridor. A special mention to Estelle for sharing her coffee machine, and to Mum for making do here while I have a speedy trip to New York.' She raised her cup, which was empty, but whatever.

Beside her, Val lifted an imaginary glass, saying, 'And to my darling Coral, for being clever and doing a workshop over there.'

Coral did a double take. She got the workshop part wrong, but *darling* and *clever*? 'Thanks, Mum,' she whispered, kissing her forehead. 'I need to get the suitcase with your things in from the car, then I'll be going.'

Heading to the car park, Coral was aware of the extra time she'd spent lingering over morning tea. Perhaps because she was finally leaving for New York, or maybe she'd just relaxed enough to enjoy herself, but she'd had fun.

She'd reversed the hire car into its slot and, beeping the locks as she drew close, she saw that a huge four-door ute had parked so close that its tow bar was almost kissing the rear of the hatchback. So close, in fact, that she couldn't stand between the two vehicles. Or open the boot.

She heaved a sigh, checked her watch, told herself not to have an anxiety attack over someone else's bad parking. Opening the rear passenger door, she wrestled the back seat down and began hauling on Val's suitcase before she realised she was doing it all wrong. She could just drive the car forward a couple of metres.

Behind the wheel, she took a second to reacquaint herself with the unfamiliar controls, pressed the start button and . . . nothing. She moved the gear selector out of park and back in; tried again.

Nothing.

Alarm buzzed across her shoulder blades. She checked her foot was on the brake, that she'd read the stops on the gear

selector properly, that there were lights glowing on the dash . . .
Oh. Oh shit.

She took a breath and, because sometimes things just worked
when you started over, she got out and got back in again. Brake,
gear, button.

Nothing.

Her heart thumped. She gripped the wheel, tried to batten
down the panic unfolding in her chest.

Okay: think. She wasn't a mechanic but no lights, no engine
turning over meant it had to be the battery. The whiteboard in her
brain appeared: call the car hire company, organise alternative
transport, retrieve luggage from boot, get to Sydney, board plane.

Doable, if she didn't panic.

Only, her phone was in her bag in Val's room, so after some
heaving and swearing to get Val's suitcase out, she headed back
down the meandering path. At double speed, too focused to take
in the garden, because experience told her to plan for the worst.

Andie

RYLEE'S APPEARANCE ON the balcony was met with a rousing welcome, which Andie thought was pretty amusing, since only minutes earlier, all three patients had been cursing the young physio for her sweet, gentle torture.

'Thought I'd drop by to see how the party's going.' She cast a smile around the group, raising a hand to Mara. Nice, Andie thought, that Mara had made a friend here.

Ben pointed a teasing finger at Rylee. 'You just came for the cake.'

'*And* cake,' Rylee pointed back. 'Not *just* cake.'

The hubbub of amused replies fell abruptly silent at a loud retort from Val's room: 'I haven't got two hours!'

No-one moved. When there was a huff of irritation, Andie went to the door.

Coral was pacing, her phone pressed to her ear, her other hand tangled in hair that ten minutes ago had been styled into neat waves.

'Okay. Okay-okay-okay-okay.' A stiff breath. 'I'll get back to you.' She hung up, saw Andie and squeezed her eyes shut.

Remembering Coral's anxiety attack, Andie aimed for calm and helpful as she said, 'What's wrong?'

Coral gave her a terse rundown: the hire car, a two-hour wait for another; why, when she spent her life making sure things arrived on time, did it have to be her that was running late? 'Fuck.' Hands on her hips and breathing hard. 'Sorry for the swearing.'

'Plenty of reason to swear.' Andie smiled. 'Right, what can I do?'

Coral held up a hand. 'I just need to find another car.'

Andie pulled her mobile from her pocket. 'Who've you called already?'

Mara stepped into the doorway, her phone out too. 'What time do you need to leave?'

But Coral was already talking to someone else, asking what and how soon and could they drop a car to her? She made three more calls; Mara took notes while Andie explained the problem to Val.

'Would either of you be able to drive me to Maitland?' Coral finally asked, looking from Andie to Mara.

Andie glanced at Val's concern then Ben's raised eyebrows, thought of the times she'd been stranded and the rest of her day with nothing to do but fill in the hours. 'I could take you to—'

'Sorry, I know it's probably well out of your way.'

'It'd be faster if—'

'I can get a four-cylinder three-door hatch in an hour. It'll be cutting it fine but I should still—'

'—I just drove you to the airport.'

Coral's face creased into an impatient, anxious frown.

'I can take you to the airport,' Andie repeated.

'It's *Sydney* Airport,' she said, like Andie was wasting time. Like Coral couldn't take much more.

'I know.'

Coral pushed a hand through her hair, looking at Andie as though she'd lost her mind. 'I can't ask you to do that.'

'You're not. I'm offering.'

Something flickered in Coral's face. Hope, perhaps. 'It's a two and a half hour drive.'

'Just as well you're not flying out of Melbourne then.' Andie laughed. She'd been stranded and late for flights before, and it was kind of fun to be someone else's godsend. And to watch Coral's face as she worked through whatever checklist she had in her head before she could run with it.

'You've got a bad elbow,' Coral finally said.

From on the balcony, Estelle called, 'Mara can share the driving.'

Coral looked at Mara then Andie. Her lips tightened and her eyes got shiny. 'Why would you do that?' she whispered.

Andie pressed a hand to her chest, all the more determined to get Coral to the airport now. 'Well, Val told us you were meant to fly out on Monday but you stayed to help her, and then Monday was,' she raised an eyebrow at Coral, 'a bad day. And,' she counted off the reasons on her fingers, 'you'll be cutting it fine if you waste time with another hire car, you can't assume you won't get held up at security, you've got a paper to deliver, and I've seen one too many runaway cars to let you drive down that motorway distracted about missing your flight.' She held up her thumb. 'Lastly, we all really want you to get to New York.'

The last part seemed to sway Coral more than the rest. She pressed fingers to her lips, swallowing hard.

'And apparently,' Andie added, 'Mara gets the rest of the day off if you say yes.'

Coral laughed, wiped her eyes. 'Thank you, yes.'

'No, thank *you*.' Mara grinned.

☕

Coral had needed help to get her luggage out of the hire car; Mara had proved to be the only one of them small and limber enough to drag it out of the boot through the passenger door. Once that was done, Andie followed Coral and Mara back into the hospital to collect their belongings and say goodbyes.

'I thought you were planning to have lunch on the balcony with your gym buddies,' Andie said when she found Ben back in his room.

'I had a visitor. The woman I spoke to yesterday.' He cleared his throat. 'She thinks there might be a rehab bed for me in Perth next week.'

Andie's pulse did a swift thump. 'Next week?'

'Yeah. I'm still getting my head around it.'

Andie glanced around his room, needing a moment. The sight of the walker reminded her of how much pain he still had. 'When would you need to leave?' Another week to heal would help.

'Apparently, they don't like to have a bed empty for more than a day or two, so if it's next week, I'd need to be there Monday or Tuesday.' He pushed a hand through his hair. 'Which means I'd be flying back this weekend.'

Andie swallowed hard. Told herself not to let him see what she was feeling. Because this wasn't about her. Ben needed to go back to the warm voices she'd heard down the phone, to the kind of life she'd lost with Zack; to let his family help him heal. 'When will you know?'

'Later today, maybe tomorrow. Enough time to organise flights and someone to be with me.'

She nodded. Smiled. She wanted this for him, she reminded herself. She wanted it for herself, too. Because she really did need to move on. From the accident and from Ben. Not linger over feeling things that could break her heart again.

'Carmel and Stuart will be so relieved,' she said.

'If it works out. It's short notice to organise someone to fly over from Perth and help me back. And of course, I don't have to take the spot.'

'Why wouldn't you?'

'If I have to share a room with six people. If it's a long way from Mum and Dad's. If it gets bad reviews on Airbnb Rehab.'

She smiled, telling herself it wasn't fair to hope for another week. 'Better get googling then.' Ignoring the thumping in her chest and fighting an urge to hug him, she hooked a thumb over her shoulder. 'I should get going.'

'You're a good person, Andie.'

How did he make her cry at the drop of a hat? Well, she wouldn't miss that.

He held out his hand and without thinking, she took it, letting him pull her against his broken ribs. She held on to him as though it was already goodbye, breathing in his musky smell; absorbing the heat, the sincerity of him. Everything she wanted to tell him about being grateful and never forgetting, about being better for knowing him, rose to her throat and threatened to choke her.

'I've got to drive to Sydney,' she whispered into his hair. Smiling at him, for him, she pulled away, kissing the tips of her fingers and pressing them to his forehead before she walked out.

Part 8

A Setback

Mara

MARA LET CORAL claim the front passenger seat; the woman was already stressed and clammy, she didn't need the limited leg room in the back to make it worse.

Val had turned into a chatterbox after Coral left for the car park the first time, finding herself the centre of attention as the authority on Coral's trip to New York. Oh, she's been wanting this assignment for years, Val told them. Yes, the doctor insisted she stay for test results; dear me, she put on a brave face. There was an outfit Val wasn't sure suited her daughter, some stairs that were likely to break her ankle, a package that had to zig-zag around the world before it got to the right place, and some bloke called Richard, whose parents were expecting so much of Coral.

It was rambling and confusing in a sweet, old lady way and Mara wasn't sure how much of it was true, but the timing had been perfect; seconds before Coral came back, they'd all reassured Val that they'd look out for her while her daughter got her much-deserved trip to New York. So Andie's offer to drive Coral to the airport and Estelle giving Mara the day off to help had felt like proof of their promise.

That kind of fun wouldn't happen if Mara went back to the Collings office, she realised. There was no guarantee it would happen if she worked for Estelle, either, but the job wouldn't be sitting in an office organising other people's lives, that was for sure. Researching a book and setting up speaking engagements sounded interesting and kind of cool. If Mara could put up with Estelle. If she decided to go back to uni.

She sighed.

'Right, so, we've got two and a half hours to get to know each other,' Andie said, as though there was no way she was driving all the way to Sydney in silence. Pulling into the traffic, she glanced at Mara in the rear-view then at Coral beside her. 'Tell us about your conference in New York.'

With any luck, Mara thought, Coral would talk all the way to Sydney and Mara wouldn't have to discuss life as she knew it, because right now, all she knew was that life was confusing.

Words seemed to spill out of Coral as though Andie's question had turned on a tap. Not an outpouring of information so much as a bullet-point list of everything leading up to New York. Five years waiting for an invitation, thrilled and terrified about presenting a paper; her daughter, her grandson, the new family business; the son's apartment, the ex in-laws, the ex; the client, the assistant. Mara had pulled her phone out, intending to do some surreptitious scrolling, but the list of Coral's calamities was like a train wreck she couldn't tune out of. She saw Andie glance at Coral a few times, making Mara hope she wasn't the only one feeling like a complete incompetent, because the woman seemed to take it all in her stride. As though each drama was just another hitch in the road, like working in logistics was the key to managing all of life's crises and all Mara needed was a whiteboard.

'How about you?' Coral said, coming to a sudden halt. She'd aimed the question at Andie, who thankfully lightened the mood as she talked about her job in recruitment: finding the right people for the right roles and vice versa. She was passionate about it, she said; she had a sixth sense about people. She'd met a guy in an internet cafe once, marched him over to meet her best friend and *voila!* Married, child, happily ever after. Her best success story.

Then it was Mara's turn, and while part of her felt these two women were exactly the kind of people she needed to talk to about Estelle's offer, a larger part just wanted to sound like she was following them down the road to clever and together. So she told them about finding Estelle at the bottom of the stairs and working by her bedside: the clothes, the tom yum, the coffee, the brain explosions. Trying to make it sound amusing, like Andie had, and all part of the job, like Coral had.

And then, thank god, Coral's phone rang and Mara could stop talking, stare out the window and tell herself that while she'd made a slow start, she too might be able to pull her life together.

'Yes.' It was just one word, but something in Coral's tone made Mara look back at her. When she pressed a hand to her forehead, Mara knew it was bad news. 'Yes, I understand. When?'

Mara turned to the window again, watching the hills and valleys speeding past, trying not to listen, trying to ignore the memory of phone calls that had left her reeling. Andie changed lanes, heading for the next turn-off. Perfect timing for the motorway stop where they'd planned for a bite to eat.

'Okay, okay,' Coral was saying. 'I'll need to get back to you. Five minutes. I just need to . . . think.'

Coral hung up and sat like a statue, eyes squeezed tight, the hinge of her jaw pulsing. The only sounds as they left the motorway were the rumble of the engine and the indicator clicking. Andie steered past a service station and pulled into a space in a large car park.

Coral's hands were pressed to her face.

Andie exchanged a glance with Mara in the rear-view. 'Coral?'

It was the same competent, bullet-pointed voice when she spoke. 'Yes. Sorry. Mum's had a fall. Looks like a broken hip. They've called an ambulance.'

Andie turned to look at her passenger.

'Sorry,' Coral said again, suddenly gasping and fumbling for the doorhandle, 'I'm going to be sick.'

Andie

ANDIE WATCHED AS Coral swung her feet out of the car and hung her head over her knees. No-one moved as they all waited for morning tea to make a comeback. Only it wasn't the coffee and cake that rose, but Coral, who shot to her feet as though thrust upright by a wave of emotion.

Andie clicked out of her seatbelt as Coral lurched through the car park. Mara gasped as a car beeped and braked, releasing her own seatbelt as Coral stumbled out of its path.

'Should we do something?' Mara asked.

'Let's give her a minute.' But Andie opened her door. 'Maybe keep an eye on her to make sure she's not hit by . . .' She pressed her lips together, fingering the fading bruises on her face.

'The cars are all going pretty slow in here,' Mara said. She joined Andie outside the car and they watched as Coral reached a blank wall at the rear of the parking area, stopping like a robot in front of an obstacle, nowhere else to go.

Andie checked her watch. 'She's got some time.'

'Do you think she'll still go?'

'No idea. I mean, it's work, she's delivering a paper. Five years' waiting, and drama after drama. If anyone deserves a break, it's Coral. But it's her mum. I'm just glad not to be making that call.' A minute later, when Coral's only move had been to press her hand to her face, Andie said, 'Right, whatever she decides, we'll need to eat.'

'I'll do the food,' Mara said, pushing her phone into a back pocket. 'You're good with people, you do Coral.'

Andie huffed a laugh, thinking Mara must be good with people too if she'd handled Estelle. Then again, maybe she'd had enough for now.

Andie went to Coral and just stood beside her for a while, remembering that sometimes talking was too hard and a comforting presence could be enough to stay sane. When Coral's sobbing eased, Andie held out the wad of tissues she'd grabbed from the car, putting a gentle hand on her back while Coral lifted her sunglasses to wipe her face. When Mara emerged from the restaurant on the other side of the car park, Andie said to Coral, 'There's a table in the sun over there.'

With a nod and a shaky breath, Coral followed her.

Mara set down a tray. 'I wasn't sure what you'd want.' She began arranging items on the table. 'I bought coffees with and without milk, lemonade, water, a cookie, fruit salad and my personal favourite in times of stress, a packet of snakes. Kind of nice to chew off a head without hurting anyone.'

It broke the tension and even Coral huffed a laugh.

'Well, I'm up for a snake.' Andie tore the packet open and said, 'I don't know what's factoring in your decision, Coral. But I just want to say it's an hour and a half to the airport from here. There's still time to make your flight, if that's what you decide to do.'

Coral's eyes were shiny and red-rimmed, but something was working behind them as she held Andie's gaze. 'You have no idea how appealing that thought is. And how guilty I feel to be sobbing about missing my flight while my mum is in an ambulance.'

'Val is in good hands,' Mara said, pushing the snakes closer.

Andie took a coffee. 'And you're so close you can almost smell the aviation fuel.'

Another laugh from Coral. 'I need to call Hepburn House again.'

Afterwards, they sipped coffee and ate snakes in the sun as Coral went through the details, her voice less machine-gun speed now that the angst had burned off. Val had fallen trying to get out of her recliner, hit her cheek as she went down, landing heavily on her side. The doctor at Hepburn House suspected she'd broken her hip, and she was on her way to the nearest Emergency Department.

'I've got to stay for Mum.' Coral took a breath and blew it out. Looked at Andie then Mara and gave a nod: decision made. 'I've been feeling bad about going all week,' she said. Not explaining so much as just talking, Andie thought. 'For two weeks, really, since Mum had her fall. I want to go to New York, I'm expected to be there, my photo is in the conference brochure, but . . .' She lined up the food packages on the table as she talked. 'I'm a planner. My plans are like Andie's people skills. I make a plan, then I make it work. It's my job. Sometimes I feel like that's my only role in life. And I got so fixated on getting to New York that I didn't stop to think about what I needed to do for myself. Like take a breath. Like shed a few of the things that I didn't need to do. You'd think the anxiety attack on Monday would have been the big hint.'

Andie reached across the table, covered Coral's hand with hers.

'That was you?' Mara said.

'Yep.' She blew out a breath. 'Why is it easier to keep doing stuff for other people than to make a decision about what you need to do for yourself?' She shook her head. 'Anyway, the upside of sobbing my heart out just now is that I know what I *need* to do. I need to stay here for Mum. I need to not worry, not feel guilty, not exhaust myself. I need to accept that some things can't be fixed, no matter how many times I shuffle the schedule about. And that in itself feels good.'

'You don't need a conference to get to New York,' Andie said. 'You can take yourself there.'

Coral straightened, brushed her fingers through her hair. 'Yeah, you're right. I can.'

As though the idea had never occurred to Mara, she said, 'I could go to New York too.'

'Yes, you could,' Andie said in unison with Coral. They glanced at each other, then back at Mara, and when all three of them laughed, they seemed to cross a threshold from acquaintances to friends.

Ten minutes later, they were back on the motorway, heading in the opposite direction. Mara was driving, Coral sat in the back and Andie was thinking about what Coral had said, and why it was hard to make a decision about what you need for yourself.

Andie knew instinctively about other people; she saw them in the way a chef understood flavour, a good teacher understood a student, like an architect saw spaces. She used to think she knew herself: what she wanted, where she fit, what made her tick. Even when her life flipped and she fell in love with Zack. But something had changed when he died. Something in herself. She didn't know if she'd lost the ability to see who was in the mirror or she'd lost the person she'd once been. Whatever it was, she had no idea what she needed for herself. To be herself.

'This has been the weirdest two weeks ever,' Mara said into the silence.

Andie turned from the view. 'You're not kidding.'

'You too?' Coral asked.

'Today's been kind of a relief, though.' Mara's gaze flicked to Coral in the rear-view mirror. 'That someone as organised as you, with that whole whiteboard thing in your head, also has no idea what you should be doing sometimes.'

'Possibly the whiteboard is a sign I've lost my mind.' Coral laughed.

'What do you have no idea about?' Andie asked.

Mara chewed her lip for a moment, said, 'Estelle offered me a job this morning.'

Andie frowned. 'Don't you already work for her?'

'A different job. Not just a job but an opportunity – a different kind of *life*.'

Andie listened as Mara explained Estelle's offer, wondering what had happened to make the older, forthright woman want to take young, quietly spoken Mara under her wing. There were obvious reasons for Mara to hesitate, not the least being Estelle herself, but Andie got the impression that the uni part of the deal was the problem.

'Wow,' Coral said when Mara had finished.

'What are your thoughts?' Andie asked her.

'That I'm . . . That she's lost her mind?'

'And that you're . . .?' Andie prompted her to finish her first thought.

Mara shrugged. 'That I'm just . . . me.' Her voice cracked on the last word.

Andie passed her a tissue, using the moment to take in the hesitant smile and the flush to her cheeks, and wondering why Mara felt undeserving. 'How do you get on with Estelle?'

'Last week she was awful,' Mara said. 'But we had a huge argument on Friday and I yelled at her and after that, she was different. I mean, she was still, you know, pompous. But it was like last week was a test to see if I'd crack, and once I'd shouted back, she decided I was okay, or worthy or something.'

'She's got a reputation for being intolerant of anyone who doesn't stand up for themselves,' Andie said. 'Maybe she's been waiting for someone to push back.'

'Last week, she told me she thought it was weak to be kind, and then today, she makes this offer.'

Coral leaned into the space between the seats. 'Maybe she's been waiting for someone who deserved her kindness.'

'What's the problem with uni?' Andie asked.

Mara didn't answer. Her hands, though, tightened on the steering wheel and her mouth straightened into a grim line.

Andie flicked a glance at Coral in the back. 'What's said on a road trip, stays on a road trip.' Andie said it gently, hoping that Mara understood there was kindness and empathy between them all now, not just conversation.

It took a moment for her to speak again, but once she did, she covered kilometres of roadway with heartbreak and loss. Andie heard her phone ping with a text, but left it unread. She considered suggesting they swap drivers so Mara could have a good sob, but decided the focus on the road might have been helping her get through her story. Several times, Coral reached forward to put a hand on Mara's shoulder, while Andie kept her supplied with tissues. When Mara was finished, Andie remembered how Ben's words had helped and said with as much sincerity as she could, 'Geez, Mara. Life can be fucking traumatic.'

It made all three of them laugh.

'So what do you think about Estelle's offer?' Mara finally said.

'I regret not finishing uni,' Coral said. 'I gave up halfway through a fine arts degree to have a baby and, to be honest, I haven't managed to put myself first since. It's a rare thing in life for someone to offer support and kindness at their own cost. And when you're the one who's usually being supportive and kind, it's easy to think your time will come again, especially when you're young. But there are no guarantees. I've been lucky; I've been able to work my way into a career that's kept me interested and financially secure, but if I had my time again, I'd find a way to finish my degree, to give myself other options, give me the confidence to pursue a different path.'

Mara nodded, glanced at Andie. 'What about you? Did you go to uni?'

'I travelled for ten years after I finished my degree,' Andie told her. 'I'm glad I didn't travel first, though. I had no money when I came back, so I couldn't have started uni then, and I haven't got the patience for the long haul of part-time study. I see plenty of people who do, but it takes commitment.' Then, not wanting Mara to feel she had no choices, she added, 'And you don't have to have a degree. I see plenty of people who didn't go to uni and still have great jobs.'

'It's not just uni,' Mara said. 'It's Estelle too. I don't want to end up being her lady's maid. Or killing her.'

That produced another laugh.

'Sounds like standing up to her will help with that.'

'Good practice for a legal career.'

Mara smiled, nodding as though they'd given her plenty to think about.

'What about you, Andie?' Coral asked. 'How's your rehab been?'

'It's been . . .' Andie dug her phone from her bag as she spoke, 'weird for me too. In a good way.' She read the text and her hand flew to her chest.

'Everything okay?' Coral asked.

'Yeah.' No. She wasn't sure. 'Ben texted. He's got a rehab place in Perth starting on Monday.'

'Oh no!' Mara said.

'Or is it good news?' asked Coral.

Andie avoided looking at either of them. 'It's good news. Great for Ben to be with his family while he recuperates.'

'Will you go with him?'

'What? No.' She flapped it away. 'We only met last week.' Not wanting to think about how he needed to be with his family, she told Mara and Coral how great it had been to have him here; the story she hadn't been able to tell Vivian. How they'd met, and then met again. How she must have felt as safe with him on the night of the accident as she had at Hepburn House, how there had been things in her life she'd been frightened to speak about until Ben opened that door. That telling Ben had freed her in some way she didn't understand yet, and that talking about it again now – something she couldn't have done a week ago – was helping her to see how she'd changed in the last two weeks.

'I was jealous that you guys were having a nice time,' Coral said. 'All that laughing was so annoying.'

'Me too,' Mara chipped in. 'I thought you were a couple.'

Turning in her seat to look at them both, Andie said, 'No, it's not like that. I couldn't stand the thought he'd have no visitors. I was only ever keeping him company until he went back to Perth.' That was the story she needed to tell herself now.

There was silence for a moment as Mara glanced at her and Coral frowned.

'Won't he need someone to help him on the flight?' Coral said.

'He's organising someone from Perth to escort him back.'

Coral tilted her head. 'You don't want to do that?'

'No.' Andie squared her face to the windscreen, not wanting to think about it.

'He could probably claim the price of your flight back on the accident insurance,' Coral said, as though cost might have been the issue.

'No.' This time the word was sharp and hard, driven by fear. 'I can't . . . I don't fly anymore. I just . . . can't.'

Andie wanted that to be the end of it, for someone to change the subject, to go back to the laughing. Only Coral reached forward and squeezed her shoulder and then it was Andie's turn to cry. She pressed fingers to trembling lips, searched the scenery for something to divert her attention, but she could sense what she'd tried to convey to Mara: that this space, her car, the bubble of their failed trip to Sydney, was a safe place to share.

So she told them about the remote island, the trip back with Zack's body, the delays and complications, the helplessness of not being able to get them both home, the fear that something worse would happen, that she'd be left there, broken and alone, and someone would zip her into a bag too. She'd spent ten years travelling the world, but the thought of boarding a plane now filled her with a heart-pounding, gasping, sweating panic.

'I'm so sorry, Andie,' Coral said with another shoulder clinch.

Andie touched her fingers, grateful for the comfort. 'It's okay. I couldn't have talked about it before Ben. I thought I should have been trying to move on from another bad experience, but lingering over this one with Ben has been . . .' So much more healing. 'Ben's exhilarated by survival. He makes the most of life and is comfortable with death. He seems to be able to embrace it all, and that's started to rub off on me. It's okay. We've done something for each other, now we can both move on.'

'Maybe he'll come back when he's better,' Mara said, as though determined to find a happy ending.

Andie couldn't let herself hope for that. Losing him now was less painful than if she let her feelings for him take root. 'He only had a six-month contract in Newcastle,' she said. 'And his dad's not well. He needs to be near his family.'

They were only twenty minutes from the hospital Val had been taken to and they slipped into a pensive silence, each of them with plenty to ponder.

'Who would have thought,' Andie said, as they turned off the motorway. 'Visit a patient in Hepburn House and get a little rehab for your soul.'

'I got the soul thing, but without the fun patient,' Mara said.

'I got an anxiety attack,' Coral laughed. 'And maybe some time to work out what I need to do for myself.'

Mara

'GOOD LUCK WITH Estelle tomorrow,' Coral said as Mara hugged her goodbye outside Emergency. 'Can't wait to hear what you decide to do.'

Mara was amazed Coral could think about anyone else after missing her flight. But then, all of today had been amazing. Who would have thought she'd finish her stint as an EA with two job offers and now two new friends?

'Good luck in there.' Thinking of her own hospital experience, Mara added, 'Make sure you have something to eat, and text if there's anything I can do.'

Andie offered to keep Coral's luggage for now. 'Pick it up tomorrow afternoon, then we can have a drink at my place,' Andie suggested. 'You too, Mara. You can tell us how your life is going to pan out, and we can toast the end of the weirdest two weeks ever.'

Mara was touched to be included, and more than happy to see off the Hepburn House experience with these two women. They swapped numbers and waved Coral goodbye. Twenty minutes later, Mara sat parked outside Hepburn House for a long time with Andie, who gave her professional advice on Estelle's offer: pay and employment contracts, positions she could apply for if she decided not to accept the role with either Estelle or Vaughn, and study that didn't include a degree.

When Mara pulled her car into the garage at home, she sat for a while longer, her brain buzzing. If she'd learned anything from the road trip with Andie and Coral, it was that life wasn't about success or failure, good or bad – it was everything, all at once, and you just had to keep picking your way through it.

'You're home early,' her dad called from his office when she came in.

'You ready for a beer yet?'

Joining her in the kitchen, he nodded at the glass of wine she'd poured for herself. 'Not like you to jump into the red when you get home.'

'It's been a big day. Can we have a chat?'

She wanted to think out loud with him, go over the pros and cons of Estelle's offer, consider the other ideas Andie had put in her head. And she wanted him to be proud that someone thought enough of her prospects to support her, whether she accepted or not. First though, she wanted to put it into perspective for him, make sure he was paying attention before she laid out the offer. Sitting at the kitchen counter with a bowl of chips between them, Mara began with how her day had unfolded, how she'd been disappointed to be told to go back to work, then upset that Estelle hadn't confided in her, then stunned by the details of Estelle's offer.

Her father sipped his beer, a frown cutting furrows into his forehead as she talked. He interrupted once to ask what was for dinner and she found a new, assertive tone, asking him to wait until she'd finished. When she was done, she said, 'What do you think?'

He took a slow sip. 'So you'd be working for Estelle, not Vaughn?'

She'd hoped he'd be impressed, but she swallowed her disappointment to explain. 'I was working for both of them at Collings. But yes, I'd be employed by Estelle if I took this position.'

'I thought you hated Estelle.'

Last week, she had. 'We sorted some things out and this week has been great. Interesting and challenging. Also, working on a book would be cool.'

'But what about Vaughn? He gave you that job at Collings when you had no experience and he's always been good to us.'

'Us?'

'I think you should be siding with Vaughn.'

'It's not about taking sides, Dad. Estelle is offering me a new job that sounds really interesting and—'

'It's only three days a week.'

'So I can do uni.'

'You don't want to go back to uni.'

She sat back on her stool and frowned at him. 'Dropping out isn't the same as not wanting to go back.'

'You dropped out twice, Maz. Your grades weren't good and you weren't happy. That's three reasons not to have another go.' He put down his beer as though he'd made the winning point.

'Come on, Dad.' Mara stretched a hand towards him, softening her voice, wanting him to remember. 'There were other reasons I wasn't happy and my grades weren't good. Mum was dying and you had a heart attack.' And before he could insist she could've gone back, she added, 'Then Pat was doing his HSC and you needed help with the business.'

He held up his hands like a footy player to the ref. 'I didn't stop you going back.'

'I've wanted to do law since I was a kid.'

'I'm just not sure you're good enough, Maz.'

It was said with kindness and a touch of pity, as though she just hadn't figured it out yet, and something wilted inside her. More quietly, she said, 'Estelle thinks I am.'

'The woman hardly knows you.'

He didn't either, she realised, the knowledge hitting her like a steel girder that had fallen from the sky, halting her in her tracks. She watched him munch a chip, his gaze flicking towards the TV as though he was ready to move on. Mara turned her wine glass round and round, thinking about how that made her feel, how much she wanted to say to him, whether he'd be hurt. Finally, she looked up at her father and said, 'Okay, thanks Dad.'

He lifted his beer bottle at her like a salute. 'So what's for dinner?'

Irritation crackled through her. At another time, she might have left it there, got up and started cooking. But she'd spent two weeks with Estelle, and all of today in the car with Andie and Coral, and she couldn't leave it there. She tipped back the last of her wine, set the glass on the counter and pulled in a breath as she stood.

'I wanted to discuss this with you,' she said, hearing the edge to her tone and doing nothing to soften it. 'Talk about the pros and cons, like you might want what's best for me. But you're not interested in what I want. You're more interested in what your client might think. And of course, you were happy to think I didn't want to go back to uni; it was easier for you that way. Having me here so you could go back to your life while I put mine on hold. For *you*.' She held up a hand when he went to speak. 'You've been great, Dad. You've taught me to be kind and thoughtful and respectful of others, but you've *never* encouraged me to do what I need to do for myself, to make a decision based on what is best for *me*. You didn't even ask what *I* want to do about Estelle's offer.'

'Okay,' a touch of defensiveness, 'what do you want?'

It was too little, too late. 'I don't know right now, but I'll be making my own decision.' She shoved her stool under the bench and turned to leave.

'What about dinner?'

She hooked a thumb over her shoulder. 'There's the fridge, help yourself.'

Andie

Despite their last tense words, Andie ended up at Vivian's place after she left Hepburn House, as though it was the natural end point to an eventful day. Viv loved a good travel story as much as Andie did, even if it was only up and down the motorway.

Andie tried to keep that in mind as she followed Vivian to the courtyard with a bottle of wine, wanting to repair Viv's hurt without wrenching the wound open again.

'Cheers.' Andie raised her glass.

'Yeah, cheers.' Vivian's smile was tentative, as though she, too, wasn't sure what footing they were on. Perhaps it was why she speed-talked about her day and Camille's upcoming ballet concert before finally asking, 'What did you get up to today?'

There was a reluctance to the question that made Andie bite down on irritation. She wanted to share with her best friend everything that had happened, the way she had with Coral and Mara, so she started with the parts of her day that wouldn't touch a nerve. She made morning tea on the balcony and their aborted dash to the airport sound like a lark. 'I wanted to wail in sympathy when Coral burst into tears.'

'Remember when we missed the flight out of Argentina?' Viv said. 'I threw something in fury and strained my shoulder.'

'Your hat.'

She looked doubtful. 'I strained my shoulder.'

'You're a really bad thrower.'

They both grinned and suddenly, it was them again. Andie took the brakes off her story then. She told Viv about Mara and Estelle, how Mara had cried, *I could go to New York!* and made Andie feel like she'd inspired someone to travel, instead of being the poster girl for how bad it could be.

'Even I thought I might be able to get on a plane again,' Andie said. Not yet, but explaining her fear to Coral and Mara had made her feel for the first time that she might work through it eventually.

'You'll travel again.' Viv flapped a hand. 'It's your natural habitat.'

The dismissiveness made Andie pause. Vivian knew enough about those long, stressful delays to understand why travel no longer felt fun or safe for Andie. It was Viv being positive, Andie told herself, but she took a sip of wine in place of a response.

The silence stretched a moment longer and, as though suddenly feeling a need to fill it, Vivian asked, 'How's Ben?'

'He's going back to Perth next week.' It came out like a declaration, as though the statement had been building in Andie's mind all day.

Vivian's gaze lifted from her glass, but she said nothing.

Andie thought that meant she didn't want to say the wrong thing, so she kept going. 'A rehab place has become available.'

'That's good,' Viv said. Then added, 'I mean, if he can fly, he must be improving.'

'I know, it's great. Although he's not mobile enough to fly on his own yet.'

Vivian sat back in her chair, incredulous. 'And you're taking him over there.'

'What?'

'I'm not stupid. One second you tell me you're thinking about getting on a plane, the next you're prepping me for, "Ben's flying to Perth and needs a companion." Don't do it, Andie.'

She hadn't for a second considered it, not even when Coral had asked her. But she wasn't about to tell Vivian that, not when her best friend thought she could tell her what to do. 'Not that it's any of your—'

'What do you think?' Camille swanned into the courtyard to show off her mini dress and leggings. 'For the party tomorrow night?'

There was a tense beat of silence before Andie rose to her feet, exclaiming, 'Oh my goodness, you're gorgeous!'

'What happened to your jeans?' Viv said without moving from her chair.

'Claire and Hazel are wearing dresses now.'

'Well, I love this one!' Andie said. 'Shoes?'

'Can you come and look?' She batted her eyes at Andie.

For the first time in her life, Andie was grateful for an excuse to leave Vivian behind. 'Love to.'

Andie was fixing a pendant around Camille's neck when the teenager said, 'Were you and Mum talking about that guy in hospital?'

'His name's Ben.'

'Mum doesn't like him.'

Andie's gaze lifted to Camille's in the mirror. 'Your mum hasn't met him.'

Camille turned one way, then the other, eyes on her own reflection as she said, 'She thinks he's using you.'

Andie stiffened. 'Okay, well . . .'

'Don't be mad at her.' It was too late for that. 'She just thinks you're not thinking straight yet, you know, after the accident.'

Andie nodded. 'Sometimes friends have to thrash things out.' She kissed Camille on the cheek, told her to send a photo from the party and went to find Viv.

'Going to Perth is a bad idea,' Vivian said as Andie crossed to the kitchen.

It had been a long time between fights, but Andie had never backed down in the face of Vivian's stubbornness, because that's all it was now. Glaring at Viv across the counter, Andie said, 'You told Camille he was using me.'

Vivian raised her hands in a, *Well, duh* gesture. 'He wants you to accompany him to Perth.'

'He's never said anything about me going with him.'

'Then he's made you feel like you should.'

'Why do you—'

'You've been at his bedside since you went to thank him for saving your life. I get that you're grateful, I am too. But that doesn't make you responsible for him.'

Andie frowned. Why wouldn't Viv let that go?

Vivian must have thought Andie's silence meant she was reconsidering her position, because when she spoke again, her tone had softened. 'You should be thinking of yourself, Andie. You should be trying to get past this accident and back to your life.'

Andie huffed in frustration. 'What life, Viv? The one where I'm fine, I'm fine, I'm fine? I'm so damn sick of trying to be fine.'

'Look, I know the accident triggered a bunch of stuff for you but you *were* fine and you will be again. You just need to get past this, not keep holding on to this guy who is a constant reminder of it.'

'I wasn't fine,' Andie snapped. 'I haven't been fine since Zack woke up clutching his head.' It felt like freedom to speak of him, of that night, without needing to brace herself. '*That guy* has helped me feel stronger than I have in two years.'

'*I know* what you went through with Zack.' Vivian pointed at her lounge room. 'I was the one sobbing on the floor with you, right there. Who watched you crumble into a thousand pieces, who helped pick you up again. I know the way back to your old self because I was with you on that journey.'

Realisation made Andie straighten and blink in surprise. 'My old self is gone, Viv. I'm not the Andie you've known for twenty-something years. I'm sad and scared and so many other things that I never was before Zack died. I *can't* be her anymore, and I don't *want* to be because that would mean denying my life with Zack ever existed. That all the joy and pain was nothing. That loving him wasn't exquisite and that losing him didn't scar me.'

'Andie . . .'

'I've been lying to you. Every time I said I was fine, it was a lie. I felt like I *should* be fine, that not being fine was failing. Only now I realise there's nothing wrong with me for feeling sad and scared. I don't need to move past what happened with Zack or the accident, I need to find a way to live with it. All of it. Maybe you do too.'

'I never said there was something wrong with you.'

Not out loud, Andie thought. But she was done arguing. 'I know I've leaned on you and Theo, I know it must have been hard to watch me go through that, and I'll be forever grateful for everything you've done for me, but that doesn't give you the right to tell me what to do.'

'You can do what you want, of course, it's just that—'

But Andie wasn't listening. She collected her handbag and slung it over her shoulder. 'Enjoy dinner. Say goodnight to Camille and Theo for me.'

'You're leaving?' Her tone was scoffing, as though Andie was being ridiculous if she left.

'I'm going home.'

'Are you going to Perth?'

Andie paused at the door, taking in Vivian's posture as she watched from the kitchen. Andie recognised the stiff uneasiness, knew her friend's inclination to keep arguing a point when she'd already lost it. Andie recognised, too, her own urge to be the peacemaker and call a truce.

But this time, she just shrugged. 'I'll let you know.'

Part 9

Healing

Coral

CORAL STOOD AT the railing above the sand as the sunrise turned the horizon pink and gold. Her eyes were scratchy from lack of sleep, her body heavy with exhaustion, her head throbbing from too many stressful conversations but the fresh, cold air felt great.

It was the same stretch of ocean she'd gazed at from the balcony at Hepburn House, which was comforting. It had always been soothing, although she wasn't feeling it yet. The jittery calm she'd woken with this morning was still there, as though her organs hadn't decided whether to relax or wind up the stress, but they were prepared for either contingency.

Coral had cleared her entire schedule for the trip to New York, which meant that now she wasn't going, she had a week free of commitments. For the first time in a long, long time, there was nothing that needed her attention. It felt like being cast into space or abandoned at sea: pleasantly floaty and palpably terrifying.

Theoretically, it was a bonus to have a week without work pressure, especially after the last fortnight – she could help Val and Summer, and get back to Wade's apartment – only it felt too much like the yawning hole of her approaching retirement. If she looked beyond this week to when she'd go back to work, the idea of cranking up her stress and splitting herself in too many directions made dread heat in her veins.

Turning away from the beach, she walked along the harbour foreshore, her mind drifting back to yesterday and the deja vu of being back in Emergency two weeks after Val's previous fall. It had been hours of waiting for a bed, for stitches to Val's cheek, X-rays, doctors, specialists, decisions. Val, at least, had had pain meds to cushion the reality of her injury and the endless delays, while Coral had spent much of the time ducking in and out of the hospital, searching for wi-fi to field emails from New York. Her bosses had offered sympathy for her family situation that had been tempered by irritation at her last-minute no-show at the conference. She'd texted information and updates to everyone who needed it, including Andrew, who'd actually called and apologised for being missing in action, explaining he'd had his own work disaster and would be arriving on Tuesday. Hallelujah. Coral finally rang Summer when Val was taken for X-rays.

'Do you want to drop in here on your way home?'

The thought was exhausting. 'No.'

'Do you want me to come to yours? Dan can drop me over.'

'No.'

'Are you okay?'

Considering everything? 'I don't think so.'

'But Nana's going to be okay?'

'Yeah, not so sure about me.'

'Why? What's wrong?'

There was alarm in her voice, but the fact Summer had to ask triggered the impatience and frustration Coral had been holding in check since she got to the hospital. 'I'm exhausted and disappointed, Summer,' she snapped. 'I've spent the last six hours waiting for doctors and bedpans and X-rays instead of being on a plane to New York. I had an anxiety attack this week trying to get on that damn plane, and now my boss and his boss are ticked off I wasn't on it. So no, I'm not okay. And I'm not good company. I need to go home and drink a bottle of wine and not do anything for days.'

It was after nine when she got home and poured herself a glass of red. She followed it up with two more glasses, a handful of nuts and half a block of chocolate then fell asleep on the lounge. She dragged herself to bed around two, woke again at five and knew she'd only stare at the ceiling if she didn't get up.

Now she was walking by the harbour, swinging her arms and breathing hard, realising how little exercise she'd had in weeks. Of how low on the list of her priorities her own health had been, and how long it had been that way. She'd spent the majority of her adult life not letting herself think about what she wanted, not wanting to yearn for things she didn't have the time or money or energy for. Her focus had been on meeting the needs of an ever-increasing number of people, ignoring the ever-decreasing list of things that might make her heart sing. She'd always promised herself that one day, she'd have time to do her own thing, whatever that was.

Only, now that she had a week to fill, she realised she had no idea what she wanted. She was already thinking of spring-cleaning Val's house in preparation for her return home, and looking at carpets for Wade's apartment. It made her wonder about her focus on work over the last few months, and whether it had been less about clearing the decks before she retired, and more about avoiding the question of what the rest of her life would look like. Perhaps it had been easier to push herself to breaking point than confront the idea that her heart might never sing again.

During one exhausted spell at the hospital last night, she'd thought the week off might be an opportunity to get her mind around the possibilities of retirement. Now, though, it felt as though it would only highlight the depressing result of a hectic life.

And yes, she told herself, it was probably tiredness and disappointment making it seem worse and it would be fine in the end. And yes, that was possibly another subconscious attempt not to think about it.

Alby did a double take when he saw her in his coffee queue, the surprise in his voice carrying over the heads of the two people in front of her. 'You're meant to be on a plane.'

'Missed my flight.' When the other customers turned to look, she added, 'Long story. Besides, the coffee's better here, apparently.'

She rested her forearms on the railing above the shoreline while she waited for her order to be called. It wasn't, though. Instead, Alby appeared beside her with a coffee for each of them.

'What about those guys?' she asked, cocking her head at his line of customers.

'I'm training someone to work a few days here and there.'

Coral squinted towards the van, seeing a fifty-something bloke behind the coffee machine, somehow pleased it wasn't a gorgeous young woman in there.

'How are you doing?' Alby asked.

Nice that he hadn't jumped straight to, *What the hell happened?* 'Tired. A little hungover. Val had a fall after I left for the airport so I turned around and came back. I'm glad I did, she's a mess. Stitches in her cheek, a black eye and a broken hip. She was admitted to a ward last night and she's having surgery to pin it on Monday.'

'How is she?'

'Pretty confused. I don't know if it was the pain meds or shock or just her brain not coping anymore.'

He nodded, the gesture confirming it could be all of those things, his eyes offering empathy and concern. She was glad she'd found his van this morning.

'Mum was upset that I'd missed my flight,' Coral told him. 'But she thought I was going to the Greek Islands. She kept talking about the pictures I'd shown her of where I was staying, blue-domed whitewashed houses and cobblestoned streets with colourful buildings. I finally realised she was remembering the posters I had in my room as a teenager. I'd been mad about going to the Greek Islands.'

'I stayed in a hot-pink house on Corfu a while back, on top of a bakery. It smelled of freshly baked pastry and had a cat that would sit on the window ledge all day. I liked it better than New York.'

You can take yourself there, Andie had said yesterday. She'd meant New York, that a conference wasn't the only way to get there. It had sounded like consolation, but now Coral realised Andie meant she could take herself anywhere. She could do it for herself, it didn't have to be for work or to accommodate someone else's plans or to fit into a schedule. Staying above a cafe with a cat on the window ledge could be the plan.

'I'd better get going,' she told Alby. 'I have to get some clothes to Mum and pack up her things from Hepburn House. I need to pick up my suitcase from Andie's, too. She suggested a drink tonight, which might be a fitting end to the week.'

He nodded again, something a little pensive in it this time. 'What are you doing with your week off?'

'No idea, to be honest. The schedule is looking scarily vacant.' She shot him a guilty glance. 'I'm not good at that, but after the last couple of weeks and the sunrise this morning, your "take the payout, buy the van" idea is appealing.'

One side of his mouth lifted. 'You want to try a couple of shifts?'

She laughed. Stopped. Glanced away from his grin to the waves, thinking of retirement. It could be research. It could be just for fun. 'If you're serious. Yeah, why not?'

'I'm taking the van up to Port Stephens on Wednesday. We could catch the ferry over to Tea Gardens afterwards, if you like?'

She frowned. 'To see some coffee vans?'

He grinned. 'I thought we could have lunch at the pub.'

Coral blinked. A hundred images of buying coffee at his window in the midst of a frantic moment flashed through her mind: was he nuts? 'Sure, yeah, I . . .' She stopped, tried again. 'Actually, that would be lovely.'

Mara

RYLEE CAUGHT UP with Mara as she was passing through the hospital foyer. 'Thought you might like to know,' she said, 'Estelle's in a good mood.'

'She offered me a job,' Mara blurted.

'Like . . . a job you'd want?'

Mara laughed, but it felt like a fizz of anxiety over the conversation she was about to have. 'It's complicated, but yes. I'm heading in to discuss the details before I give her an answer. Wish me luck.'

Rylee grinned. 'You don't need luck, you're impressively eloquent.' But she held up crossed fingers anyway. 'She advised me to call you next week.'

Mara frowned. 'About her physio treatment? That's what I was worried about, that I'd end up being responsible for everything.'

'No, it was—' Rylee cleared her throat, attempted an imitation of Estelle's voice, 'It would be my advice, where Mara is concerned, that you would both do well to stay in touch.'

Mara snorted a laugh, and they both dissolved into giggles. 'Thanks.' Mara grinned. 'That took the edge off my nerves.'

'Pleasure.'

'And that would be nice.'

'Staying in touch?'

'I mean, if you want to?'

'Ye-ah.' Rylee said it as though the question was daft. 'And I want to know how it goes with Estelle. Send me a text when you get a sec.'

Mara hesitated, then said, 'Maybe another coffee at the beach?'

'You're on!'

Mara paused outside Estelle's door, feeling too cheerful after the encounter with Rylee to concentrate. There were jobs to be done, and if Estelle was preoccupied, Mara would have to pull her attention back. Telling Estelle Collings to shut up and listen would not be a good way to start.

'Lynette will be in this afternoon to collect my suitcase,' Estelle said as Mara walked in. 'You'll need to empty my wardrobe as soon as the printer and coffee machine are packed away.'

There was a distinct *instructing the servants* tone that made Mara brace herself. 'Can we talk about your offer first?'

'Yes, yes.' It was brusque and impatient. 'Have you made your decision?'

'I have some questions I'd like to discuss before I can give you an answer.'

'I would be disappointed if you didn't.' Estelle gestured towards the chair beside her recliner. 'Take a seat.'

Mara had hoped there'd be more of yesterday's warm and generous attitude, but this was Estelle, and her fallback position was curt and all-business, so Mara would have to meet her there. 'I'd like more details on how I would work from your apartment.'

Estelle explained that if Mara chose to move into the guest suite, she wouldn't be expected to work there, unless it was for study. There'd be an office upstairs, a lunch break, which on occasion they might work through, and regular hours, which could be modified when needed.

Estelle finished with a curtness that sounded like a reprimand. 'I'm more interested in your work than making sure you arrive and leave on time.'

Mara shifted in her chair, uneasy that the cordial discussion she'd planned suddenly felt more like a cross-examination.

'Would you set minimum study requirements?'

There would be a tutoring schedule, but Mara would be responsible for her own study hours. 'I'm not concerned with how many hours your head is buried in books, only in the results. If you don't put in the effort, I'll know.'

'Okay, good to know.' She smiled, hoping to inject a lighter tone, but Estelle folded her hands, waiting for the next question. Good grief, was this what it would be like for the next two years?

'The apartment, if I decide to move in—'

'The rules for the apartment,' Estelle said without waiting for her to finish, 'are well established. The adjoining door will remain locked unless by mutual agreement. Visitors are allowed, but no loud noise at night. You will be responsible for your own cleaning, and neither I nor Lynette will enter your apartment without you being there or giving express permission.' She gave Mara a pointed glare. 'And vice versa, Mara. I'm particular about privacy, both mine and yours. I would expect the same from you.'

There was a hostility to it that made Mara want to argue her case – except, there was no case. Everything Estelle had said was what Mara had wanted to hear: privacy, independent study, regular and flexible work hours. But the information had been delivered as a reproach, as if Mara had already done something wrong.

There was another question she needed to ask, but as she gathered her bewildered thoughts, Estelle turned her eyes to the view, as though she couldn't care less what Mara decided.

Except that Mara had sat beside Estelle's bed long enough to know there was something too casual about her disregard. And for the first time, Mara looked beyond the kindness and generosity of Estelle's offer and thought about the cost to the woman herself. Sure, she sponsored other students, but this was different. This hard, proud woman had upended a lifetime of experience to give a failed young assistant another chance at a degree. Yesterday, she'd sparkled with enthusiasm, as though having Mara in her plans had been the key to a new lease on life. Today, maybe she'd realised the risk of rejection, disappointment, possibly humiliation if Mara said no; more so if Mara chose to work for Vaughn instead.

Yesterday, Mara was upset when she thought Estelle hadn't bothered to tell her she was leaving rehab. Now, Mara wondered if that was Estelle's problem: the fear that after everything they'd shared this week, Mara might reject her.

But Estelle wasn't Mara, and sugar-coating her offer with a friendly, open discussion would never be part of her game plan, not when Mara might throw it in her face. Instead, she was being clear and detailed about what to expect, and Mara had to decide if she was up for it or not.

Which, Mara decided, was a timely reminder that she also needed to be clear, that Estelle would expect it of her, and that Estelle's crusty, short-tempered response would determine Mara's future.

'There's one more issue I'd like to raise.'

'Yes?'

Mara had practised this bit, but now that Estelle had her steely-blues squared on her, she couldn't get the words out. 'It's . . . I'm concerned . . . I think that—'

'Finish your sentence, Mara.'

'Yes, sorry.' She took a breath and tried again. 'My concern is that if I work from your apartment and live next door, that I'll end up doing . . . being . . . well, like I have here.'

'Mara. A sentence please.'

Okay, be the person who deserves this opportunity. 'I looked after my mother for six months, and my father for the last couple of years. I don't want to move out to look after someone else. I don't want to be your personal assistant; I can do that somewhere else full-time. I don't want to be a lady's maid either. The truth is, you've ruined me for all that now because I don't want to fetch and carry, I want to be a lawyer. I would love to work on your book and have the benefit of your experience, but not if it means being your nurse.'

Estelle's face was a slideshow of emotions: surprise, affront, bemusement, before it stiffened to something closed and unreadable. 'Lady's maid?'

'Your clothes, the shopping, hunting down cardigans and shoes.'

There was a slight movement to her eyebrows. 'I can assure you that the work I have planned will both take advantage of and challenge your skills. For the period of time that I require a nurse, I will not rely on the skills of an undergraduate lawyer, regardless of her penchant for kindness. I will hire someone who is appropriately trained for the job and thus, less likely to kill me.'

There was not a hint of humour in the way she said it but Mara smiled anyway. A big, silly grin at Estelle's curt reassurance, the stiff-upper-lip of her fondness. And at the new bright future she had ahead of her.

Composing herself, she said, 'I am truly grateful for your offer. Estelle, I'd love to accept.'

A single nod, like a transaction had been made. 'Excellent.'

Mara ignored the formality and hugged her, enjoying the way it caught Estelle off guard, the timid clinch followed by a sudden warmth. Estelle needed a moment to pat down her hair and clear her throat before she could work past a lifetime of constraint to smile with as much enjoyment as Mara.

'You didn't enjoy shopping for my clothes?' Estelle asked.

'I've no idea about clothes.'

'Well, we'll fix that. A young lawyer needs to look the part.'

'Okay then.' She grinned.

'We'll work on finishing your sentences, too.'

'It's nerves, I get tangled.'

'I have noticed you are quite impressive when you get past all that.'

Andie

ANDIE STOOD OUTSIDE Hepburn House like she had last night after Mara drove away: both wanting and not wanting to go in. After the trip on the motorway, she'd been filled with regret for what she could no longer do.

This morning, she was sad and mad. Because today, as she looked at the balcony outside Ben's room, she understood that her heart had become invested without her permission.

Falling in love with Zack had felt like a lightning strike: instant, powerful and undeniable. She'd thought she could protect herself from that kind of thing. She hadn't understood that love could start in different ways, that a seed could be planted in her heart without her knowing, that in two weeks, it could sprout and spread roots, that it would have life even before it poked its head above the ground.

That it would hurt when it was tugged out, and that her heart would be aching even before Ben had left.

She bought coffee from the van, Alby throwing in a cookie when she told him Ben was leaving. As she paused outside Ben's room, she caught a glimpse across the hall of Mara packing the printer into a box and wondered what she'd decided.

Then she pulled in a breath to fortify herself, because she wasn't going to let Ben see how she was feeling. All he needed to be concerned about was getting home to his family.

'Do I get to keep my tartan mug?' she asked as she went in.

'You should keep both. For when I come back to visit.'

They both knew that wouldn't be for a while; it would be months before he was walking properly, maybe longer before he left Perth again, especially if his dad's cancer came back. And maybe by then, he'd have moved on. 'Sure. But don't put me in your mum's bad books if she's upset you didn't take yours home.'

'I don't think that's possible.'

'Did your parents get home okay?'

'Yeah. I spoke to them last night. Dad's exhausted. Had a great time, but he's wiped out by all the travelling. Mum too, not that she was saying.'

'They'll be happy to see you.'

Ben pushed a hand through his hair. 'Not sure they're going to. Turns out other people aren't sitting around waiting for an opportunity to fly to Newcastle.'

Andie frowned as she sat beside his chair. 'No-one wants to come?'

'Oh, everyone *wants* to. My best mate's leaving tomorrow on a trip to Paris for his wife's fortieth birthday. My other best mate is on a training mission with his police unit. And my brother-in-law currently has his head down the toilet with gastro.'

'I guess they're good excuses. Is there anyone else?'

'I've got a couple more on my list, but it's short notice.' He scrubbed a hand over his hair. 'I don't have to go, but . . .' He tipped his head.

'You want to get home.'

'I do and I don't.' He reached for Andie, then let his hand fall back to the armrest. 'But it's Mum. She was at my sister's when I called Phil. Freya texted later, saying Mum was looking at flights. She wants to come over to get me.'

'What, this weekend?'

'Yeah, when she's seriously jet-lagged.' He shook his head.

'I don't want her coming. I might have to get you to lie to her again.'

'And say what?'

'I don't know, that I'm doing great, that I want to stay. What do you think?'

Andie took a sip of coffee, her heart beating a drum in her ears. If she lied to Carmel, Ben would have to wait for another rehab place; a week, maybe more. Andie would have more time to finish healing from the inside, to cry and laugh and go on daft capers. But by then she'd feel even more for him, and losing him would be even harder.

If she didn't lie, Carmel, who'd been through so much, who'd been so nice to Andie when she didn't even know her, would exhaust herself flying across the country.

'I think . . .' She thought of the joy of being Coral's godsend and pulled in a fortifying breath, 'I could go with you to Perth.'

'What?'

'I could. I can. Help you get home.'

'No, Andie.'

'Why not?'

'Because I don't want you to.'

There was something about the way he said it that made Andie wonder if she'd misinterpreted their friendship. If for Ben, it really had been just company until he could leave. The thought cut with a sudden sharp pain, but it didn't change how she felt. 'I can fly straight back home if you don't want me there.'

'No. It's not that I don't want you there. It's . . .' He shook his head, suddenly adamant. 'I don't want you flying to Perth.'

Andie frowned. 'I don't understand.'

'Look,' he ran a hand through his hair again, as though needing a moment to work out how to explain, 'ever since the accident, your life has been turned upside down. You've spent every day for the last two weeks in here with me. You've helped my parents, you've visited on weekends, you've set your life aside. And look, I'm pretty sure I had no grand plan when I gave you that hard shove, but I didn't save your life so I could screw it up. For god's sake, Andie. You're afraid of flying. I'm not going to let you get on a plane just so I can go home.'

It dawned on her then, the thing she'd been too annoyed with Vivian to see last night. 'The thing is, I'm not scared of flying because I think the plane will crash. I'm scared of remembering the last time I was on a plane, when Zack was in a coffin. Of being up in the air and overwhelmed by heartbreak. Of being alone and frightened and having no control over what happens next. But since I told you the whole story, since I said the words out loud and you listened like it was okay to *feel*, I'm not so afraid. That's not to say I wouldn't have a few heart palpitations onboard, but I've remembered all of it, and the remembering didn't kill me. I even told Mara and Coral about it yesterday. And look at me, I'm okay.'

'That's amazing. You're amazing.'

'*You're* the one who's amazing. You saved my life.'

'That's just it, Andie. I'm more grateful to you than I can express, and I feel more for you than I thought possible after two weeks in a hospital room. You don't owe me anything for pushing you out of the way and I don't blame you that I ended up in rehab. There was never any debt, and if you thought there was, you've paid it back in spades. You're not responsible for getting me back to Perth.'

'I don't feel responsible for getting you back to Perth, and who's to say if you did save my life that night. I might not have died, both of us might have ended up in here. But you *did* save my life, slowly, over the last two weeks.' She reached for his hand. 'That's not why I offered to help you back to Perth. I want you to be with your family, I want you to recover in the best way you can, I want you to spend time with your dad. And if I take you back, I get to spend more time with you too.'

One side of his mouth tipped slowly upwards as her meaning sunk in. 'You want all of that?'

'Actually, I want something else too. I want to be *this* Andie,' she touched a finger to her chest. 'The one I found in here with you. I like her, she feels like . . . me.'

'I like her too.'

'I'd *like* to take you to Perth, Ben. It feels like something I'd do. You know, something good, different, brave.'

An upward lift of his chin, like he understood, like he agreed. 'A caper, then?'

'Yeah, exactly like a caper.' She saw it now. 'It's bold and reckless, it will brighten someone's day, and I'll be hacking a path to somewhere amazing. I've got all three rules covered.'

He did that slow, easy smile she'd seen the first day she'd met him. 'Do you think we could make it last more than a few hours in Perth?'

'Like . . . a few days?'

'Maybe longer?'

'A week?'

'A few weeks?'

Something loosened around her heart. 'What, you mean keep you company in rehab? Get coffee and papers, watch movies on a laptop, eat your leftover ice-cream. That kind of thing?'

'It could start like that. See how it goes?'

She smiled. 'Yeah, I'd like that.'

He smiled back, slid his fingers between hers.

Andie rolled her lips together. 'Do you think it's too soon to kiss you?'

'I wanted to kiss you when we were standing on the kerb that night. So, no, not too soon.'

'Really?'

'I'll tell you about it on the plane.' He smiled as he gave her hand a tug. She leaned in and pressed her lips to his.

Coral

'Coral!' Val was weak, but she could still bark loud enough to be heard across a four-bed ward. 'I owe you a trip to New York for this.'

Coral laughed. 'Sure, Mum. Whatever you say.' At least the pain meds and confusion were good for a chuckle, she thought, kissing her mum's forehead. The bruising around her eye was darker and the breathing tube was still in place, but Val had a little more colour in her face today.

'You shouldn't be here,' Val said.

She'd lost the fearful tremble in her voice too, Coral thought, stifling a sigh at the reprimand there instead. 'Of course I'm here. I've brought nighties and toiletries and,' she pulled out a package, 'chocolate.'

Val sighed as though the chocolate was all wrong. 'I knew you'd come back,' she said. 'I never doubted it. You're always there when I need you. I'm just so sorry you had to.' Her eyes were suddenly shiny and damp.

Coral frowned as she pulled a chair over. She found her mum's hand among the covers and held it. 'It's okay.'

'It's not,' she said. 'You worked hard for that trip and I was so proud of you going and now it's my fault you're not over there.'

'You didn't do it on purpose.'

Val gave Coral's hand a squeeze, as if to say, *now listen*. 'I've made up my mind. I'm paying for you to go to New York. For the full ten days. Longer, if you want.'

For a moment, Coral wasn't sure whether to laugh or ask a nurse who this imposter was. Because the real Val couldn't remember how long her daughter was going for and had thought it was ridiculous to go so far for a meeting. This Val, though, seemed clear-headed and determined. 'You don't have to do that.'

'I want to, darling. Perhaps you should write it down and I can sign it. In case I die.'

'You broke your hip and hit your head, Mum. You might be a little emotional, but you're not dying.'

'Nevertheless, Coral. I know my mind is going and I want it written down before I forget.'

A nurse appeared to check Val's drip and heart monitor, and as Coral watched from the end of the bed, she thought how much like her old self Val had just sounded. A Val from several years ago, before she lost some of her confidence, before she made up stories to cover her bewilderment. When she was feisty and indignant about older age; adamant, unfiltered and annoyingly admirable.

After the nurse had gone, Val waited until Coral sat down again and in that few-years-ago voice said, 'I never tell you how proud I am of you. But I am.'

Coral slipped her hand around Val's again. Whatever was going on, Coral wanted to hold on to it.

'You're a good daughter and a good mother.' There was something determined in her voice now, as though she'd spent the night worrying about losing her mind or dying and needed to set the record straight. 'You were a good wife too, and you didn't deserve what Richard did to you.'

Tears welled in Val's eyes again. Coral wanted to reassure her, but she was too stunned to find words.

'You're strong,' Val went on. 'You've always been strong.

I wanted to think you got that from me but I don't know where it came from. Certainly not from your father.'

'You're strong, Mum.'

'Not like you.' Val felt around for a tissue, patting carefully around her black eye. 'I was hard on you because it was the only way I knew.'

'Mum . . .'

'You were braver than me, you made choices I couldn't. Some of them were forced on you, but you didn't shirk them.' She wiped her nose, adjusted the breathing tube. 'I worried that you'd think I was weak.'

'Weak?'

'For staying with your father, for knowing nothing about all that money he spent, for having to go back to work when I could have been helping you with those little babies.' Her lips tightened. 'For forgetting things.' She closed her eyes for a moment. 'I couldn't tell you how proud I was because I was ashamed of how stupid I'd been. I'm sorry for that, Coral. You deserved better. You deserved to go to New York. I know how much you do for everyone, for me especially, and you deserve to have more time for yourself.'

There were tears leaking from Coral's eyes now. 'Oh, Mum.' She leaned over the bed to press a long, heartfelt kiss on her forehead.

'There, I've said it now.' Val patted Coral's hand. 'Now, are you sure you can't get to New York on time for your conference?'

'Even if there was still time, I haven't got the energy.'

'Then promise me you'll go. If not now, then sometime soon. So I'm still around to hear all about it.'

Coral stayed for an hour and Val was alert and unbewildered for all of it, speaking as though her life had flashed before her eyes and she didn't want to forget it. They talked about Coral's father, remembering the good and the bad. Val's uncharacteristically scathing remarks made Coral wonder how difficult it must have been to keep that hurt from her daughter; she was glad her mum could finally express it. They shared memories, retold family sagas, returned to old houses and wondered about long lost relatives. Coral had no idea if Val's sudden clarity was due to the drugs she was on or the bump to her head or a window of opportunity before whatever was happening in her brain carved another inroad. All she knew was that she cherished the time, knowing even as they talked that she'd miss this Val.

As Coral walked back through the hospital, she felt her own memories shifting about, as though Val's confessions about feeling weak and being proud had changed them somehow, reshaping and softening their edges.

Outside in the fresh air, Coral thought about New York and her promise to go while her mum was still alive to hear about it. She thought about the Greek Islands too; about the years she'd spent not thinking about what she wanted, the ever-increasing needs of others and her ever-decreasing list of things that might make her heart sing. Of the times she'd promised herself that one day, there'd be space in her life for something of her own. She still didn't know what that was – although Greece might one day feature in it – but it felt as though Val's words had changed the way she felt about that too. As though for the longest time, Coral had been trying to be better than the twenty-year-old girl who'd fallen pregnant, dropped out of uni and married a stupid, selfish man. As though she no longer needed to prove that she was worth more than the bed she'd made for herself back then. As though Val's acknowledgement that she'd been wrong, that Coral was strong and deserved better, was enough to stop trying so hard.

It had all happened a long time ago, Coral thought as she got in the car, and she should probably have figured it out well before now and given herself a break. But she'd had a wake-up call this week. She was bad at staring down an empty whiteboard, but she was good at making decisions on the run – so that's what she did.

Andie's Place

M ARA ARRIVED AS Coral was closing the boot of her car.

'How are you? How did you go today?' Coral asked as she wrapped Mara into a hug.

Mara returned the embrace, touched that Coral had asked when she'd had so much to deal with herself. 'I'm good, and it went—'

'Not yet!' Andie called from the front door. 'No news until we've poured the champagne for a toast.'

Grinning, Mara followed Coral to the townhouse, where she was greeted with another hug from Andie.

'I saw you at Hepburn House this morning. You were talking to Estelle.' Andie raised her eyebrows. 'Dying to hear all about it.'

'I spent most of the day carting Estelle's hospital office to her apartment office.' Glancing around the lower floor of Andie's large, open-plan townhouse, she set a bag on the kitchen bench. 'I've brought chips and strawberries.'

'I was meant to be drinking expensive bubbles in New York so I bought expensive bubbles to drink here instead.' Coral produced a bottle. 'French.'

'Oooh, I've never had French champagne,' Mara said.

'Perfect for toasting.' Andie grinned. 'For whatever we're toasting.' Andie had glasses ready and a plate of nibbles on a table.

'I love your place,' Coral called from glass doors that opened onto a courtyard. 'You've almost got your own Hepburn House balcony here. Just needs some plants and a couple of armchairs.'

'And a view,' Andie laughed.

'I'm not sure it was all about the view,' Mara said. 'That balcony was a lifesaver though.'

'Here's to the balcony,' Andie said, and popped the cork.

Passing around glasses, Andie held her own aloft. 'The last two weeks have been a roller-coaster for all of us, so the first toast is to us. For surviving rehab. It's been lovely meeting you both.'

'Cheers.'

'*Salut.*'

Mara had been ready to copy Andie's brief toast with one about new jobs, but Andie insisted she didn't say anything until they were settled around her coffee table with the nibbles and the rest of the champagne in reach, as though she and Coral wanted the entire story, not just the end result. Mara had forgotten how nice it was to have women in her life to share exciting news with.

'I talked to my dad last night,' she said, starting at the beginning and explaining how saying her piece had helped her make a decision.

Andie made another toast to that before saying, 'And then?'

'I followed the suggestions you both made about asking questions and not wanting to be a lady's maid.' She told them how she'd been determined to get through her list of questions before choosing her next path in life; about Estelle's spiky demeanour and the 'thus less likely to kill me' comment, enjoying Andie and Coral's hoots of laughter. Then finally, she revealed that she'd be moving into the upstairs guest rooms at Estelle's apartment next week to work and study with Estelle until she'd finished her degree . . . and that she sealed the deal with a hug that had flustered her boss.

This news was greeted with another toast before both woman got up to hug her. Mara knew it wouldn't be like this when she told Dad, but it was good to have these two new friends on her side before she did.

Andie's eyes welled at Mara's joy. Happy tears now.

She'd been planning to leave her news until last, but Coral was gazing out at the courtyard again, and Andie thought she might need more time before discussing her disappointments of the last few days.

'Well, I have news,' Andie announced as she topped up their glasses. She considered following Mara's lead and drawing out her story, but she hadn't told anyone yet – hadn't wanted to ruin the thrill of a big, new caper by trying to explain it to Vivian – and really, she just wanted to say it out loud and see how it felt. 'I'm going to Perth with Ben.'

Coral gasped and Mara clapped her hands.

'We're going to exhaust ourselves with all this hugging,' Andie laughed when they'd finished toasting and had sat back down.

'Come on, tell.' Coral grinned.

So Andie told them the whole story: about her argument with Viv, how she'd been mad with herself this morning for feeling more for Ben than she'd wanted to. Then about his friends who couldn't escort him back and his jet-lagged mum wanting to make the trip, and Ben thinking he was screwing up Andie's life when really he'd made it better.

'Then he asked me to stay for a few weeks and see how it goes.'

Another gasp.

'When are you going?' Coral asked.

'Sunday. I know, it's really soon, but it feels . . .' She glanced around the townhouse where she and Zack had lived, at their wedding photo. 'It feels right. I'm ready now. Not to move on, but to move forward.'

Good for her, Coral thought, watching Andie laugh. She looked more alive today, as though deciding to move in a different direction had lifted a ten-kilo bag from her shoulders, and switched on a light behind her eyes.

'Okay, my turn.' Coral pulled in a breath, still mentally shaking her head at what she'd done. She decided to start from where they'd dropped her at the hospital so it would make sense. Perhaps she needed to be reminded of how she'd ended up here too.

'First of all, Val's having surgery on Monday to pin her broken hip. But she's doing okay. Better than okay today.' Coral explained about the injuries and the long hours in Emergency, waking this morning feeling like she'd been hit by a truck, Val greeting her with, *I owe you a trip to New York* and making Coral promise she'd go. Then the unexpected and long overdue mother–daughter heart-to-heart. She told them how she hadn't so much made a plan as decided to see what happened when she cleared the whiteboard in her head. Which was when she realised that Andie and Mara still had no idea what she was talking about.

'So I emailed my boss from the hospital car park and, as of today, I'm officially retired.'

Their reaction was exactly what she needed: squeals and hugs. They finished the champagne, Andie opened another bottle of bubbly and they settled in to discuss Coral's retirement.

'To be honest, I'm a little terrified of the blank whiteboard.'

'There must be things you've been putting off until you had the time,' Andie said.

'Skydiving, roller derby . . .' joked Mara.

'Getting my hair done.' Coral laughed, then sighed. 'I've got a camera tucked away somewhere that I always wanted to get back to.' She shrugged. 'I always thought I'd do up the house one day. I imagined it'd be redesigning this and giving that a whole new look, but it needs so much basic work that it'd be more like replacing this guttering and fixing that leaky plumbing. I don't even like the place anymore.' She glanced around Andie's townhouse again, at the kitchen with its island bench, the highlight windows, the clever built-in shelving, the cupboards that closed and lights that worked. 'Like your place,' she said. 'I'd love something like this, but I don't want to rebuild mine to get it.'

'Want to try this one out for a while?' Andie said.

Coral scoffed a laugh.

'No, really. I'm looking for a house-sitter.'

'You're serious?'

'Yes! For a month to start with. Probably longer.'

Coral stood suddenly, swinging her gaze around, taking in the tasteful furniture, arty photos on the walls, the island bench again. She laughed.

'Is that a yes?'

'Yes. Yes, please. That would mean ... a clean whiteboard, better house, new start.'

'You could put a few plants in the courtyard and have your own rehab balcony,' Mara said.

'I could be inspired by those photos.'

'I could end up selling it,' Andie said. 'If Perth is nice, if things work out with Ben. Even if they don't, I'm not sure where I'll decide to go.'

After a tour of the rooms upstairs, they decided to get take-away and as they waited for the food to be delivered, Coral said, 'You know Alby in the coffee van? We're having lunch next week. After he shows me how to run a coffee van.'

'Rylee the physio invited me to a party next weekend,' Mara said.

'When did all the buddying up happen?' Andie asked.

'When you were falling in love with Ben,' said Mara.

Andie didn't know if she was there yet, but whatever was between them was something gentle and lovely that didn't scare her.

She raised her glass again. 'Final toast: to the weirdest two weeks ever.'

Acknowledgements

THE WRITING OF every book is a journey in itself, with fictional characters and real life not always making it smooth or simple. *The View from the Balcony*'s journey was a roller-coaster. There were emotional holds-ups and detours, story twists and turns that added kilometres to the trip, and a long, steep uphill climb before it limped exhausted to The End. I love these characters and their stories – and I've never been so pleased to get a manuscript off my desk and into the hands of a publisher.

Many thanks to Pan Macmillan and my publisher Alex Lloyd for his patience and confidence that this book would eventually get to him and make sense. Also to Brianne Collins, Vanessa Lanaway and Jo Pilgrim for their brilliant eyes on another one of my books and for finding so many clever ways to cut words without losing the story. Mietta Yans for a gorgeous cover; to publicist Kimberlea Smith, marketer Tom Evans and the whole team for their hard work on this book, and their support (and the basket at my door) when real life took an unexpected turn.

A big thank you goes to my agent of fourteen years, Clare Forster, not just for seeing me through another book, but for the support and advice through nine novels. It's been great and appreciated – and I wish you good luck for the future. Thanks also to the Curtis Brown agency and Alex Christie for jumping in quickly at the end.

There were lots of people whose support, advice and kindness helped me to finish this book, but I'd like to start with the many people who shared their stories of the challenges of helping aging parents and life in the 'sandwich generation'. Most of it wasn't research, but conversations, sometimes a shared lament, delivered with love, care and sometimes exhaustion. Some elements of those stories ended up in this book but most helped to shape it. A special mention to Lesley Dawn, who let me use her mum's, 'I owe you a trip for this!'

For research, many thanks to Bess Latouf for advice on police procedure – any mistakes are mine. Mark Hankinson for again going over and above with his engineering expertise – I think I got it right in the end. Claire Hankinson for reading a long-winded draft and talking me through her holiday to the Solomon Islands and inspiring Andie's trip, thankfully without the drama. Julie Nalbach for reading and dissecting the same long draft. Michael Ryan for his legal expertise. Judy Griffiths for throwing around broken bone ideas. Ross McLoughlin for answering editing questions.

To my writer friends who came to the rescue with coffee, drinks, emails, brainstorming, laughter and shoulders to cry on; and who get the weirdness of author life. Special thanks to Cathryn Hein, Monique McDonnell and Michelle Douglas for the get-togethers that kept me sane and the brainstorming that rescued this book from plot holes. To Fiona McArthur for being my calm rock on a drama-filled day, for another fun author tour and for everything in between. To author Trish Morey for coming to the rescue with a back cover blurb when my head was too full of story details to write it. And to the fabulous women in my writers' group for their collective experience, wisdom and enthusiasm.

To friends and family who hung in there with Paul and I over the last two years with kind messages, hugs, get-togethers and check-ins: Kay Gwynne, Peter and Juliet Clark, Phil and Sylvia Cox, Paul and Victoria Murphy, Cath and Grant Every-Burns, Brad

Wilson, Sue Myers, Denise and Kyle Loades, Gemma and Michael Ryan, Jared Pichler, Nikki Fulford, Mum, Joan and Brian.

To Bernadette Cross, who helped me to find the way back to this story when I thought it was lost, to figure out how to tackle the long, uphill climb, and to believe again in the thing that makes me a writer. It is so appreciated.

Finally, to my family, who also went through some tough times during the two years it took to write *The View from the Balcony*. To Claire, Mark, Julia and Billie, for their love and support through all of it. And to my amazing husband Paul, who had the toughest journey – and survived – and then waited for me to finish my book before we took a much-needed break.

Janette Paul
The Summer Place

As three women return to the summer place of their youth for a beach wedding, each is grappling with the cards life has dealt them.

Erin, recovering from a near-fatal cycling accident, is the reluctant maid of honour. Still coming to terms with her devastating injuries, will she find what she needs to walk down the aisle with all eyes on her?

Years ago, Jenna fell in love with the groom at his family's treasured holiday spot. Will watching him marry someone else finally allow her to get over him?

Cassie, living in Barcelona and recently widowed, is desperate to move on from her grief. The invitation to return to Australia for the wedding will give her a chance to step away from her life – and come to terms with more than she bargained for.

Emotions run high as each woman faces a crossroad, yet they will find that the place at the coast offers all of them a chance to learn to heal, love and belong . . .

PRAISE FOR THE SUMMER PLACE

'Warmth and heart shine from the pages of *The Summer Place*. Who doesn't love a novel set around a wedding with all the drama and emotion that involves? This is the feel-good novel we all need right now.' – Rachael Johns

'Clever, quirky and satisfying. Janette Paul takes women's fiction and squeezes your heart.' – Fiona McArthur

'Janette Paul's writing is wonderfully evocative. I felt the sun in my face and the sand between my toes – I wanted it to be my summer place.' – Meredith Appleyard